THE DARKLAND

A Dark and Twisted Medieval Romance

By Kathryn Le Veque

Other Novels by Kathryn Le Veque

Medieval Romance:

The White Lord of Wellesbourne
The Dark One: Dark Knight

While Angels Slept
Rise of the Defender
Spectre of the Sword
Unending Love
Archangel
Lord of the Shadows

Great Protector
To the Lady Born

The Falls of Erith
Lord of War: Black Angel

The Darkland
Black Sword

Unrelated characters or family groups:
The Whispering Night
The Dark Lord
The Gorgon
The Warrior Poet
Guardian of Darkness (related to The Fallen One)
Tender is the Knight
The Legend
Lespada
The Wolfe
Lord of Light

The Dragonblade Trilogy:
Dragonblade
Island of Glass
The Savage Curtain
The Fallen One
Fragments of Grace

Novella, Time Travel Romance:
Echoes of Ancient Dreams

Time-Travel Romance:
The Crusader
Kingdom Come

Contemporary Romance:

Kathlyn Trent/Marcus Burton Series:
Valley of the Shadow
The Eden Factor
Canyon of the Sphinx

The American Heroes Series:
Resurrection
Fires of Autumn
Evenshade
Sea of Dreams
Purgatory

Other Contemporary Romance:
Lady of Heaven
Darkling, I listen

Note: All Kathryn's novels are designed to be read as stand-alones, although many have cross-over characters or cross-over family groups.

Novels that are grouped together have related characters or family groups.

Series are clearly marked. All series contain the same characters or family groups except the American Heroes Series, which is an anthology with unrelated characters.

There is NO particular chronological order for any of the novels because they can all be read as stand-alones, even the series.

For Cindy. She said she liked them weird and I complied!

AUTHOR'S NOTE:

This novel was written several years ago, parts of which were lost to a faulty hard drive. The majority survived intact but I needed to rewrite a few lost chapters. Not a difficult task; however, I questioned even publishing this book because in re-reading it, I discovered it to be much darker and stranger than I had originally thought. I must have been on drugs when I wrote it – and I don't even do drugs!

That being said, don't be shocked at anything you read in this novel. It's an out-of-the-box and out-of-my-mind dark medieval romance. Unconventional. If things like sexual relationships between step-siblings (non-blood related) and murder bother you, then don't read the book. These things weren't unusual in those dark times. But if you have the guts, keep an open mind and discover that the heart and soul of this novel is a truly passionate love story with a hero to die for and a very happy ending. I have a feeling that this is one of those novels that people are either going to really love - or really hate. The opening scene following the prologue is probably one of the funniest you will ever read. But after that, it gets fabulous… and strange. It is what it is, and I make no apologies. But I do offer this warning….

Beware of The Darkland.

PROLOGUE

She had died like all the rest.

A cowering, foolish woman that was unable to accept the mastery of Man's strength over her fragile female soul. Not that he enjoyed killing; in fact, were it not for Johanne, he would not have killed at all. But these women, the dead ones, had been a threat to her delicate composition. And he knew he had to do away with the threat at any cost.

Johanne had wished them away, these dead women. Wished them away so that their sweet words and gentle caresses would no longer be known to the one she loved. A secret love, twisted and dark, but a strong bond that grew stronger with each successive death.

He smiled as he watched the silk-clad body sink beneath the waters of the pristine lake. It was the third lady this year to meet such a fate. And perhaps this death would deter other foolish women from pursuing the object of Johanne's love, thinking that somehow a curse was attached to the man. Left alone by the throngs of adoring admirers, Johanne was convinced the object of her desire would finally succumb to her attentions.

His smile faded as a soft mist began to fall. He could hear the birds in the trees, the whistle of the breeze through the moist foliage. Another storm was on the approach that would churn the waters of the lake and bury the body forever. And he was not sorry, not one bit. Certainly, no one should know what he had done.

No one but God. And the Lord would forgive, perhaps with enough penitence. As the man turned from the lake and made his way through the damp meadow, his thoughts turned from the dead lady to the warmth of Johanne on this wintery night. Most pleasant when the weather grew unfriendly and the temperature dropped. Johanne, his lovely step-sister, would warm his bed.

He simply couldn't explain the relationship between them. The need to dominate, to consume her. Since the moment her budding breasts had been evident, he had taken her into his bed and convinced her that this was where she belonged - with him, a man with whom she shared the same father. The only man who truly loved her.

Still, he was not the man she loved. He knew that and he didn't care. The dead women had been lusting for the true love of Johanne's life and he had listened night after night as his sister cried for a man who hardly noticed her. Therefore, to ease her pain, it had been necessary to do away with the foolish wenches. Another control he had over a woman he was completely obsessed with.

Even so, he knew the man of Johanne's dreams would never return her affection; a man like Kirk Connaught would be interested in a woman with beauty and spirit, which ruled Johanne out entirely. Her beauty was average and her spirit dark. She was sick in the mind, his sister, and everyone knew it, especially Kirk.

The rain was falling steadily by the time he reached his steed, tethered to an oak tree. Mounting the beast, he made haste for Anchorsholme Castle, known throughout southern Lancashire as The Darkland. *The House of the Death.*

With good reason.

CHAPTER ONE

Lancashire, England
January, 1515 A.D.

She had seen them coming from the distance, a hundred tiny specks against the dead winter landscape. Three massive chargers and a host of soldiers advanced like an incoming tide, the dust from their marching feet creating puffs of gritty haze. As the sky above darkened ominously, so did the lady's mood.

But she was determined to welcome the army in spite of her apprehension. After all, they were coming for her and she could not refuse them. Whether or not she was willing to accept her destiny was of little concern; the soldiers had come to take her, and she would not resist. Unlike someone else she knew, with far too much defiance for such a lovely young creature. In the face of a horde of weapon-wielding men, the lady could only pray that the stubborn stance would not bring about the death of her only sister.

A biting wind was howling from the battlements by the time the soldiers entered the shabby bailey. The lady wait patiently on the steps of the manse, watching the three knights survey the crumbling surroundings before disbursing themselves. Two went to secure the courtyard while the third, a massive man astride an enormous red charger, rode in her direction. The lady could feel chest tighten with foreboding as he drew near.

When he came within earshot, she folded herself into a proper curtsy. "My lord." She could hear the quaking in her voice. "I am the Lady Micheline le Bec. Welcome to Haslingden Hall."

The knight raised his visor, eyeing the woman in the faded blue cloak. "I am Sir Kirk Connaught, captain of Anchorsholme Castle." His Irish brogue was thick and deep. "I bring you greetings from your betrothed, Lord Edmund de Cleveley. As stated in the missive sent to Haslingden three days ago, the fulfillment of your betrothal contract came due on your eighteenth birthday, two weeks ago. Do you acknowledge these terms, my lady?"

Micheline kept her eyes properly averted. Even so, her apprehension was obvious. It seemed to cover her like a blanket. "I do, my lord."

There was something in her tone as well as her manner that went beyond the natural fear of her destiny. Something Kirk was unable to put his finger on and he tore his gaze away from the lady, noting his small escort had easily taken control of bailey. In fact, he could count on both hands the number of Haslingden soldiers and servants, and he gestured towards the slovenly group.

"How many will be accompanying you, my lady?"

Micheline looked up from the muddy ground, staring at a man the size of which she had never seen before. He was so large he seemed to blot out the sky and the Irish brogue was both fierce and intimidating. Everyone knew that the Irish were the ruthless sort, and the knight before her certainly fit the mold.

"Just me," she stammered. "And m-mayhap another."

Kirk looked at her as she choked on her words, noting the flush to her cheeks. "Mayhap another? You are uncertain?"

The mottle in Micheline's cheeks deepened. In spite of the cold weather, she was beginning to sweat.

"I-I am afraid that...." She swallowed hard, fixing him in the eye for the first time. And the strong glimmer in the stone-gray orbs was enough to jelly her spine. "That is to say, my sister does not wish to come, my lord. I have spent the better part of three days attempting to convince her, but she refuses to see reason."

Kirk remained emotionless, but he could see that the situation was causing the woman a good deal of distress. No wonder he had sensed more than the usual level of anxiety in her manner. "I see," he said. "Why does she refuse to accompany you?"

Micheline sighed, hoping her sister's resistance would not send the man into a rage. But, then again, where Mara was concerned, anything was possible. "She says that she is not the one betrothed to Lord Edmund and should not be forced to live at Anchorsholme Castle. It is her wish to be left alone at Haslingden, in peace."

Kirk scratched beneath his helm in thought, giving Micheline a glimpse of rich dark hair. "How old is your sister, my lady?"

"Seventeen years, my lord."

That seemed to draw a reaction from Kirk. "Impossible. You are her guardian, are you not?"

Micheline nodded. "Since our parents' death one year ago, it has only been the two of us."

He snorted. "Then she cannot stay. She will come to Anchorsholme Castle as the ward of Lord Edmund."

He moved past the trembling lady and into the threadbare foyer of Haslingden. It was a cavernous place, hinting at the luxury of days gone

14

by, but now, it simply looked old and worn. The stench of poverty was everywhere. As Kirk's gaze moved over the dingy stone walls, Micheline was on his heels.

"My lord, I beg you, permit me to persuade her," she pleaded fearfully. "She can be most unreasonable and... impudent. I fear she might offend you with her bold tongue."

Kirk tucked his gauntlets into the folds of his breastplate. His armor, heavy plate protection of the latest style, glimmered in the dim light. "Where is she?"

Micheline was close to tears. "Please, my lord. I beseech you...."

Kirk turned to the woman, swiftly. "I would ask again where she is. Have faith that I can be quite convincing when the situation requires, bold tongue or no." He paused, realizing he sounded rather harsh from the expression on her face. His next question was more gently delivered. "What is her name?"

Micheline twisted her hands with anxiety, wanting to protect her sister but unwilling to disobey a man the size of two average men combined. Fear won over and weakly, she gestured to the stairs, a great stone bank that disappeared into the second floor.

"Her name is Mara," she murmured. "Last door to the right. She responds better to calm reasoning than outright violence, although the latter is acceptable if all else fails."

Kirk cocked an eyebrow at the strange statement. Mounting the stairs, he found himself wondering what sort of she-cat he would be dealing with. Stubborn, young, and no doubt spoiled. A nasty combination.

The big oak door indicated by Micheline was firmly closed. And firmly locked. Kirk rapped his knuckles against the panel.

"Go away!" came the shout.

He sighed; obviously, his assumptions had been correct. Stubborn, willful, petulant; he could deduce everything simply by the tone of her voice.

"My name is Sir Kirk Connaught," he announced. "I have come to escort you and the Lady Micheline to Anchorsholme Castle. Will you come peacefully?"

There was a long pause, and no doubt a surprised one. After a moment, the voice that had once been a distant bellow was somehow closer. But the door remained locked.

"I am not going to Anchorsholme Castle, Sir Kirk." The shouting voice was now sweet in tone. Disarming if he would allow himself to think so. "I am sure my sister explained that I wish to remain at the home of my birth. There is no reason why I need go to Anchorsholme Castle."

"No need except for the fact that you will be completely alone, unchaperoned, and unprotected." Kirk leaned against the doorjamb, crossing his arms wearily. It had been far too long a ride for him to spare patience to an unyielding girl. "Does this not concern you?"

"Nay," she said flatly. "I do not need anyone to take care of me. I am quite capable of taking care of myself."

"I am sure that you are. But your sister is distressed at the thought of leaving you behind. Will you not come for her peace of mind?"

There was a stubborn pause. "Nay." She was very close now. He guessed she was leaning against the closed door. "Micheline will have a new husband to occupy her time. She will soon forget her concern for me."

"I doubt that." Kirk found himself wondering if the lady on the opposite side of the door was as plain as her sister. Certainly, her voice was terribly delicious and the pleasing tone alone was enough to ease his irritation. "Lady Micheline demands you attend her. As her betrothed's captain, it is my duty to see her wish fulfilled. Do you understand?"

There was a long, long pause. When the voice spoke again, it sounded as if it was on the other side of the room. "I understand perfectly. And unless you want a battle on your hands, I suggest you forget about fulfilling my sister's wish. I am not going."

Now he knew what Micheline had meant by acceptable violence. The young lady on the opposite side of the door was in need of a good spanking. And when he opened the panel, he planned to do just that.

"I am afraid that you are," he said, his rolling Irish accent low and steady as his irritation returned. "Unlock the door, my lady. If you do not plan on obeying my request, then you will kindly step away from the panel as I break it down."

He could hear her shriek of outrage. "Break it down and I...I shall jump from the window!"

"'Tis a long way down, lass. Opening the door would be less drastic."

Behind the closed panel, he could hear a good deal of muttering and bumping. In truth, he had to fight off a smile at her pluck. She was certainly feisty in the face of a violent threat.

"Do you hear me? Open the door or I shall break it down this instant." More muttering, more grunting. "I am jumping now!"

He cocked an eyebrow. He couldn't be positive that she wasn't bluffing and he certainly did not want her death on his hands. Standing away from the door, he raised a massive boot and lashed out at the bolted panel. In an explosion of splinters, the door came apart and Kirk was into the room before the wood had even settled.

He was concerned when he discovered the room empty. Rushing for the window, he was confronted by a rope of bed linens, secured to the heavy bed on one end and then disappearing out the lancet opening. Puzzled, he grasped the rope as he stuck his head from the window to see what was on the opposite end of the line.

He could make out long dark hair and a worn surcoat perched on the ledge several feet away. It was a rather precarious position but she was absolutely plastered against the wall, fingers clutching at the stone. For someone attempting to jump, she wasn't doing a very good job.

"My lady?" The tone was droll. "What, may I ask, are you doing?"

Pressed against the stone wall as far as she could go, the small figure refused to budge. "Jumping!"

Kirk did grin, then. "With a rope around your waist?"

"I did not want to fall before I was ready!"

"I see." He leaned lazily against the windowsill, the humor of the situation apparent. "And when will you be ready?"

The dark head twitched. "Soon. Sooner still if you do not go away and leave me alone."

Kirk snorted softly, glancing to the ground below; nearly three stories up, it was a severe drop and he could see his men gazing up with interest. In fact, the two knights that had accompanied him, Sir Corwin Martin and Sir Niles de Worth, were directly below and he waved weakly in response to their inquisitive expressions.

"I do not plan to leave," he said, simply to goad her. "In fact, I have a rather good view of the entire event. I plan to watch."

On the small ledge, the tiny figure shifted, pressing herself even closer to the wall. "Then I shan't jump. I shall stay here until you leave."

The rope was still in his grasp. With a wicked grin, Kirk tugged on it, enough for her to feel it. "Come on, lass. It's been a long time since I have seen a good jumping."

She squealed as he tugged. "Stop it! Stop it, I say!"

Kirk could hardly hold back the giggles, tugging more firmly on the rope. "Do not be shy, lass. Go ahead and jump."

She screamed and he was forced to bite back great guffaws of laughter. "Damn you for tormenting me, you brutish fiend!" she howled. "Stop pulling on the rope!"

He continued to tug mischievously. "Please?"

"Nay!"

"I promise I shall applaud loudly. I shall even throw money if it's particularly gruesome."

"Stop pulling!"

He did, but not before he gave the rope one final tweak. "Then come in here if you are not going to jump, you naughty wench. How dare you taunt me with promises of blood and pain."

17

The dark head shifted, turning toward him. Kirk's smile faded when he beheld features more beautiful than anything he had ever witnessed. Delicate, porcelain beauty with eyes of the brightest blue. Eyes that were currently blazing with fury.

"Let go of the rope, you beast," she hissed. "I am coming to the window and if you had any intelligence, you would run for your life!"

He continued to stare at her, so mesmerized by her beauty that he hardly heard the threat.

"Come back in here." He wondered why his voice sounded so peculiar. Moving to the edge of the window, he extended his hand. "Come along, Mara. I shall help you."

A well-shaped black brow lifted. "How did you know my name?"

"Your sister told me. Come back in before the rain begins."

Bright blue eyes dared to glance at the threatening sky. In fact, she could smell the imminent storm. But his outstretched hand somehow fed her stubbornness and Mara frowned, very slowly inching her way back to the window.

"Put your hand down," she grumbled. "I shall not accept it. I can do this alone."

He raised an eyebrow, drawing his hand back but not removing it completely. Her skirts were in her way as she crept along the ledge and he found himself watching her footing very carefully.

"Were you really going to jump?"

"Of course," she said boldly. "I still might if you plan to force me to travel to Anchorsholme Castle."

"I do. Jump if you must."

Her frown deepened, out of place on her lovely face. "Then untie the rope from the bed. I am going to go through with it."

He shook his head. "I am not going to untie anything. If you truly wish to jump, then unfasten the rope around your waist."

She stepped on the edge of her surcoat, tugging it carefully from beneath her slipper. "Has anyone ever told you that you are a nasty, disagreeable man?"

"Constantly."

"And this Irish accent; it offends me. Why did you not simply stay in Ireland where you belong?"

"Because my family has served the House of De Cleveley for three generations," he said patiently. "I had no choice but to come to England and associate with stubborn English females like yourself."

She scowled, taking her focus off the ledge for a brief moment. "I do not like you."

"Good."

"Mayhap you did not understand me clearly. I really do not like you. I loathe you. In fact, when my sister is married to de Cleverey, I am going to make sure that you are reduced from captain to scullery maid."

"The name is de Cleveley. And I am too hairy to be a scullery maid."

Her surcoat was caught beneath her feet again but neither one of them realized it until it was too late. Before Mara could deliver another insult, she lost her balance and plunged from the ledge.

Instinctively, Kirk snatched the linen rope, holding it tight. About ten feet below him, Mara gasped and twisted.

"Stop moving, lass!" he commanded. "I shall pull you in, but you must stop moving!"

Clutching the rope, Mara's voice was tight with fear. "I... I did not tie it about my waist very well! It is slipping!"

A bolt of panic surged through Kirk, entirely foreign to the usually calm man. It was difficult to maintain a cool, steady motion while reeling in the rope; he did not want to jerk it in his haste and end up losing her altogether.

"I have almost got you." His voice was calm. "Just a little further and I have got you."

He could hear her fearful grunts, struggling to control his own apprehension. Hand-over-hand, he was nearly to the point where he could reach down and grab her when Micheline suddenly bolted into the room. Her scream of terror was almost enough to cause him to lose his grip.

"My God!" Micheline cried, plowing into Kirk in her attempt to catch a glimpse of her sister. "Mara, darling, hold on!"

Bright blue eyes gazed up at the two concerned faces several feet above. "Misha, I am sorry!" she cried, a far different attitude from the belligerent girl of moments before. "I should not have been so difficult and I swear if God allows me to live, I shall never do anything so stupid again! And I shall go with you to Anchorsholme, I promise!"

Kirk very nearly had her. "God is not pulling you from your death, my lady, I am." He paused in his struggles. Stepping on the rope to hold it steady, he held out a hand as far as it would go. "Take hold, lass. Take hold!"

Mara could feel the tie around her waist loosening. Struggling to keep hold with one hand, she tried to reach him but missed by an inch. Feeling the rope as it continued to unwind, she gripped the linen fearfully with two hands again.

"I can't," she moaned. "I shall fall!"

Kirk knew how terrified she was. He was terrified, too. Resuming his pull on the rope, he reeled carefully. "It's all right, I shall pull you up." He heard a shaken voice, hardly aware that it was his own. A couple of more tugs and Mara let out a piercing scream.

Kirk watched as the rope spun away from her waist, leaving her free and dangling several stories above the bailey. She was nearing panic, her gasps of fright heavy as her hold slipped.

"My hands!" She looked up at Kirk with those brilliant eyes. "They are wet. I can't hold on any longer!"

She was just beyond his reach. Feeling a real surge of desperation, Kirk was about to make another attempt at grabbing her purely for the fact that he knew his time had run out when Niles and Corwin came storming into the room. Kirk caught sight of his knights, feeling a burst of hope.

"Hold the rope," he ordered, releasing it to Niles' strong arms. Throwing himself across the windowsill, his massive hands reached with desperation for the dangling lady.

"I can't hold on," Mara cried again.

"Aye, you can." He could touch her but he couldn't quite get a grip. "Niles! Pull, man, pull!"

Someone had him by the legs. Hanging from the window, it gave him the reach he needed to grab her by the wrist just as her grip failed. Mara shrieked as the rope fell away, her slender wrist straining under Kirk's iron hold and the undue stress of her dead weight.

Somehow, he made it back onto the windowsill. He had Mara by two hands now, hauling her up with him. She was gasping, panicked and weary, and he pulled her through the window and into his massive arms.

They were both panting, shaken. It took Kirk a moment to realize he was clutching her tightly, never more relieved of anything in his entire life.

"You're safe now, lass," he murmured into silken dark hair. "I have got you."

Micheline extended her arms, trying to take Mara from Kirk's embrace. "Mara darling!" she cried. "Thank God you're safe. I thought I was going to lose you!"

Mara was clutching Kirk with a death-grip. After a moment, the bright blue eyes appeared from the safe cozy of his neck. "Never," she whispered, holding out a hand. "I am so sorry, Misha. Please forgive me."

Micheline clutched the hand tightly, kissing the small fingers as she looked to Kirk. "My lord," she said breathlessly. "We are forever in your debt. No price shall be too great to ask in reward for saving my sister's life."

Kirk found he could hardly respond. The greatest reward of all was nestled in his embrace, warm and soft and trembling. But he nodded faintly, setting Mara to the ground before he grew too comfortable with the feel of her in his arms. She collapsed against Micheline, the two sisters holding each other tightly.

Kirk glanced up at Niles and Corwin, noting that the knights were fairly shaken as well. Drawing in a deep breath to regain his composure, he struggled not to appear too unnerved by the whole event.

"Since you promised your sister that you would accompany her to Anchorsholme Castle, Lady Mara, I shall hold you to your vow." He was already moving to the chamber door. As if trying to escape the unfamiliar emotions that had just occurred. "Since you are not packed for the journey, I shall give you until tomorrow morning. Considering the weather is worsening, I suspect we would do well spending the night at Haslingden."

Mara looked up from her sister's breast long enough to lock gazes with him. Before she could offer a measure of thanks, he quit the room with his knights in tow. Staring at the empty doorway, Mara was left to ponder the annoying, heroic appearance of Sir Kirk Connaught.

CHAPTER TWO

"Has she said a word to you?"

The weather had worsened since leaving Haslingden that morn, the addition of a nippy gale making life generally uncomfortable. The sky overhead was gray, the smell of rain pervasive and sharp. Astride his muscular charger, Kirk refused to glance at the wind-whipped young lady riding several paces behind him. "Not a word."

Niles, however, did look at her. Swathed in a heavy cloak that was both too large and too worn, Mara was watching the muddied road pass beneath her mare's hooves. With a shake of the head, Niles returned his attention to the bleak landscape.

"Not even a word for saving her life?"

"Nothing."

"Ungrateful wench. You should have let her fall."

Kirk chewed on his lip as his steed plodded along, refusing to reply to Niles' cruel statement. "We should see Ormskirk in another hour. We shall find a clearing to pitch camp and be gone before sunrise. Hopefully we shall reach Anchorsholme by the nooning meal."

Niles nodded, passing the information to the men-at-arms. To Kirk's left, Corwin let out a nasty burp.

"Good Christ," he gurgled. "I can still taste this morning's meal. Disgusting as it was, barley gruel."

"Considering the poverty of the keep, we were fortunate for that." Niles cast a disgusted glance at Corwin. "What about the powder Lord Edmund's physic gave you? Doesn't that settle your stomach?"

"I used it all." Corwin was struggling not to retch in front of the ladies. "Yesterday, in fact."

Niles shook his head. "For a man who has spent his entire life in the saddle, I find it extremely peculiar that your stomach has not grown accustomed to the sway of a horse."

Corwin puffed out his cheeks as another strong burp rocked him, discreetly passing it off. "The sway of the horse, the sway of a wagon, makes little difference. Any movement makes me ill." He was suddenly overtaken with another burp, so loud that the men-at-arms snickered.

Kirk was rattled by the sound, distracted from the thoughts that had plagued him most of the day and night. Thoughts involving the ungrateful, foolish, alluring Lady Mara. Forcing himself back to the world at hand, his deep voice rumbled with impatience. "We have ladies with us, Corwin. Control your repulsive habits."

"I cannot help it, my lord," he said sullenly. "You know how travel affects me."

"I know all too well." Kirk cast the auburn-haired knight a long glance. "But I ask that you control yourself just the same."

The journey progressed silently, aside from the various sounds emitting from Corwin's body, no matter how hard he tried to suppress them. The weather, strangely, was now threatening to clear, wisps of sunlight filtering through the clouds. On the outskirts of Ormskirk, Kirk spied a sheltered clearing and immediately called a halt. Men-at-arms rushed the pasture, establishing the site as Kirk moved to the ladies.

"We will camp here for the night, ladies," he said, looking down from his tall charger. "We shall rise early and be at Anchorsholme by noon."

Micheline nodded submissively while Mara eyed the busy soldiers. She had no intention of sleeping in the wet grass. "The weather is damp, my lord," she said, turning her bright blue gaze to him. "Micheline's health has always been delicate."

He met her steadily. "There will be a warm fire and adequate bedding. I am sure the lady will fare well."

As he feared, a willful eyebrow lifted. "An inn would do better. Micheline is, after all, the intended of a baron. Would a decent room not be more suitable to her station?"

She had a point. Kirk looked at Micheline who, sensing his attention, immediately flushed. "A sturdy tent will do very well, my lord. An inn will not be necessary."

Mara turned to her sister before Kirk could reply. "Ridiculous, Misha. Do you remember that bout with the chill two months ago? Why, you have only just recovered. Moreover, you are to be married to a wealthy man and there is no reason why you should not be provided with the comforts befitting his station."

Micheline's blush deepened, her plain blue eyes fixed on her sister. "Please, Mara," she hissed, refocusing on Kirk's intense gaze. "An inn is not necessary, my lord. A pitched shelter will do quite nicely."

Mara opened her mouth but Kirk blotted out her response. "As you say, Lady Micheline." He ignored Mara's frustrated expression. "Lord Edmund has sent along his very own travel bedding for your comfort."

He reined his horse in the direction of the camp when Mara's voice stopped him. "I would hardly call dusty furs and molding linens appropriate comfort." She made sure Kirk was looking at her when she spoke. "My sister deserves the best."

"And she shall have it."

23

"I am speaking of a warm inn."

"And I am not." The stone-gray eyes cooled. "This discussion is ended, Lady Mara."

Mara and Micheline watched him trample through the winter grass, gesturing to a few men and sending them running.

"You should not provoke him, Mara," Micheline said softly, eyeing the soldiers that had been left to watch over them. "He has been exceptionally patient with you. Not to mention the fact that he saved your life yesterday."

Mara looked away stubbornly. "I would not have been forced out onto the ledge had he not threatened to break my door down. 'Tis his own fault that I almost fell to my death."

Micheline sighed. "'Tis your own willfulness that almost cost you your life. And it would make my life considerably easier if you would learn to control yourself. I have enough to worry over with thoughts of a new husband."

Mara cast her sister a long glance. "I am in perfect control, Misha. And I was perfectly correct in asking Sir Kirk to take us to an inn. You deserve proper lodgings, as a future baroness."

"I am not speaking of that in particular, but everything." Micheline's gaze moved to the distant camp, a weak fire beginning to smoke. "Really, Mara. I simply do not have the strength to deal with your bold nature or Sir Kirk's resulting anger."

Mara followed her sister's gaze to the glowing encampment. She could see that Kirk had dismounted his warhorse, head-and-shoulders taller than the rest of his men as he stalked the camp to make sure everything was proceeding orderly. His men practically bowed at his feet, making haste to carry out any order or request.

"His anger is of no concern to me," she said, watching the activity. "Especially when I am correct."

Micheline's expression suggested nothing but impatience. "Correct or no, you must learn to curb your mouth. If not for yourself, then for me. Please consider my position; how would it appear for the new baroness to have a hellion for a sister?"

Mara did not reply for a moment, the bright blue eyes suddenly growing distant. "Do you recall the last time you visited an inn, Misha?"

Micheline blushed with the change of subject, lowering her gaze. "Not a word, Mara. I refuse to...."

"Father used to make you dance for money to feed his gambling habit." Mara wasn't listening to her sister's protests. "And he would leave me outside, on the street, pretending I was an orphan and begging for more money. Do you remember?"

Micheline refused to answer. Met with silence, Mara turned to her sister. "Do you?" When Micheline nodded weakly, Mara's expression softened. "That is why you do not want to go to an inn, isn't it? They hold nothing but bad memories for you."

Micheline sighed deeply, avoiding Mara's knowing stare. "The smell of ale and sweat still makes me vomit," she murmured, sickened by the painful memories. "The only reason father did not prostitute me was because he knew he could get a better price for a virgin bride."

"But in the end, he used you to pay off a gambling debt as if you were a commodity."

"To Monroe de Cleveley," Micheline finished quietly, "as a bride for his only son."

Mara observed her sister's pained expression. She had been young enough not to mind begging, her aggressive nature having served her well. But Micheline, just over the brink of womanhood, had been embarrassed to display herself like a common trollop. Dancing for drunken soldiers, or singing in her piercing soprano for the few coins they would throw. It had been a shameful way to grow up, better left forgotten. But not before Edward le Bec bestowed one final act of humiliation by using his eldest daughter to settle a substantial gambling obligation.

Mara knew that Micheline's humiliation ran deep, being likened to hard currency rather than flesh and blood. "Think on it this way, Misha." She attempted to lighten the heady mood that had settled. "A wealthy husband and the title of baroness. Mayhap Father's gambling habit will have positive results, after all."

Micheline nodded faintly, feeling the first few drops of rain cool her flaming cheeks. "I wonder what he looks like." She raised her eyes, meeting Mara's gaze. "My husband, I mean. I have been wondering for two years."

Mara smiled. "Dashing, I am sure."

Kirk's bellow echoed in the distance and both ladies turned toward the camp. "As dashing as Sir Kirk?" Micheline asked softly.

Mara shrugged. "He's a beast. A misshapen giant."

"He's terribly handsome, Mara. Or hadn't you noticed through all of your resistance?"

She had, if she were to admit it. A square jaw, thick dark lashes and a straight nose. And this morning she had even caught a glimpse of dark, shiny hair beneath his hauberk; before he donned his helm and transformed into an evil fighting machine that took delight in dominating her.

"I have noticed that he is three times my size." She turned her nose up stubbornly; there was no way Micheline would be able to wrangle a confession from her. "His fists are as big as my head."

"Who cares about his fists?" Micheline smiled, almost seductively. "I was speaking of his face."

Mara's brow furrowed, refusing to agree with her sister's assessment. Even though she realized she would very much like to. Turning away, she reined her old mare in the direction of the camp.

"I see they've pitched a couple of tents," she said. "Come along, Misha. It's been a long day for you."

Micheline followed. "I am sorry you have to sleep in a tent, darling. I just... just cannot abide sleeping in an inn."

Mara shrugged, far too carelessly. "But I can. And if I feel like going to an inn to enjoy a warm atmosphere and protection from the rain, then I shall. If Kirk Connaught is going to force me to accompany you to Anchorsholme, he'll have to pay for his decision."

Micheline looked shocked. "Why would you do this? The man is only doing his job, Mara. And inns are nothing but dens for gambling and debauchery. You know this to be true."

Mara shrugged again, noting the campfire was blazing brightly. "I spent most of my time outside of the inns, Misha. Only you and father went inside. I have always found them to be rather... flavorful."

"Flavorful?" Micheline was horrified. "How can you say that?"

They were nearing the camp perimeter and Mara shushed her sister firmly. "Not to worry, Misha. I would never do anything foolish."

"But you are thinking foolish thoughts, little goat."

From the corner of her eye, Mara caught sight of Kirk as they entered the camp. Seeing the travel-weary ladies, Kirk left the task of securing a section of tent and made his way toward them. Mara kept her eyes trained on him, the face Micheline thought was so very handsome.

"For me, these thoughts are not so foolish," she murmured. "They are perfectly normal."

"As I said," Micheline closed her eyes in silent prayer, "foolish."

***

Mara waited until the camp was quiet before making her move. The clouds had returned, as had the rain, and she made sure Micheline was asleep before stirring from her bed. The soft glow from the dying fire cast long shadows as she peered from the tent, watching the sentries pace the encampment. Waiting for the last pair of soldiers to disappear into the bramble, she slipped from the shelter and into the trees.

The village was visible about a mile down the road. Mud splashed on her worn shoes as she trudged down the thoroughfare, but Mara was unconcerned with the discomfort. She was determined to make it to town, to beg a few coins off a rich soldier as she had done so ably when she was young, and then indulge herself in a fine goblet of mead to toast her victory against Kirk.

Ormskirk was a smelly, dirty town. As Mara skipped along the road, dodging horses and men, her gaze fell on a large hostel by the edge of town. Looking through the window, she could see the laughing people and smell the smelly warmth. It was inviting and she quickly decided to become a part of it. Slipping in behind a group of well-dressed knights, she lost herself in the crowd.

No one noticed the tiny woman skirting the edge of the room, gazing curiously at what she had described to her sister as 'flavor'. Soldiers gnawing on bloodied meat, wenches with painted faces seated on their lap. There was song and gaiety and the stench of close-packed bodies filling the air. As Mara made her way to the blazing hearth, she thought all of it to be rather exciting.

The fire was scorching. Warming her hands before the blaze, the smell of beef was making her hungry. Face partially shielded by the wet hood, Mara's gaze scanned the room in search of a potential benefactor.

In the corner of the room sat a fat merchant, dining alone on a stew of turnips and mutton. Mara watched the man for a moment, sensing he was kind and hoping her instincts were right. Squaring her shoulders, she went to his table.

The man was a loud eater. Trying to appear as pathetic as possible, Mara clasped her hands against her breast.

"Kind sir," she said dramatically. "Could you find it within your heart to spare a poor widow a few coins with which to eat?"

The man paused in mid-chew, his gaze moving the length of her dripping cloak. Swallowing hard, he coughed loudly and struggled not to choke.

"A widow?" He coughed again. Then, he looked annoyed. "Go away, lass. Can you not see that I am eating?"

Mara would not be dissuaded. "But - sir! I have not eaten in days, and my children...."

"Children?"

She nodded eagerly. "Nine of them. They have not eaten, either."

The merchant raised his eyebrows. "You have nine children?" he repeated. "You're hardly more than a child yourself."

Mara drew herself up, proudly. "I am a woman grown, sir. And I would thank you kindly for helping to feed my children."

"All nine of them."

"Aye, sir."

The man took a bite of bread, chewing slowly. "You're not a very good liar, lass."

Mara looked innocent. "Sir?"

He took another bite of bread. "Who are you begging for? Your husband? Father, mayhap?"

Mara shook her head. "Myself, sir. Myself and...."

He put up a hand. "I know, I know. And your nine children."

"Aye, sir." Mara thought she could sense some amusement in his expression. "Will you help us?"

He continued to gaze at her, chewing on his bread. "How old are you?"

Mara thought quickly. "Twenty-two, sir."

"Twenty-two, eh?" He put the bread down, collecting his wooden cup. "You must have borne your first child at ten years of age."

She refused to recant her story. Once he had her confession, she was certain he would refuse to give her any coin. "Thirteen, sir. I... I was a very young bride."

"Indeed." He drank deeply of his watered ale. A dog came around looking for handouts and Mara shooed it away as it sniffed her skirt.

"Well?" she almost demanded. "Can you spare a few coins, sir? Or must I beg elsewhere?"

He raised an eyebrow. "Demanding little wench, aren't you? There is a fine line between robbing and begging."

Mara sighed. "I do apologize. 'Tis just that my children are starving and...."

He put up a hand, snorting into his cup. "No more, lass. I shall give you a few pence and be gone with you."

Mara held out her hand and he deposited five coins into her palm. Flashing him a brilliant smile, she clutched the money to her breast and made her way across the room. Just as she neared an empty table against the wall, a large hand suddenly reached out to grab her.

Mara shrieked as she plopped into an armored lap. "Let me go!"

Loud male laughter filled the stale air. "Relax, sweetling. I won't hurt you."

She twisted violently, her hood coming off in the process. Silky black hair cascaded down her back, drawing a sigh of appreciation from the table's occupants.

"Ah, what have we here?" The knight gripped her with both hands, studying her beauty. "A fine, fine catch, I'd say."

She struggled to be free, smelling the liquor on his breath. "I demand you release me immediately!"

"But why?" He shifted his grip, touching her face with a thick finger. "Christ, you're a lovely one. Name your price."

Grimacing with exertion, Mara shoved an elbow into his throat, managing to dislodge his hold. But no sooner had she bound to her feet than another knight grabbed her.

"Hold, lady," he growled. "Not so fast. He asked you to name your price."

Mara knew what they meant. She's spent too much time exposed to the atmosphere taverns to interpret any other meaning. Her indignation was joined by a healthy measure of fear as she struggled to free herself from yet another accoster.

"No price," she hissed. "Let me alone!"

The knight was strong. He and his three companions were enjoying her torment, drunk with too much food and alcohol.

"I shall give you five gold pieces, lass." The first knight who had grabbed her, an older man, was searching for his purse in spite of the fact that she had shoved her elbow into his neck.

"I told you," she grunted, succeeding in freeing one hand. "I am not for sale. Find your pleasure with another."

"The whole world's for sale, at the right price." The knight who held her captive received a slap on the chin for his troubles. "Come on, love. We shall be gentle, we promise."

With a grunt, Mara yanked herself free and stumbled over a chair, struggling to get away. The knights laughed, the older man rising to his feet in pursuit. Mara managed to get around the chair, planning to duck out through the kitchens when a powerful arm grasped her around the waist.

She could smell the ale on his breath, making her gag as his lips pressed against her ear. "Come along, sweetling. It's been a long time since I have tasted flesh as sweet as yours."

Mara's feet were dangling off the ground, her slight weight nothing against his strength. For the first time in her life, she knew what it was to sense panic. And she had a load of it. Kicking and twisting, she refused to let him take her without a fight.

Wondering, as he struggled to get her up the stairs to his rented room, if the price of her spite against Kirk Connaught would be too high.

***

It was exceedingly late. The rains had lessened again, the highs and lows of harsh winter weather, leaving the landscape wet and miserable. The only light was from the fire or the torches men carried as they went about their rounds, protecting the camp perimeter and the ladies it housed.

Kirk had been tending Corwin's charger, the animal having pulled a tendon during the journey. Leaving the charger with a wrap on its leg and a worried master, he made his way through the wet foliage and into the hub of the smoky encampment.

He passed Niles, sound asleep in a make-shift tent. The sound of the man's snoring was enough to wake the dead and Kirk kicked the knight's exposed foot as he passed by. The man rolled to his side and the obnoxious sound quieted.

The ladies tent was set away from the others purely for privacy's sake. Kirk was almost to his tent when he paused, thinking to check on the women before he turned in for the night. Wondering if the little she-devil had managed to fall asleep in spite of the fact that the drooping structure wasn't her precious inn.

He paused outside of the tent, listening. It was completely silent. Carefully, he lifted the edge of the flap, peering inside; Lady Micheline was sleeping soundly, curled on Edmund's furs. But the bed next to her was empty and Kirk threw back the covering, his stone-gray eyes blazing.

"Lady Micheline," he hissed. "Micheline!"

Micheline jolted awake. "M-My lord?"

"Where is your sister?"

Micheline blinked, looking at the bedding beside her. Touching it, as if to make sure it was truly empty, she shook her head.

"I d-do not know, my lord," she said truthfully. "Mayhap she is in the bramble... relieving herself, as it were."

"She's not in the bramble. I have sentries all over this camp and someone would have told me."

Micheline struggled to clear the cobwebs of sleep from her mind, thinking. "She was perturbed that you refused to take us to an inn. Mayhap she..."

That was all Kirk needed to hear. He was halfway across the encampment, heading for the tethered chargers before Micheline realized what was happening. Plain blue eyes wide with fright, she hovered at the edge of the tent, watching as Kirk thundered from camp astride his great red beast. Dazed and apprehensive, she had little choice but to return to the huddle of Edmund's furs.

But she did not sleep.

Oh, Mara... what have you done now?

***

The broken pitcher had cut her hand when she smashed it on his shoulder. Bleeding and sobbing, Mara remained under the bed where the knight couldn't reach her. He stomped about, issuing violent threats as she continued to resist him; refusing to sate his lust.

In hindsight, it hadn't been the wisest decision to leave camp. She should have remained, by Micheline's side, safe and sound as Lord Edmund's men watched over her. Even Kirk. He had saved her from falling to her death yesterday, but she doubted he could save her from what was about to happen. The results of her own stupidity.

But that was the problem with Mara. Always regretting her hasty actions, allowing her impulsive nature to rule her common sense. Micheline attributed her foolishness to her youthful years; Mara hoped she was right. She hoped that with age would come sensible maturity. And as the knight continued to rage and drink, Mara prayed she would live that long.

As fearful as she was, she grew even more fearful when the shouting finally stopped. She could hear footfalls pacing about the room and just when she thought, mayhap, the knight had given up, she was startled when a massive hand reached under the bed. Unable to move away fast enough, the knight had her by the skirts and pulled her out in a flash.

"There you are, sweetling." He threw her on the bed, his heavy body landing atop her. Mara swallowed the bile in her throat as he tried to kiss her. "You were a naughty girl, hiding from me. Now is your chance to make amends."

Mara twisted, turning her head and struggling not to vomit. He was heavy, crushing her slight body into the mattress. The knight's slobbering lips were on her cheek, her chin, moving down her neck. As Mara gasped and fought, he brought both of her hands up and pinned them above her head.

With one free hand he could do a good deal of damage. Starting at her round breasts, he squeezed them roughly and Mara screamed. The minute she opened her mouth, he put his tongue in it.

She spit and twisted, weeping as he laughed. The hand moved down her torso, fumbling with her skirts, and Mara's struggles increased. A calloused hand ran the length of her leg and she lashed out, managing to kick him as his attention focused on the unfurled flower between her legs. The knight grunted, using a knee to spread her legs as his hand moved to her bare buttocks.

Sharply, he slapped her white bottom. "Cease!" he growled. "Since I have no intention of releasing you, I would suggest you learn to enjoy it."

Mara ignored him, still twisting and bucking. If she wasn't enjoying the encounter, then she would make sure he did not either. She simply couldn't believe her foolishness had led her to this point, her innocence about to be taken by a drunken knight. The only thing of personal value she possessed was about to be stolen and she vowed at the moment that if God would allow her to come through intact, she would never do anything so stupid again.

But her prayers were cut short as the knight's hand moved to the black ringlets between her legs. Mara screamed again, trying desperately to avoid his probing fingers. He grinned lewdly, stroking the dry folds.

"Give me a bit of dew, sweetling," he muttered, his breath coming in heavy gasps. "'Twill make it easier on you."

She had no idea what he was talking about, panic filling her. A thick finger wormed its way inside her and she screamed again.

"Just a little bit," he rasped against her cheek. "Just a little and I shall end your torment."

There was a knock at the door. The knight turned his head away from Mara long enough to bellow at the interruption.

"Leave us!"

His finger was moving inside her, uncomfortable and foreign. Mara whimpered, tears trailing down her temples, as the knight's wriggling finger suddenly stopped. His eyes widened as he stared at her.

"You're a virgin?" He moved his finger again and she cried out in fear. Sighing raggedly, his gaze raked her pale face. "I can feel your maidenhood resisting me. Oh, sweetling, what a pleasure this will be."

His mouth tried to claim her again, but she turned her head away, sobbing. The knight, however, was unable to progress any further; the chamber door suddenly exploded in a hail of splinters and Mara saw a flash of steel and armor. The knight rolled off her, scrambling for his weapon as the intruder entered the room.

Kirk brought the blade down against the man's neck, going no further than to imply the obvious. The knight froze and dropped his weapon as stone-gray eyes glittered with unnatural fury.

"I am weaponless, my lord," he said calmly.

Kirk did not reply. His eyes remained trained on the defenseless knight as he spoke to Mara.

"Did he deflower you, Mara?"

Mara was standing by the end of the bed on quaking legs. She had no idea how she got there. "Nay, my lord," she whispered, her voice trembling. "But... but he tried."

Kirk's blade remained poised at the man's neck a moment longer before removing it with amazing speed. "Then I will spare him," he growled. "Vacate this room immediately before I change my mind."

The knight rose, collecting his armor and weapons. Kirk continued to stare at the man as he quit the room, unmoving until he heard the boot falls fade away. Then, he turned to Mara.

"What happened?"

She was shaking so terribly that she had to sit down. She could hardly look him in the eye. "I wanted to sleep in a warm, dry inn," she said weakly. "The knight thought I was a whore. How did you find me?"

Kirk sheathed his sword and suddenly, he was looming over her. "By thinking like an idiot," he said, a flash of anger coming through. "Christ, woman, what on earth possessed you to do something like this?"

She was staring at her bloodied hand. "I... I wanted to sleep at the inn," she repeated, feeling exhausted and ashamed. "Micheline does not like taverns, so I...."

"So you went regardless of the fact that had I denied you, simply to spite me," he finished for her, his anger piqued. In fact, he couldn't remember when he had been quite so angry. Or, for the second time in as many days, frightened. Working into a righteous rage, he noticed Mara's bloody hand and felt himself weaken. "Did he do that?"

She shook her head. Kirk watched as a single tear fell, bathing the bloodied flesh. "I did it whilst attempting to defend myself."

He sighed heavily, his fury fading in spite of the effort to maintain it. Glancing about, he spied a square of linen by the basin and snatched it, kneeling beside Mara and silently wrapping her hand. He was nearly finished when he glanced up to find bright blue eyes staring at him.

"This is twice in two days that you have saved me."

The vortex of her eyes was enough to erase all fury. Christ, she was so very lovely, so fragile. And so terribly headstrong. Wrestling against a same unfamiliar tenderness that had swamped him yesterday, he tore his gaze away.

"And who was there to save you before I arrived?" he asked, gruffly, to mask his emotions. "I cannot imagine that I have seen your first attempts at foolishness."

She did not say anything for a moment and Kirk forced himself to look at her. It was the first time since they had met that she appeared emotionally vulnerable. Away from all of the fire and resistance, he could see the soft little lady beneath.

"There was no one to save me," she murmured. "I did as I pleased."

He wasn't strong enough to tear his gaze away this time. The urge to give into the strange emotions was overwhelming. "Those days are gone, lady."

She continued to stare at him, without the usual hostility. "My sister calls me a hellion."

"And my men call me The Master. Who do you suppose will be the first to surrender to the other?"

"'Twill not be me."

"It had better be. Or I will do what I should have done yesterday."

"What is that?"

He rose, the stone-gray eyes intense. "Take my hand to your backside. One more infraction and I shall."

She lowered her gaze, giving a careless shrug. "My father threatened me all the time but never once carried through."

"Then you do not fear my threat?"

The bright gaze fixed on him again. He swore he saw a flicker of a smile. "I believe you."

"That is not what I asked."

"I know what you asked." She stood from the bed, deliberately avoiding his gaze and he saw the smile broaden. "I choose to give you a pleasing answer rather than the reply you truly seek."

He sighed heavily. If he had any sense, he would spank her this minute and be done with it. Even so, he couldn't seem to muster the will and his impotency confused him. Knowing only that this lack of sense had something to do with the odd warmth this little hellion seemed to provoke. Emotions he had no intention of exploring.

"We shall arrive at Anchorsholme come the morrow," he muttered. "I suggest for your own sake that you behave yourself, whether or not you give credence to my threat. Do you comprehend?"

Mara nodded faintly. But Kirk did not like the gleam to her eye; nay, he did not like it at all.

CHAPTER THREE

The following morning dawned amazingly bright considering the rain that had pounded for most of the night. The camp was quickly disassembled and a simple meal of bread and cheese provided. Before the sun burst free of the eastern horizon, the escort party was on the road, nearing home with the prize of their lord's betrothed.

At the first sight of Anchorsholme Castle, Micheline's jaw dropped and she burst into tears. Riding beside her sister under clear skies and a brisk sea breeze, Mara tried to comfort the weeping woman. A halting explanation revealed that Micheline felt herself unworthy to preside over such splendor. All anticipation of her new marriage aside, the very real fact remained that the woman was terrified to meet her destiny.

Up until the moment Micheline dissolved into tears, the air between the sisters had been strained. Kirk had remained tactfully silent, allowing Mara to explain to her sister what had happened the previous eve. She did not mention the near-rape or Kirk's heroic appearance, only the brief story about the fat merchant and nine children. Had Micheline not been so angry with her sister's show of rebellion, she would have laughed at her play-acting. For all she knew, Mara had been seized by Kirk at the inn and escorted back to camp.

With the subject gracefully skirted, it had been a long ride to Anchorsholme. The Lancashire castle was a magnificent Norman structure near the sea with an inner and outer wall to protect the mighty three storied keep. As a pair of hawks shrieked overhead, the escort party was greeted by a host of well-formed ranks. Taking a good look at their fine tunics and armor, Micheline began to weep all over again.

"Welcome to The Darkland, ladies." Corwin was riding slightly behind them, the impressive structure reflecting in his soft brown eyes.

Mara, in the midst of calming her sister, turned to the knight. "Why do you call it The Darkland?"

Over the top of Mara's head, Corwin caught Niles' negative expression. Clearing his throat, he shrugged faintly.

"Lord Edmund's Irish subjects gave it the name, I suppose, because they consider their English overlord to be the Devil himself." A very simple version of the disturbing truth.

Mara frowned, her gaze raking the structure. "It doesn't look dark to me."

Niles interrupted before Corwin could say any more. "A figure of speech, my lady."

Mara continued to stare at the castle, a single stone tower reaching for the sky. It was such a beautiful place that she could hardly justify her reluctance to come.

"I did not know Lord Edmund had lands in Ireland." She turned her inquisitive gaze to Corwin. "Where is the property?"

"Wicklow, my lady, south of Dublin," he replied. "The lands were part of his grandmother's dowry. A very large, very profitable piece of land."

"Profitable?"

"Sheep," Corwin explained. "Fine wool and Irish whisky, to name a few."

Mara nodded in understanding, noting that Micheline's hysteria had calmed. Plain blue eyes studied the structure as the woman hastened to dry her tears. She was a sight enough for her prospective bridegroom without the added distraction of red-rimmed eyes.

"Sir Kirk is from Ireland," she sniffled. "Is he from Wicklow?"

Corwin spurred his horse forward, next to Mara as he answered. "Kirk's grandfather was a great warlord. He served Lord Edmund's grandfather for many years as adjutant for the Wicklow properties. Kirk's father assumed the position after his father's death, while Kirk came to Anchorsholme to personally serve the House of de Cleveley."

Mara's gaze was lingering on the massive knight at the head of the column, his armor reflecting the weak sunlight. "Will Kirk go back to Ireland to assume the position at his father's passing?"

Corwin nodded. "Aye. Nearly half of County Wicklow belongs to the House of de Cleveley. Kirk's father commands over four hundred English troops to protect and enforce the holdings."

Mara continued to observe the distant knight, swaying in rhythm to his horse. In spite of the fact that he had become both her mortal enemy and her savior, Corwin's impressive tales about the man and his genealogy piqued her curiosity.

"Where did Sir Kirk foster?"

"Kenilworth, my lady. Lord Edmund's father pledge him to the royal household to train."

"Why?"

Corwin smiled, a lop-sided gesture. "Because when Kirk was seven years of age, he was as tall as you are and several pounds heavier. The man is a product of centuries of Celt lineage and Monroe De Cleveley recognized the natural warrior in him. Better to train him properly with strong loyalty to England than to leave him in the land of his forefathers where he can wreak havoc against the House of Tudor."

Mara pondered Kirk's pedigree, agreeing inwardly that it was somewhat respectable. But considering her lineage was also powerful in spite of her father's drain on the family funds, she continued to act as if nothing about Kirk was impressive.

"He's an Irish barbarian, no matter what his lineage," she snorted, turning away to observe the lush lands around her. Wanting off the subject of Kirk Connaught, she gestured to the landscape. "I still do not understand why Anchorsholme Castle is called The Darkland. These lands are anything but dark."

Niles was riding in front of the women, hearing every word of the conversation although he pretended otherwise. When Mara returned the subject to the dismal reference, he leapt into the dialogue.

"Lord Edmund has a sister, the Lady Johanne," he said, veering the focus away from Anchorsholme's reputation. "She is a little older than yourself, Lady Micheline. She has been very excited for your arrival."

Eyes dried, Micheline looked pleased. "She has?" She turned to smile at Mara, who returned the gesture. But when her sister returned her focus to Niles, Mara's rolled her eyes and stuck out her tongue; *that* was what she thought of Lady Johanne's excitement. "How wonderful," Micheline said, oblivious to her sister's mocking expressions. "I had no idea my betrothed even had a sister."

Niles caught Mara's gesture, shocked until he realized that giggles were very close to the surface. Unlike most finely bred ladies, the girl made no secrets of her thoughts. Aye, she was bold and spoiled and after what Kirk told him had transpired last eve, foolish too. But if he were to ignore her negative characteristics, she was also the most beautiful creature he had ever seen.

"Lady Johanne enjoys painting and poetry." He tried not to look at Mara as she continued to make faces. "I would assume you are accomplished in both?"

Micheline nodded. "I love to paint, although my knowledge of poetry is somewhat limited."

"That should not be a problem." Corwin was still in the conversation. "My wife writes poetry. She would love to indulge you."

"Your wife?" Micheline turned to the knight. "I did not know you were married, Sir Corwin."

He nodded. "Three years now. My wife, Lady Valdine, and her sister, Lady Wanda, reside at Anchorsholme."

"Are you married, Sir Niles?" Mara stopped grimacing long enough to focus on Kirk's tall associate.

The knight shook his head. "Nay, lady, I am not. Do I detect your interest?"

37

A smile played on Mara's lips even though she was doing her best to scowl. "Never!"

Niles sensed the game, smiling coyly as she turned away. "Come now, my lady. There is no need for modesty. Simply declare your interest and I shall consider you."

Mara shook her head firmly, the black hair gleaming like silk as she moved. "I am not interested and I never shall be."

Niles managed to rein his horse in front of her, his smile wicked. "I am crushed. Why not?"

Mara tried not to look at him. "Because you're too old, Sir Niles. Moreover, I do not want a husband."

"I am only twenty-six. And why do you not want a husband?"

She shrugged, watching Corwin smirk from the corner of her eye. "Because I do not. I do not need one, nor do I want one. Besides, who would be foolish enough tolerate my lively nature?"

Corwin and Niles looked at each other. "She has a point," Niles conceded. Sighing dramatically, he returned his gaze to Anchorsholme. "Lady Mara, I have decided to reject your suit. You will understand, of course. I am far too feeble a man for your bold nature."

Mara fought off a smile, giggling when Micheline whispered something in her ear. Ahead, Kirk suddenly reined his horse around and lifted a massive arm, sending the escort dividing into two long rows. Niles and Corwin, their exchange with Mara forgotten, lowered their visors and took position in front of the ladies.

Mara and Micheline watched as the great gates of Anchorsholme Castle slowly opened, the grinding of wood and rope echoing off the stone. A color guard waited on the battlements, the yellow and gray standards of the House of De Cleveley waving in the brisk wind. The sisters drank it all in, the awe of the spectacle outweighing the anxiety of their destiny.

CHAPTER FOUR

It was difficult to describe the smell of their lovemaking; somewhere between animal fat and a rotting corpse. When the heavy breathing subsided and the sweat cooled, it always smelled the same. It was a foul stench, emitting from the foul depths of their warped relationship.

A woman stood by one of three lancet windows offering weak illumination into the richly-appointed chamber. The heavy oilcloth was pulled back, a cool breeze caressing her naked body as her lover languished on the massive bed behind her.

"They've finally arrived," she said faintly. Perhaps a bit ominously.

The man on the damp, dirty sheets stirred a bit, eventually rising. He went to stand beside the woman, their gazes lingering on the activity in the bailey below.

"They are late," the man said, turning away in search of his clothes.

The lady remained focused on the scene, trying to catch a glimpse of the woman she knew to be in the party. A woman she hadn't yet decided to love or hate.

"This marriage, Edmund." She turned from the bright day, watching the man secure his hose. "You promised me that it would be in name only. Isn't that what you said, dear brother?"

He nodded, scratching his scalp before collecting his fine tunic. "Father accepted the pledge on behalf of a gambling debt, darling. I had no choice but to agree and well you know it."

The woman's naked body crossed the floor, a thin woman with tiny breasts. Even as her brother put his tunic on, she rubbed against him like a cat in heat. "You must consummate the marriage."

"I am bound to." He collected his gold-link belt. "For breeding purposes, of course. Once she's pregnant, I shall forget I even have a wife."

The woman smiled, rubbing her Venus mound on his thigh and leaving a damp streak. "And return to me, where you belong," she purred. "Into the arms of your beloved Johanne."

Edmund raised an eyebrow at his younger sister. The sister he had acquired when his father had married the wealthy widow Seymour those years ago; but his sister nonetheless. Blood or marriage was of little difference to him. "You would not be my beloved Johanne if Kirk were to show interest in you," he said, slapping her on the buttocks. When she yelped and moved away, he sat on the mattress to put on his boots. "He is the man of your dreams; not me."

She continued to smile at him, rubbing her bum where he had smacked her. "'Tis you who loves me best, Edmund. You always have. Teaching me the ways of men and woman so my flesh would not be polluted by the touch of an outsider. When Kirk finally comes to his senses, he'll be pleased with the skills you have taught me. Won't he, Edmund? Just like you said?"

Last boot in place, Edmund de Cleveley, Baron Bowland, rose from the bed and fixed his step-sister in the eye. "He shall be pleased. As pleased as I have been since you were eleven years old."

Johanne's smile broadened, rubbing herself against the canopy post and imagining it was Kirk. "And what of your new wife, Edmund? Will she be as pleasurable as me?"

"I am sure not. She's a virgin; it's guaranteed in the marriage contract. Silly, useless wench."

Johanne's smile faded, her unbalanced mind evident in the dull green eyes. "Can I wish her away if she displeases us both?"

"And how would she do that?"

"By disapproving of our relationship, of course. If she cannot be made to understand, might I wish her away like I have the others?"

Edmund paused by the door, studying the woman he couldn't seem to be without. It wasn't as if he loved her; but, truly, he had never been without her. The need to have her, to dominate her, had always been a part of his psyche. To do without her would be like relinquishing a limb; so very necessary if he wanted to remain in control.

And this wishing away business; she had started it as a child, wishing animals away that displeased her. A rabbit that bit her, a kitten that scratched. As her step-brother and protector, Edmund had made sure the offensive beasts were removed and convinced Johanne that the powers of her mind had made it so. But as she got older and her psychosis more evident, she took to wishing people away and it was Edmund's obligation to continue what he had started.

"If she does not understand our relationship, then I will permit you to wish her away as you have done the others," he said after a moment. "But not before she bears me a son. Until such time, Lady Micheline is safe from your wishing powers."

Johanne seemed satisfied, lying down on the mattress and stroking herself intimately. "I have saved my wishing powers for those women who turn their attentions on Kirk. This will be the first time I have used them for you."

Edmund lifted the bolt. "Patience, Johanne. Lady Micheline might work into our family quite nicely."

"Mayhap." Johanne closed her eyes as her orgasm began to build. Edmund paused, watching his step-sister manipulate herself. "If all else fails, mayhap I shall put the two of you in bed together and watch. And if Kirk is a good boy, I shall ask him to join me."

"Kirk would never do such a thing," she murmured. "He's far too pure. He's saving himself for me, you know."

"You mean you have eliminated all competition."

"I have had to."

Gaze lingering on his sister as her frail mind lost itself in the throes of a powerful climax, Edmund turned and quit the room.

His virgin bride was waiting.

***

The first time Edmund beheld Mara, he immediately announced his satisfaction in his bride. Mara blushed as Kirk corrected his lord, introducing the Lady Micheline le Bec as the man's intended. Edmund's response couldn't have been crueler had he slapped her.

It was obvious he wasn't pleased. Micheline stammered through her gracious speech, her cheeks flushing madly and her hands trembling. Mara remained astride her worn palfrey, fury such as she had never known filling her as Micheline offered herself to her displeased groom. When the elder sister finished her speech and gave the man a timid smile, Edmund did nothing more than turn his back and return to the keep. Leaving the escort party embarrassed and sympathetic, Kirk endeavored to make amends to the humiliated bride.

"Lord Edmund has never been the congenial sort, my lady," he said apologetically. "But he is fair. In fact, I would be surprised if he did not apologize for his conduct at the feast tonight."

Mara was off her palfrey, her bright blue eyes blazing. "There will be no feast!" she spat. "We're going home, Sir Kirk, and you are going to take us. We're not staying another moment where we're not wanted."

Kirk could hardly demand she control herself when Micheline had been righteously insulted. Maintaining his calm, he grasped Mara by the arm.

"You are indeed wanted, my lady," he said quietly. "I realize it is difficult to believe given Lord Edmund's reaction, but you must trust me when I say that he has been anticipating your arrival."

"He was anticipating the arrival of a beauty," Micheline said softly, turning for her mare. "I do not meet his criteria, Sir Kirk. Mayhap it would be best if you return us home."

Kirk watched the lady move for her horse, her movements slow and shameful. His heart ached for her, another strange emotion he had never experienced. But, given Edmund's character, he should not have been shocked by the man's behavior. He should have expected it.

"I cannot, Lady Micheline," he said quietly. "Only Lord Edmund can return you home. For now, I suggest you settle into your room and prepare for the evening's meal."

"Prepare for what? More humiliation?" Mara shook her head. "I shall not allow it, Sir Kirk. I shall cut the man's heart out if he shames her again."

Kirk raised an eyebrow. "Watch your tongue, lady. You speak of your benefactor."

"I speak of an insensitive, boorish clod," she snapped. "He's no prize himself. What gives him the right to judge my sister's appearance?"

Kirk drew a steadying breath. "Corwin," he said slowly. "Please take Lady Micheline into the keep. I suspect Lady Valdine and Lady Wanda are waiting to show her to her chamber."

"What of Lady Mara?" Niles did not like the look in Kirk's eye. "I'd be happy to take...."

"I shall take her in hand." Kirk cut him off. "You may disband the escort."

Niles did not argue. Turning to the men-at-arms, he began to bellow orders as Corwin collected Micheline's satchel from her horse. There was a small wagon containing a few trunks and other personal items and he ordered several hovering servants to see to those things. Grasping the red-cheeked bride by the arm, he escorted her past Kirk and Mara without a glance.

Mara watched her sister disappear into the castle. The moment Micheline vanished, she turned to Kirk.

"I do not care what you do to me, I am not going to apologize for my words," she said in a low voice. "Your precious Lord Edmund is a fiend and if you expect me to...."

He cut her off by yanking her across the bailey. His strides were long and Mara had to run to keep up. Even as he pulled her to a side entrance that led into the castle, still, she refused to recant her words. Just inside the door lay a cool, vacant corridor and he let go of her arm. The moment he fixed her with his stone-gray gaze, however, apprehension began to simmer.

He did not waste any time. Planting himself on a stone seat jutting from the wall, he yanked Mara over his knee and tossed up her skirts. Furious, not to mention terrified, Mara twisted and shrieked as he brought his gigantic palm to bear on her bottom not once, but twice. Listening to her yelp, he paused briefly, his hand hovering above her reddened bum.

"I told you what would happen with your next infraction," he growled. "No more unbridled words, no more rebellion. Do you understand me?"

She did not answer him, struggling to remove herself from his lap. He spanked her again and her resistance waned.

"Answer me. Do you understand?"

She was breathing heavily against his thighs; he could feel her. "Beat me if you must, Sir Kirk, but I will never surrender to your tyranny. Especially when I speak the truth!"

He swatted her again, not quite as hard, for her buttocks were becoming terribly red. Tender, white, heart-shaped buttocks he would have much rather sank his teeth into than strike with his hand.

"Correct or no, you will listen to me and you will obey." He suddenly put her skirts down, flipping her onto her back. Cradling her as if she was a very large infant, he wagged a grim finger in her face. "We will not have this conversation again. I spanked you in punishment for your actions, but hear me now as I explain the rules you will live by here at Anchorsholme. There will be no more impolite behavior, no more disobedience. You will present the model of a perfect lady or you will answer to me as you just have. Is this clear?"

Mara's eyes were wide, staring into orbs of cold steel. He was holding her tightly and had she not been so unbalanced, she might have allowed herself to experience the sensation. But she could only gaze back at him, into the face that Micheline had called handsome. And she suddenly found herself willing to admit, for the very first time, that Micheline had been right. He was handsome.

"It... it is," she heard herself whisper, hardly believing that she was giving in so easily. But she couldn't seem to control her submission, a submission accompanied by a weakening warmth. The longer he glared at her, the more powerful the warmth became.

"Good." He, too, could hardly believe she had surrendered as easily as she had. In fact, it was too good to believe. "If I need to pound out another rhythm on your buttocks to underscore my point, then I shall be happy to do so."

Mara shook her head weakly, unable to tear herself away from his incredible eyes. Beautiful eyes, she found herself thinking. Beautiful eyes of a beautiful, powerful man who wasn't intimidated by her in the least. And mayhap that was a good thing.

"No need, my lord." Her voice was sweet, faint, as he had once remembered thinking on the day she had nearly thrown herself from the window. "I understand perfectly, although I cannot guarantee the lesson will be immediately."

He cocked an eyebrow, his thoughts turning from spanking her buttocks to the wonderful warmth of her in his arms. "What does this mean?"

Mara swallowed, realizing his grip on her had tightened. As much as the new sensation enticed her, it was also frightening. Frightening that a man she had sworn to hate could create such havoc in her naive, stubborn mind.

"Would you mind letting me stand?" she asked.

He obliged, aware that he liked her much better in his arms. Mara straightened her surcoat before fixing him in the eye, far calmer than she had been when they had entered the deserted corridor.

"It means that old habits die hard," she said frankly. "I am used to speaking my mind, Sir Kirk, and...."

"Kirk."

"Beg pardon, my lord?"

"You will call me simply Kirk," he said without a hint of warmth. "Now continue."

Mara looked strangely at him but did as he asked. "I... very well, if you insist. As I said, I am used to speaking my mind and it will be quite difficult for me to rein my natural actions."

"Unbridled responses are not natural. They are the result of a complete lack of discipline. Did not your father maintain any control over you whatsoever?"

Mara looked away from him, studying the walls, the floor. "Nay," she said. "He was too busy losing money. Or drunk. And mother was sick most of the time, too ill to deal with me."

Kirk's hard stance softened as he watched her emotional vulnerability come through yet again. Last night in the inn had been only a foretaste.

"So you and Micheline took care of each other," he finished quietly. "And from what I have seen of your sister, she is hardly able to take a stand against you."

Mara nodded, leaning against the opposite wall. "We have always taken care of one another because no one else could." She fixed him in the eye, her lovely face soft with emotion. "That is why I cannot allow her to marry a man who would treat her with such disrespect. Can't you understand that I must protect her?"

Kirk sighed, resting against the wall. "You do not have a choice, love. This betrothal contract has nothing to do with you."

Mara heard the affectionate term, unsure how to react. A name that seemed to intensify the odd, quivering warmth she was already experiencing.

"I realize that, but it does not discourage my determination," she replied, her heart leaping strangely against her ribcage. "Misha is... delicate. She cannot take care of herself as I am able. And I refuse to allow this... I mean, Lord Edmund to humiliate her further. She's known enough degradation in her time."

Kirk crossed his muscular arms, his expression curious. "What does this mean? How else has your sister met with humiliation?"

For the first time since he had known her, Mara seemed to falter. She refused to look at him as she spoke.

"Father... he used Misha to support his gambling habit by forcing her to dance and sing for coin." She kicked distractedly at the stone. "That is why she did not want to sleep in an inn last night. Father used to take her into taverns to entertain the soldiers while he left me on the street, pretending to be an orphan. Somehow I always managed to make more money begging than Misha did with her talents, which only added to her shame."

He did not reply. When Mara finally looked up from her feet, she was surprised to note his expression harsh. She cocked her head curiously, gazing into eyes as cold as steel.

"Why do you look like that?"

Kirk seemed to stare at her a long, long time. "Because your father was a cruel man. And his cruelty continues as he forces his eldest to wed in order to settle a gambling debt."

Mara nodded, moving closer to him. When he wasn't taunting or threatening her, he was quite approachable. "Now you see why I cannot permit her to wed a man who will only continue to humiliate her. Our parents died within weeks of each other two years ago and since that time, we've known our only measure of peace. Now the cycle of shame threatens all over again."

She was standing beside the stone seat, level with his eyes. He found himself devouring every contour of her face. "I will speak to Lord Edmund. Have no doubt that he will be considerate of your sister's feelings when I explain the situation."

Mara frowned. "If he wasn't considerate of her feelings the moment he met her, why should your explanation make any difference?"

"Because Edmund trusts me."

"And based on the word of his servant, he is supposed to amend his attitude?"

This time, Kirk frowned. "I am not his servant."

Mara sat down on the edge of the seat, yelping when her sore bum touched the cold surface. Leaping up, she rubbed her backside as she spoke. "If you are not his servant, then what are you?"

Kirk crossed his thick arms. "My father and grandfather came into service through lands in Ireland that were a wedding dowry to Lord Edmund's grandsire. I have freely pledged my loyalty to the House of de Cleveley, and I am certainly not a servant."

She continued to gaze at him and he could literally see the thoughts tumbling through her mind. "But you had little choice in the matter to serve the House of de Cleveley if you were part of a marriage contract."

"I do not consider my fealty a matter of choice. I wanted to serve the House of de Cleveley, as it was my family's legacy. I fostered at Kenilworth at a very young age and came into Monroe de Cleveley's service as soon as I was knighted."

"Monroe de Cleveley?"

"Edmund's father."

Mara nodded, eyeing him thoughtfully. "So you fostered at Kenilworth with a host of arrogant English boys. Then why do you still possess an Irish brogue? Did not your trainers whip it out of you?"

He smiled faintly. "They tried." He scratched his ear. "God only knows, I was beaten, starved, belittled and tortured. But they could not take it out of me. The more they tried, the more I refused."

Mara's eyes widened. "They did that?"

"They did."

She stared at him, the strong lines of his face; the square angle of his jaw. "Then you have known the same shame as Micheline and I have."

He shrugged. "What my trainers did to me was not considered shameful. It was considered necessary."

Mara continued to watch him as he scratched his head again, emitting a weary sigh. Now that the chaos of their journey had ended, he seemed fatigued and Mara impulsively knelt beside him, her small hands on his tree-sized legs. Considering she couldn't sit, it was the only possible position.

"Please, Sir Kirk," she said softly. "Please help me take Micheline away from here. If you understand humiliation as you said you have, then you should be eager to help."

He gazed down at her. A massive gauntlet reached out, stroking her cheek before he could stop himself.

"I cannot," he murmured. "But I promise that I will speak to Edmund. He is not an unreasonable man."

Mara stared at him as he continued to caress her cheek, the strange warmth in her belly igniting into a raging fire. But it wasn't enough to overcome her frustration and she jerked away, turning her back on him.

"You will not touch me that way," she said, her quaking voice belying the thrill of his touch. "I do not think I like it."

He laughed. Startled, Mara turned in time to see him rising to his feet, snorting with mirth.

"Aye, you do, but you're too stubborn to admit it," he said, meeting her gaze. "Tell me, Mara; does your guard never go down?"

She turned her nose up at him. "I have never been given reason enough to lower it."

He laughed again. "Fair enough. Mayhap someday, if I am in the right mood, I shall give you reason enough."

She did not like his smug attitude. But he made her grin just the same and she kept her face averted as she picked at her nails. "Mayhap I have already had a better offer," she said, simply to poke holes in his confidence. "Mayhap another knight will declare his interest. Sir Niles, or someone else."

Kirk's smile vanished. Mara continued picking at her nails but she could feel his presence behind her, hovering.

"Did Niles declare his interest?"

She shrugged carelessly, biting her lower lip to keep the smile from spreading. "Not yet. But I have seen the expression on his face when he looks at me. Yet, I suppose it would be foolish of him to believe he could tolerate my lively nature."

It took him a moment to realize she was goading him. Staring at the back of her luscious head, he raised an eyebrow.

"I am the only man alive who would be able to tolerate your lively nature, as you call it." He turned for the door that led back into the bailey. "And I shall, when the time is right."

She cast him a long glance, somewhere between coy and doubtful. "What does that mean?"

He paused in the doorway, the light beyond giving him a surreal silhouette. Mara could see the gleam in the stone-gray eyes. "It means that someday, when I am feeling particularly foolish, I might take you off Edmund's hands."

She her lips twitched with the threat of a smile. She did not want to give into the grin, knowing that he was speaking of marriage, but somehow the thought of marriage to Kirk Connaught wasn't entirely repulsive. As much as she professed her hatred for the man, still, he intrigued her like no one ever had.

"I do not want you," she sniffed. "I would rather marry a pig."

He grinned. "I will give you time to reconsider. Or mayhap I shan't marry you at all. I haven't yet decided."

Her eyebrows rose to his careless statement. "Is that so? Then I shall decide for you. The answer is no!"

She gathered her skirts and pushed past him, out into the bailey. Smirking, he followed. "Now you make my decisions for me? Ah, just like a good wife."

She glared at him as they crossed the urine-soaked mud. "Do not say that."

47

"Why not?"

"Because I shall not have you!"

He nudged her with a big arm. "Admit it, Mara. You would have only me."

She shrieked with frustration, gaining speed to out-walk him. "No!"

Laughing, he followed.

CHAPTER FIVE

Mara had had enough of Kirk's badgering by the time they reached the chamber she and Micheline would occupy. Leaving the flushing young lady in the care of her sister, Kirk went in search of Edmund. As promised, he intended to inform his lord the details of the situation and would waste no time in doing so.

He knew exactly where to find the man and knew without a doubt that he would not be alone. Knocking loudly on Edmund's chamber door, he was met with Johanne's pale, smiling face.

"Welcome home, Kirk," she purred, gesturing him into the room. "My brother and I were just discussing you. I hope the trip to Haslingden went well?"

He eyed the woman he could hardly stand. A foul woman who leered at him as if he was something of a delightful confection.

"Well enough, my lady." He looked at Edmund, standing by the windows with a goblet of fine wine in his hand. "I would speak with you, my lord. Alone, if I may."

Edmund smiled cordially at his captain, moving to the decanter of alcohol. "Of course," he said, pouring a second cup for his knight. "I have a need to speak with you as well. Johanne, please leave us."

Johanne was staring at Kirk, a foolish grin on her face. Prancing a wide circle around the man, inspecting him closely as the knight stood stock-still, she ran an index finger down his massive forearm on her way to the door.

"We are pleased you have returned, Kirk," she said, licking the finger that had stroked his arm. Kirk refused to look at her as she opened the carved panel. "Mayhap you will tell us of the adventure tonight at the feast?"

The only thing requiring Kirk to give a decent answer was his sworn loyalty to the House of de Cleveley. Were it not for his oath, he would just as well ignore the woman.

"Mayhap." He replied, still focused on Edmund.

Johanne slipped from the room without another word. Kirk knew when she had gone because her repulsive odor immediately vanished. Whether or not it was an imagined stench, still, it seemed to reek from her like a roaring river. It was all Kirk could do to keep from gagging.

Edmund had the odor, too. But for the simple fact that he was Kirk's liege, the knight could do nothing but tolerate the fetor. He had known

Edmund the better part of his life, a young man with a remarkably level head in spite of a personal life that went beyond the boundaries of acceptable existence. Were the man not carrying on an incestuous liaison with his step-sister, Kirk might have found him likable at times.

Kirk refused the goblet Edmund offered, instead, removing his helm and setting it next to the door. He would have thrown it on the bed had he not feared contracting some of the hideous filth Johanne had left on the sheets. Scratching his head with fatigue, he waited for Edmund to speak.

Edmund eyed his moody captain, knowing the man's thoughts without being told. Kirk had long recognized the relationship between Edmund and his step-sister, a concept that distressed him now as it had from the beginning. But being a discreet man, he had never said a word. Edmund knew the tact wasn't for the benefit of his liege; it was simply because Kirk couldn't bring himself to verbally acknowledge the situation.

"Well, then," Edmund said after a moment. "What is it you wish to discuss?"

"The Lady Micheline, my lord," Kirk replied.

Edmund raised an eyebrow. "Oh, yes. My new bride." He shook his head, turning back to the decanter of liquor. "You should have left her at Haslingden, Kirk. She certainly isn't what I'd hoped for."

Kirk watched his young lord take another drink of wine. "I am sorry you feel that way," he said quietly. "She's a nice young woman, kind and obedient. She'll make a fine chatelaine for Anchorsholme."

"What of Johanne?" Edmund turned to him. "She is an excellent chatelaine. How can I ask her to share the reins of power with an outsider?"

"As your wife, the Lady Micheline should have sole power. You are, after all, the baron. And she will be the baroness."

Edmund did not like that thought. Pursing his lips, he strolled to the long windows. "Curse my father for accepting this betrothal," he muttered, gazing over the landscape. "I wanted no part of this, Kirk. I would have welcomed the black-haired girl, but her sister is below my expectations."

"Edmund," Kirk's voice was soft. Firm. "The Lady Micheline has had a difficult life. You are making it far more difficult with your obvious displeasure. But you have no choice in the matter, as she does not. If you will simply accept the situation and take comfort in the lands she brings, I am sure you will come to terms with this. I must say, I was rather embarrassed by your reaction in the bailey. You left me to make excuses for your behavior."

Edmund looked at the knight; at thirty-two years of age, he was everything Edmund could never be if he lived to one hundred. The big brother he never knew, the mentor he never had. Edmund knew Kirk respected him simply because he was sworn to him; but true respect, something that had to be earned, was non-existent. Given his relationship with Johanne, Edmund suspected he would never earn it.

"I apologize for that," he said softly. "I suppose I am not very good at masking my emotions. After witnessing her beauteous sister, the lady's average features caught me off-guard."

Kirk cocked an eyebrow. "I am not the one you should apologize to."

Edmund nodded reluctantly. "You are right, of course." He refused to elaborate further. Taking a deep breath, he moved away from the window. "We have other things to discuss, Kirk. I received a missive from your father yesterday."

Kirk was veered off the subject of Lady Micheline by mention of his father. "What did he say?"

Edmund did not look pleased. "He seems to think there is a rebellion brewing among my vassals. The harvest was poor, as you know, and winter stores are not plentiful. The serfs resent the taxes I impose on them and are growing restless as the cold spell deepens. Your father believes a revolt is imminent."

Kirk's eyebrows rose. "A revolt? Ridiculous! The House of De Cleveley has always treated her vassals fairly."

Edmund shrugged. "I take half of all harvests from my Irish subjects, which is less than some English overlords. Even so, with the countryside bordering on famine, the people are looking for someone to blame and that person, apparently, is me."

Kirk's jaw ticked. "Would you have me rally support from our allies and ride to my father's aid?"

Edmund shook his head. "Not yet." He poured himself more liquor. "Ryan Connaught is content to wait out the situation for the moment. If it intensifies, then we will have no choice."

Kirk knew is father to be an intelligent warrior, not one to panic prematurely. If Ryan said a revolt was imminent, then Kirk was inclined to believe immediate action was necessary regardless of Edmund's caution. "I shall send word to our allies nonetheless, preparing them for the potentiality," he said. "Did my father say anything about my brothers or mother? Are they in danger?"

"He did not mention the fact." Edmund went to the wardrobe and, rummaging about, drew forth the missive from Ireland. Kirk accepted it eagerly. "I am sure your younger brothers are well. Drew recently returned from fostering in Devon, did he not?"

Kirk nodded, scanning the contents of the vellum. "After Steven injured his hand in a riding accident, my father was without the power of a son by his side. But now with Drew returned...." He suddenly re-rolled the vellum, frustrated. "This missive tells me nothing. It's as if... as if he is holding something back."

"Your father holds nothing back," Edmund replied. "The missive is quite frank."

Kirk shook his head, his fatigue fading as frustration took hold. "He probably does not want to worry me. He knows I shall sail for Ireland with half of England under my command at the first sign of trouble."

Edmund watched the man work himself into a substantial fret. "According to your father, there is no trouble - yet. Trust that the man will inform us when he needs reinforcements." Kirk continued to pace, the missive clutched in his hand, and Edmund set his goblet down. "Retire to your chambers, Kirk. Rest, relax. We shall have a grand feast this night to celebrate your return."

Kirk looked up from his pacing boots. "You mean the arrival of Lady Micheline."

Edmund met his gaze. After a moment, he shrugged. "As you say. Regardless, I demand you rest until the meal. You look as if it has been a hellish journey."

Kirk did not say what he was thinking, thoughts turning from the situation in Ireland to the events of the past two days.

Not hellish, Edmund. *Hellion.*

***

The first thing Mara was aware of was the smell of roasting beef. A heavy, mouth-watering smell and she realized she was famished. Seated in the great smoky hall at the table reserved for the de Cleveley family, Mara and Micheline huddled together as the rumbled of conversation filled the room.

Kirk had explained that the guests this eve had been part of Johanne's birthday celebration a few days prior. Most of them were older, a few young men and ladies in fine court dress. Clad in the finest surcoats they owned, Mara and Micheline were sorely out of place among the wealthy visitors.

Even though Micheline was trying her best to remain dignified, Mara wanted no part of it. The crowd had been staring and pointing since her arrival a half-hour before and she was nearly wild with what she perceived to be negative attention. When Kirk passed the table on his rounds of the room, she latched onto his hand and refused to let go.

Smiling gently, he knelt beside her chair. "What's the matter with you? Are you not enjoying yourself?"

He could see she was close to tears. "These people," she whispered. "They are staring at Micheline and I. I want to leave!"

Micheline heard her sister's plea, meeting Kirk's gaze. His expression was surprisingly gentle, considering his usual reaction to Mara. Even after spanking her earlier in the day, which her sister had explained with very little outrage, it was obvious he was no longer angry. And Mara, too, apparently held no grudge.

"Relax, lass," he said. "They are simply curious and nothing more."

She shook her head, still holding his hand. He had escorted Micheline to the dining hall, clean-shaven and without his armor. Mara had followed on Niles' arm, awed by the sight of Kirk, combed and bathed and in gentlemen clothing, as he chatted pleasantly with her sister. If she had thought him handsome before, the new picture was enough to set her head spinning. And he smelled nice, too. A smell of precious oils and pine that filled her nostrils even as he knelt beside the chair and attempted to comfort her.

"They are laughing at us," she hissed, her bright blue gaze full of uncharacteristic emotion. "You promised there would be no more humiliation for Micheline!"

He sighed, patting her hand. "They are not laughing, love. I would kill them all if they were laughing."

Mara was not convinced, frustrated that he could not see the truth of the situation. "Look at us, Kirk." She let go of him and grabbed a fistful of her skirt. "Look at this surcoat; it was my mother's and it is several years old. And Micheline; she is wearing a silk surcoat that was once burgundy. Now it's pink. We're shamefully dressed, I tell you!"

He took her chin between his thumb and forefinger. "You could wear rags and you would both still outshine every woman in this room." He caught a glimpse of Micheline's grateful smile from the corner of his eye. But Mara was still frowning and he touched her cheek gently, rising. "Do not worry so, Lady Mara. Enjoy the feast and forget about these women who stare. They are simply jealous."

Mara rolled her eyes miserably. Kirk smiled at her, enjoying her animated response, when Corwin and two women approached the table. Before Mara could further lament the atmosphere of the room, Kirk turned her in the direction of the visitors.

"Lady Mara, you have not yet been introduced to Sir Corwin's wife and sister-in-law." He gestured to the identical pale-faced women. "Lady Valdine and Lady Wanda, may I present the Lady Mara le Bec."

Mara smiled weakly at the woman on Corwin's arm, who bowed crisply. As she did so, the woman standing next to her mimicked her actions perfectly. It was like watching two of the same person.

"'Tis a pleasure to meet you, Lady Valdine," she said. "Your husband's pleasant conversation helped pass the time on our journey here."

"We..."

"... thank you, my lady."

Mara blinked. Lady Valdine had started the sentence; her sister had finished it. Puzzled, she looked to Micheline for support. But her sister merely smiled.

"The Lady Valdine and her sister helped me settle into my chamber while you and Sir Kirk were... well, shall we say, in conversation." Micheline nodded her head at the two ladies. "Good eve to you, ladies."

The twins bowed again. And they smiled at Micheline at exactly the same time.

"Good eve..."

"... to you, Lady Micheline. We hope..."

"... you chamber is..."

"... satisfactory?"

Mara's mouth was hanging open. She couldn't help it. Again, Lady Valdine started the train of speech, Lady Wanda finished it. But Micheline seemed unfazed by the conversation, merely nodding at the pair. "It's wonderful, thank you. Will you be sitting with us for the meal?"

They shook their head in synchronization. "Nay, my lady. We..."

"... will be seated to..."

"... your left, with the other..."

"... knights and ladies."

Mara's head was spinning from the echo-like effect of their peculiar speech. As they bowed their farewell to the table and moved in perfect rhythm for their assigned table, Mara watched with a mixture of fascination and confusion.

"They talk at the same time!" she turned to Kirk, still standing behind her.

He laughed softly. "Nay, they do not. If you notice, they speak in perfect order. One never overlaps the other and they are very precise in what they wish to say."

"But...." Mara shook her head. "Can they not speak separately?"

"I have never heard them." Kirk glanced up, noting that the gaily-dressed crier was preparing to announce the arrival of Edmund and Johanne. "Corwin said it was quite difficult to court Valdine. Wanda always seemed to be interfering."

Mara's expression was droll. "How in the world could he tell? I'd say the man has two wives for the price of one."

Kirk snorted softly, observing as the heralds took position for the grand entrance of Lord Edmund de Cleveley, Baron Bowland. Excusing himself politely, he moved away from the table.

Mara watched him move to the grand hall entrance, a towering doorway with carved oak panels. His movements were graceful, agile, and she found herself staring at him as he waited patiently for Edmund's arrival.

"He is in a far more pleasant mood this eve than he has been," Micheline said softly.

Mara was still staring at him. "Oh... who?"

Micheline smiled. "Kirk, dear. He seems quite amiable toward you."

Mara tore her gaze away, focusing on her sister and trying not to appear too agreeable. "It's amazing what a peaceful afternoon can do for one's spirits."

Micheline continued to watch her sister as the woman's gaze returned to the towering knight. Leaning close, she whispered in her ear. "Did he really spank you this afternoon? Or did he do something else?"

Mara looked puzzled. And shocked. "What else would he do?"

Micheline kissed her on the ear. "This."

Mara nearly leapt from her chair. "I would never... I never...!"

Micheline laughed softly, grabbing the woman before she could run away. "If you say so, Mara. I will not mention it again, I promise."

Red about the ears, Mara maintained her seat but refused to look Micheline in the eye. A kiss was so intimate, so... *serious*. And it would only lead to the same actions the soldier in the inn had forced upon her. Actions that were painful and degrading and she had no intention of allowing them to happen again. Even if the actions would be coming from Kirk.

"I do not like him, Misha."

"I know."

"Nay, you do not. I am sincere when I say this."

"I realize that."

Mara looked at her sister then, just as the crier announced the appearance of Lord Edmund and his beloved step-sister, Johanne. The heralds blasted their trumpets and the lavishly-dressed guests rose to their feet, but Mara ignored the pomp; her focus remained on Micheline.

"Do not mock me, Misha. I am serious when I say that I want nothing to do with Kirk Connaught."

Micheline rose, too, her smile fading as she caught sight of her short, muss-haired groom.

"That may be, Mara," she whispered, "but he wants everything to do with you."

***

Johanne's reaction to Micheline hadn't been quite as severe as Edmund's. After the introduction by Kirk, she sized the woman from head to toe before seating herself at her brother's left. While Micheline struggled to maintain her composure as Edmund ignored her, Johanne's attention moved from her brother's future wife to the dark-haired woman seated at the end of the table. When Kirk introduced the Lady Mara, Johanne's eyes narrowed.

"I did not believe the marriage contract called for the addition of a younger sister," she said as servants began to bring out great trenchers of beef. "Will you be returning to Haslingden after the ceremony, Lady Mara?"

By Edmund's request, Kirk was seated on his right hand, between the reluctant groom and his new bride. The knight begrudgingly did so, although he was glad for his mediating presence when Johanne began her catty dialogue. Eyeing Mara, his gaze conveyed the demands of proper behavior.

"Nay, my lady." Mara wasn't the least bit intimidated by the skinny woman or Kirk's intense stare. "My sister is my guardian since our parents' death, a duty that shall go to her new husband. I am afraid I shall be staying at Anchorsholme."

Johanne's features tensed as she looked at her brother, who merely lost himself in his boiled carrots and meat. "I see," she said quietly. "Then we shall simply have to find you a husband, too. There's hardly room for you here."

Both Kirk and Micheline watched Mara's expression as she pondered Johanne's statement. Challenging would have been an accurate description.

"I do not want a husband, Lady Johanne."

"Then the cloister is preferable? Excellent. The sooner the better."

Mara lifted an eyebrow and Kirk groaned inwardly. "Why are you so anxious to be rid of me, Lady Johanne? I have only just arrived. In fact, I rather like it here." She smiled prettily, settling back in her chair. "I do believe I shall stay a long, long time."

Micheline sighed heavily, delving into her plate of beef. The head table made an odd picture; the bride and groom devouring their meal and ignoring all else as Kirk sat tall and silent in the center. On the ends, Johanne and Mara were working themselves into a serious confrontation.

"It is obvious to me why you have accompanied your sister, Lady Mara," Johanne said, her green eyes flashing. "After all, look at your clothing; it is apparent that you have merely come to seek my brother's wealth."

Mara shook her head, struggling not to lash out. "I came because I was forced to come, my lady. I have no use for your brother's wealth."

Johanne laughed shortly. "Certainly you can use it. By the state of your dress, I'd say you could use it very badly." She looked at Micheline. "And your sister, too. I must say the two of you are very brave to be seen in public, dressed like paupers."

Mara could deal with Johanne's personal attacks. But the moment she turned to Micheline, Mara's stomach twisted with fury and the tongue she had promised to bridle sprang free.

"At least the state of our dress is repairable, Lady Johanne. But I doubt there's enough money in the world to buy you the beauty and tact you so obviously lack."

Johanne turned shades of red as Edmund removed his face from his trencher.

"Enough impudence," he snarled. "Kirk, remove this... this woman immediately!"

Kirk stood. Mara, more concerned that Micheline would be left alone with two jackals once she was removed than the fact that she was in a good deal of trouble, swatted at him when he reached down to grasp her.

"Why am I to be removed when she has been deliberately baiting me?" she demanded. "If I am to be punished, then punish her as well for having the carelessness to start something she hasn't the courage to finish!"

Kirk had Mara by both arms, pulling her from the chair. Johanne, hearing the challenge, leapt from her seat. "Brazen wench! You have no idea the powers you toy with!"

Edmund rose, calming his step-sister with a gentle touch. "She is not worth the effort, Johanne. Please reclaim your seat and allow Kirk to deal with her."

With Mara and Kirk wrestling on one side and Edmund and Johanne arguing on the other, Micheline found her attention drawn to her future husband and his step-sister. The manner in which he stroked her cheek, the tone of his voice, was infinitely disturbing and the more she watched, the more confused she became. Had she not known better, she would have sworn their relationship to be more than familial.

Kirk managed to wind his arm around Mara's waist, physically removing her from the table. Her demands for Johanne's mutual punishment soon turned to pleas on Micheline's behalf and he listened in silence as he removed her from the room. Out into the stillness of the evening, he finally put her on her feet.

Immediately, Mara attempted to return to the keep. But Kirk had her firmly by the hands as she tugged and grunted.

"Please, Kirk, I cannot leave her alone with those... those wolves!" She unsuccessfully tried to pull her hands free. "She needs me!"

He cocked an eyebrow, towing her around the building and Mara recognized the entrance to the corridor where he had spanked her. Her struggles increased.

"Do not spank me again!" she half-begged, half-commanded. "I know I promised to behave, but Lady Johanne was deliberately nasty and I had no choice. Do you hear me? *I had no choice!*"

The corridor was cold and deserted, shielded from the activity in the bailey. Once inside, Kirk let go of her and she scrambled away, eyes wide with apprehension.

"There is always a choice, Mara," he said, his voice low and stern. "But you seem to make incorrect ones."

"I do not!" She stamped her little foot, fearful and angry. "I could not allow her to insult Micheline. And what of Lord Edmund? You said he would apologize for his behavior earlier."

Kirk drew in a deep breath, folding his arms across his chest. Mara was momentarily distracted by the arms, thinking that they were larger in circumference that her entire body. Warm, strong, wonderful arms.

"I did not say that, exactly." He stood beside the familiar spanking seat jutting out from the wall. "I said that I would be surprised if he did not. Obviously, I am surprised."

Mara frowned. There was no use arguing with the man when all he did was prove her wrong, again and again. Exasperated, she turned her back to him and bent over at the waist.

"Well, go on then," she grumbled. "Do what you must and be done with it. I have made an easy target for you."

He gazed at her buttocks, covered in layers of old material. Strolling up behind her, he reached down and grabbed her by the hair. Whirling her to face him, their gazes collided.

She was a tiny little thing, barely meeting with his chest. Mara gasped, although he hadn't hurt her in the least. But his control was obvious and his breath, when he spoke, was deliciously hot on her face.

"I am not going to spank you," he growled. "But God only knows I should. You're the most insolent, willful, sassy wench I have ever had the misfortune to meet."

Mara swallowed, sensing no anger in his statement. The stone-gray eyes were blazing at her, the heat from his gaze licking every inch of exposed skin. She felt naked, vulnerable, but strangely warm and protected. As if she were to allow herself, she would melt right into him.

"I tried to bank myself at first, truly," she whispered. "But when she attacked Micheline, I could not control myself."

He blinked, slowly. "Your defense of your sister is admirable but unnecessary."

Mara could feel his scorching body against her from chest to thigh. He was so massive he seemed to blot out all else. "Why do you say that?"

Kirk released her hair and she nearly collapsed. As it was, she ended up perched on the stone seat directly behind her, aware that her knees had given way as a result of Kirk's overwhelming closeness. And still, she was trembling.

"Because I shall protect her," he said softly. "This will no longer be your fight alone."

Mara blinked, her features rippling with confusion. "But... why? I never asked this of you."

"You did not, but I shall assume your battle just the same." He moved toward her, his dark hair shades of blue in the ghostly light. "And another thing, Mara. You will stay clear of Johanne. Do you understand me?"

She craned her neck back, gazing up at him. "Stay clear... why?"

He sighed, slowly, lowering himself onto the bench beside her. After a moment, he collected her small hand in his massive palm, turning it over, inspecting it.

"Because she is... not right in the head," he murmured. "I cannot tell you more than that. But know that she is dangerous. Already, she has a strong dislike for you and I am concerned...."

"Concerned for what?" Mara could barely speak as he toyed with her hand, warm sensations firing through her small body and causing her limbs to ache.

He looked up from her hand, staring into her bright blue eyes. Christ, she was such a lovely creature. "Concerned that she might try to harm you somehow." When Mara opened her mouth to question him, he shook his head firmly. "Please trust me, lass. There are things about this place you do not understand and I refuse to elaborate. Suffice it to say that I want you to stay away from Johanne, and away from Edmund if you can. Spend your time with me, or Lady Valdine and Lady Wanda. Is this clear?"

There was something in his eyes that suggested nothing but complete obedience. Without hesitation, Mara nodded.

"It is," she whispered. "But what of Micheline?"

He sighed again, squeezing her hand tightly. "I will do what I can for her. This I vow."

"Do *what*?"

He did not reply. Or mayhap he couldn't reply. Mara did not know how long they sat there, hand in hand, listening to the sentries call to one another or the occasional bark of a dog. The night around them was silent and still, the mold from the corridor tickling her nose. In spite of the fact that it was cold, damp, and eerily dark, there was no place else on earth Mara would have rather been at that moment.

CHAPTER SIX

The snorting, the grunting, had ceased for the moment. Deep in the folds of the moonless night, Edmund and Johanne lay wrapped in each other's arms, listening to the sounds of the crackling hearth. A few hours before dawn, they would make love twice more before the sun rose.

"She's a witch," Johanne murmured into her brother's stale shoulder.

Almost asleep, Edmund grunted. "Who?"

"Mara," Johanne stretched, her frizzy blond hair hanging in her eyes. "I have decided she must go."

Edmund opened his eyes, dreading his sister's words. He did not want to kill another lady, not with Kirk present. The other times, nine in all, he had sent the man out on an errand before completing the task. Always with assistance from a knight Kirk had come to trust, a man who Edmund paid well for his silence.

"What do you mean, Johanne?" his question was filled with reluctance.

But his sister seemed not to notice the cautious inflection. She raked her dirty nails down his back. "Precisely that. Either she returns home, or I shall wish her away."

Edmund sighed. "Then we will send her home. The sister I can do nothing about, but the dark-haired spitfire I would agree to remove. Either that, or betroth her to some hapless fool and be rid of her that way."

Johanne raised her head, gazing into eyes the same size and shape as her own. "Either path makes no difference as long as she is gone. And as for Lady Micheline, she seems to be quiet and respectful. Mayhap she will do well as your wife."

Edmund groaned. "Quiet and respectful and ugly," he rubbed his eyes. "I could hardly stand to look at her at dinner for fear I would lose my appetite."

Johanne laughed softly. "But she remained silent and unobtrusive and left us alone," she licked his right nipple seductively. "I do not think you said a word to her all eve."

"I did not," Edmund shuddered when Johanne licked him again. "I find I prefer to pretend she doesn't exist."

"But what about the wedding?"

He groaned again. "We shall simply get it over with, a quick ceremony and an even quicker consummation."

Johanne slithered down his body, wrapping her hands around his semi-flaccid manhood. "I shall make the arrangements, then. I am sure we can have this unpleasant business out of the way by tomorrow eve."

"Whatever you say," he grabbed her by the hair, pulling hard and loving her gasps of pain. "The sooner the better."

"And the sister?"

"Betrothed to the first man I can find. Satisfied?"

Johanne licked his phallus, grinning. "Very much. As you shall be quite shortly, as well."

***

Mara was awakened by Micheline's shrieks of pleasure. Rolling around in the large bed, she was vaguely aware of the bright day, the sounds of birds singing. Even with the brilliant light, however, the room was bitterly cold and she shivered, snuggling beneath the covers until Micheline ripped them off her small body.

"Look, Mara!" she cried happily. "Surcoats!"

Mara blinked the sleep from her eyes, growling and trying to regain her lost blankets. But Micheline was thrusting something in her face, a lovely shade of sapphire, and Mara blinked her eyes again at the fabric came into focus.

"Where did this come from?" her voice was hoarse with morning sleep.

It was then that she noticed Lady Valdine and Lady Wanda lingering respectfully at the edge of the bed. Mara sat up, staring at them; it was like looking at a mirror image.

"Sir Kirk said..."

"... that you could use these. They have..."

"... been left behind by lady visitors and he thought..."

"... they would suit you quite nicely."

Mara rubbed her eyes, unsure if she was capable of dealing with Lady Valdine and Lady Wanda this early in the morning. But the women had brought clothing, beautiful clothing, and Mara found herself willing to tolerate their strange presence. Rising from the bed, she fingered a yellow silk lying on the edge of the mattress.

"It's magnificent," she said, noting the plunging neckline. After a moment, she looked at the twins. "Sir Kirk sent you with these?"

They nodded in unison and Lady Valdine moved forward; it was the first time Mara had seen one of the twins move independently.

"Now that you are related to Baron Bowland, he suggested..."

"...that these fine surcoats would enhance your wardrobe..."

"...until we could make you some new garments. Do they..."

62

"...please you?"

"Yes, of course," Mara nodded as Lady Valdine held up the yellow surcoat, holding up to Mara's shoulders and noting the length.

"It needs to be..."

"...shortened a few inches. She's such a tiny..."

"...thing. So..."

"...beautiful. So..."

"...delicate."

Lady Wanda was standing several feet from Lady Valdine and still, they spoke in one sentence. But their expressions and gestures were kind and in spite of the oddity, Mara realized she was willing to tolerate them. They were practically the only compassionate faces she had encountered since arriving at Anchorsholme and she could hardly resist their care.

As Lady Valdine fussed over Mara, Lady Wanda went to stand beside Micheline as she examined a lovely purple brocade. Micheline insisted on trying it on and immediately removed her nightshift as Mara moved from the yellow silk to a clear red satin. Never in their lives had they had the opportunity to wear such lovely garments and their excitement was palpable. Moreover, there were armloads of surcoats and as Mara perused the pile next to the door, she turned to Lady Valdine curiously.

"You mentioned that these dresses were left by lady visitors," she said. "Why did they leave them behind?"

Lady Valdine's normally blank expression seemed to grow even more wide-eyed. "They... they simply..."

"...did," Lady Wanda had heard the question. "Sometimes we are host to such..."

"...wealthy guests that they never miss..."

"...a trunk or two left behind."

Mara did not think their weak explanation made much sense, but she remained silent on the matter. And the fact that her question seemed to have greatly disturbed the twins also deterred further inquisition. Catching sight of Micheline as the woman gasped with delight at the feel of the purple surcoat embracing her thin body, she decided that it did not matter where the surcoats came from. It had been a long time since she had seen her sister so happy.

"Then I must thank Sir Kirk for his thoughtfulness," she said, her attention returning to the clear red satin surcoat lying across the bed. "And I believe I shall wear the red surcoat to accomplish this."

"And you shall, my lady. After..."

"... we mend the length."

Mara left the pile by the door, collecting the red dress from the mussed pile of blankets. Turning to the twins, she held it up before her.

"The length is fine for the moment," she tossed the garment back to the bed and began removing her shift. "For now, you will help my sister. She is to be the future baroness, after all. 'Tis more important that she is presentable. I can wait."

The three of them turned to watch Micheline dance past them, twirling her new purple surcoat. Mara smiled as her sister waltzed with an imaginary lover to a tune none of them could hear. A delightful dance in the arms of a man who thought her beautiful as opposed to plain, fascinating as opposed to average.

The more Mara watched, the more she realized Kirk was responsible for Micheline's dose of happiness; he had promised to aid Mara in her defense of Micheline. Although he had not been able to help her yesterday in the face of Edmund's ignorance, he was helping her now by making amends for her rough introduction to Anchorsholme Castle. Bringing hope and beauty to a girl who had known little of both.

"Take care of Micheline, ladies," Mara said, tossing the red satin over her head and thinking warm thoughts of a man she was once sworn to hate. "I have a knight to thank."

***

The double baileys of Anchorsholme were dusty, smelly pools of men and animals. The sky was amazingly clear this day, the weak sun bright on the fields below. Dressed in the beautiful red surcoat that accentuated her feminine curves, Mara picked her way among the crowd in search of Kirk. The servants inside the keep had been unable to tell her where he had gone on this fine morning; therefore, she determined to find him herself.

She was almost run over near the stables by a dancing charger. Frightened, but characteristically hostile, she shook her fist at the soldier and dashed off toward the kitchen yard. It never occurred to her to ask one of the many men-at-arms what they knew of Kirk's location, but whether it was because she was too prideful or intimidated by their grizzled appearance was unknown.

The sun was drying the rain from the earth, creating dust and clouds of insects as she made her way to the kitchens. The smell of urine was sharp in her nostrils but she paid little heed to the stench, her focus on finding Kirk. Once inside the small enclosure that housed the buttery, the butcher's block, and other kitchen necessities, she saw quite clearly that Kirk wasn't in the area and, frustrated, turned to leave. Returning the way she had come, she was almost out of the yard when she noticed movement from the corner of her eye.

It was movement in the cool shadows and Mara could hear a good deal of whispering. Peering closer, she noticed several pairs of eyes stared back

64

at her. Putting her hand up to shield the sun, four dirty children abruptly came into focus.

Mara frowned. "What are you doing in there? Hiding?"

One of the children, a boy a year or so younger than herself, emerged from the dampness. He was a bit taller than she was and they gazed at each other curiously beneath the bright blue sky.

"What are *you* doing?" the boy countered. "Have you lost something?"

Mara shook her head. "I am looking for someone. I do not suppose you know where I could find Kirk?"

The boy's freckled nose twitched. "Kirk the Giant?"

Mara scowled. "You will not call him that!"

The boy shrugged, scratching his dirty blond head. "'Tis the truth. He's a giant."

Mara still did not like the term, even if the lad was correct. She eyed the boy, glancing to his three companions still in the shadows. "What's your name?"

"Robert," the boy said, gesturing to the gaggle of children behind him. "Those are my kin; Fiona, Gilly, and George."

"Do you work in the kitchens?"

Robert nodded; for a peasant youth, he seemed rather well-spoken. "Our mam assists the cook." He looked Mara up and down. "You do not sound like another Irish lady."

Mara's brow furrowed with puzzlement. "I am not. My sister is going to marry Lord Edmund."

Robert's eyes widened. He turned to look at his sisters and brother, brave enough to emerge from the cool recesses now that their brother had engaged the lady in conversation. Four pairs of astonished eyes gazed back at Mara.

"Why do you look like that?" she demanded.

The children looked to each other again, dirty youths with similar coloring and features. Finally, Robert looked at Mara.

"Is your sister forced to do this?"

"Our father betrothed her," she said, unsure how to answer the question. "Now, you will tell me why you look so distressed."

Robert gazed at her a moment, his intelligent eyes studying her striking features. "What's your name, lady?"

"Mara."

"Are you hungry, Lady Mara?"

"I ate not an hour ago but... aye, I suppose I could eat."

Robert motioned her with him. "Then come along," he said as his siblings collected around Mara in an eager group. "Mam will feed us."

Surrounded by grinning children, Mara had no choice but to accept.

***

Robert's mother was a round woman who gave the children as much food as they could carry. Munching on a wedge of tart white cheese, Mara followed the group from the kitchen yard and through a small tunnel carved into the outer wall. Emerging into the knee-high grass of the surrounding fields, the five of them tramped down a small hill and into a grove of gnarled oak.

It was cool and pleasant among the trees. Mara finished the cheese and crunched into a small green apple as Robert graciously brushed off a rock for her to sit. Smiling, she accepted.

The lanky youth plopped to the dirt at her feet, smacking loudly on pumpkin seeds. "Now," he said, licking his fingers. "You have got to send word to your da. He must come and take your sister away from Anchorsholme before she can marry the Devilboy."

"Devilboy?" Mara repeated. "You mean Lord Edmund?"

Robert nodded, his unkempt blond hair waving like grass in a breeze. "He is evil."

Mara stopped mid-chew. "How do you know this?"

Robert picked more seeds. "Because I have lived here all my life, lady. If your sister stays, she'll end up dead like all the rest. Mayhap you will, too."

Mara could hardly swallow. She tossed the apple aside and spit out the contents of her mouth, her bright blue eyes wide on the boy. "Dead? For Heaven's sake, Robert, what are you talking about?"

Robert's younger brother retrieved Mara's half-eaten apple, brushed it off, and finished it. Robert ignored the boy, finishing his seeds. "Did not anyone tell you about The Darkland?"

Mara nodded hesitantly. "Well, yes... Sir Corwin told me that is what Lord Edmund's Irish subjects call it."

"Did he tell you why?"

"Not really," she sat forward on the rock, her expression intensely curious. "Why do they call it The Darkland, Robert?"

Robert finished his seeds and met Mara's demanding gaze. "Because women die here. Any young woman who comes to this place never leaves."

Chills of foreboding raced up Mara's spine. "How do they die?"

"No one knows," Robert shook his head. "One minute they are here, the next they are gone. No one ever sees them again. Nine in all, in fact."

Mara did not reply for a moment, digesting his story. "And you believe my sister and I to be in danger?"

Robert's expression tensed. "All young women are in danger."

"But Sir Kirk will protect us."

"He cannot. He is always gone when the women vanish."

Mara swallowed, her sense of dread growing. "Is he somehow involved with these... disappearances?"

Robert shook his head and Mara sighed with instant relief. "Sir Kirk is a just man. But he always seems to be away when the women vanish." The youth gestured at her new surcoat. "I saw that dress on a lady in early winter, a lady come to serve Lady Johanne from Ireland. The dead ladies are always from Ireland, you see, vassals of Lord Edmund. Lady Jessamyn wore that same dress the night before she vanished."

Mara looked at the garment, horrified. "How do you know it is the same dress?"

The lad shrugged. "Sometimes I help serve the soldiers. She was sitting with Lady Johanne in that dress, eating her last meal. I remember noticing the dress because Gilly liked the silver thread around the sleeve."

Mara was pale as she looked at the young girl seated on her left, no more than twelve years of age. The girl smiled weakly, her cheeks flushing, and Mara returned her focus to Robert in dismay.

"You are sure, Robert?"

"Positive."

"But you said the women disappeared. How do you know for sure that they were killed? Mayhap they simply left and no one saw them depart."

Robert shook his head, slowly. "They are dead, lady. Lord Edmund told everyone that the women returned home, but my mam once helped bury the possessions of one of the ladies."

"By whose order?"

"No one is for certain. And no one is willing to ask."

Mara felt sick. And terrified. Slouching on the rock, she shook her head as she pondered the lad's stunning account on the happenings at Anchorsholme.

"So that is why they call it The Darkland," she murmured, more to herself.

Robert nodded. "The House of the Death. Young ladies never leave here alive."

Mara's gaze snapped to him, trapping him within her intense focus. "Well, I am leaving here alive," she hissed, rising swiftly from the rock. "My sister and I are leaving and never coming back, betrothal or no!"

Robert and his siblings were instantly on their feet as Mara gathered her too-long skirts. Retraced her steps up the hill, the collection of children followed.

"How are you going to leave?" Robert pulled her skirt free of prickly bramble when it snagged. "Do you have horses, a wagon?"

"We have palfreys," Mara said firmly. "We are leaving and no one is going to stop us. I shall kill anyone who tries!"

"Even Sir Kirk?"

"Especially Sir Kirk. How dare he not tell us of the danger we are in!"

"Sir Kirk was the reason the ladies died," Gilly's soft voice came from behind her brother.

Mara came to an abrupt stop, causing the children to bump into each other. Bright blue eyes were fixed on the pale young girl with the untamed curls.

"Tell me all," her voice was hoarse with dread.

Gilly swallowed hard, struggling for courage. She had been bold enough to make the statement, but explaining her words were clearly another matter. "The dead ladies all had eyes for him," she said softly. "It was known that he did not return their feelings, but the ladies died just the same. Mayhap by their own hand. Some have come to think that Kirk Connaught is cursed."

Mara's eyebrows rose in shock. "Cursed?" she repeated. Taking a deep breath to soothe her shattering composure, she turned her eyes toward the dark stone bastion reaching for the heavens. "Dear God. Why did not anyone tell us this before?"

Robert was standing beside her, his blue eyes sympathetic and fearful at the same time. She was such a pretty lady, far prettier than any lady he had ever seen at Anchorsholme Castle. And she was nice, too; none of the other ladies had ever spoken to him. But Mara had.

"We shall help you leave, lady," he said, nodding to his siblings. "Get your things together and we shall whisk you from Anchorsholme before anyone is the wiser."

Mara should have been grateful for the lad's assistance. But instead, she was overwhelmed with despondency over Kirk's apparent hex and found herself unable to focus on anything else.

"Do you believe that Kirk is cursed, Robert?" she asked softly.

He shrugged weakly. "I do not know, lady. But some say he is."

"Who?"

"Servants mostly. The soldiers defend him, saying he had nothing to do with the ladies' deaths."

"What of Edmund and Johanne? What do they say?"

Robert's gaze faltered. After a moment, he shrugged again. "Who can say? Everyone is a'feared of them because of Johanne's madness."

"Madness?"

The boy nodded. "She rages with the change of the moons. She's been known to beat serving wenches, or burn them with pokers. One time she bit a wench on the hand and tore off her finger."

Mara's eyes widened with horror. Without another word, she returned to the kitchen yard through the tunnel in the wall. With a hasty farewell to Robert and his silent siblings, she made way to her chamber as fast as her feet would carry her.

***

Micheline was trying on her sixth surcoat by the time Mara reached her. Huffing with exertion, she raced into the room and slammed the door, bolting it from the inside. But when she turned and saw Lady Valdine and Lady Wanda hemming one of Micheline's new dresses, she screamed at them to leave and, in perfect synchronization, they did so.

Mara bolted the door again when they were gone. Puzzled and incensed, Micheline came down from the stool she had been perched on.

"Mara!" she scolded. "What is the matter with you?"

Mara's face was white with fear, her breathing rapid from having mounted three flights of stairs in a panic.

"Misha," she grasped her sister by the arms. "We have got to leave this place. Now!"

Micheline could see the terror in her sister's eyes. "Why, Mara? What has happened?"

Mara couldn't answer. Releasing her sister, she ran to the massive wardrobe and threw open the doors. Grabbing the worn satchel that had once belonged to her mother, she began stuffing garments into it.

Micheline went to her, struggling to calm the hysterical woman. "Tell me what's the matter, darling. What has upset you so?"

Mara dropped the satchel in her haste. Growling in frustration, she turned to her sister, both hands clutching the clothing she was trying so desperately to pack.

"This place," she hardly knew where to begin. "Do you remember when Sir Corwin called it The Darkland?"

When Micheline nodded, Mara swallowed hard before continuing. "It's called The Darkland because young women die here. These dresses that were brought to us are from those dead ladies. Do you remember Lady Valdine and Lady Wanda explaining how the garments had been left behind? With hesitance and uncertainty, as if they did not want us to know!"

Micheline wasn't any better at masking her horror than her sister. "Are you certain?" she hissed. "Who told you this?"

"Children of a servant. They have lived here for a very long time and explained the evil of this place to me," Mara shuddered involuntarily, struggling to go on. "Thank God someone had the courage to enlighten us.

69

But Kirk... they say he is cursed. Every young woman who died had eyes for him."

Micheline gasped. "But... Mara! He is so fond of you and...!"

There was a sharp rap on the door. Mara shrieked, dropping the garments in her hands. Frozen with fright, the sisters stared at the panel as the caller rapped again. And a third time. Finally, a voice echoed from the opposite side of the door.

"Mara?" It was Kirk. "Lady Micheline? Are you there?"

Micheline gasped again and Mara shushed her sternly. Her entirely body trembling, she moved swiftly to the door, making sure it was bolted before replying.

"Go away, Sir Kirk," she half-demanded, half-begged. "We do not wish to see you."

In the corridor, Kirk's brow furrowed at the sound of Mara's voice. She sounded so... weak.

"Mara?" he tried the latch; it was locked. He rattled it loudly. "Mara, what's wrong? Open the door."

The sound of his deep, soothing voice was enough to drive her to tears. Terrified and confused, Mara sobbed softly against the old, scrubbed wood.

"Please," she whispered loudly. "Just... go away. Leave us alone, Kirk."

He rattled the latch again, more firmly this time. "I will not. Open the door or I shall break it down."

"Nay!" she knew he was fully capable of carrying out his threat. "Do not break it down. Please do as I ask!"

Hand still on the iron latch, Kirk was distressed by Mara's attitude. But he was even more distressed by the quaking of her voice. To become angry would only inflame her, so very calmly, he leaned against the seam where the door met the frame.

"I won't break it down, love," he murmured, knowing she could hear him. "But please open the door. Why are you so upset?"

He could hear her sobbing. "I am... I am simply fatigued. Micheline and I wish to be left alone."

"I will leave you alone if you open the door and prove to me that you're well."

"Do you not trust my word?"

"When I do not know the reason for your tears, I must say that I do not."

Mara stared at the latch a long, long time. Finally, and very slowly, she released the bolt. And after another lengthy pause, she cracked the panel open.

Kirk's stone-gray eyes were staring at her. Mara sniffled, meeting his gaze and struggling not to crumble.

"There," she said hoarsely. "As you can see, I am well. Micheline is well. Now will you leave us?"

"Nay," he pushed the door open, his gaze roving the room. Seeing there was no obvious threat that would drive Mara to tears, his gaze immediately fell on the satchel and discarded clothing heaped on the floor. His eyebrows knit together. "What is this?"

Micheline was still standing by the wardrobe, her cheeks flushed. Hastily, she bent down to collect the falling things. "I... it was merely my own clumsiness. I was clearing the wardrobe for our new garments and this fell out."

He did not believe her for a moment. His accusing gaze immediately turned to Mara. "Where were you going, Mara?"

She wasn't a very good liar and it had never been her habit to excuse her way out of a situation. Fully prepared to tell him that her intentions were none of his affair, one look at the intense gray eyes and her control shattered like fragile glass.

"I am leaving!" she gasped, the tears that has so recently fled returning with a vengeance. "And Micheline is going with me!"

He moved toward her simply to comfort her but she screamed, moving away from him as if he carried the plague. "Stay away from me!"

He froze, his gaze tracking her like a cat watching a mouse. "What is the matter, Mara? What have I done?"

She was standing next to the bed, sobbing. "You..," she gasped, hardly able to continue. "You are cursed!"

He stared at her. "What do you mean?"

She wept into her hand, close to hysteria. But the bright blue eyes were intense. "The Darkland, Kirk. I know why Anchorsholme Castle is called the House of the Death."

He did not say anything. Outwardly, his composure never wavered, but inwardly, his heart was breaking. He'd never known it to break before.

"Why is that, love?"

His gentle tone inflamed her. "Because young women die here!" she nearly shouted, angry that he would act as if he had no idea what she was talking about. "Nine young ladies who have come here to serve Johanne, women who have simply vanished into the night. Why did you tell us the truth from the beginning?"

He took a deep breath, aware that his control was slowly weakening. And that had never happened, either. Especially not where a woman was concerned. Carefully, he pondered his reply.

71

"Is that what you wanted?" his voice was oddly hoarse. "To hear stories of Anchorsholme Castle, frightening you to death when you were already reluctant to come?"

Near the wardrobe, Micheline nearly collapsed with the confirmation of Mara's wild stories.

"Dear God," she gasped, groping for the nearest chair. "Then what she has told me is true."

Kirk eyed the woman a brief moment before returning his attention to Mara. She was sitting on the bed now, facing away from and sobbing pitifully.

"I do not know the extent of what she has told you, Lady Micheline," he said softly, moving slowly for the bed. "But I would like to hear everything."

Mara could feel him standing by the foot of the bed, too weak to resist him. Face in her hands, she simply shook her head. "Dead women, Kirk. Ladies come to Anchorsholme Castle but they never leave. Isn't that so?"

"There's more to it than that, lass."

"But what of Johanne?" she demanded. "You told me to stay away from her because she was dangerous. Now I know she burns people and bites off fingers!"

He sighed deeply, gazing at her glorious black head. After a moment, he turned away and marched to the chamber door, calling for a servant. When two women appeared, wide-eyed and eager to do his bidding, he instructed them to escort Micheline to Lady Wanda's chamber. He wanted to speak with Mara, alone. To see if he could undo, or at least ease, the damage done.

Micheline was reluctant to leave, but did so obediently. Kirk closed the door, returning his attention to the bed where Mara remained huddled and weeping. Silently, he approached.

"Did you kill them?" she asked.,

Her voice was soft. Kirk sat down on the mattress beside her before replying. "Of course not," he said softly. "I would know who has told you the tales of Anchorsholme Castle."

She sniffled, struggling to calm herself. She had a terrible headache as a result of her crying jag. "It does not matter," she said, with less force. "But I know everything and I demand that you let Micheline and I leave before we fall victim, too."

"That is not going to happen," he said firmly. "I would never allow any harm to befall you."

"It befell the other women."

"If you know the tales as you have said, then you would also know that I wasn't at Anchorsholme Castle at the time of their disappearances. Had I been here, I most certainly would have protected them."

"Did you never try to find out what happened to them?"

"By the time I returned, all evidence had been removed. And Edmund's story was always solid. As my liege, it was not my place to question him. But, unfortunately, there was no one who could tell me much more than what I already knew."

"So you ignored the disappearances?"

"I wasn't given much choice, Mara. One does not question the activities of one's liege, no matter what the circumstances. I realize that excuse is weak, but you must understand that as lord of Anchorsholme Castle and head of the House of de Cleveley, Edmund is answerable only to his liege, the Earl of Carlisle, to the king, and to God. I have no right accusing him of something I cannot prove."

"But did you ever *try*, Kirk?"

He nodded. "I did as much as I could," he replied. "I would follow clues that servants or soldiers would tell me but they always led to a dead-end. After the last disappearance, I had some of my men dig around in newly disturbed earth outside of the walls in the dead of night to see if we could come up with a corpse, but there was nothing. Mara, lass, I am not an ignorant or cowering wretch. I understand what justice is. But even if I were to find the bodies of the women who had disappeared, what could I do with them? Confront Edmund? If he denies any knowledge, then I must believe him. I have no choice because no one, save God himself, will bring him to justice because I promise you the earl and the king would do nothing. Edmund is nobility and he is untouchable. 'Tis the way of the world."

Mara continued to sniffle, wiping her eyes and digesting his words. She could tell that he was pained by his helplessness, a big dark shadow that he was unable to shake. After a moment, she cast him a long glance.

"I was told that all of the women had eyes for you," she said quietly.

He met her gaze, a smile creeping over his lips. "Now I see why you are so worried. Certainly you fit the pattern."

She frowned. "What pattern?"

"Having eyes for me."

Her bow-shaped mouth opened in outrage. "I do not!"

He grinned. "Pity. After all, I have eyes for you."

She turned her nose up at him, looking away. It was purely a defensive reaction, however; she did not want him to see that his words had pleased her.

"You are wasting your time, Kirk Connaught," she said, though she did not mean a word of it. "I have no interest in you."

"You do. Admit it."

"I will not."

He leaned close, burying his face in her silken hair and inhaling deeply. Mara froze, feeling his hot breath against the back of her head as chills enveloped her body. Closing her eyes, she could hardly repress the mad trembling that had suddenly taken control.

Kirk smiled into her hair, taking an inky tendril and wrapping it around his finger. "Then if you have no interest in me, kindly explain why rumors of my curse have upset you so?"

Mara shuddered violently, scarcely able to reply as his massive body pressed against her back. "I... I was afraid."

"Afraid of me?"

She nodded, unaware that she was listing against him. As her eyes remained closed, she had no idea that she was literally collapsing in his arms. "Afraid of you."

Mara was cognizant of his lips against her temple. Somehow, she was falling, falling into the curve of his strong embrace and she had neither the desire nor the strength to resist him. And if she had learned one thing from the very beginning of their association, it was that Kirk Connaught had strong, warm, wonderful arms. Arms that made her feel more protected, more cherished, than anything on this earth.

"You need never fear me, love," his mouth was moving down her face, his hands caressing her cheeks. "I am the last person you need dread. But you, on the other hand..."

She was lost as his lips roved her chin. "What... what of me?"

His mouth hovered above her luscious lips, quivering with desire. Mara opened her eyes long enough to meet his liquid gaze.

"You scare me to death."

It was the truth.

CHAPTER SEVEN

Mara had no idea what Kirk meant by his strange statement. And he never gave her the chance to ask. One moment she was gazing into his stone gray eyes, and in the next his mouth was consuming her luscious lips with a hunger. It was the first time a man had ever kissed her, slow and warm and insistent, and before Mara realized her actions, small hands were weaving themselves into his hair.

He was oh so tender with her, like a tiny fragile flower. He tasted gently, tickling her lips with his tongue until she opened wide to his seeking warmth. Mara gasped, squirmed, and gasped anew as his massive arms pulled her against his chest. Focused on the new experience of his wonderful mouth, she was unaware when he lay her on the bed, partially covering her with his enormous body.

One hand still held her tightly as the other forged into virgin territory. Delicately, he touched the swell of her breast, listening to her purr like a kitten. Feeling bolder, he gently enclosed the entire breast, his kisses more passionate, more forceful, as she responded. He released her lips, intending to taste every inch of her beautiful face when she suddenly turned the tables on him, peppering his jaw and cheeks with hot little kisses.

"Dear God," he breathed, caressing the firmness of her breast as she attacked his face. "Mara, Mara... you're a hellion more than you know, lass."

She heard him, kissing his eyes, clinging to him with a fervor. For a sheltered young lady who had known little of the ways between men and women, it was apparent that Kirk brought out her animal instincts. Fingers anchored in his dark hair, she was in the process of raining kisses across his forehead when he suddenly lowered his head, dragging his mouth over the swell of her breasts.

The too-long surcoat was loosening. Kirk pulled Mara away from his face, forcing her back onto the mattress as his hands sought her bare breasts. She moaned softly as he pinched a nipple, rolling it into a hot little bud. Consumed with the need to taste her, to suckle the life from her pert breasts, Kirk realized through his haze of lust that the neckline of the surcoat was too constricting for his needs. But the moment he moved to lift her skirts, she balked.

"Nay!" she gasped, slapping at his hands. "Not... not that!"

He frowned with concern. "Not what, love?"

Panting with desire and a surge of fright, she tried to squirm away from him. Kirk grasped her wrists to prevent her from leaping off the bed.

"What is the matter?" he asked, his voice gentle but firm. "What have I done, Mara?"

She refused to look him in the eye, her cheeks flushing bright. Seeing her obvious discomfort, and fear, Kirk gently kissed her hands, hoping to ease her. Not a moment ago she had been alive with awakening desire; now she was withdrawn and fearful. And he would know why.

"Tell me, lass," he whispered, straightening the neckline of her surcoat where it drooped. "I would know what I have done to upset you so."

She struggled with herself for a moment. Finally, the bright blue gaze lifted hesitantly. "I... I do not want you to touch me... there."

"Where?"

She lifted an eyebrow with as much force as she could muster. "*There.*"

He understood immediately. "I wasn't going to," mostly truth, although it had been his next target after her delicious breasts. Still clutching her wrists, he pulled her toward him in a gentle, comforting manner. "Mara, you realize that when men and women mate, at some point, touching is necessary. And when we marry..."

"I never said I'd marry you."

He acted as if he hadn't heard her. "*When* we marry, it will be necessary for me to touch you there in order to produce children. It's perfectly natural, lass. Why does it frighten you so?"

Her expression was suddenly filled with shame and she turned her face away. True to her forthright nature, however, she made no attempt to cover the truth. No matter how humiliating. "The soldier in the inn... he touched me there and it was painful," she could feel his gaze on her. "I hated every minute of it."

Kirk was quiet a moment. "You told me that he did not take your maidenhood."

"He did not," she forced herself to look at him. "But his fingers... *they* touched me."

He did not say any more. Pulling her stiff body against him, he lay back on the soft pillows, holding her tightly. Mara gave in to his comfort, his heat, sighing with contentment as he gently caressed her.

"Are you angry?" her voice was small.

"Why should I be?" he said softly. "I understand your fear and I am sorry that you are frightened of something that can be quite wonderful. Obviously, your first experience was dreadful. But you must realize that it will be different with me."

"Why?"

76

"Because I will be gentle, lass. I shall take the time needed to introduce you into the world of desire."

"But it will hurt, will it not? My mother told me once that it is painful for a woman to lose her virginity."

"I have heard that it is," his voice was quiet as he turned, capturing her against his chest and gazing down into her wonderful eyes. "In truth, I have never bedded a virgin before. I suppose this will be a new experience for the both of us."

She raised an eyebrow and he caught a glimpse of her stubborn nature returning. "You speak as if I have already agreed to this. I told you quite clearly that I did not want to marry you."

"Would you rather have someone else?"

"And if I did?"

"Then I will kill him," Kirk sounded entirely sincere. "I shall kill any man who tries to take you from me, Mara. I swear it."

The gently-taunting air of their conversation had turned serious. Mara raised her head, leaning on an elbow as she studied his strong, handsome face. "You once told me to jump from the window ledge to entertain you," she said, reaching out a timid hand to stroke his cheek. "I told you that I hated you. And still you want me?"

He smiled faintly. "I think I have from the moment I first saw you. I'd never seen anything so beautiful in my entire life."

"Then why did you tell me to jump?"

His smile broadened. "So I could save you and you would be forever indebted to me. Why else?"

She matched his smile, giggling when he enfolded her in his arms and rolled across the bed. Mara ended up with her head hanging over the side of the mattress, quickly succumbing to the scorching kisses Kirk was depositing on her neck.

"I still say that I do not want to marry you," she breathed, the blood rushing to her head. "But supposing I have a weak moment and agree, will we live here?"

He grunted, tasting her sweet flesh. "I think not. One of my brothers can come and serve Edmund and Johanne. You and I shall return to Ireland. You will not stay at Anchorsholme any longer than necessary."

"Because you fear for me?"

He stopped kissing her. Mara raised her head, gazing into intense gray eyes. "Because I fear what I might do if you are threatened," he sighed heavily, his gaze raking her face. "My family has served the House of de Cleveley for three generations, Mara. I would hate to be the link in the chain that destroyed the standards of service my father and grandfather set."

"By killing for me?"

He nodded faintly. "Aye, love," he whispered. "By killing for you. By killing them all."

***

The evening feast was a less fanciful affair than it had been the previous evening. Most of the guests had departed, leaving the cavernous grand hall rather empty. Aside from a few senior soldiers, the knights and their ladies, all was silent and somber as the meal of pork and boiled vegetables was served.

Mara and Micheline sat at the head table, a bank of smoking tallow candles burning brightly before them. They were clad in surcoats they had brought from Haslingden, faded garments in contrast to Johanne's brilliant scarlet frock. But there was no humiliation in their appearance this night; proudly, they wore the old dresses. For no amount of convincing from Kirk or the twin ladies could convince them to wear the beautiful dresses of the dead women.

Kirk sat between Edmund and Micheline again this night, silently consuming his meal. Micheline ate silently as well, as did Mara. The only conversation, soft and intimate, was between Edmund and Johanne as they tittered and whispered privately.

Kirk ignored his young lord, casting long glances at Mara as she picked at her food. An afternoon spent in her arms had been more than enough to convince him that he could not, would not, live without her whether or not she agreed to his marriage proposal. He made feeble attempts to catch her attention, clearing his throat or banging his spoon. But she deliberately ignored him, pretending not to hear his overtures.

He had to grin at her, stubborn little wench. The harder he tried, the more she ignored him. Just when he was about to throw a piece of bread at her, Johanne broke from her conversation with Edmund and focused on pale, subdued Micheline.

"I thought you would like to know that wedding arrangements have been made," she said, mockingly-sweet. "The priest will arrive on the morrow from Crosby and you and my brother shall be wed."

Micheline's cheeks flushed. "I... I thank you for making the arrangements, my lady," she said politely. "I hope it wasn't too much trouble for you."

Johanne smiled thinly. "Not at all. A simple missive sent to the priest was the only undertaking. I would expect that by noon will see you and my brother as husband and wife."

Micheline nodded submissively, though the entire idea shocked and sickened her. *So soon.* "If I may be of any assistance to you in the final preparations, please let me know. I should be happy to help."

"You're the bride, dear, you're not supposed to help," Johanne said. "To marry my brother and spread your legs is all that is required of you."

Kirk looked to Mara as Johanne spouted her uncouth remark and was not surprised to note her turning shades of red. But, remarkably and with a great deal of effort, she kept her mouth shut.

Micheline, ever lady-like, refused to dignify the remark. Self-control and poise that impressed Kirk tremendously. "I look forward to becoming a member of the House of De Cleveley." It was a lie. She wished she could run far, far away and never look back.

Edmund finished his wine, turning to look at Micheline for the first time since their introduction. His green gaze was bland. "Did your mother only bear two daughters?"

Micheline looked up from her trencher, aware that her betrothed was speaking to her and wondering what sort of belittlement she would be facing now. "Aye, my lord."

He grunted, motioning the serving wench for more drink. "Worthless. You will bear me only sons, is that clear?"

Micheline's mottled cheeks deepened. "I... I can only try, my lord."

"She has no control over the sex of the child," Kirk was looking at Edmund, his gray eyes glittering. "We take what God gives us, male or female."

Edmund looked at him. "But your mother had three sons, Kirk. I have heard that there are things women can do to assure the sex of the child."

Kirk sat back in his chair, toying with his goblet. "Like what? I would be interested to know."

Edmund shrugged. "By eating certain foods or rinsing their womb with herbs. I have heard of a woman in Liverpool who makes potions to insure male offspring. I do believe I shall contact her."

Kirk snorted into his chalice. "Fool's tales, my lord. I have never heard of such a thing."

Edmund gaze moved to Micheline, sitting meek and submissive and red-cheeked. "Nonetheless, for my bride's sake the potions had better work. I have no use for a woman who can only bear females."

"Or what?" Mara could keep silent no longer and Kirk visibly perked. "Or you will kill her like you have killed all the rest?"

Kirk was on his feet, coughing loudly to cover the impact of Mara's words. "My lady is fatigued this night," he growled through clenched teeth. Before Mara could protest, he was literally scooping her up by the arms in his haste to remove her from Edmund's rage. "Allow me to escort you to your chamber."

But his liege would not be put off so easily. Edmund leapt to his feet before Kirk could move Mara from the table. "Hold!" he commanded. "Whereby does she spout such nonsense?"

Kirk cast Mara an expression that suggested nothing other than complete silence from her. "The lady strolled the grounds this morn and was told some of the local folklore," he said evenly. "Surely nothing you have not heard before, my lord."

"But she has accused me of murder!" Edmund said with outrage. "I would know who told her such lies!"

Kirk looked at Mara, who immediately thrust up her chin stubbornly. Even in the face of an angry lord, she was characteristically brave. And mayhap foolish. "I do not know their names, my lord," she said.

Kirk knew it was a lie. He watched as Edmund approached, his freckled face taut with emotion. Kirk was also quite aware that he himself tensed, preparing to defend Mara from any physical punishment Edmund might choose to deliver.

"Then if you do not know their names, you will describe them," Edmund demanded. "Tell me now!"

Mara wasn't the least bit intimidated by him. "It will not help to shout at me."

"I am not shouting!"

"You are, my lord, and I find that your howling has upset my head," she turned away from him as if entirely disinterested in the conversation. "If you will excuse me, I shall retire for the evening."

Edmund reached out and grabbed her by the arm. Raising his open palm, his downward motion was stopped by a grip so powerful that he yelped in pain. Gazing up, he realized with shock that that Kirk had prevented him from venting his rage on the obstinate young girl.

The gleam to the stone-gray eyes was most disturbing. "That," Kirk growled, "would not be wise, Edmund. I suggest you return to your meal and permit me to escort Lady Mara to her chamber."

As Edmund stared into his chilling expression, he realized that he was frightened of Kirk. Truly frightened. But he was also terribly offended.

"You *defend* her?" he hissed. "I am your liege, Kirk. 'Tis your duty to support me without question!"

"Not when it comes to beating helpless women," Kirk released Edmund's hand. Grasping Mara by the arm, he struggled to maintain his calm; he, too, could hardly believe what he had just done. "Trust that I shall deal with the lady in a less painful manner. You will excuse us."

He whisked Mara from the room before Edmund could express his astonishment. Once sheltered by the long, cool corridor leading to the foyer of Anchorsholme, he thrust Mara into a secluded alcove and pulled the tapestry closed. When he faced her, she could read nothing but fury on his face.

"Kirk," she said softly. "I...."

His piercing gaze cleaved her words. "You will listen to me, lady, and listen well. Never again will you show such stupidity by spouting accusations that are hardly concrete. The tales of the Darkland are not to be trivialized in any way, for they hold more power and terror than you can imagine. Do you understand?"

He was rigid with anger. Fearful of him for the first time since their introduction, Mara nodded weakly. "I... I am sorry, Kirk. But he was threatening Micheline and..."

"And did I not tell you that I would protect her?" he fired back, his tone harsh. "Do you not trust me, Mara? Or are you so young and foolish that you would place yourself in jeopardy simply to gain a small measure of revenge on your sister's behalf?"

She lowered her gaze, close to tears of anger and shame. He was right and she was well aware of the fact; still, his scolding upset her. Even more than the spanking had.

"I suppose I am young and foolish, my lord," she said, refusing to look at him. "I have always been outspoken, flagrantly so. I would have thought you to realize that by now."

He loomed over her, jaw ticking with emotion. "Curb it, Mara. Or it will be the end of you."

She was wedged into the corner of the alcove, picking distractedly at her nails. "Then let it end me. At least my end will be honestly met, speaking my mind for what is right and just. If it is not to your approval, then that is your misfortune."

He shook his head slowly. "Christ, you're a stubborn creature."

She turned to him, then. "Aye, I am. And I refuse to go through life being reprimanded by you every time I open my mouth. If you were serious when you proposed marriage, Kirk Connaught, then I suggest you reconsider. You will not find a perfect wife in me."

He stared at her. Long and hard. "Mayhap you are right. Mayhap I have been fooling myself all along."

Mara felt as if she had been hit in the stomach. She hadn't expected him to agree so readily. Before she could respond, however, he grasped her by the arm again and pulled her from the alcove. Silent and brooding, he escorted her to the chamber she shared with Micheline and left without another word.

When Micheline came to bed less than an hour later, she noticed that Mara's pillow was saturated with dampness. As she stood and watched her sleeping sister with concern, more tears trailed down her temples and onto the linen. Puddling, weakening. Expressing her sorrow.

When the dawn finally came, the tears were still falling.

***

"Another missive, Kirk."

Niles was in Kirk's chamber before daybreak, a rolled message in his hand. Kirk rose from his bed, naked, and snatched the vellum.

"Where's the rider?" he asked, his voice scratchy.

"In the kitchens," Niles replied, his blue eyes shadowed. He had been on sentry duty all night and was particularly weary. "He said the missive was for you alone."

Kirk unrolled the parchment, his gray eyes struggling to read the contents under the weak candlelight. Reaching the bottom of the page, he sighed and re-rolled the vellum.

"Well?" Niles demanded softly.

"It's from Drew," Kirk put the parchment aside and went in search of his hose. "Apparently, the potential of a revolt is greater than father indicated. Drew is worried that father will wait until it is too late before summoning help. They need a mediator immediately."

"You?"

Kirk pulled on his breeches, securing them. "Drew requests that I come," he said. "I must speak with Edmund on the matter."

Niles watched the man as he donned his tunic. "After what happened last night, are you sure Edmund will receive you?"

Kirk cocked an eyebrow. "I am his captain, Niles. Of course he will receive me."

Niles sighed, sitting on the edge of the bunk as Kirk splashed water on his face and wiped it off. "You're quite smitten with her, aren't you?"

Kirk did not say anything. Collecting his boots, he sat next to his friend as he pulled them on. "She's a handful, Niles. A hellion of the worst sort."

"And how is that?"

Kirk snorted softly, rising from the bed and peeling back the oilcloth on his lancet window to reveal the lightening horizon. "She's knows she's a hellion and she doesn't care. As much as I like her spirit, she must learn to control herself."

"Before or after you marry her?"

Kirk continued to stare at the sky, turning shades of pink and gold. "Who said anything about marriage?"

Niles chuckled, rising from the mattress. "No one, my friend," he put his hand on Kirk's broad shoulder. "Back to the subject at hand, do you wish for me to prepare an escort bound for Ireland?"

Kirk nodded faintly, thoughts still on Mara as he ran his fingers through his dark hair. He'd hardly slept all night thinking of her. "Better still, I plan to solicit our allies for support. Prepare a small party to accompany me to Quernmore Castle. After Edmund's marriage, I shall ride north and ask Lord le Vay for military commitment. The man owes us after we aided him in ridding his territory of gypsies last year."

Niles opened the door. "Ah, yes, Edmund's marriage," he shook his head. "I heard yesterday that Johanne sent for the priest. Going through with this rather quickly and unobtrusively, are they not?"

"Edmund simply wants to be done with it, I think."

"What is going to happen when Lady Micheline realizes her husband is sharing his bed with his sister?"

Kirk shook his head with disgust. "God only knows. For Edmund's sake, he had better be kind to the woman. She's an extremely decent woman, far too decent for Edmund."

The corridor was heavy with smoke as they stepped into it, the result of low-burning torches. "So you are Lady Micheline's protector as well, are you?" Niles smiled knowingly. "How chivalrous. The little hellion certainly has you wrapped around her finger."

Kirk couldn't deny the truth. No matter how much he wanted to.

***

The priest from Crosby was a tall, thin man with a hooked nose. He looked rather unassuming standing before Micheline and Edmund, wedding the two as if he were simply carrying on a conversation rather than a wedding mass. Clad in pale yellow brocade that had been her mother's finest dress, Micheline stood regally as the dreaded union took place.

Edmund yawned, sighed, and picked his nose as the mass was intoned. Johanne was amazingly attentive on her brother's right, while Mara, Lady Valdine and Lady Wanda stood silent just behind Micheline. Niles, Corwin and Kirk brought up the rear.

Mara could feel Kirk standing behind her, her stomach twisting painfully as the priest conducted the mass. Niles had escorted Micheline to the grand hall for the ceremony while Mara had been left in the company of Lady Valdine and Lady Wanda. Kirk was nowhere to be found and nearly missed the ceremony altogether, rushing in from the bailey at the last moment clad in worn battle armor.

Mara had been aching since last night to catch a glimpse of him. But the moment she heard his voice, she turned her attention to the priest and refused to look in his direction. Miserably, she listened as her sister wed a man the entire castle thought to be a murderer while Kirk's presence seemed to creep all over her, invading her senses and mind.

She should have been focused on Micheline but found she could not concentrate. Even this morning, helping her sister dress, her attention had been obviously diverted. Micheline never did find out what had happened, what had made Mara cry all night, but she suspected the reason. When Kirk did not appear first thing in the morning to greet them, her suspicions were confirmed.

The ceremony was over as quickly as it began. Edmund turned away from the priest, asking Kirk to pay the man as he cast a reluctant glance to his pink-cheeked bride. With a weak wave of his hand, he summoned the woman to follow and quit the hall with Johanne on his heels. Chagrinned and miserable, Micheline struggled to remain composed as the knights and ladies congratulated her.

Kirk finished paying the priest, watching as Mara and Micheline lost themselves in private conversation. They held hands tightly, Mara whispering something he couldn't hear. But the compassion on her face, the ache for her sister, spoke volumes and Kirk felt himself weakening.

Even if she was a hellion, a willful wench with an uncontrollable mouth, she was still the most beautiful, sensitive woman he had ever met. Her untamed words had always been in defense of her sister, or another worthy cause, never selfish or trite. If there was one thing Mara le Bec was not, it was self-centered. The woman had a heart of gold.

Aye, he had been angry at her last night. Angry that she proven her control over him, control he had freely given. If he should be angry at anyone, it should be himself; he was the one who allowed himself to become smitten with her. Smitten enough to the point of falling in love with the bright-eyed beauty.

The grand hall cleared, Niles and Corwin escorting Lady Valdine and Lady Wanda into the solar. The wedding had taken place after the morning meal and the servants were eager to prepare the hall for the nooning feast, but Mara and Micheline remained huddled together, ignoring all else around them, as Kirk hovered several feet away. When the wait became excessive, Kirk gently cleared his throat.

"Lady de Cleveley," he addressed Micheline softly. "Your husband awaits, madam."

Micheline was crying. As Kirk approached, she wiped her face quickly and struggled to regain her composure. "I... I know," she whispered. Then, her pale eyes turned to him. "Will you be escorting me to him?" Kirk nodded faintly. "It would be an honor."

Mara was still clutching Micheline, her lovely face dark. "I shall go with you and help you prepare."

Kirk shook his head, reaching down to dislodge the sisters' grip. He did not want Mara near Edmund or Johanne, irritating an already strained situation. "That will not be necessary, lady."

Mara flared as he took Micheline away from her. "Of course it is necessary," she snapped. "She needs me."

He refused to look at her, focused on Micheline. "Are you ready, my lady? We shall take the long route if it pleases you."

Micheline managed to smile weakly. "How long? Hours?"

He cocked an eyebrow. "By way of Paris if you like."

Micheline laughed softly, eased by Kirk's gentle manner. "Paris will not be necessary, I think. Mayhap it is best if I simply get this over with."

Mara couldn't stand it; she turned away, closing her eyes against the injustice about to happen. "Connaught, if you have any sympathy at all, you will take her back to our chamber and bolt the door," she hissed.

Kirk gazed at her dark head. "Lord Edmund is her husband, Lady Mara. He has every right to his bride." Putting Micheline's hand on his elbow, he smiled encouragingly as he led her away. "Have you ever been to Paris, my lady?"

Mara listened to their conversation as they neared the stairs, her heart shattering for her sister's plight. She could only imagine the horrors Micheline would be going through in the next few hours. And Kirk was speaking so gently to her, as if nothing in the world was awry. She adored and hated him all the more for it.

She heard the conversation fade as they mounted the stairs. She sat in the vacant hall for some time after that, pondering the misery the future had brought. For both of them. When Kirk did not return after a nominal amount of time, she rose and went into the kitchens in search of her four little friends. Wondering, and hoping, if they could distract her from her sorrows.

CHAPTER EIGHT

By the time Kirk reached Edmund's chamber with a composed Micheline on his arm, thoughts of Mara were faded and he was more reluctant than ever to subject the woman to her husband's callous attentions. He felt as if he was leading her into the lion's den. But he had no choice in the matter, a sense of duty that did not falter even as he knocked on the door and Johanne answered.

Micheline seemed comforted by the fact that Johanne was present; mayhap she believed there was safety in numbers. Whatever the case, she gave Kirk a brave smile and entered the room with her customary dignity. Kirk watched, feeling sickened, wishing he could warn her of the appalling reality she was about to face. But his sense of duty prevented him from doing so. Still, it did not stop him from assuring her he would be right outside the door should she require him.

A statement that seemed to anger Edmund. Kirk's strange loyalty to the le Bec sisters was something he had not anticipated, nor desired, considering he needed the man now more than ever. The Irish were preparing to rebel and he needed his captain's strength and military wisdom if he were going to protect his holdings; clearly, the last thing he wanted was a souring relationship.

Although he did not want to argue with the man he admired above all else, the fact remained that Kirk was sworn to obey him and not the other way around. But the arrival of Micheline and Mara le Bec was creating division between him and his mighty captain, an uncomfortable situation that Edmund was struggling to come to terms with. A division that seemed to be growing wider by the moment and Edmund was desperate to stop the rift.

A rift that was apparent as Micheline entered the bridal chamber, accompanied by her new sister-in-law, and Edmund. Kirk locked gazes with him. Edmund had no idea what to say to the obviously displeased knight, waiting for him to shut the door, but instead Kirk beckoned him with a crooked finger.

Edmund labored to remain neutral of expression as he graciously honored the request. Quietly, Kirk pulled him into the corridor where their conversation could not be heard.

"Lady Johanne will be leaving, I trust?" Kirk asked.

Edmund nodded. "After she prepares my bride. Truly, Kirk, this is of no concern to you. She is my wife, after all."

Kirk's gaze was cold. He had always disengaged himself with Edmund's personal habits but found at this moment he could not. He had promised Mara that he would protect her sister and felt strongly, even above his oath of fealty to Edmund, that he enforce his promise. Especially when he knew what Edmund was capable of.

"That may be, Lord Edmund," his voice was a growl. "But Lady Micheline is a fine and dignified woman and I shall be most displeased if I discover the marriage bed does not meet with her expectations."

Edmund tried not to appear intimidated. "And what does that mean?"

Kirk's jaw ticked, dangerously close to insubordination. "I believe you already know," he moved to the opposite side of the corridor, assuming his post at a discreet distance. "Congratulations on your marriage, my lord. May you be truly blessed."

Edmund stared at him; thinly veiled threats one moment, best wishes the next. But his apprehension quickly turned to rage and he whirled about, slamming the door to his chamber hard enough to rattle the walls.

Kirk continued to stare at the door, wondering if his intimidation would do any good for Micheline's sake. Wondering, upon reflection, if Edmund would do unspeakable things to the woman simply to show his captain who was truly in charge of Anchorsholme Castle. A battle of wills had begun, the lines of conflict drawn, and Kirk knew there could only be one winner.

And it would not be Edmund.

***

Mara was trying desperately not to think of her sister's plight as she strolled the kitchen yard, searching for the quartet of dirty children. The more she walked, however, the more difficult it became for her to forget what was happening. Micheline had married a fiend, Kirk had decided she was indeed a hellion, and the world in general was looking rather dismal.

Dismal and depressing until four familiar faces suddenly appeared out of the buttery. The younger children shrieked and danced around Mara, delighted to see her, while Robert greeted her with a dignified bow. He had seen the knights offer the gesture to fine young ladies and mimicked their manners perfectly.

"Heard there was a marriage this morning," he said. "Was it your sister?"

Mara nodded, he smile fading. "She had no choice, Robert. But Kirk has promised to protect her."

Robert shook his head sadly. "He canna. Not if Edmund wants to kill her. Nothing can protect her. Or you."

87

Mara stiffened, turning away. "I can protect myself." In the distance, Niles caught her attention, waving at her as his charger was brought around. She waved back, shading her eyes against the bright sun. "He's dressed in full armor. I wonder where he's going?"

Robert followed her gaze. "To hell, most likely."

Mara turned to him sharply. "Why do you say that?"

The lad cocked an eyebrow. "Because he's evil, like Edmund."

"How do you know?"

"Everyone knows."

"Knows *what*?"

Robert looked around to make sure no one was listening. Moving close to Mara, she tried not to shy away from his strong stench. "They say that Niles helps Edmund murder the young ladies," he said quietly. "You should stay away from him."

Mara's eyes widened. "He does? Why did not you tell me this yesterday?"

"Would you have believed me?"

Mara continued to stare at him, shaking her head after a moment. "You must be mistaken, Robert. He's a fine knight and a kind man. Kirk trusts him implicitly."

"He blinds Kirk to the truth. He has a dark, dark soul."

Sighing heavily, Mara put her hands on her hips. "Is that all you do, spout words of doom and gloom? Yesterday, you told me stories of the Darkland and today, you weave tales of Niles' dark soul. Is there anything else so terrible around here?"

"I have lived at Anchorsholme a long time, Lady Mara," Robert said, an odd wisdom flickering in his eyes. "Sometimes we servants know more than the lord. Or The Master."

"You mean Kirk?"

The lad nodded, hushing his sister impatiently when she tugged on his sleeve. "Fiona found a litter of fox pups yesterday. She wants you to come and see them."

Distracted from stories of Niles, Mara found herself gazing at the thin young girl, perhaps seven years of age. Her eyes were a pale blue, the same color as Micheline's, and Mara suddenly found herself lamenting her sister's situation all over again. Her depression threatened, even as Fiona politely begged her to come and see the pups, and Mara forced herself to put her fears aside for the moment.

After all, she had come to the kitchen yards in search of distraction. Now that she had been provided with four lively distractions, she realized she might as well allow the diversion to swallow her. If not, surely she would make herself ill with thoughts of Micheline. And of Kirk.

Sighing, she took Fiona's offered hand and permitted the giggling girl to lead her from the shielding walls of Anchorsholme. Flanked by her escorts, the soothing bramble of Lancashire served to ease her cares for the moment. Away from the turmoil, the anguish, of the Darkland.

***

If he was any judge of time, Kirk had been standing guard outside of Edmund's chamber for a little more than an hour. In that time, he had heard no sound whatsoever coming from the bridal bed and he was increasingly curious as to what was transpiring. Johanne had yet to leave the chamber, as Edmund had promised, and Kirk seriously wondered if all was proceeding smoothly.

He soon received his answer. When the door finally opened, he was not surprised to see Johanne emerge. But he was terribly surprised to see Edmund on her heels, closing the door behind them. Puzzled, Kirk moved forward to inquire if everything was all right when Edmund looked him in the eye, his expression uncharacteristically hard.

"I would assume the escort is ready to ride to Quernmore Castle on the morrow?" he asked.

Off-guard, Kirk slowly lifted an eyebrow. "As we discussed this morning, Niles is in charge and I am sure the escort is set. Is... is everything well, my lord?"

Edmund was decidedly defensive. "That is none of your concern, Kirk. My sister and I are going for a stroll about the grounds and my wife, when she is recovered, shall join us for the nooning meal."

Kirk did not like the emotions he was sensing, hard and careless and defiant. "Is Micheline all right?"

Edmund paused a moment before answering, his dull green eyes intense. "Listen to me well, Connaught. What transpires in the bedchamber between my wife and me is none of your concern. If you try to interfere, I shall have you clapped in irons for insubordination. And if you still insist on continuing this role of protector for Lady Micheline, then I will have no choice but to send you back to your father. He has other sons who will serve me quite well in your stead."

Kirk remained calm. He knew that Edmund relied on him too strongly to carry out his threat. "Steven is crippled and Drew is still a boy. There is no one in England or Ireland who would serve you with as much strength and devotion as I have," he paused, surprised that Edmund's expression remained firm. "If you believe I am interfering, then I apologize. It was not my intent. My intent was simply to make sure the lady was treated with the respect deserving Baroness Bowland."

Edmund studied him a moment. Then, he cocked his head as if a thought suddenly occurred to him. "Are you in love with her, Kirk?"

"Nay."

"Then why do you insist on protecting her?"

"Because she needs protecting."

"From me?"

Kirk stared at him a moment. Then, he smiled humorlessly. "Most of all."

It wasn't an insult, simply the truth. Edmund continued to gaze at the man a moment longer before turning away, moving quickly down the hall. Johanne skipped after him and Kirk watched the pair until they disappeared from view. Then, his attention turned to the closed door. He couldn't help but open it.

The room was dark. The oilcloths remained secured over the lancet windows and the hearth was dark and sooty. Kirk paused a moment as his eyes grew accustom to the dim light, noticing a slight figure seated on the edge of the bed. Puzzled, not to mention concerned, he moved for the heavy window dressings.

"My lady," he said. "Allow me to open the..."

"Nay," Micheline's voice was loud and dull.

Kirk paused in the middle of the room, looking at the woman as she sat motionless. Her eyes were distant, her back straight and proud. Kirk could sense a terrible sorrow.

"Misha," he said softly. "Are you well, lass?"

She blinked. Then, she looked as if the question confused her. "Is this what it will always be like?"

"Will what be like?"

She turned to him, then. "My marriage. Is this is what it is meant to be?"

He shook his head, unsure of the question. Slowly, he lowered himself into an oaken chair next to the bed. "I do not understand you, lass. What do you mean?"

Micheline stared at him and he could see the tears coming. Closing her eyes, as if she could hardly stand to recall the events of the past hour, she turned away from him in soft sobs.

"My dear God...," she gasped.

Kirk swallowed. "What happened, Misha? Can you tell me?"

She shook her head, her entire body trembling. "I... I cannot," she whispered. "It is too... too...."

"Did he hurt you?"

She did not reply for a moment. "There was supposed to be pain."

90

Kirk was struggling to help her without squeezing the truth free. It wasn't any of his business, yet, he was eager to know. Almost frantic. "That's not what I mean, lass. Other than the obvious, did he hurt you?"

She remained silent, sobbing into her hands. Kirk was preparing to ask again when her voice, muffled and faint, suddenly filled the room. "He made me... watch."

He gazed at her, laboring to maintain his composure as a creeping sense of dread took hold. "What did he make you watch?"

She wept painfully, believing that the mere words describing her torment would surely make her vomit.

"He... he and Johanne," she whispered. "He made me watch them, together, and told me to learn well from their actions. He expects the same from me."

Kirk closed his eyes, shocked and sickened. But in the same breath, fury such as he had never known welled within his chest and he reached out, grasping Micheline's hand. Instead of pulling away, recoiling from the man who had delivered her to her nightmare, she clutched him tightly.

"Oh, lass," he breathed. "I am so sorry. I never... I never imagined he would do something like this."

She continued to cry, so terribly pitiful. "That wasn't the worst of it," she gasped. "When they were done, Johanne... she stood by and watched as Edmund forced...forced me to...."

Kirk hung his head. He wasn't sure he wanted to hear any more. Literally, the pain from Micheline's humiliation reached out to grab him like a vise and he found it difficult to breath for all of the heartache and outrage he was experiencing.

"Misha, I am sorry," he whispered, feeling as if he had contributed to her agony. "I am so very sorry. Had I known...."

"And she laughed, too," Micheline's voice was high-pitched, strained with emotion and hysteria. "When I cried in pain, she laughed. She told me to bear it well."

Kirk thought he might vomit. But Micheline wasn't finished, compounding his illness with each successive word until he thought he might literally go mad.

"Edmund invited her to touch me," she was gasping for air, struggling to tell her sordid tale. *Needing* to tell someone. "As he continued to... oh, Kirk, he told her to touch me. And she did. *She did!*"

Kirk shot to his feet, blind fury filling him. He simply couldn't stand it any longer and was determined to punish Edmund for his vile doings no matter what the personal cost. Before he reached the door, however, Micheline threw herself at him, pleading for calm.

"Nay, Kirk," she begged, clutching his arms with all her frail strength. "You have no right to condemn them. He is my husband and has every right to do with me as he pleases."

The gleam in Kirk's eyes frightened her. "He has no right to treat you like...."

Micheline nodded firmly, struggling to gain control of her tears. She could see that Kirk was beyond his limits and the sooner she regain her composure, the better for them all.

"It is his right," she insisted, sniffling. But her gaze was steady as she faced him. "You know as well as I do that you have no control over what he does. No matter how barbaric. And certainly it is not your station to judge or punish his actions."

"But...."

"You have no *right*."

Kirk stared down at the woman, his heart aching for her plight. Never had he imagined Edmund or Johanne capable of such debauchery and he grappled furiously with his outrage, so much so that beads of sweat peppered his brow. After a moment, he shook his head in a helpless gesture.

"But I promised Mara..." he sighed heavily, turning away from Micheline. "Dear God, I promised your sister that I would protect you. I alone would prevent further humiliation to your fragile character. And see how I have failed."

"You have not failed," Micheline was calmer now, watching the broad back pace away from her. "You have done all you can, Sir Kirk, and I am grateful. To have failed would have been to confront Edmund when it is not your place to do so. And I could not allow you to jeopardize yourself, not when Mara loves you so."

He froze in mid-pace, his chest heaving with emotion. Slowly, with great wonder, he focused on the pale, trembling lady.

"She told you this?"

Micheline smiled weakly. "She spent the night crying over you, though she would not tell me the exact circumstance. I know my sister well, Sir Kirk, well enough to know that she loves you and would be lost without you."

Kirk's face was pale, the stone-gray eyes wide. "I... I do not know what to say."

Micheline wiped the last of her tears from her cheeks, her smile steady as she approached him. "Say that you love her, too."

He did not hesitate. "I have from the start."

"And you will marry her?"

"She does not want to marry me," he shrugged. "And... last night, I said things I should not have. But she was so stubborn, so pugnacious, I simply couldn't...."

Micheline put her hand on his chest before he could finish. "The trick with Mara is to be more stubborn and more pugnacious than she is. She loves a good fight, but she respects someone who can beat her at her own game. It's the Irish in her, I suppose."

He lifted an eyebrow. "Mara has Irish bloodlines?"

Micheline nodded. "On our mother's side. Her grandmother was from Dublin."

Kirk chuckled, his composure returning as Micheline succeeded in calming his rage with talk of Mara's stubborn nature, of all things. "She has a lot of fire in her. Certainly it could only be Irish blood."

Micheline laughed softly, feeling her mood lighten and her horror fade; to have Kirk's support was more of an emotional boost than she realized. If he wasn't already smitten with Mara, she might have declared interest in him herself.

"You will promise me something, Sir Kirk," she said after the laughter faded.

"Anything, my lady."

"Promise that you will not tell Mara what happened here today. I shall think of something to tell her, but she must never know the truth."

Kirk gazed into the pale blue eyes before answering. "Of course," he said softly. "There is no telling what she will do if she learns what Edmund and Johanne subjected you to."

Micheline turned away from him, sighing heavily as her composure, her wits, returned. "Have you always been aware of their... relationship?"

He paused a moment. "Aye," he muttered. "But it is something we do not speak of simply for the fact that it is too vile to comprehend. I... I am sorry I did not forewarn you. I truthfully do not know if it would have made a difference even if I had."

Micheline nodded, running her hand over the mussed coverlet, smelling of sweat and sex. "It would not have," she murmured. "I would have been forced to marry him regardless."

Kirk watched her as she gazed at the bed, pondering the course of her future. "Still, I will speak to him," he said quietly. "Mayhap he will listen to me."

"And mayhap he will take your interest out on my hide," Micheline looked at him, amazingly composed now that her cleansing cry was complete. "For my sake, I ask that you not intervene. This is my marriage and I must take responsibility as best I am able."

Kirk sighed heavily; there was nothing he could say against her sound logic. "As you request, my lady," the stone-gray eyes twinkled. "Tell me; did you inherit all of the common sense in your family?"

Micheline smiled. "Mara has a good deal of common sense, though she pretends otherwise. Have you never shared a calm conversation with her, Kirk?"

Now he grinned. "Once, after I spanked her. She harbors a great deal of wisdom in her little brain, wisdom I should like to nurture. Mayhap it will overshadow the wild nature, someday."

"But not entirely."

He chuckled. "Nay, not entirely. I rather like a hellion."

Micheline laughed with him, holding out her hand. He collected it gently, so very respectful of the new Baroness Bowland. Edmund did not deserve the woman in the least and if the man was standing before him at this very minute, he wasn't at all sure he could refrain from killing him.

"And I rather like the hellion's beau," Micheline said softly, laughing again when he shrugged modestly. "Thank you, Sir Kirk. For everything you have done for my sister and I, I thank you."

The moment was genuinely warm and Kirk maintained his smile, hating Edmund more by the second for subjecting Micheline to his immorality. It was a battle not to become grieved with the circumstance all over again. "My pleasure, my lady."

***

The seasonal rains had greened the countryside now basking under the new winter sun. Mara had spent well over an hour inspecting the fox pups that Fiona had so delightfully discovered, hiding in the bramble as the mother fox nursed her young. In fact, the magnificent morning had been enough to distract her from her depression and by the time she returned to the keep, her fragile composure was well fortified.

Her hands were full of winter blooms that she had discovered in the foliage, small flowers with blue and white petals she did not have a name for. Robert and his siblings followed her into the kitchen yards, demanding she lay the flowers aside and play a game with them, but Mara declined.

Even though her frame of mind had been calmed by the lovely weather and playful children, she was nonetheless eager to see to her sister. And possibly see what had become of Kirk if she could spare the time. Bidding her friends farewell, she crossed into the inner bailey only to come face to face with Edmund and Johanne.

Immediately, her fine mood dissolved, replaced instead by a burgeoning dislike. The bright blue eyes simmered with hostility as Edmund and Johanne came to a halt, hand in hand, before her.

"Ah, Lady Mara," Johanne said with feigned delight. "Out foraging in the fields, I see."

Mara's gaze moved between the two pasty-faced siblings. "I was enjoying the day. At least, I was until this moment."

Edmund shook his head. "Are you always so confrontational? My sister was merely making an observation."

Mara fixed on him. "Speaking of sisters, where is mine?"

Johanne shrugged lightly, snuggling up to her brother in more than companionable gesture. "In my brother's bower, where we left her, I suppose," she looked to her brother, touching his cheek. "Shall we continue our walk, dear? I do not think I like the atmosphere here."

But Mara refused to allow them to pass. Clearly, she was uncomfortable with Johanne's flippant answer. "What do you mean 'where *we* left her'? Is she well?"

Johanne's green eyes focused on her. She seemed to do most of the talking while Edmund smirked and gloated. "Well enough. What would you expect after surrendering her virginal body to her husband?"

Mara visibly paled, her pulse quickening. When she spoke, it was directed at Edmund. "You were... kind to her, my lord?"

"That is none of your affair."

"I realize that. But I am asking nonetheless."

Edmund sighed, eyeing her a moment before replying. "Kind enough, I suppose. Far more than I was willing. Was that the answer you were seeking?"

Mara swallowed hard, seeing the carelessness in his eyes and it only served to inflame her. "You never wanted her to begin with. Why did not you simply dissolve the contract or sell her to another? Why must you insist on continuing this... this torment?"

Edmund cocked an eyebrow, suddenly realizing why Kirk was so protective of Lady Micheline. The little sister was quite defensive of her sibling, echoing Kirk's actions perfectly. Or, as Edmund's suspected, Kirk was merely echoing Lady Mara's. Leaping to defend the sister of the woman he was smitten with.

He did not know why he hadn't realized the truth before; the actions in the dining hall when Kirk had prevented him from striking the wench, or the constant attention he paid her, pretending to be stern. Mayhap with his concern over his unwanted bride, he simply hadn't given thought to anything else. Even something as obvious as Kirk's infatuation.

Aye, the knight's shift of loyalty made sense now. And truthfully, he couldn't blame the man. In spite of her unruly mouth, Mara was a lovely creature. Too lovely to kill should Johanne figure out what Edmund now understood. But his sister, too, had been focused on Micheline's arrival. Enough to deter her from her usual scrutiny of Kirk. For the moment, at least, and unless Edmund intended to commit murder in the near future, he had better plan for the girl's immediate removal.

"You call your sister's plight torment?" He let go of Johanne's hand, moving to stand before a shaken Mara. Gazing over her lovely face, he realized well what Kirk saw in the girl. "Think of my plight, if you would. Betrothed to a woman I never wanted, forced to wed against my will. Sound familiar?"

Mara refused to step back from him, although his foul breath was turning her stomach. "Indeed. But do you have to make an undesirable situation worse with your treatment of my sister? She simply wants to be a good wife."

Edmund stared at her a moment. Then, turning to glance at is sister, he laughed. "She *was* good. For both of us."

Mara had no idea what he meant. But she certainly did not like the tone of his voice. "Both of you? How do you mean?"

Edmund continued to snicker, returning to his snorting sister. "Precisely that. A rather tasty bit of flesh. Unseasoned, but tasty."

Mara was lost to their meaning as Johanne latched on to her brother again, rubbing against him in a manner that made Mara's skin crawl. "She's simply inexperienced," she murmured, loud enough for Mara to hear. "Time will improve her performance. And I will teach her what she needs to know in order to please you."

Mara stared at them, baffled and nauseated. "How... how can you teach... those things? How would you know...?"

Johanne laughed, looking at Mara as if she were the most foolish creature on the face of the earth. "Ask your sister what I know, Mara. If she's brave enough to tell you."

They turned away from the perplexed young lady in a snickering pair, continuing their walk of Anchorsholme's grounds. Mara was about to follow them to demand clarification when a rumbling male voice caught her attention.

"Let them go, love."

She turned to see Niles standing next to her. The bright blue eyes were filled with distress. "But...."

He shook his head firmly. "Not those two, Mara. You would do well to stay far, far away from them."

Mara passed a lingering glance at the pair, sighing with frustration. "But they spoke so strangely, Niles. I do not think I like their inference at all."

Niles' gaze was fixed on the couple as they disappeared into the kitchen yard. "And what inference was that?"

Mara thought a moment. Then, she shook her head. "Truly, I do not know. But I must find my sister and make sure she is unharmed."

Niles took her arm, gently, before she could dash away. "That will not be necessary, I am sure," he said quietly, putting her hand on his elbow. "Kirk will see to your sister and she is in far better hands than if God himself was watching over her."

Hesitantly, Mara allowed Niles to lead her at a leisurely pace toward the keep. "Niles?" she asked softly.

"What is it, my lady?"

"Why... why does Johanne tend her brother as if he were her lover? Are they so close?"

Niles did not reply for a moment. "'Tis their way, Mara. Never ask more than that."

She was more puzzled than ever. "But Johanne said she would teach my sister what she needed to know in order to please Edmund." She came to a halt under the bright winter sky, looking to the tall knight. "What on earth did she mean by that? How could she possibly know?"

Niles sighed. "Trust me, Mara, you would not like the answer," he said, resuming their walk. "Have you spoken with Kirk this morn?"

Mara knew he was attempting to change the subject. "Nay, I have not. And I have no intention of speaking with him ever again." She cast the knight a long look. "Why won't you tell me what Johanne meant by her strange words? And why wouldn't I like the answer?"

Niles sighed again, heavily. He did not like the determined look in her eye.

***

The kitchen yards vacated, not strangely, the moment Edmund and Johanne entered. Edmund kicked at a dog that came too close as they moved for the postern gate cut into the fortified wall.

"Why did not you simply tell her the truth?" Johanne asked as the passageway enveloped her.

Edmund followed behind. "Because it is none of her affair. Moreover, I do not believe we will have to worry over the Lady Mara much longer."

"She does not worry me," Johanne snorted, casting her brother a long look. "Even so, you sound rather sure of yourself. What did you have in mind?"

Edmund smiled as they emerged into the knee-high grass beyond the wall. "I have been considering the situation and I do believe I have come up with a brilliant plan." He took his sister's hand again. "Kirk is traveling to Quernmore Castle tomorrow, is he not?"

Johanne nodded. "He is. And I am rather displeased with the fact that he will be seeing Lady Lily again. You know how infatuated she is with him."

"Never mind about Lady Lily. She is already pledged and certainly no threat to you," Edmund grasped her by the shoulders, returning the subject to its original course. "As I was saying, Kirk will be meeting with Lord le Vay. A widower, is he not?"

A flicker of understanding glimmered in his sister's eyes. "You do not mean to suggest...?"

"Of course I do."

"Oh, Edmund," she gasped. "Of course! How perfectly convenient!"

Edmund nodded smugly. "Kirk will carry not only a request for military assistance for my Wicklow holdings, but he will also carry a sealed missive proposing a betrothal."

Johanne threw her arms around him and they giggled happily. "Le Vay has expressed the desire to wed again, especially after his son died of the fever two years ago and left him without an heir," Johanne kissed her brother loudly on the cheek. "He'll wed the little chit and we shall be done with her."

Edmund patted her on the cheek. "Mayhap we shall even send her along with Kirk for the baron's inspection."

Johanne giggled again and Edmund was relieved that she had agreed to sending the woman away rather than wishing her away. That was what she called it; wishing, as in wishing for death. But Johanne's mood was particularly good today and Edmund was thankful; with Kirk's interest in the girl, arranging her disappearance would have been difficult enough, if not impossible. Even so, he suspected the betrothal to Lord le Vay, once revealed, would not be well met and he realized he walked a fine line between keeping Johanne happy and avoiding Kirk's wrath.

But family came first, and his sister's delighted expression was an indication of his supreme devotion. "Now you will not have to wish her away," he said. "Save your powers for something worthwhile."

"Like what?"

Edmund shrugged as they headed down the hill toward the grove of gnarled oak. "My wife, of course," he snorted. "While the sister's at

Quernmore, mayhap we shall have a chance to see if she will fit well into our lifestyle. If not..."

"If not, she'll vanish like all the rest."

"Precisely."

The birdsong was sweet overhead as the shielding branches of the old oaks swallowed them. "Let's take her to bed with us tonight," Johanne grasped her brother's hand affectionately, savoring the power she commanded over Life and Death. "Mayhap she'll be more... cooperative."

Edmund lifted an eyebrow. "For her sake, I hope so," his voice was serious as well as frightening. "Indeed, I do."

CHAPTER NINE

The nooning meal was less than an hour away. Kirk sat in the chilly solar, going over the maps of Edmund's Wicklow holdings and struggling to keep his thoughts from lingering on Mara. He was faced with a very important task and was in desperate need of his mental facilities, even those that would rather seek out the little hellion and apologize rather than focus on the task at hand.

He convinced himself he could not spare the time to apologize to her. He had more pressing duties and his personal feelings for Mara would simply have to wait. So he had planted himself in Edmund's dimly-lit solar, refusing to cower at Mara's feet simply to ease the tension between them. He had hoped she had learned something from their negative encounter, although he would have been truly surprised if she had. All he had learned was that he missed her terribly.

Time passed at a painful pace as he endeavored to lay out a plan of containment against the Wicklow estates. Having no knowledge of the true scope of the revolt, a general course of action was the best he could do at the moment. And in the interim, he realized he had managed to quell his surging emotions somewhat and was pleased with his self-control. Self-control against a woman who inflamed and entranced him at the same time.

Hunched over the map table, sturdy boot falls approached from the foyer and he glanced up as Niles entered the room. The expression on the man's features was enough to distract Kirk from his turbulent thoughts.

"What's the matter?" he demanded. "Why do you look like that?"

Niles was beyond grim. He was miserable, actually. "Kirk, I have done a terrible thing, I think."

Kirk cocked a droll eyebrow. "Pray tell, lad."

Niles shook his head. "This is serious, Kirk. I have just come from Mara and...."

The mention of her name stirred Kirk intensely, dashing his recently-managed emotions. "What about Mara? Is she well?"

Niles nodded quickly, seeing the urgency in Kirk's eyes. "She is fine, Kirk. But we had a long conversation today and somehow I managed to tell her of Johanne and Edmund's relationship. Christ, I have no idea how it slipped out, but it did. She badgered me and badgered me and before I realized what had happened, she knew the truth of it."

Kirk looked at the man as if he wanted to strangle him. "Damnation," he hissed. "How could you, Niles? Mara, of all people, should know nothing!"

Niles wished the earth would open up and swallow him. Surely it would be less painful than Kirk's wrath. "I do not know, I tell you. She pestered me until I was crazy!"

Kirk shook his head, the veins in his temples pulsing. "Where is she now?"

"She ran to her chamber. I can only imagine she's with Micheline."

Kirk's face paled. "Oh... Christ!" he bolted past Niles, heading for the foyer. The knight raced after him.

"What's wrong, Kirk?" Niles was having difficulty keeping pace. "I thought you would be pleased to know she was with her sister. Surely Micheline will calm her!"

Kirk mounted the stairs three at a time, hardly pausing to reply. "Under normal circumstances, I would," he breathed as they topped the landing and headed down the corridor. "However, Micheline's first experience with Edmund's husbandly attentions was not a pleasant one. If Mara forces her sister to tell her...."

They rounded a corner, picking up speed. "Tell her what?" Niles demanded.

Kirk did not reply until they reached the ladies' chamber. Scarcely stopping, he cast Niles a long look as he grasped the latch. "Johanne was a participant, Niles. Out of respect for Lady Micheline, I shall not tell you more than that."

As Niles struggled to overcome his shock, Kirk was already into the chamber, his eyes searching for Mara. But the only face he came into contact with was Micheline's.

"Where's Mara?" he demanded.

Micheline's eyes were wide. Accusing, he thought. "What did you tell her, Kirk?"

Kirk shook his head. "Nothing, my lady. I have not seen her. What hap..?"

Micheline cut him off, as livid as he had ever seen her. "Some fool told her of Edmund and Johanne. After she realized I was not going to tell her all that had transpired in my wedding bed, she ran from here like a madwoman. I have no idea where she might have gone."

Niles, lingering by the chamber door, cleared his throat guiltily. Kirk glanced at him, a look of pure exasperation on his face before returning his focus to Micheline. "When did she leave?"

"A minute or so before you arrived. I was just coming to find you myself."

"Did she say anything that might lend clue to where she was heading? Anything at all?"

Micheline shook her head. "Nothing. I tried to keep her here, but she shoved me to the ground," she sighed, her anger replaced by a genuine fear. "I am worried for her, Kirk. There's no knowing what she might do."

Kirk scratched his head, a nervous gesture. "Why are we so sure she is going to do anything," the itching hand dropped to his side. "I came up here merely to prevent her from forcing the truth from you and thereby preclude a hysterical situation. Since you refrained from telling her anything, mayhap she's simply run off to sulk."

Micheline shook her head. "Even if I did not tell her, it was evident that she suspected... something," she kept her voice low lest Niles hear of her shame. "Mara is not stupid, Kirk. She suspects something humiliating happened. But she does not know what."

Kirk stared at the woman a long, long moment. "And the only other person capable of telling her..."

"And gladly, I would think."

"...would be Edmund."

Kirk was already moving for the door, a sense of urgency filling him like nothing before. Micheline ran after him, her chest swelling with terror.

"She is capable of using a dagger," she gasped. "I have seen her!"

Kirk paused long enough to cast her a disturbed expression. "You have seen her?"

Micheline nodded, pale and trembling where she had been furious not moments before. "When... when she was young, nine or ten years of age. She defended me in a tavern against a zealous soldier. She was forced to stab the man while our father stood by, drunk, inactive, and involved in his dice game. There was no choice, mind you; if she hadn't stabbed the man, he would have done unspeakable things to me."

Kirk stared at Micheline before letting out a sharp, ragged sigh. "Christ," he muttered. "Has she always been defending you so, Micheline?"

"Always," Micheline whispered in reply. "She will do what she feels necessary."

Kirk did not like the sound of that at all.

***

Mara hadn't been hard to follow. There were very few raven-haired ladies running about Anchorsholme with murder in her eye. Kirk and Niles tracked her to the kitchen yard, helped along by four children who indicated that Lady Mara had left the enclosure through the tunnel in the wall. Emerging into the tall grass, the knights continued their pursuit.

The children in the yard were chatty enough to inform Kirk that Edmund and Johanne were also beyond the walls; feeding Kirk's anxiety that Mara was either intent to do them great bodily harm. Either that or in doing so, she had been overcome and now lay dead or dying. Either scenario was terrifying. As he entered the cool grove of oak, he found himself praying for Mara's safety; a fervent prayer that hadn't touched his lips since his knighting ceremony.

He and Niles quieted as they reached the shielding trees, alert for any sounds or movements. Kirk split away from the knight, taking a path through the heavy foliage, hoping he could find Mara before it was too late. Knowing that, in spite of her hasty judgment and foolish nature, her true motivation was the protection of her sister. In however form that protection might come.

Aye, the woman had a heart of gold. And the mind of an imbecile at times. Kirk shook his head even as he moved silently among the trees, thinking that mayhap he should spank her again for being foolish enough to take the offensive against Edmund and Johanne. And after he spanked her, he would plead forgiveness for his harsh words and beg her to marry him once again. He simply couldn't stand to be away from her, not even for a few lonely hours.

Twisting his way along a holly bush, Kirk suddenly came to a halt. In the distance, he could hear the faint rumble of conversation and immediately recognized Edmund and Johanne through the trees. Crouching low so they would not see him, he saw Niles do the same from the corner of his eye. If Mara was after the pair, then she had to be close. Very close.

And he wanted to get to her first.

***

The bark of the tree was scratchy. As Mara pressed herself against the bark, bright blue eyes watched Edmund and Johanne as they moved through the dense brush, holding hands and giggling softly. And the more Mara observed, the more sickened she became.

To have an intimate relationship with one's own sibling was beyond her comprehension. Niles had been delicate when had explained their association, but even so the pure wickedness of their actions was more than she could bear. And poor Micheline had been thrust into the middle of it, unknowingly.

There had been a time when Mara had cursed Kirk violently for not having had the courtesy to inform Micheline of the situation; but the truth was, there was nothing any of them could have done even if Micheline had known. And Mara accepted the truth, even though her anger had not yet abated. Anger now directed at the two twisted siblings strolling through the trees.

Their taunts in the kitchen yard had upset her. Niles' reluctant explanation had upset her further. But the final straw had been Micheline's staunch refusal to tell her anything more. Even when she could look into the woman's eyes and see what her lips were incapable of bringing forth.

Therefore, she was determined to find her own truth. Out in the wood, where no one could hear the vile conversation. Aye, she was determined to learn the truth of whatever Micheline was in the middle of. To learn the truth and then protect her sister as best she was able.

Edmund and Johanne paused in a small clearing, kissing and fondling one another until Mara thought she truly might become ill. But it only served to reinforce her conviction to clarify the situation and she stepped away from the tree, completely focused on the two wicked participants of incest. Taking a step in their direction, she made her advance.

Until a hand clamped over her mouth. A huge arm went about her waist, hoisting her into the dense trees before she could utter a sound. But the shock quickly wore off, turning into an explosion of panic and she kicked violently, struggling to free herself. Deeper and deeper she was dragged, the canopy above blocking out the sun, until her attacker suddenly dropped to his knees and took her down with him.

"Not a word, Mara." It was Kirk, hot on her ear.

Shaken and disoriented, Mara tried to twist away from him. But he held her tight, grasping her wrists when she tried to hit him. In their battle, Mara ended up on the carpet of leaves and Kirk was pressed atop her, his stone-gray eyes blazing.

"Enough!" he hissed.

Chest heaving with exertion and fright, Mara met his intense gaze with her usual defiance. "Let me go!"

He shifted his weight in response, nearly crushing her. "Do you have a dagger somewhere on your person that I should be aware of?"

She grunted as his body smashed her, finding it difficult to breathe in more ways than one. "A... a dagger? Of course not! Where would I get one?"

He shushed her sternly, glancing over his shoulder to see where Edmund and Johanne were. He caught sight of Niles, watching him from several yards away, and nodded his head curtly at the man. Niles took the hint and disappeared in the direction of the Castle.

Kirk remained silent as Edmund and Johanne, completely oblivious to the chaos going on around them, continued their walk and faded into the distance. Then, and only then, did Kirk rise and haul Mara to her feet.

"What are you doing out here?" his tone was not kind.

She brushed off her bum, rubbing her ribs where his torso had bruised her. "Looking for answers," she said boldly. "If no one will tell me what I wish to know, then I shall find out for myself."

"By attacking Edmund and Johanne?"

"I wasn't going to attack them. I was going to speak with them and demand they tell me the truth."

Kirk's expression was stern. "It's none of your affair, Mara. Micheline told you as much and you would do well to heed her."

He could see the hurt, the confusion, in her eyes. After a moment, he saw the wall of defiance crumble and suddenly he was looking into a very sad, very lost, expression.

"Why?" she demanded, her voice a hoarse whisper. "Why won't anyone tell me what is going on?"

He felt himself weaken. But when he instinctively reached out to touch her, she pulled away. Kirk gazed at her, feeling her rejection to his soul.

"What do you want to know?" he asked softly. "And, more importantly, does your very life hang in the balance if you do not discover these answers?"

Mara turned away from him, her worn slippers crunching the moldering leaves. "Something happened to my sister in Edmund's bedchamber and no one will tell me what it was. Not even my sister."

Kirk watched her deliciously petite figure, wishing he could simply reach out and hold her. "What happens between a wife and her husband is a private matter, Mara," he followed her, slowly, as she moved away. "And what led you to believe that anything out of the ordinary happened?"

She paused, picking at her nails as she so often did when subdued or confused. "Edmund and Johanne inferred as much. Edmund said my sister pleased them both. And Johanne said she would teach my sister what she needed to know in order to please Edmund," she suddenly turned on him, the brilliant eyes filled with emotion. "If it was your sister they were speaking of, how would you react?"

He sighed heavily, looking away as he pondered his reply. He couldn't stand the pain in her eyes. "I would want to know, of course. But that still does not make the matter any of your affair."

Mara was silent a moment, watching his beautiful face, realizing he was reluctant to meet her head-on as he usually did. It suddenly occurred to her that he knew more than he was telling her and she swallowed hard, approaching him as he stared at the ground and chewed his lip.

"Was it truly awful?"

He looked up, meeting her gaze. "Why would you ask me this?"

"Because you know. I can tell. Was Edmund truly awful to Micheline?"

His expression wavered, the consummately controlled facade weakening in the face of her softly-uttered question. After a moment, he weakly lifted his shoulders. "What would you have me tell you, lass?"

She moved closer to him until the toes of her slippers were against the toes of his massive boots. Craning her neck back, she could literally feel the heat and power radiating from his body. But the look in his eyes reflected a weakness only she was capable of understanding. A characteristic flaw that occurred every time he gazed at her.

"Tell me it was awful and I will ask no more."

His features softened, the reluctance evident on his features. "It was awful." She hardly heard him.

"Did he hurt her?"

"I thought you said you would ask no more."

"I lied. You answered one question, you might as well answer the rest. Did he hurt her?"

He sighed. There was no avoiding her logic or questions. "Aside from the obvious, he did not."

"Was he cruel? Did he shame her somehow?"

Kirk nodded. He simply couldn't lie to her. "He did."

Mara continued to gaze into his eyes before closing them tightly, turning away. After a moment, Kirk saw the delicate shoulders heave.

"You promised," she whispered tightly. "You promised to protect her."

"I have my limits," his entire body ached with sorrow. "There was nothing I could do for her."

"But you promised," her voice cracked. "You asked me to trust you, once. And now I see my trust has been destroyed."

He drew in a deep breath, wanting so badly to whip her into his arms and tell her the entire story simply so she would understand how helpless he had been. But he had promised Micheline that he would not tell, and he intended to keep his vow. Even if Mara thought him a failure.

"I did not destroy your trust," his voice was tight. "I did what I could, as much as I could. Mara, love, I could do no more. You must believe me."

Her answer was to turn away from him and walk through the bramble. He followed on her heels, feeling desperate. She simply had to understand.

"Please, Mara," he said softly. "Do not do this to me. I can take anything but your silence, lass."

Mara wiped at her nose, her eyes. She had no idea what she was feeling, only intense pain that Micheline had somehow been shamed by her husband and that Kirk had stood by and allowed it to happen. If he wasn't going to elaborate, she could do nothing more than draw her own conclusions.

"I have nothing to say to you," she said, crossing the small clearing where Edmund and Johanne had titillated one another. "For the bitter words you dealt me last night or for your failure to protect my sister. You will stay away from me, Kirk. Go about your life and leave me out of it."

He did grab her then, only to receive a sharp rake of nails across his face. His head snapped with the unexpected action, coming away with three bloodied lines just under his cheekbone. Slowly, and very deliberately, he ran his fingers through the gashes and stared at the blood.

Mara, her eyes wide, watched his movements. She'd only meant to strike him, to break his hold on her, but instead her nails had clipped his face. Her apology died in her throat when his stone-gray eyes fixed on her. She couldn't have felt their harsh impact more if he had slapped her.

"Christ," he breathed slowly and with great regret. "What I fool I was to ever think I was in love with you."

He pushed past her, bloodied face and all. Mara watched him move across the dense foliage with tears in her eyes, wanting so badly to apologize, yet still embittered by his failure to Micheline and by the entire turbulent situation. Nonetheless, she had to literally bite her tongue to keep from calling out to him.

He disappeared in the grove of oaks. Mara could hardly follow, the pain in her heart rendering her weak and helpless. Collapsing in the rotting leaves, she wept through the nooning meal. The afternoon passed and still, she alternately wept and reflected on the course her life had taken. And when night eventually fell, Corwin found her dirty and asleep, her misery too deep for the tears that could no longer heal.

***

By morning, Mara was miserable with the chill and an aching heart. Sniffling and sneezing between bouts of tremendous sadness, she answered a knock on her chamber door only to find Niles' wan face smiling at her.

"What do you want?" she wasn't in the mood for pleasantries.

Niles was vastly uncomfortable. More so in her company because he had seen evidence of her rage on Kirk's face, an event which he had refused to discuss. And the fact that Kirk had spent the entire night drinking only fed Niles's guilt that, somehow, he had contributed to this nasty situation with his loose tongue. "Lord Edmund is sending a party to Quernmore Castle within the hour, my lady," he said. "He asks that you accompany them."

She sneezed, her foul mood worsening. "Why?"

"I do not know," Niles said, trying to avoid her when she sneezed again. "He only asks that you prepare yourself for the trip."

"And he gave no reason at all?"

"He did not. But mayhap, given yesterday's events, a few days away from Anchorsholme might do you well."

Mara sneezed, her raven-colored hair shaking violently. "This is madness," she said irritably. "There is no reason why I need travel to this Castle. What if I do not wish to go?"

Niles met her gaze steadily. "It is not a choice, my lady. Lord Edmund asked that you travel to Quernmore this day."

Mara stared at him, frowning, before slamming the door in his face. So Edmund wanted her to ride to Quernmore Castle, did he? Most likely to be rid of her, as Niles suggested. Or, mayhap, he was hoping the party would be set upon by bandits and she would fall victim to their murderous rage.

Whatever the case, she had little choice in the matter. And since Micheline was nowhere to be found, having spent the night with her new husband, Mara quite frankly did not care where she went or what she did. Micheline was keeping secrets, Kirk hated her, and she was doomed to a life of misery of her own making. It had started when she agreed to come to Anchorsholme Castle in the first place.

So she packed a small satchel. Sneezing and coughing, she donned the warmest dress she owned and pulled her hair away from her face, securing it in a loose braid at the nape of her neck. Her mother's worn brown cloak served its purpose as she slung it over her shoulders, collecting her bag. The moment she opened the door, however, Lady Valdine and Lady Wanda were there to greet her.

They bowed in perfect unison. "Good morn,.."

"... my lady. Sir Niles informed us that..."

"...you were not feeling well. May we..."

"...assist?"

Mara hadn't the strength to reject them. Or the will. Depressed and ill, she simply shook her head. "I do not know what you can do for me. 'Tis a simple bout with the chill that only time will cure."

Lady Valdine suddenly produced a pewter flask. Mara eyed the steaming contents. "What is that?"

The ladies smiled at the same time. "Herbs. And..."

"...secret ingredients. It will..."

"...heal you if it does not make..."

"...a drunkard out of you first."

Mara couldn't help but grin. "How much do I take?"

Lady Valdine put the flask in her hand. "A few sips now. And a..."

"...few sips after the morning meal. A few..."

"...sips here and there throughout the day. But not..."

"...all at once."

Mara smelled the contents and, with a shrug, took a long, deep swallow. Smacking her lips, she shrugged again. "I taste whisky."

"Irish..."

"...whisky. And how would a..."

"...lady know the taste of whisky?"

Mara grinned again and took another swallow before the ladies could stop her. "My father was a drunkard, ladies. I have been exposed to whisky since I was old enough to know what it was."

Lady Valdine and Lady Wanda were fixed with identical grins, suggesting to Mara that the ladies were not so prim and proper as they appeared. She raised the flask.

"Would you like some?"

They tittered and she smiled, taking another sip. And still another. Feeling the warmth from the alcohol fortify her, she clutched her satchel in one hand and the flask in the other, moving down the corridor with the pair of ladies in tow.

"I have been ordered to travel to Quernmore Castle this day," she said as they reached the stairs, taking yet another swallow of the 'medicine'. "Do either of you ladies know where my sister is?"

Lady Valdine and Lady Wanda shook their heads, a wagging pair. "Nay, my lady. Your..."

"...sister is still with Lord Edmund in..."

"...his chamber"

Reaching the bottom of the stairs and cross the old stone of the foyer, Mara felt the familiar depression grasp at her. Since her marriage the day before, Micheline had been distant and withdrawn and somehow, Mara felt as if a wedge had been driven between them. A wedge of secrets that both grieved and bewildered her. Taking another drink from the flask, she smacked her lips as the great doors of Anchorsholme loomed before her. Open to the bailey, she could see that a small army was formed.

Her brow furrowed as she saw Kirk and Niles at the edge of the formation, speaking between themselves. Coming to a halt, Lady Valdine and Lady Wanda moved up on either side of her.

"Is something..."

"...the matter, Lady Mara?"

Mara took a deep breath. Then she took another drink. Shaking her head, she proceeded into the weak sunlight.

Niles saw her coming. He said something to Kirk, who immediately moved for his charger without so much as passing her a glance. Mood dampening, Mara ignored him as well, allowing Niles to help her mount her palfrey. The knight took her satchel, leaving her with the flask clutched in her palm.

As Lady Valdine and Lady Wanda bid the party farewell, Kirk and Niles moved the men into marching rhythm, purging themselves from the great double baileys of Anchorsholme.

CHAPTER TEN

The journey to Quernmore Castle was a little more than a day's ride. Mara sat atop her old mare, listening to the chatter of birds as the escort party passed through the small forest on the border between Anchorsholme and Quernmore. She made a point of focusing on the landscape, the road, her horse's mane. Anything to avoid looking at Kirk, riding tall and strong at the head of the column.

But she had stolen glances at him now and again, never once catching him looking at her in return. Niles tried to make polite conversation, but she quickly ended his attempts with one-word replies. She did not want to speak with anyone, save Kirk, if he was so inclined to apologize for the events of the past two days. And if he were to apologize, then there would be nothing to stop her from apologizing, too.

Noon came and went. The army did not stop for a meal, merely passed around bread and jerky. Niles provided Mara with bread and delicious cheese, which she washed down with the whiskey concoction. By mid-afternoon, the flask was empty and Mara was showing distinct signs of intoxication.

It all started with a slight tune, off-key and muttered. But the tune grew louder, much to Niles' amusement, and Mara seemed quite happy with her ear-piercing song. The alcohol only served to enhance her turbulent emotions and when the last verse of the tune ended, the bright blue eyes focused on Kirk's distant back.

"He hates me, you know." She turned to look at Niles. "Kirk hates me. Did you see his face? I did that."

Niles' expression remained even, wondering if Kirk could hear what was going on. The Kirk Connaught he knew had eyes and ears all over his person and, if Niles suspected correctly, the man had heard every syllable of conversation since leaving Anchorsholme. He wondered how much he would allow Mara to carry on before intervening.

"It was an accident, I am sure," the knight said, eyeing Kirk in the distance. "Mere scratches."

"Aye, it was an accident," Mara said loudly, waving her arm to emphasize her point and nearly falling off her mount. "He grabbed me and I meant to break away. But I gouged him instead."

Niles glanced at Kirk again, wondering if he shouldn't discreetly back away from the lady so that she would cease her conversation. Without an audience, there would be no need for chatter.

"Nothing is right any longer," Mara muttered, swaying in the saddle and oblivious to the discomfort of the knight. "My sister is married and Kirk hates me and I... I want to go home!"

She burst into tears. As Niles debated whether or not to calm her, Kirk suddenly reined his charger around and plowed through the column. Those who did not move out of his way fast enough were nearly run over. Reaching Mara, he ordered the knight away with a brusque jerk of his head.

"Enough tears, Mara," he said quietly, reining his horse next to her. "There's no need..."

Her weeping grew louder and she turned away from him. Kirk raised his visor, looking seriously at her. Catching sight of the flask clutched in her hand, he snatched it. Smelling the alcohol, he turned accusingly to Niles.

"Who in the hell gave her this?"

"She had it when she emerged from the keep," Niles replied steadily. "I thought mayhap it was mead, or even flavored water."

Kirk shook his head with disgust. "It's whiskey." He focused on Mara again. "My lady, who gave you this?"

Mara sobbed dramatically. "You... you called me 'my lady'! You haven't addressed me formally since we kissed!" The bright eyes were suddenly on him again. "It was a good kiss, wasn't it? Wasn't it good, Kirk?"

She was so intoxicated it was comical. But Kirk did not smile, merely nodding, as he had little choice. "It was good."

"Better than any lady you have kissed?"

"The best."

"The very, very best?"

"Aye, Mara. The very, very best."

That seemed to satisfy her somewhat. He thought she might smile, but she suddenly burst into even louder sobs. "The very best and the very last!" she wept. "Now that you hate me, there will be no more kisses!"

Kirk did not change expression, although inside he was shrinking from the stares of his men. Mara moaned and sobbed into her hand and Kirk decided to put an end to her performance. Motioning to Niles, he grasped Mara by the arms.

"Secure her palfrey," he told the knight, lifting the lady off the small beast without effort. Placing her across his thighs, he ignored her weak protests and spurred his charger forward.

Well in front of the column, he finally responded to her squirming. Squeezing her tightly, he listened to her gasp with the force of his strength.

"Enough," he hissed. "You're causing a scene."

She balled her fists, pounding his mailed hands weakly. "Let me go," she sobbed, but there were very few tears. Mostly frustration. "I d-do not want to ride with you."

"Nonetheless, you are," he said quietly. "Tell me who gave you the whiskey."

Mara sniffled and coughed, wiping her nose most unladylike. "Lady V-Valdine and Lady Wanda," she hiccupped. "They care more for me than you do."

"By giving you whiskey?"

"By giving me medicine to help my cough." She sniffled again, feeling weak and dizzy and emotionally drained. "They told me it was a cure for the chill, which I contracted last night whilst in the woods where you had left me."

He did not reply, wondering if he shouldn't steer clear of that particular subject. Being that Mara was drunk on the ladies' potent cure, she probably wouldn't remember the conversation were they to reconcile. And he wanted her to remember.

"I am sorry you are ill," he replied softly.

In her exhaustion, she leaned heavily against him, too weak to maintain her fight. "You left me all alone, for the thieves and animals and elements. Do you know that I stayed in the trees until Corwin came looking for me?"

He was silent a moment, his stone-gray eyes grazing the landscape. "I knew."

"But you did not care."

"'Twas I who sent Corwin looking for you."

"Why did you not come yourself?"

Because I was drunk. Kirk wasn't sure how to answer her, the fact that he had immersed himself in liquor to help ease the confusion of their relationship. He'd never been more tormented in his life. "I could not come, lass." It was the truth. As of this morn, still, he could hardly walk a straight line.

Mara suddenly turned in the saddle, her bright eyes filled with sentiment. Kirk could smell the alcohol on her breath as she reached up, touching the parallel lines she had left on his face.

"Would not come, isn't that what you mean?" Sobs were close to the surface again. "Oh, Kirk, I did not mean to hurt you. It was an accident. I only meant to push you away, truly. Do you hate me?"

He gazed at her, feeling himself weaken, surrendering to the power of her emotions. Slowly, he shook his head. "I do not."

"But you said you were a fool to think yourself in love with me. Did you mean it?"

"Nay."

"Then why did you say it?"

He sighed faintly. "Because a tortured man says many things."

She continued to gaze at him, looking far more clear-minded than she had moments earlier. The hand still touching his cheek began to caress it. "Kirk, I am afraid."

The corner of his mouth twitched. "I do not believe it. What could you possibly be afraid of?"

She was serious; he could read it in her expression. "I fear I have lost my sister to her new marriage and I cannot bear the thought of losing you, too. After all we have said to one another, after all I have done, have you truly reconsidered your proposal of marriage?"

He was silent for a moment. "I thought you did not want to marry me."

The brilliant eyes bore into him, reaching deep to pull at his heart. "I have changed my mind. Will you not reconsider?"

He tried to avert his gaze but was unable to. He knew he loved her, but her words and actions had cut him deeply. Frightened him, even. It would take courage to marry the little hellion, he knew, and he had spent all night asking God to give him the courage. The beautiful lady with the bright blue eyes had taken his heart captive and he had not the strength to resist her. No matter what she had said or done.

"Mayhap," he heard himself whisper. He knew it was a lie; he had always known he would marry her regardless. But fear and confusion halted any further acknowledgement.

Mara saw his reluctance. For the first time in her life, she found herself wanting to please another, wanting to make amends for something she had done. Never had she been so compelled to ease tension or erase the past. Kirk had been kind to her, unafraid to discipline her in order to mold her wild character. And she had repaid him by gouging his face. Accident or no, the damage was obvious and she was eager to prove her remorse.

She forced a smile. "I promise I shall behave myself from this day forward. No more arguments and fighting. And I shall listen to whatever you say."

He lifted an eyebrow. "Time will tell, lady."

Her smile faded as she struggled not to give in to the sorrow his reluctance provoked. "But I am serious, Kirk. I shall truly put forth my best effort."

He nodded faintly, glancing to the rear of the column when someone shouted. Mara sensed his doubt, his disinterest in the conversation. As if he could not afford to believe her after what had happened. Hanging her head, she picked at her worn cloak, the pain in her heart uneased by the alcohol.

"Oh, Kirk," she whispered, more to herself. "Have I truly lost you?"

He heard her, feeling his heart tug. "Nay," he murmured, watching the raven-colored head come up, the blue eyes on him. "You haven't lost me."

"But you are angry?"

He shook his head slowly. "Not angry, Mara. Disappointed."

She sniffled, tears suddenly brimming again. "With me, I know. But I swear if it takes the rest of my life, I shall make amends. You are the only person in my life, other than Micheline, who has ever shown me any true kindness." She shrugged, blinking away the moisture as she lowered her gaze. "Mayhap I simply do not know how to react to true kindness. I react to you as I have reacted my entire life to the situation around me; with force and determination. I... I have never known another way."

He felt himself relenting completely, knowing her words were insightful and true. Before he could respond, however, she sneezed violently and pulled her cloak more tightly about her body. Snuggling against him, she sneezed again.

"Please do not hate me, Kirk," she murmured. "You are all that I have now."

He felt her go limp, knowing the sway of the horse and the strength of the liquor had lured her into unconsciousness. Gathering her tightly in his right arm, Mara never felt the kisses to her forehead.

***

The corridor was dim and musty, reeking of smoke. Soft footfalls echoed against the floor as Micheline made her way to her husband's chamber, more determination in her heart than she had ever experienced. Having spent the night with the man and his sister, she should have stayed far away from the pair. Yet, she could not help but remember her words to Kirk, declaring that she would take charge of her marriage as best she was able.

A marriage that had been a disaster from the onset. Submissive by character, Micheline had no idea where her sudden burst of determination had come from. But as she sat in her morning bath, washing away the reminders of her husband and his sister, it became apparent that she would not tolerate this situation. Mayhap it was in knowing that she was now the baroness and the strength of the title was behind her. Or mayhap it was because she refused to be a pawn in Edmund's sick games, manipulated and abused until she could stand no more.

Whatever the case, Micheline was inclined to take charge of the situation before it harangued out of control. Considering it was the only marriage she would ever know, she realized she had to voice her objections now unless she wanted to remain miserable for the rest of her life.

Still, the courage to do what was necessary was a hard thing to come by. Pausing before the great chamber door, she took a deep breath and knocked. After several moments, Johanne's breathless voice answered. "Who comes?"

Micheline's reply was to boldly open the door. Closing the panel behind her, she focused on her husband and his sister, intertwined in the bed sheets. After the hell she had been through the previous night, the sight of the pair no longer jolted her.

"Ah, Micheline," Johanne purred seductively. "You have returned for more?"

Micheline raised an eyebrow. "I have not," she said flatly. "First, I have come to ask where my sister has gone. Lady Valdine and Lady Wanda informed that she left for Quernmore Castle this morn."

Johanne answered irritably. "The woman is a thorn in our side. We have sent her to Quernmore Castle in the hopes of finding her a husband."

Micheline's eyes widened but she said nothing; apparently, Johanne knew nothing of the relationship between Kirk and Mara, and Micheline had no intention of elaborating. But she had also been told that Kirk had led the escort to Quernmore, and she wondered if the man was aware of the motives behind Mara's presence. Surely, he had asked. Surely, he knew.

But still... Mara was on her way to Quernmore. Perplexed, Micheline struggled not to be diverted from the subject at hand.

"I see," she said quietly. "With my first question answered, there is but another matter to discuss. I have come to say that I refuse to tolerate this... this lewd behavior any longer. The relationship between the two of you is nothing short of ghastly."

Edmund fixed her with a bland expression. "We do not require your opinion. Leave the room unless you plan to join us."

Micheline refused to back down, musing that some of Mara's boldness had finally taken its toll on her. "I do not plan to join you nor will I leave. I have come to settle this situation and I would see that accomplished."

Johanne propped herself up on an elbow, her smile fading. "What do you intend to settle, dear? Last night you made no mention of your displeasure with our arrangements."

Micheline swallowed, recollecting the events of the previous night and struggling not to succumb to bone-numbing shame. "It was my wedding night, Lady Johanne." Her voice quieted. "I was not even allowed the privilege of knowing my husband privately, but with you to comment and explain every move, every step. Your mouth to my breast, his mouth to my breast, it made no difference to either of you. I was like a new toy, to be explored and belittled. I could have allowed the circumstance to destroy me, but I will not. I refuse to allow the two of you to do what you please with me."

Edmund sat up, annoyance on his face. "You are my wife, woman. You will do as I say, without reserve or question, and I am unmoved by your pathetic speech."

"'Tis no speech, my lord, but fact."

Edmund lifted his eyebrows. "Fact? If that is so, then you have failed to realize that above all else, you are my wife. It is your duty to do what you have been told and bear me strong sons to carry on my dynasty. That, woman, is the only true fact!"

Micheline labored to keep the quiver from her voice. She wasn't very good at maintaining her courage in the face of strong opposition. "I shall be an obedient wife and bear children for the House of De Cleveley, but I will not be used as... as an object of lust. The more I think on this situation, the more it sickens me. Let Johanne find her own husband, for by the rules of marriage, you belong to me and I will not share you with your own sister."

Edmund was up, his usually pale face pinched with emotion. "You will do as I say," he hissed. "I never wanted you to begin with. How dare you confront me with your demands as if they hold any meaning to me!"

Micheline could feel her entire body trembling. "They should hold meaning to you, as I am your wife. And it is not a demand I give you, but a threat. You will cease this sinful relationship or I shall inform the church of your deeds. And they, my lord, have the power to punish you for your actions and well you know it."

Edmund stared at her. He couldn't help it. After a moment, he glanced at Johanne as if hardly believing what he had heard. "You seek to threaten me?" he repeated, his pale eyes focusing on Micheline once again. "Are you so daft, woman? Are you truly so daft that you would threaten the man who holds your very life in his hands?"

"I am not, my lord. But what you do with your sister is wrong and I refuse to tolerate it."

"But you tolerated it last night when..."

"I had no choice!" Micheline's voice soared with emotion. "I was numbed by the circumstance and you, my lord, saw fit to take advantage of me. But now that I have had time to clear my head, I realize that I will not tolerate such abuse and the rules of conduct must be established. The first rule states that Johanne is never to share our marriage bed again, and the second that you will cease this horrific relationship with her."

Edmund's neck bulged with pulsing veins. Gazing into Micheline's blue eyes, he shook his head with disgust. "You have no idea the powers you toy with," he breathed. "I would sooner squash you like a bug beneath my boot than bow to your demands."

Micheline labored to maintain eye contact; the urge to shy away from him was overwhelming. Just this once, she vowed to stay firm. She had come too far to turn back.

"I am not asking you to bow. I am asking that you graciously conform to the rules of marriage. This is a union between you and I, not the three of us."

Edmund studied the woman, finding himself wondering how Kirk would react when he returned from Quernmore to find her vanished. But he certainly could not permit her continued existence, not after she threatened his relationship with Johanne. If the church were to discover their liaison, he could expect nothing but trouble. And there was only one way to avoid the trouble.

Micheline never saw it coming. One minute she was standing her ground, and in the next she was sprawled on the floor somewhere between light and dark. The room was spinning, a great pain pounding in her head. She tried to rise but the moment she made an attempt, another blow to her head brought a curtain of darkness.

Edmund stared at his wife, collapsed in a heap. His knuckles hurt from striking her and he rubbed them gingerly as his sister hovered at the edge of the bed, her eyes wide.

"Oh, Edmund," she breathed. "I must. I truly must."

Edmund nodded unsteadily. "Aye, you must." His heart was pounding in his chest. "Do it, Johanne. Wish her away and be done with it."

Johanne nodded, madness in her eyes. "We tried, dearest. We tried to accept her, but she refused to see the rightness of our devotion. We simply cannot allow her to tell..."

"I know," Edmund said, his apprehension mounting. *Kirk had sworn to protect this woman.* But he couldn't think of that now. His desire to rid himself of the threat outweighed the fear of his captain for the moment. "Do it now, Johanne. Wish as hard as you can."

Johanne glanced at Micheline, completely emotionless. Unlike the other ladies she had wished away, Micheline's interest hadn't been in Kirk. It had been her condemnation of her husband's relationship with his sister that had brought about her ending. Closing her eyes, she bowed her head in prayer. A prayer for death.

Edmund watched his sister as she lost herself in a stupor. Opening the door, he barked breathless orders to a guard and the man disappeared down the hall. Edmund closed the door, biting his nails as Johanne continued to hex Micheline.

A knock on the door came several minutes later and Edmund yanked the panel open.

"My lord requires me?" Corwin asked quietly.

Edmund nodded, practically dragging the man into the room. When Corwin saw the heap on the floor, his nostrils flared.

"Dear God," he breathed. "You... you cannot mean...."

Edmund refused to listen, shoving him in Micheline's direction. "Take her," he commanded. "Johanne has wished her away and it is your duty to fulfill her desire."

Corwin was pale. "Not again." He turned beseechingly to Edmund. "Kirk will return tomorrow. There is not enough time to..."

"There is plenty of time!" Edmund shoved him again. "Take her and be rid of her. It is your duty!"

"My lord, I cannot!" Corwin was trying to stand his ground. "This woman is not like the others!"

"She is!"

"She is your wife, my lord, and Kirk has taken a personal interest in her. He already suspects my participation in these vanishings!"

"He does not. 'Tis Niles he suspects thanks to the seeds of doubt I myself planted. Now move!"

Corwin would not be swayed. "But Niles is with him. He'll know it is me if...!"

Edmund grabbed him, slapping his open palm over the man's mouth. Hurling Corwin against the wall, Edmund's face was ashen as he faced off against the reluctant knight.

"We are only doing as Johanne demands." His lips were against Corwin's cheek, the foul stench of his breath pervasive. "This is her doing, not ours. We are merely instruments through which her mighty powers work. We are but servants!"

Corwin was terrified of the glint in Edmund's eyes. "We are murderers!"

Edmund yanked him away from the wall, tossing him toward the fireplace in his dementia. Corwin stumbled over the billows, landing next to Micheline's feet. Before he could scramble away, Edmund leapt on top of him, grabbing him by the hair and forcing him to look at the lady's limp form.

"Look at her," he hissed, yanking the knight's hair until the man gasped in pain." *Look at her!* She is not worth the price of your worry, Corwin, for just as easily she could be your wife if you do not cooperate. Do you understand me clearly?"

It was always the same threat. A threat Corwin always succumbed to because he believed Edmund would carry it through. Ever since Corwin had married his cousin, a woman he had been in love with since childhood, his wife had been wielded against him like a weapon.

"I refuse to do this again. You cannot threaten me with...!"

"Do it or I tell Kirk the vanishings were all of your doing. He will have no choice but to believe me and after your execution has been carried out, I will make sure Lady Valdine and Lady Wanda live nothing short of a hellish existence!"

God help him, Corwin knew he spoke the truth. And he was disgusted that the man was able to control him so easily. Edmund released his hair, rising unsteadily from the floor. Corwin rose to his knees, struggling to recover his composure.

"Remove her, Corwin," Edmund said again, taking a deep breath to calm himself. "Remove her and we will see her no more."

Swallowing hard, Corwin cast Edmund a loathsome glare as he stood on quaking feet. As Johanne continued to pray and Edmund poured himself a chalice of wine, Corwin scooped Micheline up from the floor. He was silent as he moved to the door.

"Corwin," Edmund called to him before he could quit the chamber. "Leave the lady's clothes in her chamber. Everything shall remain untouched."

Corwin paused. He could hardly speak through his disgust. "And what will you tell Kirk?"

Edmund savored his wine, feeling the calming alcohol flood his veins. "We shall tell him that the lady threw herself from the tower window; her reasons unknown." He turned to the pale-faced knight. "That is what you intend to do with her, is it not? I believe the tower would be a proper exit for my distraught wife."

Corwin did not reply for a moment. "I suppose, considering you drown the last one. And the one before her. If I drown another, the lake will be floating with bodies and our activities will be obvious."

Edmund looked to his sister, eyes closed as she wished her brother's wife far, far away. He knew her simple mind hadn't heard a word of what had been said. "Not our activities, Corwin." He gestured to his sister with a raised goblet. "Johanne's activities. This is her doing, after all."

Corwin shook his head, slowly. "Why must you blame her? Her thoughts may be evil, but it is you and I who carry out the sentence."

Edmund drained his cup, moving to the bed where his sister continued to pray. Reaching out, he stroked her tangled hair. "We must keep Johanne happy, Corwin."

Corwin left the chamber without another word, Micheline's limp body flopping in his arms. The sun was setting, intermittent rays of light streaming through windows as the knight mounted the stairs for the tower.

The cylinder was narrow, the steps winding an endless circle skyward. Micheline stirred, groaning softly as Corwin neared the top. Just as he entered the dusty, unused chamber at the summit, Micheline raised her head, her eyes struggling to focus.

"Sir Corwin," she mumbled. "What... happened?"

Corwin was beyond all rational thought. He dumped Micheline on the floor, his eyes wild.

"You will stay here," he gasped, wiping the sweat from his brow. "You will not leave this place if you value your life. Do you understand me?"

Micheline stared at him, her stomach lurching and her head spinning. Tears filled her frightened eyes. "What has happened?"

Corwin struggled with his control. "Your death is what will happen if you leave. Kirk will return in two days and we must wait for him. Until that time, you must stay here and remain completely silent. No one must know of your presence." He suddenly grabbed her by the arms, shouting. "Tell me you understand what I have told you!"

Micheline burst into terrified tears. "I do," she sobbed. "Did Edmund... is he...?"

Corwin did not answer. Releasing the dazed woman, he stumbled from the chamber and slammed the door. Micheline heard the rusty bolt as it slid across the panel, locking her in. His footfalls faded down the stairs, leaving Micheline confused and scared.

Looking about the cobwebs and broken furniture of her new home, she covered her face and wept.

CHAPTER ELEVEN

The rain had returned by the time evening fell. Quernmore Castle was only a few more hours, but as the weather worsened, Kirk decided to seek shelter for the night. With Mara wrapped up in her worn cloak, snoring softly in his arms, he ordered his men to find shelter in a grove of oak trees.

There was a small village in the distance, the smoke from cooking fires choking the damp air. Leaving Niles in charge of the camp, Kirk spurred his charger in the direction of the settlement.

The few merchants along the main avenue had closed shop for the night. The massive destrier plodded along the muddied street, his hooves echoing off the small homes as Kirk went in search of proper shelter for Mara. She had shivered and sneezed all afternoon and he was unwilling to allow her to spend the night in the freezing rain.

On the opposite side of the berg sat a small tavern, a warm light emitting from a partially-open door. Kirk reined his charger around the side of the establishment, providing the animal with shelter from the rain. There was a pool of water collecting from the rain gutters and the animal drank noisily as Kirk gently roused Mara.

"Mara," he murmured, brushing a stray lock of hair from her cheek. "Wake up, lass."

She stirred, but mostly she ignored him. Sighing, he managed to dismount with her still in his arms. As the rain pounded and the wind began to whip up, he walked to the front of the inn and opened the door with his boot. Hit in the face by a blast of warm, stale air, he ducked beneath the doorjamb.

There were several people enjoying their ale and food, hardly glancing up when the massive man with the lady in his arms entered. The innkeeper looked up from behind his bar, wiping his hands on his stained tunic.

"What'll it be, m'lord?"

Kirk shifted Mara, who was beginning to come around. "A room on this hellish night."

The innkeeper nodded, shoving a nearby serving wench on the arm to get her moving. "Verenia'll show ye a room," he said, eyeing Kirk more closely now that Mara seemed to be showing signs of life. "Food for ye, then? A bath for yer lady?"

Before Kirk could answer, Mara suddenly raised her head and scowled viciously. "Good Lord, no food!" she put her hands to her head, groaning. "My head is threatening to explode. Why is this damnable room spinning?"

Kirk couldn't help but grin. He wasn't feeling particularly well, either, but he knew that in their current state, food would be the best thing for them both.

"Send it to my room," he told the innkeeper.

The man nodded, listening to Mara moan and grumble as Kirk carried her down a short corridor, following the direction of the serving wench. Snapping his fingers to his toothless wife, the woman began to serve up the knight's supper as ordered.

The chamber provided was small. Kirk could hardly move about as he set Mara to unsteady feet, glancing around their dismal surroundings. But Mara ignored the state of the room, smelling of sweat and dirt, as the serving wench turned back the bed and quit the room. Finally alone, Mara sat down on the lumpy bed and fell backward.

"My head," she groaned softly. "It hurts so!"

Kirk unlatched his helm, removing it with a grunt of relief. "Let this be your lesson against the evils of whisky."

The bright blue eyes were closed against the rocking room. After a moment, she peeped open a lid. "It was medicine," she insisted softly. The other eye opened and she focused on him as he went to work removing his armor. "Where are we?"

He did not look up as he dislodged his gauntlets, his chaffing breastplate. "At an inn," he cocked an eyebrow, meeting her gaze. "I seem to remember a certain young lady telling me that sleeping on the damp grass like a hardened soldier was unacceptable."

She continued to gaze at him as the plate protection came off piece by piece, carefully set aside against the wall to drain. Slowly, she sat up, gripping the bed when the room swayed. Kirk pretended to ignore her as she unfastened her worn cloak, laying it by the small hearth. He finished removing his mail hauberk when he noticed she was staring at her shoes.

"What's the matter?"

She kicked off the shoes in response, setting them by the cloak. As Kirk watched, she reached up her skirt and fumbled about, coming away with two ribbon garters. As he watched with increasing interest, she proceeded to peel off her woolen stockings.

They were wet and she lay them carefully on the warm stone. They were also full of holes. Kirk continued to watch her, distractedly removing his damp tunic, as she meticulously flattened out the wool so that it would dry better.

"I did not realize you had gotten wet," he said softly. "Wrap yourself in the coverlet if you are chilled."

She shook her head, her bare feet sticking out from beneath her surcoat as she knelt beside the fire. "I am used to the wet and the cold."

She had made the statement without a hint of self-pity. Simply stating a fact. Kirk moved up behind her, tearing his eyes away from her long enough to glance at the saturated cloak, her worn shoes. Scratching his dark head, he fingered the cloak.

"I shall have to see about purchasing you some new clothes," he said. "Bright colors, I think. Your coloring is far too striking for unspectacular shades."

He seemed rather nonchalant in his statement, almost normal in fact. As if they hadn't spent a day and a night in violent conflict. As Mara glanced up to reply, she noticed that he had removed his tunic.

Suddenly, it was very warm in the little room. Mara had never seen a man's naked chest before, tanned skin as it covered bulging muscles and hair that matted his chest and trailed down his abdomen. She couldn't help but stare at his trim belly and arms that were as large as oak branches. In fact, she was so involved in her observations of Kirk's magnificent form that she had yet to notice his amused smile.

"What's the matter, lass?" his voice was soft. "Have you never seen a man before?"

Her cheeks flushed a brilliant red and she looked away, fumbling with her hose once again. "You... you have removed nearly all of your clothing," she stammered. "I was merely... what I mean to say is that... Oh!"

She grunted in frustration, angry that he had caught her staring at him and saw fit to laugh at her innocence. Kirk continued to chuckle.

"What was I supposed to do? Leave the wet garments on?" he gestured at her. "You yourself treated me to a titillating show when you removed your hose as if I was not in the room."

Her gaze was fixed on the hearth, her cheeks glowing like the white-hot embers. "I...I simply wasn't thinking," she said. "I am not used to having men about. Only Micheline."

He snorted. "No more, lass. Had you put your hands up your skirt in Niles' company, the man would have attacked you in a fit of lust and I would have been forced to kill him."

She pursed her lips with embarrassment, defiance. "I would have never done such a thing in front of him. I simply did not think, I tell you. It's nothing to laugh over!"

The more agitated she became, the more he snorted. "Aye, it is. You are more comfortable with me than you care to admit."

She rose abruptly, moving to the large bed and throwing herself on the coverlet. Annoyed with Kirk, she was in the process of wrapping her cold feet in the smelly warmth of the blankets when Kirk leaned over the bed, collecting both sides of the coverlet and winding them around her. Before Mara could protest, he had her snuggly swaddled in the linens.

"There," he stood back, hands on his hips. "Is that better?"

Mara lifted a black eyebrow. Christ, how he knew that expression. "If I do not suffocate first, I suppose it is."

A faint smile continued to play on his lips as he turned away, laying his tunic next to her hose. Outside, the rain continued to beat and the wind to howl, but the stenchy little room was remarkably cozy. And in spite of her aching head and irritation, Mara realized she was rather comfortable. And hungry.

But she was more interested in watching Kirk at the moment. On his haunches next to the fire, she watched his naked back as he stoked the hearth, coaxing it into a blaze. She could see every muscle as it moved beneath the tanned skin, shoulders so broad that they were wider than a door. As the warmth of the room and blankets saturated her, the harsh emotions, the churning of her stomach, seemed to fade.

"Kirk?"

He turned around, his face illuminated by the glowing fire. "Hmm?"

"Have you realized that Micheline is alone at Anchorsholme?"

He shook his head. "She is not alone. I left Corwin behind to see to her."

Mara did not seem particularly comforted by his answer but remained silent. He returned his attention to the fire when she spoke again, softly.

"Why am I here?"

He gazed at her a moment, setting the poker aside. "Because it is raining."

"Nay," she shook her head. "Why am I going to Quernmore? Am I to be banished there?"

His brow furrowed as he rose. "Banished? Who told you such nonsense?"

"No one," she watched him move for the bed, his weight sinking the mattress dangerously as he sat. "Niles said that Lord Edmund ordered me to travel to Quernmore, but he gave no reason. Do you know why?"

Kirk scratched his head, averting his gaze. "Most likely because I told him I was going to take you with me."

She frowned. "*You* wanted to take me with you? Why?"

The scratching hand dropped to his side. "Foremost, because I was afraid of what would happen if I left you alone, without my guidance. I thought a few days away from the situation would settle your emotions. When I broached the subject with Edmund last night, he heartily agreed. It seems that he wants you away from Anchorsholme as well, although I cannot understand why."

The last few words were delivered sarcastically. Mara's frown deepened and she unwound herself from the covers. "Settle my emotions? The need to protect my sister from her deviant husband will never be settled!"

Kirk did not want another argument on his hands, not when the peace between them was new and easily damaged. "We have been through this, Mara. This is Micheline's marriage and she does not want any interference, from you or from me."

Mara was working herself into a righteous rage when she saw the expression on his face; it was somewhat saddened. "Did she tell you this?" she asked.

He nodded, his stone-gray eyes gazing into the fire. "She is correct. It is her marriage and if there is to be any respect at all, she must be the one to establish it. As much as I am reluctant to obey her wishes, I will not always be around to make sure Edmund treats her well. Misha must do that for herself, I am afraid."

Mara stared at him, sensing his frustration. He had wanted to help Micheline, but her sister had firmly declined his offer. And she could see that the rejection bothered him deeply.

"You called her Misha?" she reached out, touching his arm.

Kirk tore his gaze away from the hearth, finding himself swallowed whole by brilliant blue eyes. "I have heard you address her as such. 'Tis an endearing term of affection between family."

Mara's cheeks flamed again, the heat from his naked arm sending a blaze of excitement through her body. "But you are not family."

"Not yet."

She raised an eyebrow. "I thought you were reluctant to reconsider your marriage proposal."

He couldn't have removed his gaze from her if he had tried. He did not want to try; the magnetism between them was more powerful, more intense, than he had ever known it to be. "There was truly nothing to reconsider, lass," he sighed; it was useless to resist the obvious. "God help me, I cannot stay away from you, not even if my common sense tells me otherwise."

She smiled radiantly. Great hands suddenly came up and the bed shifted heavily as he pulled her against him, his lips devouring her tender mouth. Mara gasped with delight, feeling his overwhelming warmth envelope her, melting her completely. All of the heartache of the past two days was forgotten as his seeking lips told her how eager he was to make all between them well again.

"Kirk, Kirk," she moaned, her hands in his hair as his teeth nibbled on her jaw. "I am so glad you have not abandoned me. I was afraid I had driven you away."

"Never," his voice was muffled against her flesh. "The more you abuse me, the more I want you."

She giggled, quickly turning to sighs of pleasure as he devoured her neck. "You're insane to think so," she whispered. "But know... know I truly never meant to hurt you."

He heard her, incapable of replying as his lips moved to the swell of her breasts. Mara's hands touched his face, still terribly concerned with the parallel lacerations as he focused on other, more pleasurable, targets.

"Do they hurt?" she asked, running her fingers over the scabs.

He shook his head, pulling her surcoat off her shoulders. Before Mara realized it, she was bared to the waist and his mouth was suckling heartily on a rosy nipple. With a gasp, she stiffened with new, ripe pleasure and the three ugly wounds vanished from thought. Clutching Kirk's head against her breast, she fell back on the bed and took him down with her.

She was sweeter than he had ever known a woman to be. Soft, delectable, tender for the taking. Pinning her arms above her head, he kissed a delicate circle around each breast, rewarding himself after each turn by sampling a hot nipple. Mara writhed and panted, experiencing his mouth with the greatest of joy.

Between each breast he moved, blazing a scorching trail up one arm and down the other. Releasing her arms, his massive hands kneaded and explored as her slender fingers anchored themselves firmly in his hair. Just as he was forging into the new territory of her abdomen, a soft knock rattled the door.

He almost shouted them away. But Mara lifted her head, panting and dazed.

"The food," she breathed.

He knew she was hungry. With a heavy sigh, he nodded in resignation and pushed himself off her.

"A moment!" he couldn't help the frustration in his voice, pulling Mara off the bed and helping her straighten her surcoat. When she was properly secured, he discreetly adjusted his bulging hose and opened the door.

The innkeeper's wife and the serving wench had their hands full of steaming food. Kirk pointed silently to the small table next to the hearth and the women quickly deposited their load. Bowing and scraping their way from the room seemed to take a small eternity and Kirk slammed the door irritably when they were finally gone. Turning around, he was not surprised to see that Mara was almost halfway through with the meal.

He lifted an eyebrow as he approached. "Did you not think to save any for me?"

Her mouth was full of mutton. "Nay," she said, pushing his hand away when he tried to take a slab of meat. "This is all mine."

He grinned and she batted at him, pushing him away and pretending to horde it all. In a flash, Kirk reached down and lifted her from the small chair, taking it himself. As Mara sputtered and shrieked, unable to protest with her mouth stuffed, he deposited her on his lap and took a helping of bread.

"There, you gluttonous wench," he slopped the bread in gravy and took a healthy bite. "I will claim you and your food."

She grinned at him, pieces of mutton on her lips. He kissed her, licking the debris clean. One kiss led to another, and still another. Before either one of them could control their actions, the food was back on the wooden trays. They were on the bed, continuing where they had left off before the intrusion of their meal.

The surcoat came off more quickly than before. And this time, Kirk pulled it completely free, leaving Mara naked beneath him. Between heated kisses, he somehow managed to remove his boots and finally, his damp hose. But Mara never noticed; as long as his mouth remained where it was the most pleasurable, she would pay little attention to anything else. When his hot, naked body covered her on the stale sheets, the only thing she was aware of was her own awakening desire.

Thunder rattled the walls as Kirk's pace increased, his kisses fast and furious. Mara gasped with unrestrained delight, her experience with the drunken soldier all but forgotten. The rude introduction to desire had not scarred her so deeply that Kirk was not able to erase the memory with his scalding hands and searching mouth. Pulling, tugging, tasting; the delights multiplied as the night deepened.

His knees wedged between her slender thighs, sure fingers stroking her gently. Mara leapt with uncertainty but Kirk purred in her ear, words of desire and beauty that calmed her innocent heart. When his finger slipped inside her, discomfort was virtually unknown; she was slick, ready for his throbbing member. No pain, no fear; only rousing passion.

Thunder rolled again, filling the smelly room and all but drowning out Mara's pants of pleasure. Kirk inserted another finger into her, listening to her groan and nearly exploding with his impatience. His tongue fondled her nipples and he could feel her slippery passage contracting around his fingers, a physical response to the timeless ritual of mating.

He removed his hand from her, no longer capable of restraining himself. Her soft, responsive body called to him and he was shaking with anticipation as he answered, placing his heavy arousal against her and pushing gently. Wet and pulsating, he slipped forward without effort.

He was anchored, sliding deeper by the moment. Mara squirmed, her pants of pleasure less evident as he gained headway. Kirk kissed her deeply, murmuring against her mouth and promising the pain would be momentary. She was so tiny that he was surprised with the ease thus far; still, it was becoming uncomfortable for her and he was acutely aware of the fact.

Gathering her tightly against him, he drew back and coiled his buttocks, driving into her again and feeling her maidenhood breach. Mara yelped into his mouth, the fingers clutching at him digging crescent-shaped wounds into his scalp. She continued to gasp with pain as he rolled onto his side to remove his tremendous weight off her. Holding her close and seated to the hilt, he did not realize that he was gasping, too.

"No...no more," Mara groaned, feeling crushed and impaled by his huge body. "I do not want to do this anymore."

He kissed her face, her hair. "The pain is over, lass, I promise," he murmured tenderly. "You must trust me. 'Twill only become more pleasurable from now on."

She struggled feebly with him but there was no possible way to escape; he had her tightly, his throbbing manroot clutched deep within her sugared walls. When she failed to respond to his soothing words, Kirk decided to show her what he meant. Holding her against his chest with one hand, the other cupped her heart-shaped bottom and he began to move.

Mara groaned miserably with the first couple of thrusts, feeling full and overwhelmed. But his gentle nurturing, his tender whispers, broke through her haze and instinctively she began to respond to him, experiencing the friction of his manroot as he penetrated deep. Soon enough, the discomfort gave way to a burgeoning fire that grew brighter by the moment.

But Mara's fire was nothing compared to Kirk's. He was far gone with passion, feeling her silken body in his embrace, experiencing every throb of her feminine core as the most erotic of caresses. Within seconds he had reached his peak, breathing her name as he released himself deep within her. But he continued to move, feeling the slippery wetness he had put in her, wondering fleetingly if she would be with child by the time they married. He was a selfish man in that he hoped so.

Mara felt his spasms, hearing her name on his strangled groan. But his thrusting continued as he reached between their sweating bodies, his fingers probing her wet curls. A gasping scream erupted from her lips as he gently pinched her throbbing nub, bringing her to a powerful release.

Thrashing about as the waves of pleasure consumed her, Mara was vaguely aware of Kirk's soft laughter.

"So you like this, my little hellion," he murmured, kissing and nuzzling every inch of her face. "I thought you would."

As the waves settled, Mara rasped for air. "My... my God, Kirk. What has happened?"

He laughed again, his trencher-sized hands caressing her buttocks. "Delicious, is it not?"

She swallowed, gasped, and swallowed again. She wasn't sure how to answer him. "I feel so... weak. Weak and wonderful."

He was still in her, cradling her trembling body against his broad chest. "Aye, lass, weak and wonderful describes me as well. As if I have waited for this moment all my life."

Mara was silent a moment, listening to her heart pounding in her ears. Brushing the hair from her eyes, she lifted her gaze to meet his. "I had no idea that feelings like this were possible," she said softly. "And I certainly would never have thought you capable of bringing them about."

He lifted an eyebrow. "And why not?"

She smiled faintly, a gesture he found utterly beautiful. "Because I hated you, once."

"You do not hate me now."

She shook her head, slowly. "Nay," she reached up, touching his stubbled cheek. He kissed her fingers, the warmth and tenderness of the moment evident. "I do not."

The thunder rolled again and the rain pounded as he took her mouth with his own, kissing her tenderly until she fell asleep in his arms. More content that he had ever been in his life, sleep claimed him before he realized it.

CHAPTER TWELVE

Lord Lionel le Vay, Baron Wyresdale, was a big man with bushy black eyebrows and gray hair. He greeted Kirk as one would a lost son, welcoming him into the Norman stronghold of Quernmore Castle. And the same warm greeting went for Lionel's flame-haired daughter as well.

Mara tried not to lash out when Lady Lily le Vay turned her pretty smile in Kirk's direction. And she further kept her mouth shut when the graceful young woman took his arm and escorted him into the great hall of Quernmore's tall and block-shaped keep where a lavish table had been set. With Niles as her escort, Mara's spirits continued to sink as she watched Lady Lily tend to Kirk hand and foot.

The fare served by Lord Lionel was premium. He was a very wealthy man, having gained much of his wealth in shipping so close to the sea. Roast beef, ale, vegetables and sweet cakes filled the lengthy dining table as Niles helped Mara to her seat. The fair-haired knight served her himself but Mara had little appetite; her bright blue eyes were riveted to Kirk as he politely responded to Lady Lily's attentions.

He met Mara's piercing stare, several times, winking reassuringly at her. But Mara refused to respond to his gesture, instead, glaring headily at the lovely young woman so obviously infatuated with him. Even after Kirk introduced Mara as Edmund's sister-in-law, she maintained her grim mood in the face of Lady Lily's bubbling personality.

She seemed to be nice enough, but Mara could hardly see past her own jealousy. Lady Lily's ladies-in-waiting joined them for the refreshments and Mara found herself contending with not one, but four women all eager to speak with Kirk. Her cheeks flushed but she said nothing, as hard as it was for her to control herself. She had promised Kirk that she would behave and was determined to keep her promise no matter what the circumstance.

Kirk did not seem particularly interested in the women, his gaze mostly on Mara or on his food. She had long since stopped glaring in his direction, instead, focused on her trencher lest she be forced to break her promise. Next to her, Niles' voice lifted in greeting and much to her reluctance, Mara found herself pulled into the conversation.

Lifting her gaze, she found herself staring into the pale blue eyes of a very large, very blond knight. He was a handsome fellow with a wide, toothy grin and he took Mara's hand chivalrously.

"Sir Spencer de Shera, my lady," he kissed her fingers gently, his eyes never leaving her. "At your service."

Mara was a fast thinker. Gazing into the face of the handsome knight, she suddenly saw the opportunity to make Kirk pay for Lady Lily's attention. If she could only make him jealous enough that he would shun the woman and drop to his knees to beg Mara's forgiveness, then she would ask no more. Smiling brightly at Sir Spencer, she gestured him to sit between her and Niles.

"A pleasure, Sir Spencer," she scooted over to allow the man room. "Would you share our meal?"

Spencer continued to grin, practically shoving Niles to the ground in his haste. "'Twould be an honor," he sat heavily, his scabbard pinching Mara's thigh. She yelped and he was mortified. "Forgive me, my lady. I should have been more cautious!"

She rubbed her leg, smiling weakly, wondering if Kirk was watching the exchange. "No harm done, truly," she removed her hand from her throbbing thigh, collecting her chalice. "Tell me; how long have you served at Quernmore?"

"Six years, my lady," he could hardly eat with such a beautiful lady by his side. "Lord le Vay knighted me personally and I have been commanding his troops ever since."

Mara acted as if truly involved in their conversation, hoping Kirk was beginning to boil. "How splendid. Where were you born?"

"York. My mother was Scots, royal by blood."

"Is that so?" she could see Niles' expression over Spencer' shoulder and she imagined that he looked rather on edge. And she could guess the reason. "Very impressive. I have had several uncles that have served various kings, but I have no direct blood relation to the crown. Is your mother still living?"

He nodded, warming to her and feeling like a giddy squire. "She and my father reside near Alnwick Castle in Northumberland. I have six younger sisters that they are trying to marry off as we speak."

Mara laughed. "If the ladies are anything like their brother then I am sure your parents will have little difficulty," his freckled cheeks flushed profusely and she laughed again. "Your modesty is astounding, Sir Spencer. Surely you have been snatched by some fortunate lady?"

He shook his head. "I have not," his voice softened, his pale blue eyes intense. "Are... are you spoken for, my lady?"

Mara never had the chance to reply. Kirk was suddenly between them, cleaving any further conversation. Spencer glanced up, startled by the abrupt appearance.

"Sir K-Kirk," he stammered, leaping to his feet. "An honor, my lord. I did not want to interrupt your conversation with Lord Lionel, else I would have greeted you already."

Kirk struggled to keep from wrapping his hands around Spencer' throat. He was a good knight, intelligent and strong, and Kirk liked him a great deal. Or at least he had until the man turned his interest on Mara, who did little to discourage the attention.

"If you will notice, Lord Lionel has left the room to tend to a brief matter," he was growling. "Now you may properly greet me. And you will vacate this seat immediately."

Spencer did as he was told. Mara was sorry she had caused the man trouble, but the end result was what she hoped for; Lady Lily was alone at the head of the table. And Kirk, even though he wasn't begging forgiveness for allowing another woman to occupy his attention, was nonetheless standing by her side.

"I... I apologize, my lord," Sir Spencer said respectfully. "I was not aware that I was offending anyone."

"You were not," Mara said, rising from the bench. "I enjoyed meeting you, Sir Spencer. Mayhap we can continue our conversation at another time."

Kirk gazed down at her, suspecting what she had been up to and greatly perturbed. He was about to remove her from the room and explain his displeasure with the palm of his hand to her buttocks when Lord le Vay re-emerged into the great hall. Motioning to Kirk, the knight had no choice but to go with the man and deliver his message privately.

But not before he looked to Mara and then to Niles. "Take her in hand, Niles," he said deliberately, ignoring Spencer altogether. "I shall trust you and you alone."

Niles nodded, watching as Kirk passed a heady glare at Spencer before departing. And Spencer, normally mild-mannered and quite congenial, glared in return. Without benefit of spoken word, Niles realized the battle lines had already been drawn.

Mara, too, wasn't oblivious to the intense expressions between the men and it was oddly flattering. Not that Spencer had any possible chance in pursuing her; still, it somehow made her feel more secure. As long as Kirk was willing to obviously establish that she belonged to him, then she was satisfied.

As Kirk marched away, she called after him. He paused, waiting as she caught up to him. His expression did not soften even when she smiled.

"Where are you going?" she asked.

"To meet with le Vay."

She gazed at him a moment, studying his hard features. "Why are you so angry?"

He lifted an eyebrow. "You know why. And you are not behaving yourself in the least in spite of your promise."

This time, she hardened. "I believe I have behaved myself quite well. I did not tear Lady Lily's hair out by the roots when she put her hands on you, did I? And when her ladies vied for your attention, I kept silent, did I not? How dare you accuse me of breaking my promise!"

His jaw ticked and she could see his facade wavering. "Lady Lily is certainly no threat and her ladies are barely mentionable. I am used to their silly games. But as for de Shera...." He cast a long glance at Spencer, now in conversation with Niles. "You will stay away from him, Mara."

"Will you stay away from Lily?"

He sighed with frustration, laboring to keep his voice quiet. "It is different with her. I must be polite lest I offend le Vay. But with de Shera, there is no reason for you to even communicate with the man. Am I understood?"

A smile played on her lips. "You are jealous of him."

He growled. "You are mine, lass, body and soul. I shall kill the man if he comes near you again."

Her smile broke through. "Then why do not you announce to the world that I am yours? That should keep Lily and Spencer away from us."

"I cannot announce anything until I speak with Edmund and he makes our betrothal official. Not that I have any doubts, but it is best to remain silent until we have his blessing."

Mara regarded him a moment before turning a coy gaze in Spencer's direction. "He seems very nice, actually."

He was in no mood for her foolery, taunting him with her mastery over him. "Enough of that nonsense or I shall spank you as I did before." He pointed a mailed glove in the direction of the table. "Now, go and sit with Niles and behave yourself. I do not know how long I shall be with le Vay and I do not want to worry over you while I am gone."

Her smile faded as she sensed more than irritation in his manner; he had failed to respond to her teasing in his usual fashion. Reaching out, she grasped his arm. "You will not," she said softly. "Is something the matter, Kirk? You seem... edgy."

He found himself swallowed by the brilliant eyes, thoughts of the previous night filling his veins with warmth. "Nothing you should concern yourself over, love," he patted her hand. "Go with Niles. I shall seek you when I am finished."

As Mara watched him disappear from the great hall, a thought occurred to her; he had never clarified why they had come to Quermore in the first place, aside from the fact that he wanted her away from Anchorsholme. Obviously, there was a motivation and she wondered seriously what it might be. Kirk had been perfectly calm until they had arrived, but now, he seemed preoccupied and harsh.

Thoughtfully, she turned for the table laden with a half-finished feast and chattering people. Niles and Spencer had finished their conversation, Niles waiting patiently for her to return as Spencer seemed focused on his drink.

Niles served her a fresh helping of meat and she delved in with gusto. Ignoring Lady Lily's inquisitive stares and Spencer's brooding silence, her mind remained focused on Kirk as he met with Lionel le Vay. She wondered why he seemed so edgy even though he had told her not to be troubled by it. Anything that worried him, she was naturally concerned.

But there was nothing she could do about it at the moment. Her more prevalent concern was staying clear of Sir Spencer now that she had enticed the man. As she approached the feasting table that looked as if it had been picked over, she was considering all manner of behavior to un-entice him.

Unfortunately for her, he proved rather resistant to her revolting charms.

CHAPTER THIRTEEN

"This has just arrived, Lord Edmund," Corwin's voice was tight, his face beaded with sweat from racing up three flights of stairs. "From Wicklow."

Edmund snatched the missive, damp and stained, from the knight's hand. He nearly tore it in his haste to unroll the parchment, his faded green eyes greedily consuming the message contained. After a moment, he sighed with great remorse.

"My God...," he breathed, his eyes still glued to the vellum.

"What's happened?"

Edmund sighed again. The sun was beginning to set on the winter-dead fields of Lancashire, a break in the storm permitting a few weak rays to caress the landscape. The small solar was musty, dim, lit only by a tallow taper and a fire in the hearth. As Edmund rounded the large desk, the vellum still in his hand, Corwin struggled to make sense of the expression on the man's face.

"So it comes," Edmund said slowly, letting the parchment fall to the desktop. Running his fingers through his hair, he sighed again as if his entire body was deflating. "My foolish Irish vassals have finally managed to overrun the Castle. Kirk's father has been killed in the siege."

Corwin visibly blanched. "Christ," he hissed. "We must send Kirk a missive immediately."

Edmund nodded, watching the weak flicker of the hearth. "I have lost him completely."

"Who?"

"Kirk," Edmund turned away from the blaze, pacing. "The arrival of the le Bec sisters has driven a wedge between us. Kirk appointed himself their protector and his loyalty to me was weakened."

"Foolishness, my lord," Corwin chided softly. "Kirk is ever loyal to the House of de Cleveley."

Edmund stopped pacing, shaking his head. "Not at all," he insisted. "Certainly, I cannot give him what the youngest sister has. My loyalties would be swayed, too, by a beautiful face and sensual body."

Corwin was silent a moment, knowing his liege spoke the truth. "It matters not that he thinks himself in love with her. His fealty is still sworn to you and he takes his oath very seriously."

Edmund appeared not to have heard him. "He asked to take her with him on his journey to Quernmore," he resumed his pacing, losing himself in thought. "He gave me some foolish explanation about her distress with her sister's marriage and the disorientation of a new home, but I knew better. I knew it was because he was afraid to leave her here, alone."

Corwin watched his liege, his expression guarded. "Do you blame him?" He turned away, jaw ticking with disgust. "Look what we've done to her sister. And should Johanne realize that Kirk is in love with Mara, then..."

"She shall never know," Edmund's expression was unusually harsh. "She does not suspect and I wish to keep it that way. With her attention on Micheline, Kirk's feelings for the little hellion went unnoticed."

Corwin cast a long glance at the fidgeting man. "When he leaves for Ireland, he cannot take her with him. What then?"

Edmund shrugged. "She will be untouched."

"Why?" Corwin was genuinely curious. "There have been ten ladies in all, my lord. All but your wife showed Kirk too much attention and Johanne was determined to do away with them. Why would you leave the one woman Kirk has responded to untouched?"

"For the very reason you give," Edmund's voice was barely a whisper. "He feels for her, Corwin. I suspect that if something happened to her, I would see my last day upon this earth. Kirk would stop at nothing to seek vengeance."

Corwin thought on that a moment. "So Kirk leaves her here while he sails to Ireland to quell the rebellion. There is a very strong chance that Johanne will learn the truth of the matter the longer Mara stays. Whereas you and I are capable of respecting the emotions Kirk holds for the lady, Johanne is not. She is fully capable of injuring the girl, if not worse."

Edmund lowered himself into a chair next to the hearth. "She will not be here."

"I do not understand."

Edmund was silent a moment, contemplating the course of his actions. "When Kirk rode to Quernmore, he carried two missives with him. He was aware of the contents of the first. But he was unaware of the contents of the second."

"And what was that?"

"A marriage contract," Edmund turned to look at him. "A proposal of marriage between Lady Mara le Bec and Lord Lionel le Vay. If le Vay reacts to Mara as most men do, then I suspect he will accept and while Kirk is fighting to free my holdings, the young lady who has managed to turn him against me shall wed another."

Corwin's eyes widened. "And you do not think he will seek vengeance for your treachery?" he could hardly believe what he was hearing. "He'll return from Ireland and kill you!"

Edmund looked away from the man, studying the weak flame. "After she is married, there is nothing he can do. He'll simply have to resign himself to the inevitable and killing me will not solve the problem."

Corwin shook his head. "Why would you do this, Edmund? To Kirk, of all people. You love the man!"

"Exactly," Edmund struggled against the guilt Corwin was attempting to evoke. "I love him and I want this woman away from him. Away from us all so that things can return to normal. In time, he'll understand. He must."

Corwin stared at the man, long and hard, before turning away. "He'll never understand," he muttered, raking his fingers through his auburn hair. "He'll kill us all."

Edmund heard the knight, ignoring the truth of his words. He simply couldn't think on the long-term implications of his actions, not with his Wicklow holdings in jeopardy. The flames in the hearth continued to snap and crackle as each man lost himself to his own turbulent thoughts.

"Send word to Kirk this night," Edmund's voice was faint. "He must be prepared to sail to Ireland immediately. In fact, tell him you will meet him at the port with our troops. He can ride from Quernmore with le Vay's support."

Corwin sighed heavily, feeling the familiar disgust for his liege. A man he was helpless against. "Do I tell him of his father?"

Edmund nodded. "Aye. It will feed his sense of vengeance against the rebels and move him faster to his duty."

Corwin turned to glance at the man one last time, a man he wished he had the nerve to stand against. Without another word, he moved for the door.

"Corwin," Edmund stopped the man in his tracks. "If you are also thinking to send word to Kirk regarding my plans for Mara, I would reconsider. You will be sailing to Ireland as well, leaving your wife at my mercy. Quite a bit can happen while you are away."

Corwin turned shades of red, biting his tongue as he quit the room.

Within an hour, a messenger was speeding for Quernmore Castle.

CHAPTER FOURTEEN

Clad in a bright blue surcoat that, even with its simplicity, was the very best surcoat she owned, Mara was escorted to the evening meal by Niles. The sun had set and an expensive display of torches lit the corridors as she was led from her comfortable chamber to the smoky and crowded hall below.

Kirk had remained with le Vay all afternoon, affording Mara a good deal of time alone. A chambermaid came late in the day to help her with her surcoat, the only surcoat she had packed, and the woman pressed it as Mara sat in a big copper tub. Lady Lily had sent her a bar of scented soap and Mara felt like a hypocrite for accepting a gift from a woman she had sworn to hate. But her guilt did not prevent her from stashing the bar in her satchel.

The chambermaid had styled her hair, brushing it until it gleamed with auburn highlights. Pulling it away from her face, the woman secured it with an old clip that had once belonged to Mara's mother. Dressed in a surcoat that was far too thin for the winter air, Mara passed the time until supper gazing from the window overlooking a neat bailey and very high walls.

Twice, she saw Sir Spencer. He waved to her and she responded weakly, retreating from the window until he moved on. He was a nice man, but she truly wasn't interested and she was coming to regret her attempts to make Kirk jealous. She suspected, if Spencer persisted, that it would be necessary to inform the man he was barking up the wrong tree.

The afternoon had passed into evening and still no Kirk. Niles appeared at her door shortly after sundown, his eyes gleaming with appreciation at the sight of her. Cold in the thin surcoat but without anything to wear other than her mother's worn cloak, Mara braved the chill and allowed him to escort her to the hall where a great feast had been set.

Having never attended a lavish supper, other than the meals at Anchorsholme, Mara was entranced with the beauty and warmth. Banks of tallow candles graced the corners of the room and a massive fire blazed in the hearth. Several people were already seated, including Lady Lily's women. But she turned her nose up at them as she passed their table, snubbing them for having paid attention to Kirk. Niles grinned when he saw what she was up to.

"If you put your nose any further into the air, a bird will nest in it," he murmured in her ear.

139

Mara struggled not to crack a smile. "I am sure I have no idea what you mean."

He laughed softly. "You cannot blame them, Mara. Kirk is like a god to them. Instead of showing your disregard, mayhap you should show your pity. You have, after all, what they want."

She hadn't thought of it that way. Her stance began to soften. "But Lady Lily...."

"Lady Lily is to be married at the end of the month, to a great knight in Henry's court. You needn't worry over her, or the rest of these women. Kirk has eyes only for you."

Her smile broke through, weakly. "And I have eyes only for him." Her smile suddenly faded as her gaze moved across the room. "Oh... my goodness, Niles. I see Sir Spencer. And he is waving to us."

Nile's head snapped in the direction she was indicating and his eyes narrowed. "I think it would be best if we sit over here, away from him." He stopped at the next available space, seating Mara while still keeping check on Spencer. "All we need is for the man to pay you more attention and we shall have a bloodbath on our hands."

Mara's back was to Spencer. "Kirk would really kill him?"

Niles took his seat. "You have no idea what the man is capable of when provoked." He motioned for wine. "I have seen him... well, it does not matter. But he is most protective of you and I...."

"So you have chosen to sit here?" Spencer was on her other side, helping himself to the vacant seat. "Then this will suit me fine, as well. Good eve, Niles."

Mara smiled weakly as Niles cast the man a heady look. Spencer, however, ignored the knight, bringing Mara's hand to his lips.

"My lady looks ravishing tonight," he said smoothly, his pale eyes glittering. "I trust you have a healthy appetite for tonight's fare? Wild boar I killed myself."

Mara pulled her hand away as discreetly as she could manage, glancing about to see if Kirk had entered the room. "How... how impressive, Sir Spencer. I am sure your skill is amazing."

He shrugged modestly, taking a chalice offered by a serving wench. In the balcony, a cluster of minstrels began to play and Mara glanced up, watching the performance. Across the swell of her breasts, Niles and Spencer exchanged glares.

"I have always been rather fond of the hunt," he said, still hexing Niles with his stare. When Mara looked away from the musicians, he smiled warmly. "And you? Do you hunt, my lady?"

She shook her head. "I do not. But I am rather good at catching rabbits. Unfortunately, they are so cute that I have a difficult time killing them."

Spencer laughed, deep and hearty. "Take heart, my lady. Boars are ugly, so you may be guilt-free when consuming their meat."

Mara smiled at his humor, noticing over his shoulder that one of Lady Lily's women seemed to be glaring at her. Her smile faded and, without tact, she pointed at the woman. "Sir Spencer, who is that lady? She is frowning at me."

Spencer glanced over his shoulder, clearing his throat when he realized who Mara was indicating. "That is the Lady Juliet." He turned his back on the woman. "And it is not you she is frowning at, but me."

"You?" Mara lifted an eyebrow. "Have you angered her somehow?"

Spencer wriggled his eyebrows, turning his attention to the guests filling the hall. "I suppose so. I rejected her suit."

"Oh." Mara looked at the lady again, rather small and average-looking. "No wonder she is frowning."

Niles was gulping his wine, his gaze scanning the room in anticipation of Kirk's arrival. He ignored the conversation between Mara and Spencer, mostly because Mara kept it very generic. Whenever he would ask her something of herself, she would give him a vague answer and change the subject. And the message, as Niles saw it, was obvious.

Pleased that she was making an attempt to disinterest the man, Niles was feeling rather comfortable with the situation when his gaze suddenly came to rest on the balcony directly above their table. And who should be staring down at them but none other than Kirk himself.

Niles nearly choked on his wine. He sprayed it over the table, his tunic, leaping to his feet as Mara and Spencer turned to him with concern. He assured them that he was well, already moving away from the table in an attempt to intercept Kirk, who was leaving the balcony and heading down the stairs. Covered with red wine, Niles met his captain halfway down the steps.

"How long were you standing there?" he demanded.

Kirk was in no mood to be interrogated. "I told you to keep him away from her. Now I see I must take matters into my own hands."

Niles put his red-stained hands on Kirk's chest, preventing him from descending. "She is handling him quite well, Kirk. The conversation has been very limited and she has made it obvious that his presence is of little interest to her." When Kirk tried to push past him, Niles asserted himself and shoved Kirk against the railing. "Listen to me! 'Twill be much simpler and far less bloody if Mara discourages the man herself. How do you think le Vay will react if he learns you have challenged one of his knights?"

Kirk eyed him, righting himself where Niles had pushed him off-balance. "Le Vay is aware of my feelings for Mara. He will understand if I must defend what is mine."

"Officially, she is not," Niles reminded him quietly. "Technically, Spencer has every right to pursue her. You have hardly told him otherwise."

A dark eyebrow rose. "But I inferred as much. If the man cannot understand that she belongs to me, then I will gladly teach him a lesson."

"And what lesson is that? That you are bigger, stronger, and by far more skilled? Before this afternoon, you liked Spencer a great deal, Kirk. Now you are determined to kill him?"

"He has eyes for Mara."

"Every man in the room has eyes for Mara. Are you going to kill them all?"

Kirk sighed, his hard stance softening in the slightest. After a moment, he scratched his scalp irritably. "Then what would you suggest? That I simply look the other way while he pants and paws over the woman I will marry?"

Niles shook his head slowly. "I have already suggested the solution. Allow Mara to discourage him in her own way. She was doing quite well when I left."

Kirk pursed his lips, eyeing Niles as he continued to scratch and pace on the narrow stair. "She all but encouraged him this afternoon."

"Because she was seeking revenge against the attention Lily was paying you. Truthfully, Kirk, it would have been well had you informed her of Lily's infatuation."

He shrugged. "It was never an issue. Certainly not enough to explain it to Mara as if it was a viable threat."

Niles grabbed Kirk by the shoulder, shaking him gently. "So you have both punished one another with your schemes and petty jealousies. I would say the time has come to put this foolishness behind you." He released Kirk and began to descend the steps. "Come along, my Irish hooligan. The time has come to return to Mara and forget about Spencer's weak challenge."

Kirk growled in response and, reluctantly, followed Niles into the great room.

The tables were full. The only seat at Mara's table was the one vacated by Niles and the man graciously allowed Kirk to occupy the spot. Ignoring Spencer altogether, Kirk lowered himself onto the bench and kissed Mara's hand sweetly.

"You look lovely, love," he said as if they were alone. "I apologize that my business kept me all afternoon. I hope you were not bored."

She shook her head, beaming into his handsome face. She was terribly glad to see him. "I spent the time looking from the window, watching the happenings of the bailey. I watched the blacksmith shoe a large black charger and when the horse tried to bite him, he punched him in the nose."

Kirk smiled drolly. "Such lady-like entertainment. Is that all you did?"

"I took a bath, with some soap that Lady Lily sent me." She giggled when he held her arm to his nostrils, inhaling deeply. "What do you smell?"

He closed his eyes, lingering in the fine scent. "Jasmine. Rose." He growled and sank his teeth into her arm as Mara squealed with delight. "Christ, you taste good enough to eat. I take it that you and Lady Lily have spoken?"

"Her maid brought the soap. I have not seen nor spoken to Lady Lily."

Kirk glanced over his shoulder at the table behind them, reserved for the le Vay family. He knew that Lionel would insist he sit with the family and he smiled, thinking of Mara struggling to maintain her anger in the face of Lady Lily's overwhelming sweetness.

"You shall have the chance to thank her personally," he said. He was still holding her arm, caressing it, as Spencer watched. "When Lord le Vay and his daughter arrive, we shall sup with them."

"Hardly, my lord." Spencer was cool, his eyes fixed on Kirk over his chalice of wine. "Lord Lionel's sister and her family are visiting from Kent. There is no room for you at the head table."

Kirk sensed the man's pleasure to have informed him that he was being displaced from Lionel's table. With equal calm, he collected his own goblet and took a large swallow.

"I hope you like ships, Sir Spencer," he said casually, "because you shall find yourself aboard one very shortly. Your liege has graciously pledged you to my service when I sail for Ireland later this week to quell a minor rebellion on de Cleveley lands."

This was the first Mara had heard of such a thing. She sat straight in her seat, the brilliant eyes wide. "Ireland? You are going to Ireland?"

Kirk had meant to unbalance Spencer, forgetting the fact that Mara knew nothing of his plans. His expression softened when he saw the shock in her eyes.

"In a few days, love," he said softly. "I shall hardly be gone long enough for you to miss me."

Her jaw dropped. "But... you have said nothing of this. Why did you not tell me before?"

He could see the rising storm and hastened to ease her emotions. "Because nothing was for certain until a day or two ago. I saw no need to worry you."

"*Worry* me?" Mara would not be soothed. She was angry as well as surprised. "You are going to Ireland to quash an uprising and you do not have the courtesy to tell me of your future plans?"

Spencer smiled smugly over his goblet, enjoying Kirk's distress. Kirk could sense the taunting gaze and it only served to inflame him.

"You are not directly involved in my military operations, Mara," he said quietly. "I need not clear my plans through you before I proceed."

She gasped with outrage. "I never indicated that you must. Certainly, it would have been polite to tell me what was happening. Simply so I am prepared for your departure which, I find, may not be soon enough for my taste."

Even though he was remorseful for his snappish statement, he refused to be baited into a verbal brawl. Collecting Mara's chalice, he pushed it into her hands. "Drink."

"But I do not..."

"Drink!"

He nearly shouted at her. Mara took a large swallow, her expression a mixture of fury and fear. Kirk made her take another drink before they continued their conversation, and still another. He was determined to calm her before she veered out of control. And, as he had so often experienced, she could veer out of control quite easily.

"Now," he said softly, shifting in his seat so that Spencer could not hear him. "I apologize for my remark. But I am truthful when I say that the business I handle for Edmund is none of your affair. And I did not want to spoil our last few days together with thoughts of my departure looming over our heads. Can you understand this?"

Her lips were jutted out in a pout, but she nodded. "Aye." The wall of anger crumbling. "But how long will you be gone?"

He collected both of her hands, bringing one and then the other to his lips. "I am not sure. Certainly a few weeks. Maybe months."

"Months?" she repeated, distressed. "But... you cannot leave me!"

"You will be well taken care of."

"Not at Anchorsholme!" She shook her head firmly, fearfully. "All of those women were murdered while you were away and...!"

Kirk shushed her sternly. Even though the rumors regarding The Darkland were common knowledge, still, he did not want Mara adding fuel to the fire.

"No one will touch you." There was urgency to his tone that she dare not dispute. "Do you understand me? No one will touch you. Or Micheline."

Mara would not be convinced. "This is all a convenient ploy," she hissed. "Edmund is sending you away so that he can kill me!"

"Nonsense," he said patiently. "He will not touch you. Have faith in my word, lass, that no harm will befall you. Please?"

He was terribly sincere. Still, Mara was frightened. Frightened for Kirk facing a rebellion and frightened for herself. But most of all, she simply did not want to be separated from him.

"Then I shall come with you." She scooted closer to him, her expression eager as if she thought her idea grand. "I shall be very quiet and obedient and I shall take care of you while you fight."

Kirk shook his head sadly. "You cannot come, lass. A battle is no place for you."

Mara could feel the sting of tears, the painful ache of distance already piercing her heart. "Please, Kirk," she whispered. "Please let me come. I promise I shall not be any trouble."

He touched her cheek tenderly, feeling the painful swell of longing in him as well. "You would come along on a ship full of men, distracting me with your beauty and sweetness when I should be concentrating on my duties?" He shook his head. "You would be the death of me. Not to mention the fact that I would be quite useless."

Mara's brow furrowed and Kirk saw the glimmer of tears. Grabbing her chalice, he forced her to down the contents in the hope of staving off the tide of emotions. But the alcohol was not having the desired effect and the tears began to fall as he gestured to the serving wench for more wine.

Just when he thought he had lost her completely, Lord le Vay and his richly-dressed daughter entered the room and Mara's attention was diverted. A few smiles and a good deal of chatter regarding Lily's elaborate dress caused Mara to forget her sobs. With another dose of wine and a barrage of kisses to her hands, Mara was calming admirably.

Though Spencer wished it was he who was doing the calming. The knight had thus far sat silent throughout the exchange, hearing little of the conversation but aware of the body language. Obviously, there was a good deal of emotion between the lady and Sir Kirk and, being a gracious knight, Spencer should have been willing to relinquish his pursuit. But he realized, as he had when he had first seen the lady, that she was one prize worth fighting for. And he further realized he was determined to win.

Lord le Vay motioned to Kirk as Spencer continued to stare at Mara. Kirk kissed Mara's hand and left the table without as much as a glance to Spencer. While Kirk found himself being introduced to a flock of le Vay relatives, Spencer saw his opportunity arise.

Great platters of food were brought from the kitchens, much to the delight of the famished guests. As a huge boar was set in the center of their table, Spencer immediately sliced off a portion for Mara and placed it neatly on her plate.

"This bugger was a feisty one," he said, cutting his own meat from the thigh. "He nearly gored me before I could kill him."

Mara, still emotionally fragile, found she had no appetite. But Spencer smiled at her encouragingly, going so far as to cut her meat when she simply sat and stared at it. It took a good deal of coaxing for her to taste it, and even then, she chewed slowly and without enthusiasm.

Spencer watched her lethargic movements, setting his knife down after a moment. "Is it not to your liking, my lady?"

Mara shook her head. "It is very good." She swallowed hard, forcing it down. "I... I am simply not hungry."

Spencer was to the point. "Because of Kirk?"

Mara looked at him. Then, she looked away sullenly. "I find I must apologize for my behavior earlier, Sir Spencer. I never meant to... that is to say, I believe I encouraged your attention and I should not have. Sir Kirk and I are... involved."

"Are you betrothed?"

Her brow furrowed and she stared at her hands. "Well... nay, we are not. But he is going to ask Lord Edmund for permission when we return to Anchorsholme."

Spencer stared at her a moment, her silken hair and exquisite profile. She seemed to provoke feelings in him that he had forgotten himself capable of and the desire to continue those warm feelings, and expand them was more than a want. It was a need.

"Tell me, Lady Mara," he said quietly. "Is Kirk the only suitor you have known?"

Mara was thoughtful. "In the true sense," she admitted. "I have known many men, mostly friends of my father or relatives. But Kirk is the only man who has pursued me."

Spencer smiled faintly. "Then tell me; were you to go to the dressmaker, would you simply purchase the first dress offered or would you demand to be shown her selection of patterns before making your choice?"

Mara turned her brilliant blue eyes on him and Spencer was swallowed by their beauty. "What does that have to do with suitors?"

His pale eyes twinkled. "I mean that you should choose carefully your suitor. Not simply take the first man who comes along."

Mara regarded him carefully. "I do not need to sample a variety of men before making my selection. I love Kirk."

Spencer's smile faded somewhat. "Are you sure it is not infatuation?"

"Why would you say that?"

"Because you said yourself he is the first man who has wooed you. Is it possible that the thrill of his attentions has caused you to believe yourself in love with him when, in fact, he has merely succeeded in blinding you with his charm?"

Mara frowned. "I am not a fool, Sir Spencer. I love Kirk and he loves me and we shall be married. "

Spencer cast a long glance at Kirk, currently in conversation with a wrinkled dowager. But the Irish knight caught his stare, the stone-gray eyes blazing across the room. Spencer merely turned back to Mara.

"Kirk Connaught is a career soldier," he said quietly. "The man is thirty-three years old and has never been married. Have you never wondered why?"

Mara shook her head slowly. "Nay."

Now that he had her attention, Spencer focused on his food. "Mayhap you should consider that he is not the marrying kind. You could find yourself taking second place in his heart, well behind his love for fighting and his oath to the House of de Cleveley."

Mara stared at the man as he devoured his meat, turning wide eyes to Kirk as he chatted politely with the old woman in the severe wimple. She simply couldn't believe there was any truth to Spencer's words but was appalled to realize he had given her food for thought. Being rather innocent of men and their games, it was difficult to resist the confusion.

"You are wrong." She turned away from Kirk and from Spencer, taking another bite of meat simply to occupy herself. "Kirk and I shall wed and he shall love me best of all."

Spencer continued to eat. "I certainly hope so, my lady," he said softly. "Speaking for myself, of course, I would most certainly love you best of all. There would be nothing to stand in the way of my devotion."

Mara looked at him sharply. "Sir Spencer, I hardly know you. And I have no interest in becoming your wife."

Spencer's expression did not waver. He wiped his mouth and took a long drink of wine. "Mayhap not at the moment. But know that if your betrothal with Kirk fails to come about, I shall be eager to take his place."

A few of the guests had finished their meal and took to the floor as the musicians played a delicate ballad. Mara refrained from answering Spencer's declaration, partially because she was uncertain how to respond, and instead turned her attention to the dancers. A few more couples joined the gaiety and it took Mara a moment to realize she knew one of the dancers very, very well.

Kirk and Lady Lily were enjoying themselves as they whirled around the floor. Even though Kirk was holding the lady at a proper distance, Mara was infuriated. Intending to interrupt their cozy clutch, she hardly noticed a wrinkled hand in her face.

"Lady Mara." Lord le Vay was smiling at her. "Would you care to dance to a truly Irish folk ballad?"

Mara was caught off-guard by his handsome, old face. Spencer leapt to his feet, swallowing the bite of food in his mouth.

"Good eve to you, my lord," he said formally. "I apologize for my bad manners, but I did not see you coming."

Le Vay waved him off. "Of course you did not see me. You were too busy gawking at Lady Mara." He thrust his hand in her face again, the implication obvious. "Certainly, I can hardly blame you, but now I intend to occupy the lady myself. A dance, if you please?"

Mara stammered. "But... surely you have not yet eaten, my lord. You have only just arrived."

He waved her off. "There is the rest of the night for eating. Now, I wish to dance with a lovely lass."

Mara had no choice. As le Vay guided her onto the stone floor, Spencer caught a glimpse of Kirk and Lily as they enjoyed the dance. Pale blue locked with stone-gray and Spencer realized that Kirk was quite unhappy for three very good reasons; forced to dance with Lady Lily, being separated from Mara while Spencer took the offensive, and also with the fact that le Vay was very busy swinging Mara around the dance floor.

But Spencer wasn't unhappy in the least. In fact, things were going rather well. Taking a drink of his wine, he turned his back on Kirk and Lily as they whirled by. Glancing over his shoulder as Lily's brilliant green surcoat moved away from him, he drained the contents of his chalice; aye, things were going very well indeed.

As Spencer gloated in triumph, across the room Mara was wallowing in misery. Lord le Vay was a nice man but she had no interest in his conversation. Her only concern was Kirk, still holding Lady Lily as the Irish ballad ended and a snappy jig began. Le Vay was rattling on about something and she ignored him, instead, watching as Kirk tried to pull away from his dance partner. But the woman was persistent and as Mara found herself forced to jig with the father, Kirk found himself forced to jig with the daughter.

Fortunately, Mara could jig like the devil himself. She could easily out-dance le Vay and the old man began to huff and chuckle as he struggled through the dance. Bright blue eyes met stone-gray across the floor and Kirk smiled, his gaze never leaving her even as Lily laughed gaily before him.

Warmth and emotion flowed between them even though they were several feet apart. But Mara found her attention diverted as le Vay scooped her up in his arms, tossing her to the man next to him. It was part of the dance and she was not surprised nor offended, but she soon lost sight of Kirk as she was tossed from man to man.

Mara found herself hoping she would eventually be tossed into Kirk's arms and he would sweep her away from these strange, lively people. And then, once they were alone, he would make her forget all of Spencer' disturbing words. A tender touch, a soothing word, and the confusion would leave her.

A pair of strong arms caught her. Very large arms that held her tight and refused to let go. As the men laughed and the women shrieked in the midst of the lively dance, Mara found herself being whisked from the hall. It took her a moment to realize that Spencer was taking her through the kitchens filled with smoke and stench, carrying her out into the chilly night.

The kitchen yards were quiet. Mara was genuinely startled by his actions, finally recovering enough to demand he put her down. But Spencer merely grinned, taking her through an arched gate and emerging into a small, well-manicured garden. Only after he closed the gate did he put her to her feet.

Mara was angry. And she was also very cold in her thin dress. Arms wrapped protectively about her torso, she stamped her foot at Spencer.

"Why did you bring me out here?" she demanded.

He smiled lazily, standing in front of the gate so that she could not escape. "It is far more pleasant out here, away from the crowds and the smoke of the hall. Moreover, you were looking rather miserable. I thought you might enjoy a change of scenery."

"I am cold. And I want to go back to the hall this instant."

He moved toward her. "Then if you are cold, I shall warm you."

She did not like the look in his eye. "Sir Spencer, I can guarantee you shall be sorry if you touch me. You needn't worry about Kirk's wrath, merely my own. Trust me when I tell you it shall be painful."

He stopped, his smile fading. "I... I meant no offense, lady. Certainly I will not touch you if you do not want me to."

"I do not," she said firmly. "I want to go inside."

He watched her walk around him, heading for the gate. But he did not follow, instead, strolling toward a bench resting beside the moon-lit pond.

"I was betrothed, once," he said, loud enough for her to hear. "She died two years ago, one month before we were to be married. I suppose... I suppose that when I saw you, it brought back the feelings I held for Genevieve all over again and naturally, I have had a difficult time controlling myself."

Mara paused by the gate. Against her better judgment, she felt herself softening and she let go the latch, half-open, as she gazed at the knight. His back was to her as he lowered himself on the bench, staring over the waters of the pond.

"I am sorry for your loss," she said softly. She did not know what else to say. "How did she die?"

He tore a leaf from a dead foxglove, picking at it distractedly. "Some strange female ailment. Her mother would not tell me everything, only that she bled to death somehow." He could hear Mara's footfalls as she came up behind him and he repressed the urge to look over his shoulder. As long as she was listening to him, he intended to keep her occupied. Even with a story that brought tears to his eyes. "She was a lovely girl. Tiny, with long brown hair and big brown eyes. And she could sing like an angel."

Mara knew she shouldn't be listening to him; he had been trying to confuse and intimidate her all evening and she had no reason to believe that this was anything other than a ploy. But because he sounded so sincere, she could not help but listen.

"I cannot sing," she said, still standing behind him. "My sister can, a little."

Spencer tossed the leaf he had been toying with into the pond. "I miss my Genevieve. I miss her laughter, her smile. And I suppose when I saw you... well, the attraction was instant. And I saw a chance for happiness again."

Mara was feeling rather torn; he sounded so pathetic. But the fact remained that she wasn't interested in him no matter how sorrowful his past. No matter how much he was attempting to draw her to him. Impulsively, she plopped onto the bench beside him.

"I feel for you, Sir Spencer, truly," she said. "But the fact remains that I am not Genevieve and I am not interested in marrying you. When I flirted with you earlier today, it was for no other reason than to make Kirk jealous. I am truly sorry if I gave you false hope, but you must understand that I love Kirk and I shall be his wife. There will be another woman to heal your heart, I am sure. But that woman is not me."

Spencer turned to her, studying the beauty of her face. "You say that with such certainty. How can you know?"

She lifted an eyebrow. "And I ask you, how can *you* know that I am the woman to replace your Genevieve? If, in fact, she truly existed at all."

His brow furrowed slightly. "I would not lie to you, my lady."

"Not even to entice my pity and, mayhap, even my comfort?"

"Nay," he shook his head slowly. "Is that what you thought?"

She shrugged. "You have spent the evening truly to dissuade me from Kirk. What else am I to think?"

"I was simply trying to help you think clearly, but I will admit it was for purely selfish reasons." His gaze raked her. "But Genevieve... she was very, very real. And the woman who was casting you the evil eye all night is Genevieve's older sister."

Mara's eyebrows rose in mild astonishment. "Lady Lily's woman? But you said you had rejected her suit."

He turned away, his eyes lingering on the pond. "I did. When Geni died, Juliet took it upon herself to marry me. Only I wanted nothing to do with her and she resents me for it."

Mara shook her head, rubbing her arms against the chill of the night. "How terrible for all of you," she said. After a moment, she cast Spencer a long glance. "Then surely you of all people should see the reality of what I am telling you. As you rejected Juliet's suit, I am rejecting yours. I am simply not interested."

He refused to look at her, instead, tearing off another dried twig and tossing the pieces into the pond. "I can change that."

"I do not want you to change it," she said firmly. But her tone was kind. "Spencer, I love Kirk. If you loved Genevieve, then you can understand my position. Please do not make this difficult."

His jaw ticked, his face ghostly beneath the haunting moon. "It was not my intention to be difficult," he said softly. "But I know I can make you happy if you will only give me a chance. Kirk is the only beau you have ever known; how do you know he is the man to love and cherish you for the rest of your life? He guards The Darkland, for Heaven's sake. The man has allowed several murders to happen, overlooking the fact that his liege is a vicious monster simply because he is afraid to confront the truth. Is that the kind of man you wish to marry? Loyal to his oath to the point of injustice?"

Mara never had the chance to reply. A soft hum filled the air and Spencer bolted to his feet, his hand moving to the sword strapped to his thigh. Mara gasped, stumbling away from the bench as flashes of moonlight against metal blinded her. And she knew, even before she saw the face, who had come upon them.

Stone-gray eyes that were as cold as the blade of his broadsword.

CHAPTER FIFTEEN

Kirk faced off against Spencer beneath the silver moon, blade upon blade, will against will. And from the look in Spencer' eyes, Kirk knew it would not be an easy fight.

"So you bring her into the night to feed her lies against me." Kirk shook his head slowly. "I once considered you my friend, Spencer. I can see that I was mistaken."

Spencer did not waver. His hand was steady, his broadsword against Kirk's. "You were not mistaken, my lord. But there are times when friendship pales in comparison to desire. And in response to your accusation, I did not feed the lady lies against you. Nothing I have said has been untrue."

Kirk regarded him carefully, his words directed at Mara. "Has he been bold against you, lass?"

Terrified of what was to come, Mara shook her head. "Nay, Kirk. He never touched me."

"But he has tried to turn you against me."

Tension filled the air. And Mara knew, once the battle started, it would only end when death claimed one of the combatants. And the thought that Kirk might fall victim scared her to death.

Quickly, she moved to his side, a gentle hand on the arm that held the sword. "He could never turn me against you," she said softly. "Please come back to the hall with me. I want to dance."

"In good time, lass," he said steadily. "After I take care of your suitor."

"I do not want you to 'take care' of him." She tugged on his arm. "I want you to come with me, now. Please?"

Kirk moved away from her, placing her out of the line of fire. "Return to the hall and find Niles," he told her. "Tell him that I have need of him."

Mara watched the men tense, preparing for the first strike. "Nay!" she cried. "Kirk, please do not! I promise I shall..!"

"There will be rules established, my lord." Spencer interrupted Mara's pleas. He sounded so terribly cold. "To the death."

"As expected."

"No mercy."

"None given."

"And the lady belongs to the winner."

"The lady belongs to me."

Spencer cocked an eyebrow, watching Kirk as the man circled around, bringing them further and further away from Mara. When the blows started, they would be hard and furious and if she happened to be in the way, the results could be deadly.

"If I win, my lord, she will belong to me."

Kirk continued to move back, away from the wall lest he be trapped against it. Spencer' blade was still poised against Kirk's as he followed the man's movements, his young face determined and fearless.

"You shall not win."

The first blow came heavy, sparks flying into the damp night air. Mara screamed with fear as Kirk plowed into Spencer with an unearthly strength. Knowing she had been forgotten, she did not try to stop the battle. She suspected there was only one man who had a chance of bringing about a bloodless cessation. Turning on her heel, she raced for the keep as fast as her legs could carry her.

The men locked in combat never saw her leave. Spencer was meeting Kirk's onslaught admirably, but in truth he was having a difficult time. Kirk was larger, stronger, and had the advantage. But Spencer was young and quick, providing a reluctant target for Kirk's rage. Sparks from the broadswords burst against the backdrop of the dead garden as the battle raged.

Kirk backed Spencer against the small bench overlooking the pond. But the young knight deftly leapt over the seat, sloshing through the water with Kirk in pursuit. The noise was deafening as broadswords met with each other, the old bench, and in one case several stalks of dead foxgloves.

A few servants had heard the commotion and came to watch, joined by several soldiers. It wasn't often that they were treated to a true swordfight, with the grace and skill that made the spectacle exciting to watch. But it was also apparent that the stakes of this match were high, higher still when Kirk landed a heavy blow to Spencer' armorless forearm. Blood streamed from the wound, sprinkling the ground with every move.

"Why do not..." Spencer grunted as he countered Kirk's thrust. "... you simply leave the lady to a younger man. Do you truly think you can..." he grunted again as he narrowly avoided being gored. "... make her happy?"

Kirk would not be distracted with chatter. With a growl, he lunged for Spencer, anticipating the man's reaction and thereby countering. The result saw Spencer stabbed in the shoulder.

"You have no idea what you're saying," he breathed, taking a step back as a wounded Spencer took the offensive. "We are very happy. More so after I marry her. Why couldn't you have simply left her alone?"

"Because I want her." Spencer backed Kirk against a cluster of dead daisy bushes. Kirk simply plowed through the bramble, fending off the younger knight's energetic blows. "When you saw her for the first time, did you not feel the same?"

"I did."

"And if she had been involved with another man but not yet betrothed, would you have still pursued her?"

The vicious thrusts slowed, coming to an unsteady halt. Panting and sweating, the men stared at one another.

"Mayhap," Kirk said quietly. In truth, he would have done exactly what Spencer had done. "But tell me; if it were you she was involved with and I attempted to woo her away from you, would you not react as I have?"

Spencer's expression tightened. "I would have killed you."

There was nothing more to be said. The swords came up again.

***

The great hall was warm and smoky, smelling of meat and dogs. Mara raced into the hall, searching frantically for Lord le Vay. But the only familiar face she saw was that of Lady Lily, seated at the head table with her relatives. All jealousy for the woman aside, Mara pushed her way through the crowd of people and servants.

"Where is your father?" she demanded breathlessly.

Lily looked shocked. "I... I believe he has gone to his solar with my uncle. Is something wrong, Lady Mara?"

Mara realized she was very close to tears. And Lady Lily's kind eyes somehow intensified her anguish. "Kirk... he and... oh, I must find your father!"

Lily did not question her further. It was apparent that something was very, very wrong. "Then I shall take you to him immediately."

They ran from the hall. Lily led her through the tall, narrow foyer and into a smaller corridor. To their left a warm room beckoned, scented of hides and liquor. Lionel was seated before the fire, laughing softly with an older man as his daughter and Mara stumbled into the room.

"Father!" Lily said. "Something is...!"

"It's Kirk, my lord," Mara gasped. "He has challenged Spencer and even now they are battling in the garden. You must stop them!"

Lionel leapt from his chair, his bushy eyebrows aloft. "They are battling?" he boomed. "Great Gods! I told Kirk to leave Spencer alone!"

He propelled his girth from the room, leaving Lily and Mara to follow. Lionel took the long route to the garden, not wanting to enter the great hall and create havoc for his guests with his brusque manner. Skirting the perimeter of the keep, he passed through a small fortified door and emerged into the bailey. He could hear the clash of broadswords almost immediately.

Mara hadn't realized that Lily was holding her hand as they reached the entrance to the garden. Lionel burst through the gate with the fearful ladies in tow, watching in horror as Kirk backed a bloodied Spencer against the wall with merciless strikes.

"Kirk!" he roared. "Enough!"

Kirk immediately came to a halt, breathing heavily as he turned to the source of the shout. Spencer, seeing that Kirk was distracted, brought up his sword. But Kirk caught the movement, turning away before the man could spear him deep in the belly. Instead, the broadsword passed cleanly though the muscle of his torso, just below the ribs. Had Spencer's aim been an inch to the right, he would have missed altogether.

Mara screamed as Kirk whirled away from Spencer, bleeding profusely. Lionel rushed forward, putting his rotund body between the two knights.

"Enough, both of you!" he bellowed, his hard gaze on Spencer. "An unfair move, Spencer. You're too good a knight to indulge in such unethical tactics!"

Spencer pushed himself off the wall, trembling as a result of his blood loss. "It was perfectly legal. My opponent was distracted and, as we know, distraction can be deadly."

Lionel glared at him. "When I called a halt to this battle, I meant the both of you." He glanced at Kirk, standing tall and strong in spite of the fact that blood was streaming from his wound. "And you. I told you not to kill Spencer, did I not?"

"He gave me little choice, my lord," Kirk replied steadily. "I warned him against pursuing the lady and he chose to ignore me."

Le Vay sighed heavily, looking to his blond-haired captain. "You knew the lady was spoken for and still you pursued her? I find this difficult to comprehend, Spencer."

Spencer emitted a ragged sigh, wiping the sweat from his brow and gingerly touching the wound in his shoulder. "Some things in the world are worth fighting for, my lord," he said quietly. "She is one of them."

Le Vay did not reply for a moment, waiting for Kirk to erupt. But the knight remained silent and Lionel maintained his gaze on the young knight.

"No more, Spencer," he said, more gently. "It is obvious that you are not meant to have the lady. I would demand you leave her, and Kirk, in peace."

Spencer eyed his liege before gazing at Kirk. The reluctance, the defiance, was obvious. But the young knight said nothing as he turned away, wearily moving for the gate.

Le Vay watched him stagger his way through the garden, a genuine sadness filling him. Spencer had been devastated by Genevieve's death two years prior and this was the first occasion the man had shown interest in another woman. An interest that had been proven tumultuous. Still, it showed that the death of his lady had not permanently damaged him; indeed, he was capable of feeling again.

"Lily," le Vay indicated his daughter, "assist Spencer if you would."

Lily obeyed, helping the weary knight from the shadowed garden. Mara was left standing alone, her eyes wide, as Kirk and Lionel faced one another.

"This does not please me." Le Vay's voice was quiet. "You knew better than to challenge him."

Kirk's stance was unwavering. "I explained my reasons, my lord. I was given little choice."

Le Vay sighed heavily, pondering the situation as Kirk's wound continued to ooze. The knight had broken out in a cold sweat, indicative of his pain and exhaustion. After a moment, Lionel simply shook his head.

"You will understand when I withdraw my permission for Spencer to accompany you to Ireland," he said. "And I would suspect you will have little objection."

Kirk's stone-gray gaze was even. "I plan to leave before the end of the week. Spencer's shoulder wound will take longer than that to heal."

Le Vay cocked an eyebrow. "That is not what I meant and well you know it. I shall not have you two battling each other when it's the bloody Irish you should be focused on." He turned away, glancing at Mara as he moved for the gate. "Tend your knight, lady. And I would suggest you keep him out of my sight for the remainder of the eve."

Mara nodded obediently, watching the old man leave the garden. Slowly, she turned to Kirk.

"I am so sorry," she whispered. "Please forgive me for causing all of this."

He stood there, staring at her. After a moment, he sighed heavily and attempted to sheathe his sword. "You are not responsible, lass. There is no one to blame but myself and Spencer."

He was struggling wearily with the sword, his left side soaked with a growing red stain and Mara moved forward, practically yanking the weapon from his grip. "Give this to me," she demanded quietly. "Let us go inside where I can tend your wound."

He let her take the sword, although it was a struggle for her to simply hold the thing. He continued to gaze at her as she put his great arm around her shoulder, his blood staining her dress. Gently, she urged him forward.

The servants and soldiers that still lingered fled in all directions when Mara and Kirk emerged from the gate. Kirk's pace was slow as Mara nursed him across the courtyard, exhausted herself from lugging his sword. Kirk wasn't particularly weak from the battle, but he found himself emotionally drained more than anything. When they entered the dark corridors of the keep, he took the sword from Mara lest it drag her to the ground.

By the time they reached her chamber, blood had stained the top of his hose but the wound was sealing itself. Mara had him remove his tunic, sending a serving wench for hot water and rags. Waiting for the woman to return, Kirk stretched out on Mara's pretty bed and smeared blood all over the coverlet.

Mara moved to the edge of the bed as he lay with his eyes closed, timidly examining the puncture. It was clean, about two inches in length, and she decided it would be best to simply clean it and bind him tightly. In truth, she had never sewn a wound in her life and was nauseated with the thought of sticking a needle into Kirk's flesh. Peering closer at the rather sickening injury, she was unaware that his eyes had opened.

"It should take about eight stitches," he said quietly, watching her turn shades of green. "Small ones, if you please."

She swallowed hard, daring to look him in the eye. "I... I have never sewn a wound. I do not think I can."

He smiled faintly. "Certainly you can. I shall help you."

She made a face of disgust. "Kirk, I do not think...."

A sharp rap at the door interrupted her. Gladly, she answered and Niles burst into the room. One look at Kirk's bloody torso and the man came apart.

"Christ!" he exclaimed, rushing to the bed. "What in the hell happened?"

Kirk was quite cool. "Spencer pressed his attentions and I was forced to defend my interests." He cocked an eyebrow at Niles' dismayed expression. "The lady was not persuasive enough in her attempts to be rid of him. I had no other choice."

"There is always a choice," Niles insisted. "The entire castle has heard of the clash and considering this is Spencer' domain, they are siding with him."

"I care not who the people of Quernmore side with. Spencer did all he could to take Mara away from me and I did what I felt necessary to dissuade him."

Niles looked at Mara, standing rather pale next to the bed. She looked terribly guilty and he refrained from comment; it was no one's fault in particular, but Niles was concerned with the fact that le Vay seemed to be taking a good deal of grief from his vassals who wanted Kirk sent home to

Anchorsholme in disgrace. He had been in the great hall for the past several minutes, listening to the rising displeasure.

"I suppose we can thank God that you did not kill the man," he muttered, casting Kirk's wound a long glance before turning away. "Were that the case, I am sure we would have a mob on our hands. You must remember, Kirk, that Spencer is very much loved here at Quernmore. Whether or not he tried to steal your lady."

Kirk was well aware of the situation and the consequences that could have transpired. And he certainly wasn't blind to le Vay's disappointment or the fact that his military support was now in jeopardy. With a grunt of effort, he swung his legs over the bed.

"Then I suppose I should soothe the situation before it grows out of hand," he said, wincing as he rose to his feet. "Clearly I am to be made the villain in all of this."

Mara rushed to his side. "You cannot! I must tend your wound!"

He cast her an amused expression. "How? With kisses and magic? Not a minute ago you informed me that you had no intention of sewing it."

She frowned. "I never said that I did not intend to sew it. I simply said that I had never sewn a wound before."

He looked around for his stained tunic, his voice mockingly high as he repeated her words. "'Kirk, I do not think I can sew your hideous gash.'" When Niles snickered, Kirk turned to Mara with a smirk on his face. "Fear not, you spineless creature. I shall survive without your needle and thread."

Her cheeks pinkened, torn between extreme anger and the urge to giggle. "How dare you taunt me." She stamped her little foot. "Very well, then. Go and make your attempts to soothe the vicious mob and I hope they tear you limb from limb for your efforts!"

He grinned broadly, pulling the tunic over his head. Putting his fingers in the hole left by Spencer, he gasped like a woman and pretended to faint at the sight of his wound. Mara rushed at him, slapping him with her little hands.

"You're a horrible, nasty man!" She struggled with him even as he grabbed her, laughing deeply. "Out of my sight before I use your own sword against you!"

He tried to kiss her but she slapped his lips, drawing guffaws from Niles. Laughing as she continued to wrestle with him, Kirk groaned when he moved suddenly to avoid being hit in the belly. All struggles and frivolity came to an end.

"Kirk!" Mara gasped. "Did I hurt you? Are you all right?"

He eyed her, his hand to his left side. "You have sorely taxed me, you brutal wench. If you will not sew this scratch, then I suppose I shall have to find someone who will."

"Lily sews a rather beautiful stitch," Niles said, a grin playing on his lips. "Mayhap you should seek her skills."

"Lily is tending Spencer," Mara said before Kirk could reply. Casting Kirk a long glance, she nodded with resignation. "I suppose I shall have to do it if you're going to whine about it. Niles, would you procure a needle and thread for me, please?"

Niles dipped his head. "With pleasure, my lady."

It wasn't as bad as she had imagined. With Niles' expert guidance, Mara managed to put seven stitches in Kirk's side and, rather pleased that she hadn't vomited in the process, smiled triumphantly at her pale patient. Kirk patted her on the head, his fatigue and blood loss rendering him weak and sleepy.

Still, he intended to find le Vay and apologize for his actions. But the longer he lay on the soft mattress, the more tired he became. By the time Niles left the room, Kirk was snoring softly on the blankets.

Mara bolted the door after Niles departed. A fire blazed brightly in the hearth and she moved to douse the spirit candles, two by the bed and another on a small table by the door. The strange bedchamber was warm and dim, shadows from the flickering flames dancing on the walls as she stood beside the bed and removed her surcoat.

It fell in a heap on the floor. Carefully, she peeled back the linens and crawled into bed, being sure not to disturb Kirk. He lay on the top of the coverlet, sleeping an exhausted sleep, and she kissed him tenderly on the cheek. Gazing at his masculine beauty, memorizing every line of his face, she smiled faintly as she snuggled beneath the covers.

But sleep did not come as easily for her as it had for him. Mara did not know how long she lay there, listening to the strange sounds around her and Kirk's soft snoring. It was cold in the room in spite of the fire and she pressed against him, relishing his heat. But still, she could not sleep.

His shoulder was next to her face and Mara found herself tracing the powerful lines of his muscles, touching the large veins that bulged through the skin. Her small fingers moved upward, feeling the stubble of his neck and tickling the cleft in his chin. Involved in her exploration, she propped herself up on an elbow to inspected his ears, noting that the lobes were perfectly formed. Finding a tiny scar just under his jaw, she was in the process of examining it when Kirk groaned softly.

"You're going to be the death of me, lass."

She smiled. "What do you mean by that?"

His eyes rolled open, clouded with sleep. "What I mean is that I would like to sleep. I *should* sleep, considering I have lost a good deal of blood." A great hand came up, cupping her chin. "But all I can think of at this moment is making love to you until the sun rises."

She put her face in his neck, nuzzling his scratchy skin. "I thought I might lose you today, Kirk. And the thought of you going to Ireland to quell a rebellion frightens me to death. If you were to die..."

"I will not," he said firmly, grunting as he rolled off the bed. Pulling back the coverlet he had been sleeping on, he removed his hose and climbed into bed beside Mara. Gathering her in his arms, he sighed raggedly at the feel of her delicious body. "Trust me, love. Never doubt that I shall return to you."

Her naked skin against his, Mara was giddily content. "But what if you do not? What if you die and I am left with nothing?" She wrapped her arms around his neck, bright blue eyes melding with stone-gray. "Give me something to remember you by."

He grinned, kissing her chin, her cheek. "Gladly. Other than my body and soul, what else would you have?"

She stared off into the darkness of the room as his lips moved down her neck. "A son."

He stopped. Abruptly, he pulled away, staring at her. "What did you say?"

Mara was resolute. "I want a son." She touched his face, smiling in response to his shock. "Why does this surprise you? We are to be married, are we not? Whether I conceive now or on our wedding night will make no difference."

Odd that she was reflecting his own thoughts on the night he had taken her maidenhood. A son. But not so odd considering how much they thought alike. Or how very much they felt for one another.

"But... Mara, we shall not be married until I return from Ireland," he said. "There will not be time before I leave. And I could be gone months, lass. Time enough for your condition to announce to the world our ill restraint."

"You would be ashamed, then?"

"Never. But I would not want you to feel ashamed or humiliated."

"Bearing your child would make me proud." She continued to smile. "You once told Edmund that we take whatever child God gives us, male or female. And the same can be said for the timing of the child, Kirk. We have no control over such things. For all we know, I have already conceived considering this sin we have committed was established by God to create a child. Has that not occurred to you?"

160

He nodded vaguely, swallowed by the emotion from the bright blue eyes. "It has. And so has something else."

"What is that?"

His eyes twinkled. "Your sister was right. You do have a good deal of common sense, though you like to pretend otherwise."

Mara laughed softly. "And my common sense tells me that I want your son, no matter what the cost. A son for the great Master of Anchorsholme."

"It could be a lass."

"Would you be disappointed?"

"Perish the thought."

Mara gazed at him, feeling the pull of emotion overwhelm her. Lowering her head, she brushed her lips against his. "Then give me your son, Kirk Connaught," she breathed against his mouth. "Give me your life so that you will never, ever leave me."

He growled, pulling her tight against him and plunging his tongue into her mouth. Mara wrapped her legs around him as he rolled on top of her, feeling his weight and power with the greatest of joy.

"Kirk," she gasped as his lips moved to her breast. "I do love you. I love you with all my heart."

He paused, his gray eyes filled with emotion. "Oh, Mara," he whispered. "You know the feeling is very, very mutual. I cannot remember when I have not loved you."

There were tears in her eyes. "When I raked my nails across your face?"

He shook his head. "Not even then." He lifted himself so he was level with her gaze. "But if it worries you so, then make amends to me."

She kissed his scabs, so tenderly that Kirk could literally feel her reverence. "There," she murmured. "Better?"

"Hmm, much." He kissed her in return, gathering her against him once more. "And it shall be better still."

Mara wrapped her legs around his hips, feeling his arousal push at her. Kirk's hand was to her breast, his lips against her forehead, her cheek, as he murmured words of love and desire. With every caress, every kiss, the fire in her loins grew and she thrust her pelvis forward, capturing the tip of his seeking manhood. Kirk groaned, bracing himself, as he finished what she had started by pushing deep into her body.

The first heavy thrust rocked her. Mara gasped with pleasure, lifting her arms and grasping the bedpost for support as he thrust into her again and again. She was slick with passion, fully prepared to accept all of the maleness he had to offer.

"Harder, Kirk," she breathed. "Do it... harder."

He nearly exploded, her words of lust driving him to the brink. But he controlled himself, obeying her command by pumping firmly into her responsive little body. Mara squirmed and panted, lifting her pelvis to meet him, demanding pleasure only he could supply.

The world rocked. Mara could feel Kirk's hand on her breasts as he drove into her, pinching her nipples into hard pellets. Her legs held him tight, squeezing him against her as the heat of desire mounted.

Mara savored the exquisite blaze in her loins, remembering how Kirk had so ably doused the fire with his magical touch. And she wanted to experience the same pleasure again. Releasing the bedpost, she pulled his mouth to her swollen lips.

"Make me feel as you did last night," she whispered between heated kisses. "The pleasure... the feelings, Kirk. Bring them back to me."

"In time, love." He suddenly rolled onto his back, still joined to her. "All in good time."

Mara gasped with the swift movement as she ended up on top of him. Kirk grinned up at her, both hands moving to her supple breasts.

"You wanted feelings, love?" He thrust his hips upward, slowly. "The make your own feelings. Ride me as I ride you."

Hair wildly askew, Mara looked puzzled. Kirk moved again, encouragingly, until she timidly took the lead. Pushing herself up, she grinned wickedly when he groaned.

"Like this?" She slid down on him and pushed up again. Repeating the process, she watched Kirk twitch and moan. "Do you like this?"

He nodded weakly, his eyes closed. "Christ, woman. I am mere putty in your hands."

Mara grinned. She could make her own wonderful feelings by impaling herself on him, sliding the length of his shaft and feeling her body shudder with delight. The rhythm soon became steady, the pulse pounding, and in little time Mara felt the familiar explosion ripple through her groin. Kirk held her hips firmly, feeling her muscles milk him, demanding his seed. He could not help but answer.

Mara felt him erupt deep inside her and she smiled, eyes closed and head lolling. "That's right," she murmured, squirming atop him to drain every last drop. "Give it all to me, Kirk. Give me your son."

In spite of his pleasure and exhaustion, Kirk laughed softly. "Is that all you want me for?"

Her eyes were still closed. Lazily, she smiled. "Aye."

He took a deep breath as the waves of rapture faded, pulling her against his chest. Weak and sated, Mara dozed to the sound of his pounding heart.

Kirk's lips caressed her forehead, his thoughts turning from their lovemaking to his impending trip to Ireland. The urge to take her with him was tremendous, but he knew in his heart she must stay behind. Still, the thought of separation ate away at him like a cancer and he gathered her closer, pulling the linens over them both in a protective cocoon.

"Kirk?"

He had thought she was asleep. "What is it, love?"

"Do I have to stay at Anchorsholme while you are gone?"

Her head was tucked under his chin and he caressed her back, gazing into the darkness. "There is little choice. Where else would you stay?"

"Haslingden Hall." She lifted her sleepy face to meet his gaze. "Mayhap you could supply an escort to guard me while you are away."

He sighed; truthfully, the idea wasn't a bad one. "What of Micheline? She will have to remain at Anchorsholme."

Mara pushed the hair from her eyes, making a face. "Edmund doesn't like her, anyway. Mayhap he will allow her to return to Haslingden simply to be rid of her."

He lifted an eyebrow. "I doubt that. But supposing I allowed you returned to Haslingden, the place is in shambles. Do you truly wish to return to such poverty?"

She could see he was trying to talk her out of it. Mara stared at him, realizing that if he truly had confidence that nothing would happen to her at Anchorsholme, then he would have discouraged her idea from the onset. Instead, he actually seemed interested. And that worried her.

"I would rather return to Haslingden that meet my death at Anchorsholme," she said. "And I can see that you agree."

"I told you that nothing would happen to you at Anchorsholme."

"But you do not fully believe that, else you would not have allowed me to entertain the thought of returning to Haslingden." She eyed him a moment. "If neither place is acceptable, then you could always ask Lord le Vay to watch over me."

He looked as if he had been struck. "With Spencer waiting to steal you when my back is turned?" He snorted rudely. "I think not, lady."

She shrugged. "It was merely an idea. I did not say that I wanted to stay here."

"And you shan't," he said firmly, miffed by her suggestion. "The mere idea is ludicrous."

"Fine, fine," she agreed simply because he seemed so agitated, "I apologize for even mentioning it."

He glared at her and she smiled sweetly, kissing him on the nose. "You shall stay at Anchorsholme," he said, struggling to maintain his stern attitude in the face of her kisses. "You and Micheline shall be safe from harm, I swear it."

"But you will be in Ireland," she said, kissing his chin and feeling his body react to her. "How can you be sure?"

He softened, his affront fading as she began to kiss his broad shoulder. "By threatening Edmund's life," he rumbled, his hands moving from her back to her buttocks. "If anything happens to you, I shall make sure his death is not pleasant."

"And you are sure he will listen?"

Kirk's hands were moving down her slender thighs, pulling her knees apart as he wedged his big body between them. "He will listen. Especially if I threaten Johanne."

Mara paused in her kisses, casting him a strange glance. "You would harm a woman?"

One hand moved from her knee to her private core, fingering the thatch of dark curls. "Johanne is not a woman, Mara," he muttered. "She is a mad beast and I suspect it is she, and not Edmund, who is behind the vanishings."

Mara did not like the sound of that at all. "What makes you believe so?"

Kirk was silent a moment. "Because the women who vanished had all shown me undue attention. I never responded to any of them, but it is well known that Johanne is rather fond of me and her jealousy feeds her madness." His hands moved to her buttocks again, caressing them. "And that is why we will live in Ireland, far away from Anchorsholme and far away from Johanne's insanity. But until then, I have no doubt that you shall be untouchable to the evil forces of Anchorsholme. You are the only woman I have ever loved and that fact alone shall place you above harm. If some mishap befalls you, the wrath of The Master shall be severe."

Mara gazed at him, wanting so desperately to believe him. "Promise?"

"I do."

She would not dream of disputing his vow. Smiling weakly, she kissed his smooth lips. "Then I shall wait for your return at Anchorsholme."

His hands moved to her thighs again, pulling her closer as he responded to her kisses. "And have no doubt that I will return," he breathed, feeling her love-slick sheath draw him in. "I love you, Mara. Always remember that."

The sun rose before they realized it.

CHAPTER SIXTEEN

Micheline had spent an entire day and night in the small, dingy little tower room, peering from the skinny lancet window that emitted light and air into the room and wondering what on earth was going to happen to her. Now, as dawn broke, she was terrified, hungry, and cold. It would seem the curse of The Darkland was infecting her as well.

Thank God Mara is away, was all she could think. Stoic in her fate, she comforted herself by knowing that Mara was safe with Kirk, far away from the hellish walls of Anchorsholme.

The chamber had become her tomb, both comforting and terrifying. Huddled against the wall beneath the lancet window, she could hear the activity below as the people began to go about their day. She wondered when, or if, Sir Corwin would return with something to eat or perhaps something to stay warm with. She had nearly frozen during the night as the tomb turned to ice in the cold temperatures. The walls bore no warmth. She had felt as if she was in a grave.

With the cold and the fear came the reflection of her actions. Perhaps she should not have confronted Edmund and Johanne as she had. Perhaps she simply should have accepted things as they were. At least she would have been safe, but the cost would have been her self-respect and, in a manner, her very soul.

She cringed every time she thought of the pair, trying not to think of them, now wondering what her destiny would be. Would Corwin tell Kirk what had become of her when the man returned from Quernmore? If he did, Kirk surely would tell Mara, and her sister was not very good at keeping her mouth shut. She might even go after Edmund and Johanne for what they did and... Micheline shuddered. The situation might go from bad to worse.

As Micheline sat in the corner and chewed her nails, the door rattled. She jumped, terrified, her gaze on the door and positive that Edmund was about to come charging through with a dagger in his hand. She could hear the old bolt being thrown and she stumbled to her feet, preparing to defend herself. As the door swung open, she shrieked, but two familiar faces shushed her harshly.

"My lady!" Lady Valdine hissed, holding up her hands for silence. "You must not..."

"... make a sound lest Lord Edmund..."

"... hear you!"

Wanda shut the door swiftly as the two rushed into the room. Micheline was so startled, and so relieved, that she ended up stumbling back against the wall and sliding to her buttocks. The women had bundles in their arms and immediately went to Micheline as she cowered against the wall.

"My husband told me what happened," Valdine said. "Are you..."

"... injured, my lady?"

Micheline shook her head as Wanda knelt on her other side. "I am not injured," she said. "But I am cold and hungry."

Valdine nodded as she pulled out a sack from amongst all of the items she had brought. "We have brought you food," she said. "We have also..."

"... brought fresh clothing and water with which to bathe. Do you feel strong enough?"

Micheline accepted a hunk of brown bread from Valdine and tore into it, starving. "What of Corwin? Where is he?"

Valdine looked rather somber and because she dampened, so did her sister. "There is great trouble in de Cleveley's Irish lands," she said. "My husband..."

"... has taken an army and gone to meet..."

"... Sir Kirk on the docks of Fleetwood. They leave..."

"... for Ireland tomorrow morning."

Micheline swallowed what was in her mouth. "Leaving for Ireland?" she repeated. "Kirk is going to Ireland? But where is my sister?"

Valdine produced a bladder of wine and handed it to Micheline. "We can only assume she..."

"... is still at Quernmore Castle with Lord le Vay. Perhaps..."

"... Sir Kirk has asked that she remain there while he away. It would..."

"... be the safe thing to do."

Micheline thought on that as she sipped the wine. "Then I am glad," she murmured. "I am terrified of what will happen if she returns here."

Valdine and Wanda nodded in unison. "We can only assume..."

"... that Sir Kirk will not want her returned here while he is unable to protect her. Corwin..."

"... had hoped that Sir Kirk would return shortly to escort you from Anchorsholme, but..."

"... he is leaving for Ireland on the morrow and we do not know when he shall return. Therefore..."

"... we must find someone else to take you from this place."

Micheline gazed at the pair as she took a big bite of tart, white cheese. "Take me where?"

Valdine shrugged. "There is..."

"... a priory in Crosby. Corwin thought perhaps..."

"... you could seek sanctuary there. You must..."

"... leave Anchorsholme, my lady. If Edmund finds you..."

"... he will kill you himself. He ordered you..."

"... dead and you are clearly not dead."

Micheline knew that. Still, to hear them speak of it was terrifying and sickening. Her chewing slowed. Swallowing the bite in her mouth, she sipped at the wine again. She was pensive.

"How do you plan to remove me from this place?" she asked. "It will not be a simple thing. You must disguise me somehow."

Valdine and Wanda nodded, mirror image. "We will seek help," Valdine said. "We will..."

"... collect peasant clothing and..."

"... find a soldier who will escort you to Crosby. We promise we..."

"... will take you from this place, my lady. We do not want..."

"... to see you end up as the others have."

Micheline didn't have much of an appetite any more. Her pale eyes moved between the two women, seeing that they, too, were afraid but nonetheless willing to help her. She was truly touched that they should risk themselves so. But in their eyes she saw more than fear; she saw anguish. It was a telling expression.

"You know who has done the killing," she murmured, a statement more than a question. "You know who does these terrible things."

Wanda looked at her sister, but Valdine was looking at Micheline. She didn't reply for a moment. "We have a suspect," she said quietly. "But there..."

"... was nothing we could do to help. The young women..."

"... were taken in the night before..."

"... we could do anything to help. My husband..."

"... would never speak of the disappearances. He said..."

"... it is better to let the dead lie before the same thing..."

"... happens to us."

Micheline studied them intently. "Did Corwin ever try to help the women?" she asked. Then, a dark glimmer came to her eye. "Or... dear God, was he a party to the crimes?"

Valdine lowered her gaze. "We suspect that..."

"... Edmund threatened to harm us if..."

"... he did not do as he was told."

Micheline's eyes widened. "Do as he was told?" she repeated. "*What* was he told?"

Valdine shook her head, her features paler than usual. "Please," she begged softly. "Do not..."

"... ask questions that you will not..."

"... like the answer to. My husband has asked us to..."

"... remove you from Anchorsholme and that..."

"... is what we shall do. Do not ask more than that."

Micheline didn't like any of what she was hearing. Too much pointed to Corwin as a source of guilt in The Darkland's disappearances but she didn't say anymore. Perhaps she was wrong. He had, after all, saved her. All she could think of at the moment was getting out of Anchorsholme. The rest she would worry about when she wasn't in mortal danger.

"I will not," she told them. "I am deeply grateful for your help. And I shall be ready to leave as soon as you have found someone to escort me."

The women didn't say much more after that. As Micheline finished off the remainder of the food, Valdine and Wanda helped her change into warmer clothing. They also fashioned a pallet for her out of the blankets they had brought. They tried to make her as comfortable as possible in her tower prison, all the while thinking of the plans that lay ahead. They had to remove Baroness Bowland and inconspicuously as possible, which would not be an easy task. Although Corwin had sworn them to secrecy, the ladies knew that they would need help.

The population of Anchorsholme held no love for Edmund. There was too much fear and contempt there for the man, something that was ingrained into the history of the castle. They would have to depend on that hatred in order to save the baroness' life.

***

"The missive arrived this morning," Le Vay said softly. "I have already read it. I am sorry, Kirk."

It was just after sunrise in Lionel's lavish solar with its hide rugs and glass from Venice. It spoke of a man well-traveled and wealthy, but Kirk didn't pay any notice. He had been summoned from his bed several minutes earlier with news of a missive for him newly arrived from Anchorsholme. He had been curious but not concerned, and that had been his undoing. He had been caught off guard.

Now, he was staring at a piece of vellum upon which was inscribed hastily written words. He recognized Edmund's writing, almost unrecognizable scrawl. All he could feel as he read the words, over and over, was grief. Pure, unmitigated grief.

"I suppose in hindsight it is not a surprise," he finally said. "We knew there were winds of revolt, but my father...."

He sighed heavily, unable to continue, as Lionel watched him carefully. The missive had carried bad news indeed and he was not without compassion.

"I never knew your father," he said quietly. "I understood he was a magnificent knight."

Kirk nodded slowly, thinking on the man he favored greatly, now cut down by rebels. *My father is dead.* It made him feel sick to think about it.

"He was," he murmured, realizing his throat was tight with emotion. "I shall miss him."

Lionel could feel the man's sorrow and he was deeply sympathetic. "I know what it is like to lose someone you care for," he said after a moment. "I lost my son several years ago when he was newly knighted. He was cut down by archers during a siege at Kenilworth Castle. It was perhaps the worst day of my life."

Kirk glanced up at the man. "I remember when that happened," he said. "I knew your son, if you recall. Michael was a fine man."

Lionel shrugged, not particularly wanting to relive that agony. It was still his daily companion, like a ghost that never went away. He gestured at the vellum.

"What else does Edmund say about the siege?" he asked. "Don't you have brothers at Wicklow as well?"

Kirk looked back at the missive. "I do," he replied, "but he does not mention them. Just my father. He says I am to meet Anchorholme's troops at the port tomorrow morning. We sail for Wicklow immediately."

Lionel nodded. "Of course," he said. "I shall have Spencer muster six hundred troops for you to take with you but I think, given his injury, that I will keep him here with me. I will send another knight in his stead."

Kirk nodded faintly, not giving much thought to the fact that Spencer's injury wasn't that serious and le Vay was more than likely keeping him behind because he was afraid he would lose the man to Kirk's temper were he to send him to Ireland. Kirk had more important things on his mind, reflecting on his father, his mother, his brothers, and losing himself in a world of anguish and sorrow. The more he tried to fight off the feelings, the more they swamped him. Eventually, he set the missive aside and leaned forward in his chair, head in his hands. Grief swallowed him.

Le Vay rose from his padded chair, moving away from Kirk to give the man a bit of privacy to mourn. He went to stand near the lancet window, watching the bailey of Quernmore Castle come alive in the early morning. This small Norman fortress had been in his family for three hundred years, close to the western coast of Lancashire where it had fended off Celtic invaders and other marauders during that time. It had seen much action.

"What more can I do for you, Kirk?" he asked softly, turning away from the sights and sounds of the bailey to face the distraught knight. "How can I help?"

Kirk removed his face from his hands, wiping the tears from his eyes. "You have already pledged men and support, my lord," he said hoarsely. "You have already done much that I am grateful for."

"You would do the same for me."

Kirk nodded, rising wearily to his feet. "I will help Spencer muster the troops."

"Kirk," le Vay came away from the window, his gaze intense. "Spencer can do this without your help. In fact, I would prefer if you stayed away from him."

Kirk knew what he meant. He waved the man off. "I will not harass him," he assured le Vay. "This is business. I do not mix it with personal feelings."

Le Vay sighed faintly, thoughtfully. "I would not presume to question your honor, but I would feel better if you stayed away until the troops are prepared," he said. "I am an old man. I worry. You will do this for me."

Kirk smiled weakly. "If I were to swear on my oath, would you believe me?"

"I would. But I still want you to stay away."

Kirk simply nodded, not having the energy to argue with the man. But there was one more thing on his mind as he headed to the solar door.

"My lord, you asked if there was something more you could do for me," he paused by the big oak panel, open to the darkened keep beyond. "I believe there is."

"Name it."

Kirk hesitated a moment before speaking. "Lady Mara," he said. "I will not be able to return her to Anchorsholme myself."

"I will send her with an escort."

Kirk was visibly relieved. "Thank you, my lord. I appreciate it."

Le Vay's dark eyes twinkled. "I will make sure not to send Spencer as her escort."

Kirk rolled his eyes. "A wise choice, my lord," he said. Then, he sobered. "In fact, it would be wise to keep the man away from her. Permanently."

Le Vay sobered as well. "I will make sure he understands that."

Kirk nodded shortly and left the room without another word. Lionel watched him go with a heavy heart, feeling sad about the circumstances at Wicklow that had robbed Kirk of his father. But such was the way of the world. Battles, and death, were part of the common fabric. They had all known their fair share of it.

As he turned away from the door, he noticed Kirk's missive on the floor and bent over to pick it up. As he put it on the table, he noticed the second of the two missives Edmund had sent him. He'd only opened the first one because Kirk had been insistent about it. Kirk hadn't known the contents of the second missive so Lionel had set it aside as the more pressing issues in the first missive had taken over. In fact, he'd forgotten about it until now.

Alone in the solar, Lionel popped the seal on the second missive and read the contents. He read it again. His mouth popped open and his bushy eyebrows lifted. He read it three more times before the meaning actually began to sink in. Even then, he could hardly believe it.

What he read shocked him to the bone.

***

Kirk had been summoned shortly after sunrise by a servant and had left Mara to their cozy bed, warm and snug. She drifted in and out of sleep as the sun broke the horizon, her dreams on Kirk when she slept and her thoughts on him when she was awake. She could smell him in the bed linens, on her hands, and on her body. Everything about the man made her feel deliriously warm and happy and safe.

But those thoughts ended when a gull took rest upon the windowsill, squawking. Mara lifted her head, eyeing the gull unhappily as it preened its feathers and squawked. Hanging over the side of the bed, she grabbed the nearest thing she could grab, her shoe, and tossed it at the window. Insulted, the gull flew off as the shoe clattered to the floor.

The gull reminded her of the sea, and the sea reminded her of Kirk and his departure for Ireland. Sadness swamped her but she fought it, not wanting to be an emotional wreck about it. She had been given the chance to rage about it, to beg Kirk not to go, but that was over with now. She was coming to see that no amount of pleading would keep the man from going. She needed to come to terms with it. She thought, perhaps, he would want it that way. Perhaps she needed to grow up a bit, as befitting the future wife of a warrior.

There was cold water in the basin next to the bed and she remembered the bar of soap Lady Lily had given her. Rising in the chill of the room, she found the precious soap in her satchel and used it to wash with, cold water and all. She hooted as she splashed the water on her face and swabbed off her body. The smell of freesia was heavy and delicious. Having existed for so long with only the bare necessities of life, something luxurious and feminine was thrilling. Once she was washed and moderately dried, she tucked the precious soap away again.

As she pulled her shift over her head, there was a knock at the door. Hesitantly, Mara went to open it a crack, peering out into the darkened landing.

Lady Lily stood in the weak light, swathed in finery and smiling timidly. "Good morn to you, my lady," she said pleasantly. "I… I thought you could use some assistance in dressing this morning. I have not had much opportunity to properly speak with you and I should like to remedy that."

Mara wasn't quite sure what to say. Seeing Lily's lovely face brought on stabs of jealousy that she quickly pushed aside. She remembered how kind and accommodating Lily had been the night before when Mara had been in a panic about Kirk and Spencer's battle. In fact, Lily had gone out of her way to comfort her, something Mara didn't really think about until this very moment. Suddenly, she didn't feel so resistant. She opened the door wider.

"Come in," she told her.

Lily entered the room, followed closely by two servants bearing a variety of garments and other things. Mara looked at them very curiously.

"What have you brought?" she asked.

Lily's smile grew. "Well," she began, pulling one of the garments out of the servant's arms. "I truly hope you do not mind, but when I saw you last night, a thought occurred to me. You see, my mother died some time ago and I have trunks full of her garments that I cannot wear simply because I am too tall, so they have been packed away in storage with no one to wear them. They are too fine to donate to the poor and no one I know can fit them, so I was hoping to perhaps gift them to you because you are the perfect size. Will you at least look?"

Astonished, Mara watched as Lily held up an exquisite shift made from soft lamb's wool with tiny gold thread woven through it. As Mara reached out to touch the fabric, Lily held up another garment, a matching surcoat that was layered with golden fabrics and lined on the edges with white rabbit fur. It was absolutely exquisite and Mara couldn't help her jaw from dropping.

"Me?" she asked, stunned. "For me?"

Lily could see how surprised Mara was. Truthfully, she had come this morning because she felt guilty for virtually ignoring the lady since her arrival. She'd had Kirk to keep her occupied and a host of visiting relatives. In fact, she had only gotten a good look at the lady last night as Kirk and Spencer had battled it out, and she had noticed the worn nature of Mara's surcoat. Surely a woman would have worn her very finest to a feast so if that was Mara's finest, Lily came to think that perhaps the woman didn't have much at all. As her ladies in waiting whispered and giggled about Mara's rags, Lily felt a good deal of compassion for her.

Although she didn't know anything about her other than the fact she was Edmund de Cleveley's sister-in-law and that in of itself caused her to feel good deal of pity for her. Everyone knew what a horrible place The

Darkland was. There was something about Lady Mara that invited compassion. Moreover, Kirk had spoken so fondly of the woman at the feast the previous night and she had seen how Kirk had battled Spencer when the man had gotten too close. If Mara was worthy of Kirk's respect, then Lily wanted very much to know her.

"Try them on," Lily said as she tossed them over onto the mussed bed. Snapping her fingers at the servants, they began to lay them all out over the enormous bed. "My mother spared no expense with her wardrobe. I shall be so happy if you feel you can use it."

Mara stood rather dumbly as the activity went on around her. She wasn't honestly sure what to do or say, lured by the beautiful new clothing and Lily's kind manner. Lily was sweet and mothering, and in little time, Mara was dressed in the fine lamb's wool shift and the surcoat with the rabbit lining. One of Lily's maids was an excellent seamstress so when the woman was finished taking note of what needed to be altered, that clothing was pulled off in favor of a red silk. And then a green brocade, a yellow silk, and finally a very fine linen that was the color of a ripe peach. Mara stood on a stool while all of the frivolous madness went on around her. She'd never known anything like it.

The last dress to go on was a magnificent blue that magnified Mara's eye color. It fit her snuggly on the torso while draping off her shoulders into sleeves that trailed to the floor. A silver ribbon cinched up the front, crisscrossing across her breasts and making her look absolutely delectable.

Lily and her maids fussed over Mara and the dress. In fact, it needed very little altering and as the women tugged here and there, fitting the garment on Mara's shapely frame, Lilly began to talk.

"Where were you born, Lady Mara?" she asked.

Mara watched the maids work on the hemline of the gown. "Haslingden," she replied. "It is two days' ride south of Anchorsholme."

"You have lived there your entire life?"

"Aye."

"Where did you foster?"

Mara glanced at the woman, embarrassed to answer. "Well," she began reluctantly, "I was sent to foster when I was seven but I did not stay long. I came home at nine years of age."

Lily's pretty brow furrowed. "Why so early?"

Mara sighed heavily, making a face. "I did not like it," she said. "I lived at Rochdale Castle. Lord de Worth was an acquaintance of my father and when my father approached him to ask if my sister and I could foster in his household, he was very gracious. But we soon found out why; he was a vile old man who preferred young girls. His wife was an invalid so he did much as he pleased without her knowledge. He tried to... well, suffice it to say that when he approached my sister, we paid a soldier to escort us home."

Lily's eyes were wide with shock and sadness. "How terrible," she said sincerely. "Yet you remain a strong and noble young woman. It did not affect you overly."

It was a kind thing to say of a shameful situation. The more Mara spent time with Lily, the more her jealousy faded and the more she came to like the woman. Truth be told, Mara had never really spent any time around women other than her sister, so her experience with friends was limited. She wasn't quite sure how to react.

"Where... where did you foster?" she asked timidly.

"Warwick Castle," she replied. "I went there at nine years of age and returned home at sixteen."

Mara lifted her arms as the maids began to work on the sleeves. "Did you like it at Warwick?"

Lily nodded, supervising the maids closely on the sapphire-blue coat. "It was a very big place," she said. "Do you know much of Warwick, my lady?"

Mara shook her head. "I do not," she admitted.

Lily helped the maid with the hem of the sleeve as she spoke. "It used to belong to the Earls of Warwick, but the last one died several years ago," she said, happy to share her knowledge. "It belongs to the Crown now and the castellan is Sir Augbert de Gilles. Sir Augbert and his wife, the Lady Eve, were my hosts. The Lady Eve taught me to paint. She also taught me Latin, Italian, and Portuguese."

Mara looked at the woman, feeling utterly inadequate in the presence of such an educated lady. But Lily didn't speak boastfully. Her delivery was easy and almost dismissive. In fact, Mara found herself quite interested in what the woman was saying.

"You can speak Italian?" she said with some awe. "I have always wanted to go to Rome. Have you been there?"

Lily shook her head. "Nay," she replied. "But I am to be married soon. Perhaps I can convince my husband to take me there."

Mara smiled, a genuine gesture. "If he does, perhaps... perhaps you will tell me of your travels when you return."

Lily was thoughtful. "Perhaps I will not need to," she said as if concocting a great plan. "Perhaps Kirk will marry you soon and you can join us. Would that not be exciting? We could be traveling companions and spend all of our husbands' money."

She giggled and Mara found herself giggling, too. But it occurred to her that Kirk must have told Lily about their relationship during all of that time that Lily was monopolizing his time.

"Then he told you about... me?" she asked.

Lily grinned. "Even if he had not, fighting Spencer to the death would have told me everything I needed to know," she replied, her blue eyes twinkling. "He is very fond of you, is he not?"

Mara flushed furiously, fighting off a grin. "I believe we are both very fond of each other."

Lily laughed softly at Mara's embarrassment. As the maids wandered away, she moved in close.

"I also know that you have been sleeping in his chamber," she whispered, watching Mara's uncertain expression. "My ladies have told me such things. They are terrible gossips."

Mara cheeks flushed a dull red. "I notice you did not bring them with you."

Lily shook her head, a dismissive gesture. "They are jealous of you," she said. "I have told them to stay away from you and if I hear them whispering any more gossip, I will slap them all silly. They are amusing companions but at times they can be very petty."

Mara was pleased by the woman's defense of her. "Thank you, my lady," she said sincerely. "But... but they have not told anyone else?"

"Never," Lily insisted. "Have no fear; my father does not know. He also does not know that my betrothed and I have also shared the same bed. Wicked, are we not? Well, I do not care a lick. I like being wicked."

It was a great secret and Mara's smile hesitantly returned. "I did not look at it that way," she murmured. "Kirk and I have such feelings for one another... we are in love, my lady. When there is love, I am not sure how sharing the bed of the man you love is wicked."

Lily giggled. "It *is* wicked before the marriage bed," she said. "Perhaps it even makes me a whore. I do not care, I tell you!"

She said it with such glee that Mara couldn't help but giggle. "Tell me of your betrothed," she said, feeling a kindred spirit with Lily now that they had shared their naughty secrets. She'd never known female companionship like this in her life. "Is he strong and handsome?"

Lily half-shrugged, half-nodded as she began to fuss with the collar of Mara's dress. "He is quite handsome and strong," she replied. "His name is Sir Thomas de Ryce and his brother is very close to King Henry. Thomas is Welsh and his family is very powerful. It will be a wonderful marriage, I am sure."

She said it as if she was trying to convince herself. Mara watched the woman's face as she fingered the surcoat. "Do you love him?"

Lily met her gaze. "I am quite fond of him," she said softly. "He is kind and generous. He will make a good husband."

Mara nodded faintly, silently accepting the explanation although she didn't believe the woman. She spoke without much enthusiasm.

"Then perhaps we can convince Thomas and Kirk to take us to Rome," she said. "Kirk has spoken of taking me to Ireland but I would much rather go to Italy."

The twinkle returned to Lily's eyes but before she could speak, the chamber door opened and Kirk stood in the doorway. As the women turned to him, he surveyed the chaotic state of the room with a mixture of amusement and curiosity.

"What goes on here?" he asked.

Lily, ever-chatty and right with wording, moved in his direction. "Lady Mara is doing me a great favor," she insisted. "When my mother passed away, she left a great many fine garments that I have had to store. Mara has agreed to take them off my hands. Does she not look marvelous?"

Lily pointed proudly to Mara, who was still standing in the middle of the chamber where she had left her, arms up as the maids finished with the sleeves of the too-long gown. Kirk lifted an appraising eyebrow as he sauntered in her direction, inspecting her closely.

"She does indeed," he said with appreciation. "She looks beautiful."

Mara, who had been watching Kirk with some trepidation when he first entered the room, grinned when he gave his approval. With a still-upraised arm, she pointed to the bed.

"Look at all of the garments," she said eagerly. "Lady Lily has had them all this time with no one to give them to. Are they not lovely?"

Kirk glanced over at the pile of clothing on the bed. "Indeed," he said, but his gaze returned to her in the exquisite blue silk. His eyes were warm on her. "Do you like them, love?"

Mara nodded excitedly. "I love them all," she said. "Lady Lily was very kind to think of me."

"Indeed she was," Kirk said, turning to look at Lily. "My lady, you are most generous. We thank you."

Lily smiled broadly as she went to Kirk and looped a hand through his elbow. "Marry her soon, Kirk. I like her very much. In fact, you are going to escort her to Rome when my husband and I go. Mara and I will travel very well together and I forbid you to deny her the journey, do you hear?"

Kirk fought off a grin. "You sound much like Mara when you say it that way."

"What way?"

"Demanding."

Lily laughed. "She is *not* demanding," she said as she let go of Kirk's elbow. She moved back over to the bed and began collecting the surcoats.

"My maids will finish with these dresses, my lady, and will return them in time for supper. I should love to see you looking finely dressed tonight."

Mara nodded. "As would I," she replied. "Do you want to take this blue dress with you?"

Lily handed over the garments in her arms to the nearest maid. "I think not," she said, her gaze warm. "It fits you well enough. Kirk can hardly keep his eyes off of you. I do believe you should keep it on. I shall return to finish it later."

Mara smiled at the woman as she finished collecting the shifts and surcoats, chasing her maids out and closing the door softly behind her. When they were finally alone, Mara turned to Kirk.

"Do you really like the dress?" she asked.

Kirk's gaze was steady, but inside, the weight of the news he bore was dragging him down. He just needed a few moments with Mara to settle himself, to breathe, and perhaps even to grieve privately. His mind was whirling and his heart was heavy. His smile faded.

"You are the most beautiful creature I have ever seen," he said with soft sincerity. "No woman can compete with your glory."

Mara smiled modestly, her cheeks flushing. She bobbed a stiff curtsy. "My thanks, my lord."

He grinned, his gaze moving over her face, the lovely dress. "Am I to understand that you and Lily have become friends?"

She nodded, somewhat embarrassed. "She has been very kind."

"She is a kind lady."

"I am sorry I was so jealous of her before I came to know her. It was silly of me."

Kirk's attention lingered on her a moment longer before moving over to the bed. As he sat, heavily, he held out his hand to her.

"Come here," he murmured.

Mara obeyed. When she came within arm's length, he reached out and pulled her onto his lap. As she wrapped her arms around his neck, he felt both comforted and weakened. The woman had the ability to stir emotion within him, making him feel vulnerable and strong at the same time. He buried his face against her shoulder and closed his eyes.

"You left early this morning," Mara said softly, her cheek against the top of his head. "Where did you go?"

He was silent for a moment. "A missive came from Anchorsholme."

Mara's pleasant mood fled. She stiffened. "Micheline?" she asked in a panic. "Has something happened to my sister?"

Kirk calmed her. "Nay," he assured her. "It contained nothing about Micheline. It was for me."

Mara still wasn't over her fright. Her hand was on her chest as if to soothe her racing heart. "Thank the Lord," she said. "What did the missive say?"

He gazed into her blue eyes. "There has been a rebellion on de Cleveley's Irish lands," he said quietly. "Wicklow Castle fell. My father was killed."

Mara's eyes widened. "Oh... Kirk," she breathed. "I am so terribly sorry."

He went back to resting his head on her shoulder. "As am I," he muttered. "I am sorry that he will never meet you. He would have liked you."

"As I am sure I would have liked him," she said, so very sad at Kirk's obvious distress. "Did the missive say how it happened?"

Kirk lifted his big shoulders. "It does not matter how it happened, only that it has. My father is dead and nothing can bring him back."

Mara wasn't sure what to say to that. He didn't seem to want to discuss it. She held Kirk tightly, her arms around his neck.

"What will you do now?" she asked softly.

His embrace tightened as he turned his face against her skin, smelling her. "I am instructed to take le Vay's troops to the docks at Fleetwood where we will meet de Cleveley troops, board de Cleveley vessels, and sail for Ireland on the morning tide."

Mara processed the information. She could feel the angst rise, not wanting him to leave her. She was terrified for him going to war, terrified for herself because she was returning to Anchorsholme. But contrary to her nature, she didn't voice her concerns. For the first time in her life, she kept her mouth shut because she knew Kirk had enough on his mind. His father's murder was surely killing him.

"You leave tomorrow?" she asked softly.

"Aye. And so do you."

"Back to Anchorsholme?"

"Aye."

Mara didn't say anymore after that. They'd already spoken of it and the subject was already settled. Still, she couldn't help the tightening in her gut. She pressed her face into the top of his head.

"I am truly sorry about your father," she whispered. "What of the rest of your family?"

"I do not know," he replied. "The missive only mentioned my father."

She sighed faintly. "I have spent nearly all my life at Haslingden," she said softly. "I have never been around a battle. I would be lying if I said I was not frightened for you. Please take great care."

He hugged her. "I will, I swear it," he said. "I have much to live for."

She pulled her face from his head, looking at him with a smile on her lips. "Me?"

He met her grin, gently tweaking her nose. "You."

Her smile faded as she gazed into his eyes. "Will it be a big battle?"

He shrugged. "Possibly," he said. "When the Irish are angry, there is no knowing how many will answer the call to aide."

"Then mustn't you go and muster your troops? Surely you have duties to attend to."

Kirk shook his head. "Le Vay has asked me to stay away from Spencer as he prepares the men," he said. "I have nothing more to do than spend the remaining hours with you, for which I am grateful."

Mara was thrilled. She toyed with his dark hair, memorizing the texture to tuck away in her memories for days when she was feeling particularly lonely. She watched Kirk's expression, seeing such sorrow in it.

"When was the last time you were in Ireland?" she asked quietly.

"About four years ago. A lot can change in four years."

"What... what should I do if you do not return?"

His gaze grew intense. "Raise my son in the manner you see fit."

A twinkle came to her eye. "The son you gave me last night?"

"The same."

"Are you so sure I carry your son?"

"I have prayed for it since last night."

The humor vanished from the conversation. He was deeply sincere and it frightened her. The man was sailing into the unknown, to face tragic circumstances, and she could read his uncertainty. Without another word, she threw her arms around his neck and he swallowed her up in his big embrace. There wasn't much more either one of them could say that hadn't already been spoken of.

Fear of the future, grief from Kirk's father's murder, and their longing for one another came together in a cataclysmic clash. Kirk took Mara back to bed and didn't leave her until he was forced to the following morning before dawn.

Mara's last vision of Kirk was as he rode from Quernmore's gatehouse, astride his massive charger as he faded out into the breaking dawn.

CHAPTER SEVENTEEN

"My lord?" Spencer was startled to see Lionel in his chamber. "Have you need of me?"

It was early morning following the departure of Kirk and over half of Quernmore's army for the green shores of Ireland. Now the bailey was a quiet and somewhat still place, drained of the men with weapons and knights on horseback.

Le Vay shook his head to Spencer's question, holding out a hand as the knight tried to climb out of bed. Recovering from his bout with Kirk, he was still rather weak and the physic had prescribed bed rest. Still, the man was fully prepared to rise up and do his lord's bidding no matter how poorly he was feeling. Mustering the troops to leave with Connaught had just about finished him.

"It has been years since I have entered the knight's quarters," Lionel said, eyeing the small, windowless chamber with its dark stone walls and dirt floor. It was a dark chamber except for the fat tallow candle near the bed. "I had forgotten how dismal they are."

Spencer looked around the room as well. "I have not noticed," he replied. "Other than sleep, I do not spend any time in this room."

Lionel wriggled his eyebrows as he looked around for a chair. "I shall have you moved into the keep. That is where you belong."

Spencer didn't reply. He was more interested in why le Vay had come. The man was correct; he hadn't been to the knight's quarters in years, so his appearance had Spencer curious and, if he thought about it, perhaps on edge. It was an odd happening. Something was afoot.

But le Vay wasn't looking at him. He was more interested in finding a chair. All he could locate was a squat stool, so he pulled it up next to Spencer's bed and sat heavily. He lifted the ends of his fine robes and tried to keep them out of the dirt. When he finally focused his attention on Spencer, the knight was watching him intently.

"How can I be of service, my lord?" Spencer asked quietly.

Le Vay shrugged. Then he sighed and scratched his head. "Are you well enough, Spencer?"

"I will heal. In fact, I suspect I will be back to my regular duties by this evening."

"That is good."

"Do you have a task for me, my lord?"

Le Vay sighed heavily again. He seemed contemplative or, at the very least, ill at ease. He paused for several seconds before replying.

"With all of the conflict between you and Kirk, I have not yet had the opportunity to tell you why the man came to Quernmore," he said. "Kirk and I had a lengthy conference yesterday afternoon and it would seem that he came on behalf of Edmund to solicit support for a revolt on his lands in Ireland, as you well know. You saw the result last night and this morning when the army was mustered."

Spencer nodded. "I know, my lord."

Lionel eyed the young knight. "I told you to remain behind but I did not tell you why. I felt that your wound should be allowed to heal. You are still quite weak."

"My wound is not that bad."

Lionel cocked an eyebrow at him. "Then I shall be plain. I did not send you to Ireland with Kirk given what happened between the two of you. That would be a volatile situation and a bad decision on my part. That is why I sent Albert in your stead."

Spencer knew as much but he still wasn't pleased with the directive. He had been excessively furious when the brash young knight had ridden off with Connaught.

"Albert d'Uberville is a young knight, my lord," he argued feebly. "He does not have excessive battle experience."

"He will learn. Kirk will teach him. The call him The Master, after all."

"Albert can be reckless."

"He will not be for long with Kirk as his commander. The first time he makes a foolish decision, Kirk's wrath shall be fierce."

Spencer could see there was no changing le Vay's mind. With nothing more to say, he simply nodded his head and averted his gaze. His disappointment was obvious. "As you say, my lord."

Lionel watched Spencer's face for any sign of rebellion but saw nothing other than the displeasure. He continued. "There is something else," he said softly.

Spencer turned to him, struggling to force the disappointment aside. "And that would be, my lord?"

Lionel averted his gaze and looked at his hands. It was apparent that he was searching for the correct words to describe whatever 'something else' was. It took him several long seconds before he spoke again.

"You have served me for six years," he said.

"Aye, my lord."

"You are aware that I had a son who was killed in battle shortly before you came into my service."

"I am, my lord."

"In fact, you have been something of a son to me in the absence of my own."

"Thank you, my lord."

Lionel shook his head. "But the fact remains that you are *not* my son," he said. "When I die, Quernmore will pass to Lily and her husband. That is not how I wish to bequeath my inheritance."

Spencer wasn't following the man in the least. He finally lifted his shoulders. "Very well, my lord." He wasn't sure what else to say. "Lily's betrothed is a fine man."

"But he is not my son, my flesh and blood."

"No, he is not."

Lionel was still looking at his hands. The pause was lengthy before he spoke again. "It would seem that I have an opportunity that I never thought I would have again."

"And what is that, my lord?"

Lionel lifted his head, then, and looked at him. "The opportunity to have another son."

Spencer still had no idea what he was talking about. He finally gave up pretending that he embraced the conversation. "I do not understand, my lord."

Lionel knew that. He hadn't been very clear. But he was confused, hopeful, and bewildered all at the same time. He stood up and began to pace.

"When Kirk arrived from Anchorsholme, he carried two missives with him," he said. "The first missive was the request for support in Ireland. The second was a marriage proposal."

Spencer was genuinely surprised. "A marriage proposal?" he repeated. "For whom?"

"Me."

Spencer's shock only grew. "From Anchorsholme?" he said. Then, a disturbing flicker came to his eye. "Not Johanne...?"

Lionel shook his head quickly. "Nay," he said. "Not that madwoman, thankfully. It would seem that Edmund is proposing a marriage between me and the Lady Mara le Bec, sister of Edmund's new wife. He has sent Lady Mara along with Kirk so that I may have a look at her."

Spencer stared at him. "Mara?" he repeated, astonished. "*Kirk's* Mara?"

"The same."

Spencer's jaw dropped. "The woman we were *fighting* over?" his astonishment grew, so much so that he had to spell out the obvious just to make sure he understood correctly. "Lord de Cleveley has proposed a marriage between you and Lady Mara?"

Lionel nodded, carefully gauging Spencer's reaction. He couldn't tell if the man was pleased or outraged but he suspected it was the later. He felt defensive.

"I am a wealthy widower," he said. "Lady Mara is young, beautiful, and healthy. It is perfectly acceptable to marry her so that she may bear me a son."

Spencer couldn't believe what he was hearing. "And if she doesn't bear you a son?"

"Then she shall be a wealthy and respected wife nonetheless."

"Is that all she is to you, my lord? Someone to breed with?"

Lionel could hear the judgment in Spencer's tone. He went from a calm demeanor to a frustrated one in a flash.

"That is the purpose of marriage," he pointed out. "It is not for young knights to live out romantic and lusty dreams. It is to breed empires, of which I intend to do. If you cannot accept that, then I shall release you from your oath and you may seek your comfort and fortune elsewhere."

Spencer cooled. He could see that Lionel would not be berated or judged for his decision. It was a reasonable one, that was true, but Spencer was not thinking with reason. He was thinking with his loins and with his heart. He was also thinking about Kirk; he couldn't help it. He pondered his liege's words, forcing himself to settle.

"That will not be necessary, my lord," he replied, returning to his obedient demeanor. "But I would assume that Kirk knew nothing of this proposal."

Lionel was eyeing Spencer for any further hint of rebellion. "I would assume not," he replied. "If he did, I am sure he would have destroyed the missive."

"What do you think he will say when he finds out?"

"That is not my concern. My concern is with my family and my holdings." Lionel was coming to realize how harsh he sounded simply by Spencer's expression. He was not a harsh man by nature; in fact, he didn't like to take a stand of any kind. He was fairly passive. After a moment, he took a deep breath and cooled. "Kirk is an excellent knight, Spencer. I admire him a great deal. But he has his choice of women. I do not. This... this is my last chance, lad. When I die, the House of le Vay dies with me and this I cannot abide. I have to do what I can to remedy the situation before it is too late."

Spencer's brow furrowed, caught up in le Vay's passionate speech. "What do you mean before it is too late?" he asked. "You speak like a desperate man. If you want to marry so badly to have another son, I am sure there are many women who would be more eligible than a minor baron's second daughter."

Le Vay shook his head firmly, rising from the stool. He gathered his fine robes up around him to keep them off the floor. There was agitation in his movements.

"But it would take time to find such a woman," he said. "Lady Mara is here, now. I could marry her today without delay."

Spencer was growing increasingly baffled. "My lord, I have never heard you express importance in another marriage," he said. "I do not understand your sudden interest."

"It is not sudden. It is something I have been thinking of for some time."

"But I do not understand why...?"

Lionel cut him off. "Because I *must*," he fired back with more passion that Spencer had seen from the man in a long time. "Time is running out."

"What time?"

"*My* time," Lionel insisted, his words overlapping Spencer's question. When he saw the look on Spencer's face, he realized how abrupt he had come across. He backed down, but not entirely. He put a hand to his chest, gesturing to himself in an impassioned plea. "My time, Spencer. The physic says I do not have much longer to live. When I die, the House of le Vay dies with me. Now I see a chance to save it and I cannot let it slip away."

Spencer sat in stunned silence for a moment. "You are dying?"

Lionel nodded. Suddenly, he wasn't so passionate. He was exhausted. He returned to his stool and sat heavily. After a moment, he sighed.

"You know that I have not been feeling my best as of late," he said quietly.

Spencer was very concerned. "For at least a year," he said. "The physic said it was infirmaries of old age."

"That is because I told him to tell everyone I was simply feeling my years and nothing more," he said. "It would seem that I have a mass growing in my belly. It has affected everything about me from my eating to the ability to relieve myself. I do not wish to get into graphic detail but suffice it to say that the mass has grown so much that it is affecting my ability to walk. Soon, I will be crippled and soon thereafter, it will kill me. Whatever it is grows swiftly. The physic thinks it is a cancer."

Spencer was horrified. But he also understood now why le Vay was so anxious to marry and produce a son before he was unable to move at all. It made perfect sense. After a moment, he simply shook his head.

"My lord," he said softly, "I do not know what to say to all of this. I take it that Lady Lily does not know?"

Lionel scratched his head. "She does not," he replied, subdued. "I do not want her to know. She will be a mess, mourning me before I have even passed on. I do not wish her final memories of me to be those of sadness."

"She will find out soon enough if this cancer overtakes you."

"Then we shall confront the subject at that time. But until then, not a word to anyone."

"I swear it, my lord," Spencer assured him. He eyed the man as he sat on the stool, brushing the dust from his robes. "But I still do not believe marriage to Lady Mara is wise."

Lionel looked up from his robes. "Why not?"

"Because Kirk loves the woman," he said softly. "She loves him. Would you ruin her life simply to satisfy your own wants?"

Lionel's jaw ticked, causing his jowls to quiver. "She is young," he replied. "I will die soon and all of this will be hers. Kirk can have her when I am finished with her. Meanwhile, I would have you deliver a missive to Edmund when you are feeling better that I accept the terms of betrothal."

Spencer's first instinct was to refuse but he knew he could not. "If I must, my lord."

"You must." Lionel rose unsteadily from his stool, eyeing the knight on the bed. "For now, I do believe I will attend Lady Mara and explain the course her future is about to take."

Spencer met the man's gaze, his disapproval evident. He simply couldn't help himself. "Would you like me to go with you? She may need comfort."

Lionel paused by the door. "Let me make this clear, Spencer; from this day forward, the Lady Mara is my betrothed and you will cease any notion you ever entertained where it pertains to her. You will behave perfectly and act perfectly towards her, or I will throw you from the castle myself. Is this in any way unclear?"

Spencer didn't rise to the obvious challenge. In truth, he had no choice. "It is, my lord."

Lionel's gaze lingered on him, cold as ice. "Good," he muttered. "Spencer, do not pretend that your reaction to this betrothal is on Kirk's behalf, for it is not. It is simply because you are jealous that I now possess what you wanted. It is envy, pure and simple."

"Perhaps, my lord."

"It ends now."

After the man left the chamber, Spencer sat in silence, mulling over the course the conversation had taken. He was still in shock, over many things. But even with his shock, and his contention with Kirk, all he could think about was how le Vay was stabbing Kirk right where it would hurt him most. Certainly there was jealousy there, but surprisingly, it was not overwhelming. Spencer had always believed le Vay to be a fair and decent man, but in light of the recent conversation, that opinion was now changed.

Dying or not, it didn't give him the right to take a woman that clearly belonged to someone else. If Lionel had done to him what he was doing to Kirk, Spencer would have killed him.

He knew that if Kirk was aware of the contents of Edmund's missive, he would do the same.

***

Lionel found Mara, conveniently enough, in Lily's light and beautiful rooms. He had only sought to speak to his daughter but finding Mara there was a stroke of fortune in his opinion. He thought perhaps that if he delivered the news with Lily present, Mara would have comfort when the information settled and it would be better for them both. He knew, deep down, that what he was doing was wrong, but he didn't care. His sense of self-preservation ruled above all else.

"Greetings, Father," Lily set her needlepoint onto the table next to her chair and rose to greet her father. "How lovely of you to visit."

Lionel kissed his daughter's cheek as he collected her hands. "How fortunate that I have found the two most beautiful women at Quernmore in the same room," he said, looking around the chamber. "It seems quiet in here. Where are your other ladies, Lily?"

Lily waved a dismissive hand. "Off being silly somewhere, I suppose," she said. "Today, it is simply Mara and me. We are very companionable."

Lionel's gaze fell on Mara. "As well you should be," he said. "Greetings, my lady."

Mara, a paint brush in hand and a small palette of paints and half-painted vellum on the table before her, stood up.

"My lord," she greeted.

Lionel's gaze lingered on her; she was wearing the same sapphire blue silk that she had worn that morning when Kirk had ridden off into the dawn. The dress had belonged to Lionel's dead wife, although his wife had never worn it as beautifully as Mara did. He found he couldn't take his eyes off her.

"You look quite lovely in that dress," he told her. "I am so glad you could use my wife's garments. It seemed a shame to keep them stored away and unused."

Mara looked down at herself, in the fine dress she could have never imagined owning. "You are very generous to give them to me," she said. "I can never thank you enough."

Lionel's gaze lingered on her delightful rosebud mouth before forcing a smile. "Your enjoyment of them is thanks enough," he replied. Then he noticed the paint brush in her hand. "What are you doing?"

Mara grinned, somewhat embarrassed. "Lady Lily is teaching me to paint," she said. "I do not think I am a very good student."

Lily laughed. "She is a wonderful student," she corrected. "Mara and I have been here since Kirk left this morning. She was sad at his departure and I did not want her to be alone, so I brought her here and we have been painting ever since."

Lionel's gaze moved from Mara to the painting on the table and back again. "She seems to be doing a marvelous job," he said. "Please; do not let me disturb you. I merely came to see my daughter, whom I have not seen all morning."

"Sit with us, Father," Lily insisted, indicating one of her fine chairs. "Please sit and tell us stories to entertain us. In fact, tell us of the days when you used to live in London. Mara, did you know that my father was friends with Henry Tudor?"

Mara was impressed. "King Henry?" she looked at Lionel with some awe. "Was he your good friend?"

Lionel shook his head. "I was friends with Henry only as much as he found me and my army useful," he said. "I supported him at Bosworth. That was a long time ago."

"Only thirty years ago," Lily insisted. "It is not that long ago."

"You must have been a very young man," Mara said to him.

Lionel shrugged. "I was young indeed," he replied, thinking back to that great and bloody day. "That was the last time I saw significant battle. It was such a glorious and tragic day. In fact, I was near Richard when he was killed. I saw it all. I was also near Matthew Wellesbourne when he lost his hand."

Mara nodded, enthralled. She didn't pay much attention to history or battles, but everyone knew of the battle of Bosworth Field when Richard the Third was killed by Henry Tudor's forces. She had never actually met anyone who had been eyewitness to the event.

"I have heard of Matthew Wellesbourne," she said. "Was he not a comrade of Gaston de Russe?"

Lionel nodded. "Great Gods, you have never seen such big and powerful men," he said, reflecting. "In the presence of The White Lord and the Dark Knight, men cowered, including me. I swear the ground shook when they walked."

He said it so dramatically that the women giggled. "What became of them, Father?" Lily asked. "Did they survive into old age?"

Again, Lionel nodded. "The last I heard they had both survived into old age," he said thoughtfully. "They are still alive but very old, and I have heard tale that they both had gaggles of descendants. In fact, Wellesbourne has sons that serve our king and I believe de Russe's sons have conquered half of the known world."

The women grinned. "It is a wonder anyone survived that battle," Lily said as she collected her sewing. "I am so glad you did, Father. You were not married to Mother at the time, were you?"

Lionel shook his head. "I was barely twenty years and one when Bosworth was etched into the annals of history," he said. "I did not marry your mother until I was well past thirty years and she was sixteen years of age. It was an arranged marriage, and advantageous. All good marriages are. Lily, your marriage is also a contract marriage."

Lily nodded, stabbing at the material. "But I happen to like my future husband," she sighed. "I am fortunate. But Mara is even more fortunate; she and Kirk love one another. Father, you loved Mother, did you not?"

Careful, Lionel told himself. He could see a window opening and he was about to climb through. He was extremely cautious as he proceeded in the minefield between pleasant conversation and life-changing information.

"I did," he said softly, his gaze on Mara. "I learned to love her. She was a good woman and I was very fortunate. But she was not my first love; no. First loves are not meant to last. They are the loves that teach us what it means to feel for someone and to adore them. That way, the second time around, it is much easier."

Mara was listening with interest in between brush strokes. The conversation was engaging and flowing easily. She had no idea he was setting her up for the kill.

"How long where you married?" she asked innocently.

"Over twenty years," he told her. "I miss her. I miss the companionship and the affection. It is something I never imagined I would have again, with anyone. But it seems that I was mistaken."

Lily looked curiously at her father. "What do you mean?"

It was the obvious question, one that Lionel was looking for. *Now is your chance*, he told himself. *Be careful!*

"Since your brother died, I am without an heir," he told his daughter quietly. "You know this, and you know how I have lamented the fact. All I had was to go to Michael but instead, it will pass to you and your husband, and the House of le Vay will cease to exist. That has always deeply saddened me, as I have wished that your mother and I had been blessed with at least another son to carry on the name. It is a prayer I have had since your brother died but one that has gone unfulfilled until now."

Lily was still looking at him curiously. She set her sewing down. "Be plain, father," she said. "Has something happened?"

Lionel stood up; he had to. He was too close to the lovely faces and when he delivered the news, he didn't want to be so close that he could feel Mara's tears. He paced away from them, across Lily's lovely sitting room, and paused by the lancet window overlooking the bailey.

"Something has happened indeed," he said quietly. "It would seem that I have been presented with a marriage proposal and it is one I intend to accept. I understand that this young lady, the bride that has been offered to me, has a suitor but she must understand that marriages are not made of love and dreams. They are made of politics and breeding and standing. I will offer this young lady the Barony of Wyresdale, of course, and all of the wealth related to it. All of this I will offer her; she will never want for anything. Do you not think she will be amiable to such an offer?"

He turned to look at the young women as he said it. Lily nodded, as did Mara. In fact, both girls looked very sincere in their response.

"The young woman will be most fortunate, Father," Lily insisted. "I am very happy that you have received the offer. But you said that she has a suitor?"

Lionel nodded, coming away from the window as he moved back in their direction. "A knight," he said. "An infatuation, I am sure. It will pass. What I offer her is much more substantial."

Lily's brow furrowed. "That is true; it is," she said hesitantly. "But... but what of her feelings? If she has a suitor, she must care deeply for him. Have you not considered that?"

"Of course I have," he said. "I have considered her feelings fairly and I hope dispassionately. Although I am not unsympathetic, I am sure she will understand that marriage to me will be best for her. She seems to come from an impoverish family so the wealth she will acquire when we marry is beyond her dreams. In the end, her suitor will fade from memory because she will know that marriage to me was the right choice. It is the reasonable choice."

Lily was more confused than ever. "She is impoverished?" she repeated. "How in the world did you come to an agreement with a bride who carries no dowry?"

Lionel was very serious. "She does not need a dowry," he said. "She will provide me with a son and that is worth a thousand dowries. Make no mistake; I am agreeing to this marriage because it is my chance to have a son, another heir. Lily, as much as I love you, you are my daughter. A man needs a son. I marry again to have one so that the le Vay name will not die. In exchange for a son, I will make this young woman wealthy beyond her wildest dreams."

Lily didn't know what to say to all of that. In fact, she was rather embarrassed that Mara had heard all of it. Her father's thoughts were deeply personal; *too* personal to be spoken in front of a mere acquaintance like Mara. When she looked at Mara, rather apologetically, she could see

189

that Mara's attention was on Lionel. She held a rather innocent expression, as if the passion of Lionel's words truly had no meaning to her. She didn't know the man at all, so her opinion of his feelings was superficial at best. Lily returned her attention to her father.

"Then I am happy for you," she finally said. "Who is this young woman? Do I know her?"

Lionel nodded. "You do," he said softly, his gaze finally trailing to Mara. "You are sitting at the table with her."

Lily's eyes widened as she looked at Mara, but Mara had no immediately reaction. She had just completed a brush stroke on her half-finished painting so her focus was on her art and not Lionel's words. But the words eventually sank in and her head came up, looking at Lily and seeing the woman's shock.

When Mara saw the look on Lily's face, it began to occur to her that she was the only other woman at the table and surely Lionel would not be speaking of his own daughter. *Impoverished. Her suitor, a knight.* All of these clues began to go off in her mind like lightning hits and the paint brush clattered to the table.

"What... what's this you say?" she looked at the man with horror. "Surely... surely you do not mean *me?*"

Lionel nodded patiently. "I do," he said, almost apologetically. "Edmund de Cleveley, your guardian and the man entrusted to look out for your welfare, as offered you in marriage to me and I have accepted."

Mara just stared at him. "That is not possible," she said flatly. "It is not true."

"It is. I have the missive from Edmund to prove it. I will be happy to show you."

Mara was coming to realize that this wasn't some kind of horrid joke. The room began to sway. "But Edmund is my sister's husband and..."

"And your legal guardian," Lionel cut her off, though not unkindly. He could see that she was building up to an explosion and he hastened to calm her. "Lady Mara, do you not understand what an honor you have been given? You shall be Baroness Wyresdale. You will be respected and loved by all. You will wield power and money such as you have never dreamed. All I ask of you is a son to carry on the le Vay name. It is a great honor, my lady, to be the mother of a legacy."

Mara's mouth popped open and she stood up, knocking over her chair. When Lionel reached out to keep her from falling, she flailed away from him and ended up on one knee. The look in her eyes was wild.

"Never," she hissed. "I will never marry you. I am to marry Kirk!"

Lily stood up, putting herself between her father and Mara. "Mara, please," she begged for calm as she turned to her father. "Father, you will leave now. Please get out of here."

Lionel stood his ground. "I will not," he said. "I am not trying to be unkind, but you must understand that there is no choice in all of this. The sooner Lady Mara understands her destiny, the better for us all. I am truly sorry if I have upset her, but the facts cannot be changed. She will be my wife."

"No!" Mara screamed. "I will not marry you! 'Tis Kirk I love and Kirk I shall marry!"

"Mara, love," Lily rushed at her, trying to calm her down. "Please do not...."

Mara ripped free of sweet Lily's grasp, hurling herself towards the lancet window. Before anyone could stop her, she leapt up into the window sill.

"I shall throw myself to the ground if you intend to go through with this... this *outrage*," she cried. The tears were beginning to come now, fast and furious. "Edmund had no right to make such a contract. Kirk will be my husband, do you hear? I will not marry you."

Lionel could see that she was beyond rational. "Lady Mara, please calm yourself," he pleaded. "I understand your feelings for Kirk. I like Kirk a great deal. But in marriage, feelings do not come in to play. You must understand that this is for the best."

"The best?" Mara shrieked. "The best for you but not for me. You cannot force me to do this!"

"I am afraid you have no choice."

"I will marry Kirk!"

"You will not. I am sorry, but you will not."

"Then I will have no husband at all!"

Lily threw herself at Mara, grabbing her around the body and trying to pull her out of the windowsill. Lionel rushed to the pair, pulling them both out of the window, but Mara was like a wild animal. She screamed and fought and scratched as Lily tried to calm her and Lionel tried to talk reason to her. But she ended up sobbing, and Lily was sobbing, and Lionel had a mess on his hands. He tried to calm them both but neither one of them wanted anything to do with him. They huddled together on the floor and wept.

Defeated, disappointed, Lionel moved away from them and settled in a corner, watching them from the shadows. Mara's reaction wasn't surprising; he'd seen the way Mara and Kirk had looked at each other. But he was still convinced it was infatuation and still convinced that Mara

191

would eventually see the advantages of a marriage to him. At least, that was the hope.

Spencer was upset with him. Lily was upset with him. Mara was shattered. Lionel could only imagine how Kirk was going to react but by the time he was informed, they would be married and there would be nothing he could do about it.

Yet, somehow he didn't see Kirk Connaught simply fading away. It was just a feeling he had. He began to wonder what would kill him first; Kirk or the disease.

CHAPTER EIGHTEEN

Kirk could smell Ireland before he ever saw the coast. The green, lush lands and softly rolling hills. When the three de Cleveley ships docked with their load of one thousand men, horses, wagons and supplies, Kirk found himself frantic to reach Wicklow. But it was a three hour march by his calculations and the army set forth at a strong pace.

Niles and Albert had charge of the advance party, sent ahead of the main army to determine the state of the Castle. Kirk and Corwin remained with the column, Corwin still terribly ill from his day-and-night trip across the Irish Sea. The sway of his charger only seemed to worsen his condition and Kirk ignored the man as he wretched bile over miles of rocky road.

Retching and burping that continued until they reached Wicklow. Niles and Albert met the army a mile out, indicating that a sizable rebel force was occupying the estate. Bringing his men to arms, Kirk lowered his visor and, with rage feeding his determination, spread his ranks into a sweeping pattern that marched on Wicklow like a plague of locusts.

The battle had been ugly from the start. The Irish rebels were prepared for the approach of the de Cleveley army and put up a hellish fight. Kirk lost Sir Albert in the first few hours of fighting, and Niles died in his arms just after midnight of the following day. A far too costly war, in Kirk's opinion. And it only grew worse.

When dawn broke the next day, Kirk threw caution to the wind and sent a suicide force of men into the keep, literally burning the place free of invaders. He lost a good deal of seasoned men, mostly de Cleveley troops, but was rewarded with a full retreat of the enemy by noon. Licking their wounds, the rebels skulked into the surrounding countryside as Kirk raised the gray and yellow de Cleveley standard over the keep he had been born in.

His father's impaled body had been the first sight greeting him upon entering the large, and now devastated, inner bailey. Ryan Connaught had been strung up by his wrists, spread between two large poles as an object of inspiration for the Irish insurgents. Kirk had promptly vomited at the sight and then ordered his father cut down. He himself carried the man to a resting place against the inner wall, tears falling on the corpse as he brushed away the flies and maggots.

But he had no time to spare his grief or his rage. Corwin located his two brothers, dirty and beaten, shackled in the moldering vault. But they were alive and unharmed for the most part, greeting Kirk with kisses and tears.

The eldest Connaught learned that his mother had been taken by the rebels, her whereabouts unknown. A short search of the surrounding area had discovered the woman murdered, and Kirk's rage developed into full-blow madness.

The second night after nearly two days of continuous fighting, Kirk, Steven and Drew found themselves on the battlements as six hundred English troops patrolled the grounds and Castle perimeter. To gaze at the three men would have been to notice identical characteristics, an expression here or a gesture there. Whereas Kirk and Drew had similar coloring and features, Steven was fair, his blue eyes and blond hair in direct contrast to his brothers' dark countenance.

The Irish eve was amazingly mild, the smell of rain in the distance. Kirk was weary, but his murderous emotions kept him from seeking his pallet. With his mother and father killed, his thoughts lingered solely on those of revenge.

And his brothers were aware of the fact. But they were also aware that unless Kirk intended to kill every peasant in the county of Wicklow, he would never find the culprits.

"Why do not you sleep, Kirk?" Steven asked his brother quietly. "Drewie and I have the watch. You have been awake for days, lad, and it shows."

Kirk grinned in spite of himself, rubbing his stubbled face. "So I am not my beauteous self, am I?"

Drew shook his head. "Christ, you're an ugly man. No wonder you have never married."

A dull twinkle came to Kirk's eye. "A few months will see that changed, lads."

Both Steven and Drew turned to him with surprise. "Is that so?" Steven snorted. "God's Blood, I pity the woman. How much did you pay her, Kirk?"

Kirk chuckled. "There's not enough money in the world to buy this woman. She's priceless."

His brothers grinned. "Priceless? Do tell, lad." Drew was snickering.

Kirk sighed heavily, leaning against the parapet as he gazed into the clear night sky. "She's a beautiful lass. Silken dark hair and the brightest blue eyes I have ever seen. Her name is Mara and if you so much as sneeze in her direction, she'll put her fist through your nose before you can blink."

Drew raised his eyebrows. "A fighting wench, eh?"

Kirk grinned. "Not when handled correctly."

His brothers let up a collective "oh", a knowing sound that suggested they understood their brother completely.

"You have bedded her, then," Steven said.

Kirk crossed his thick arms. "It wasn't like that, Steven. I am in love with the girl."

"And she loves you?"

"She does."

"Foolish wench."

The brothers shared a laugh. Kirk sobered, watching the great bonfires in the distance as the dead were burned. Their parents' burial was slated for the morning, in the graveyard where Connaught ancestors had been interred for centuries. Still, Kirk was having a difficult time coming to terms with what had happened. Even thoughts of Mara seemed unable to distract him.

"You cannot do anything for them, Kirk." Steven's voice was soft.

Kirk turned to his brother, his crippled right hand a painful reminder of the once-great knight. "What do you speak of?"

"Mother and father," Steven clarified. "You cannot do anything for them. Those who killed them are long gone, or dead themselves. We shall never know exactly who did it."

Kirk hardened. "We will if I interrogate every rebel in the land, or burn every village. Someone will tell me."

"You will destroy everything if you do this," Drew said. "The actual number of rebels are few. But through threats and intimidation, they coerced the loyal peasants to aid their cause. You cannot destroy everyone simply to capture a few."

Kirk's jaw ticked. "How can you say that?" he demanded. "You saw what they did to father, to mother. How can you be so willing to stand ignorant while murderers roam free?"

"I told you why," Drew returned, with more force. "What do you plan to do, completely obliterate the county, punishing everyone for the crimes of a select few?"

Kirk cocked an eyebrow. "When we came upon Wicklow two days ago, I would say that more than a select few occupied the castle. I'd say hundreds."

Drew shook his head. "Untrained peasants forced to comply with the few trained rebels in their midst. The men who captured Steven and I were hardly more than children. And the only reason we were captured was because of their sheer number."

"What about the men who killed father? Or beat mother to death? Were they children, too?"

"Hard to the core, Kirk. And we shall never, ever find them. They are too clever. And too intimidating."

Kirk sighed with frustration, wrinkling his nose to the pungent smell of the burning dead. "I simply cannot abide by all of this," he said after a moment. "I return home to find my parents killed, the home of my birth all but destroyed. Can you not see the basis for my rage, lads?"

"Of course we do," Drew said softly. "But we also know there is nothing you can do about it. We will rebuild and we will strengthen our ranks with more soldiers. Then we will meet with the village chieftains and see if there isn't some peace we can come to. There is nothing more we can do than that."

"I disagree."

"What would your Mara say to your need for revenge, Kirk?"

It was Steven, always the voice of calm. Kirk looked at his younger brother with frustration when he realized what he was driving at. Pursing his lips, he turned away.

"Most likely the same as you," he grunted. "But Mara is not a soldier. It is right for women to believe in peace and harmony. Without them, the world would know little."

"Do you want to return to her soon, Kirk?" Steven's tone was pointed, soft. "Or do you want to spend the next year searching for men whose identities will never be revealed? The peasants respect the English, Kirk, but they fear the rebels more. Have you been away so long that you have forgotten that?"

Kirk did not like what he was hearing, mostly because it was the truth. Feeling frustrated and impotent, he merely shook his head.

"Nay," his voice was hoarse. "I haven't forgotten. But with all of the might I command, I should think I could do more to bring these men to justice."

To the north, the sound of distant thunder could be heard, dying away just as Kirk's determination for vengeance was. His brothers were correct and he realized he would have to resign himself to the fact. But the knowledge that vengeance would be useless did nothing to ease his anger.

"I so wanted Mara to meet father," he said after a moment, feeling his fatigue as the night deepened. "She's such an exquisite creature. I wanted him to see the woman I had chosen to pass along the Connaught lineage."

"A spirited woman who throws her fists around?" Steven laughed when Kirk pretended to punch him. "I think I like her already."

"You will fall in love with her, as I have," he said. "But you cannot have her. I have already had to fight off one bastard and I swear I kill the next man who looks at her."

Steven and Drew, aware that they had deterred their big brother's taste for vengeance, gladly delved into the subject of Lady Mara once again. It was good to see Kirk smile and they realized that his mood was the direct result of Mara's name. Any mention of her sent him grinning like a fool.

Corwin mounted the ladder to the battlements, approaching the brothers as they conversed and snickered. Smiling wearily, he fixed on Kirk.

"The scouts have returned from the surrounding area, Kirk," he said. "The trees are clear of rebels. In fact, they seemed to have disappeared altogether."

Kirk lifted an eyebrow. "But they have not, of course," he said. "Make sure the sentry posts are tripled, Corwin. And I want mounted guards outside the walls, patrolling in foursomes."

Corwin nodded, eager to carry out the orders and get to bed. He, too, was exceedingly weary.

"Corwin." Kirk stopped the man before he could dismount the wall. "You have met the illustrious Mara. Tell my brothers of her, as they seem to have difficultly believing that one woman can be so perfect."

Corwin glanced to the expectant brothers, his stomach twisting with renewed nausea. But not because of the travel or the battle he had recently fought. It was because he knew something Kirk did not, something that was tearing him apart. The longer he gazed into Kirk's smiling face, the more powerful the urge became to drop to his knees and confess everything. But for fear of Valdine, he remained silent. For her, he had always remained silent.

"She is... well, she is certainly beautiful," he offered weakly. "But ask Kirk about the scars on his cheek if he thinks she is so perfect."

He was out of the conversation as Steven and Drew turned to their brother, demanding to know of the parallel wounds. Corwin slid off the wall, hating himself for his disloyalty to Kirk. Moving to complete his assigned duties, he tried to forget what he knew about Micheline's situation, or Mara's future. But, God help him, he simply couldn't. And the feeling was growing stronger by the moment.

   ***

Spencer stood stoically in Edmund's small solar, watching the thin young lord pace about the room with glee. Spencer, however, could not reciprocate the emotions he was witnessing and with very good reason.

"So he has agreed to my marriage proposal?" Edmund repeated the knight's missive. "How marvelous!"

Spencer could hardly agree. For seven days he had lived with bitterness such as he had never known. And Mara, poor Mara, was beyond devastated. She was lifeless.

"Aye, my lord," he replied stiffly. "He has asked me to thank you for sending the lady to him."

Edmund laughed joyously, shaking his hands in the air. "Thank God!" he crowed. Then, he looked to Spencer with sudden suspicion. "He kept the proposal from Kirk, did he not? I asked that he not tell him."

Spencer could literally taste his disgust. "As far as I know, he did not. He told no one at all and I must say we were quite surprised by the news." He eyed the delighted baron, wishing he could simply run him through and be done with it. The man had no idea the number of people affected by his treachery. "Lord le Vay has already sent for the priest from Crosby. The man should be arriving within the next day and I have been asked to escort Lady Micheline De Cleveley to attend her sister's wedding."

Edmund's giddy demeanor vanished. It was odd, truly, as if a fire had suddenly been doused. "Just... Micheline? Not I, nor my sister?"

Spencer shook his head. "'Tis to be a private wedding, my lord. Immediate family only."

"But I *am* immediate family," Edmund insisted. "After all, he will be marrying the sister of my wife."

Spencer remained firm. He had no love for Edmund de Cleveley, nor did le Vay, hence his exclusion from a wedding Spencer wished would never happen. "I understand, my lord, but Lord le Vay was specific. Lady Micheline only."

Edmund stared at the knight. He had arranged this marriage, after all, and now he was not even invited. But rather than lodge a protest, he wisely decided to obey le Vay's wishes. After all, the man had just sent three hundred men to support the reclamation of the Wicklow estate. Edmund wouldn't dream of taxing the man further with his petty demands.

"I see," he said quietly, but it was obvious he was disappointed. "But his demand that only my wife attend brings me to a rather unpleasant confession."

A seed of apprehension blossomed deep in Spencer' belly. He knew, before Edmund even elaborated, what that confession would be. Given the sinister reputation of The Darkland, there was no other alternative.

"And what is that, my lord?"

Edmund was emotionless as he spoke. "My wife threw herself from the tower the day after our wedding. I am afraid you will have the unpleasant duty of informing both le Vay and his wife that Lady Micheline is dead."

Spencer's body tensed, struggling to bite off words of condemnation that begged to come forth. But his control was not so strong that his cheeks did not flush, nor his pale blue eyes glitter with rage. Edmund noted the reaction, his own stance hardening.

"She did it herself!" He nearly shouted. "How dare you look at me as if... as if I had something to do with it. I never touched her!"

It was all Spencer could do to keep from refuting him. To do so would surely be to jeopardize his own life and freedom. Instead, he lifted his shoulders weakly.

"I never suggested otherwise, my lord." He was struggling to maintain his calm. But he simply couldn't hold himself back. "Given the reputation of Anchorsholme Castle, you will hardly blame le Vay or Lady Mara if they believe otherwise."

Edmund exploded. "I do not care what they think!" he bellowed. "This is my keep and the vassals within belong to me. I command the power of life and death within Anchorsholme, but I cannot control everything. Especially a distraught young woman determined to end her pitiful life. You will tell them this, de Shera, and you will make them understand!"

Spencer's jaw ticked. He had already said too much, as indicated by Edmund's over-defensive rage. But, God help him, he simply couldn't help himself and more words spilled forth before he could stop them.

"I cannot make them understand when I do not understand, my lord." His voice was tight. "And there is something else I do not understand; why have you not had the courtesy to tell Kirk of your plans for his lady? Do not you think he will find out, eventually?"

Edmund grabbed the nearest weapon, a gilded candleholder with three thin tapers. Hurling it across the room, he narrowly missed Spencer's head.

"Get out!" he screamed. "Get out before I kill you myself! This is none of your affair and I shall kill you if you interfere!"

Spencer was wise enough to leave. Edmund raged and stormed, destroying anything he could get his hands on as Spencer marched from the room. By the time he reached the front door, he was very close to breaking himself. *Lying bastard!* he thought furiously.

His charger was still in the bailey, being tended by a stable hand. Spencer stormed up, yanking the reins from the young man. The servant scurried away and Spencer mounted, feeling desperate to put distance between himself and Edmund De Cleveley. If only for Mara's sake, he would like nothing better than to throttle the man. Punishment that was a long time in coming.

The charger snorted irritably in response to Spencer's frustrated movements. His stirrup was twisted and, muttering curses, he struggled to turn it around when a soft voice caught his attention.

Spencer glanced up into a pair of plain brown eyes. Actually, there were two pairs of identical brown eyes. Clinging to one another, the duplicate women emerged nervously from the shadows of the inner wall.

"My lord," the first lady began. "I am Lady Valdine Martin. My husband Corwin is serving with Sir Kirk in Ireland."

Spencer was still frustrated and angry. He paused in his struggles with the stirrup, sighing impatiently.

"And?"

The first woman swallowed. "My sister and I watched you..."

"... ride in and we heard the argument..."

"... with Lord Edmund. Is it true that Lady Mara..."

"... is marrying Lord le Vay?"

Definitely not a subject Spencer was willing to discuss. He cast the sisters an annoyed look and finished straightened out his stirrup.

"That is none of your affair," he said shortly. "If you will excuse me, I am expected back at Quernmore."

"Wait!" Valdine threw herself in front of the charger as Spencer spurred him forward. The animal danced and shrieked, thoroughly angering Spencer.

"Foolish wench, move aside!" he commanded.

But Valdine refused to move. "My lord, I cannot!" she said earnestly, glancing about to make sure there was no one to hear her. "Please, we must speak with you!"

Spencer had had enough of the pesky woman. "Move aside or I shall run you over."

Valdine swallowed hard, but she did not budge. "Lord Edmund lied, my lord."

Spencer stared at the woman. Her simple sentence had been enough to delay his departure. "What do you mean?"

Valdine moved closer to the horse, followed by her cowering sister. The two huddled together as they spoke.

"Lady Micheline is not dead," Valdine murmured. "Lord Edmund wished..."

"... her dead, but Sir Corwin saved her."

The speech pattern was strange but Spencer could not spare it any thought; at the moment, the message they bore was far more intriguing.

"Your husband?" He looked to Valdine. "But why did Lord Edmund tell me she was dead?"

"Because he does not know she lives." Valdine's voice was hoarse with emotion, with urgency. "My husband took her..."

"... to the tower in the hope that Sir Kirk would..."

"... return to escort her to sanctuary. But Sir Kirk..."

"... is in Ireland now, not to return for some time."

Spencer' anger cooled as the story unfolded. "Is the lady still in the tower?"

The women nodded in unison. "Since we cannot rely on Sir Kirk, we must..."

"... help her ourselves."

"And how will you do this?"

Valdine looked at her sister, the two of them obviously terrified. Spencer dismounted his charger.

"Tell me."

Valdine took a deep breath. "We had hoped to dress her in peasant clothing and whisk her from the keep."

"A valid scheme."

Valdine nodded hesitantly. "We were planning to do it today. Lady Micheline has the clothes in her possession, but..."

"... finding an escort to take her to the monastery at Crosby has..."

"... been difficult."

"How so?"

Valdine glanced about as her sister trembled. "The soldiers who remain are reluctant to go against their liege. I sincerely believed we would..."

"... have their support, but it would seem that out of loyalty to the House of de Cleveley, they are fearful of the consequences should..."

"... their aid to Baroness Bowland be discovered."

Spencer glanced to the battlements, noting the positioning of sentries, old soldiers who had seen better days. Scratching under his hauberk, he sighed heavily.

"I see," he said softly. "And you would have me assist you?"

Valdine almost collapsed. "Oh, my lord, we were fearful to ask. Other than a few peasant children and servants, we have no help..."

" ... at all. It has been terribly frustrating!"

"What on earth are they afraid of?"

"Of the curse of The Darkland. They are fearful that it..."

"... will turn against them if they defy Lord Edmund."

Spencer sighed again, turning to glance at the structure behind him. "So the fear of the evils of The Darkland has prevented anyone from going against the grain." He returned his focus to the trembling women. "Well, I for one do not fear The Darkland or her reputation. And if Lady Micheline needs a champion, then I am determined to help her."

Valdine reached out, grasping his mailed hand. "Thank you, my lord. We truly feared we were at an end."

Spencer was feeling the slightest bit of satisfaction that he would be bringing shame to Edmund by rescuing his wife from under his nose. But more than that, he was determined to prevent the death of another young woman at the hands of a man who had no concept of the value of life. Spencer was brave and strong, and he was not afraid to do what was right.

"You have come to the right man, ladies," he said confidently. "I shall escort Lady Micheline to Crosby and take great pleasure in doing so. Now, it would seem we must solidify the plan. Do you think you can bring her down from the tower without incident?"

Valdine and Wanda nodded. "The plan is to take her through..."

"... the kitchens and out through the tunneled gate."

"Where is the gate?"

"On the north side, by the kitchen yard," Valdine replied.

Spencer tightened his gauntlets. "Bring her. I shall be waiting."

Valdine and Wanda dashed away without another word. Spencer mounted his charger, passing a final glance at the towering structure of Anchorsholme and resisting the urge to smile.

Not another, you bastard. You will not take another!

***

Johanne entered the smelly solar, locating her brother by the lancet window. He seemed preoccupied, staring over the bailey, as she approached and rubbed against his leg.

"What did Spencer have to say?" she purred, grabbing his flaccid member through his hose.

Edmund pushed her hand away, still gazing over the bailey. "He came to tell me that le Vay is marrying Mara. And to escort Micheline to the wedding."

Johanne would not be deterred. She lifted her skirt and straddled Edmund's leg, bumping her Venus mound against his thigh. "There was never any doubt that the old man would take to her," she replied. "What did you tell him of Micheline?"

"That she threw herself from the tower." He was thinking on pushing her away again but his physical reaction was difficult to ignore. "He did not believe me, I could tell. Now, why on earth would he be speaking to Valdine and Wanda?"

The change of subject captured Johanne's attention and she stopped rubbing against him long enough to peer from the window, following his gaze. After a moment, she shrugged and returned to masturbating.

"I suppose they want to find out if Spencer knows anything about the conflict in Ireland." She licked her brother's ear. "On your desk, dear. I need you now."

Edmund ignored her, watching curiously as Valdine and Wanda suddenly rushed away from Spencer. The knight mounted his horse and bolted from the inner bailey, leaving Edmund thoroughly puzzled by their behavior.

"Not now." He moved away from his sister. "I want to see what Valdine and Wanda are up to. Something is not right; they were acting very strangely."

"They always act strangely." Johanne followed her brother as he quit the solar. "Where are we going?"

Edmund gestured to the door leading to the bailey. "Where *they* went."

"And if they went nowhere?"

Edmund paused by the door, the dust from the bailey filling his nostrils. "They are up to something, Johanne. And I must discover what it is. They had no valid reason to speak to Spencer, and suddenly they dash away from him as if he has sent them on an errand. Though I cannot imagine what that would be."

Johanne pursed her lips irritably. "Something subversive, I am sure."

"Do not mock me. The man stood in my solar not five minutes ago accusing me of killing my wife. There is no way of knowing what treachery he is up to. Enlisting Valdine and Wanda to help him, no less!"

Johanne was impatient. She did not believe her brother's suspicions and was impatient for him to take her. Throwing up her hands, she agreed. "Fine. Let's discover what they are all up to. And then I demand you pay attention to me."

"Later." He pulled her after him.

CHAPTER NINETEEN

Micheline found that the garments worn by the serving wenches were hardly different from her own clothing. Coarse, simple, without flair. But her surcoats were clean, whereas the rags Valdine and Wanda had brought her were filthy and louse-ridden. But she put them on, willing to subject herself to such squalor if it would help in her escape.

There was no time frame for her break to freedom; day or night made no difference. When Valdine and Wanda deemed the conditions safe, they would escort Micheline through a secured route. But what had been most disheartening was the fact that no one seemed eager to help. Aye, everyone knew of Micheline's predicament. But when the twins went about soliciting assistance, no one was willing to involve themselves in a risky situation. No one but the children, that is.

Robert, Fiona, Gilly and George. They had stolen the peasant clothing, and they pestered people to aid Micheline's cause. Determined little buggers, they had gone so far as to steal one old soldier's breeches in an attempt to force him to their will. But the ploy had only managed to get Robert a whipping, from his mother no less, who was helping in her own right by giving Valdine and Wanda food to take to the baroness.

Micheline could have very easily been discouraged by the fact that the servants who hated Edmund were likewise unwilling to go against him. But she wasn't, for she could understand their fear of a man who held their lives in his demented hands. Still, she had Valdine and Wanda and four little peasants who were determined to aid her. And for that, she was grateful.

It was just prior to the nooning meal on the ninth day of her incarceration. Micheline was standing by the window, itching her bug bites, when the rusty latch was thrown. She rushed to the door to be met by the twins, more pleased than she had ever seen them.

"It is time!" Valdine announced.

Micheline's stomach twisted in knots of excitement and terror. "Then you have managed to find me an escort to Crosby?"

Valdine and Wanda were grinning. "Better than..."

"... that, my lady. A very powerful knight..."

"... has come to your rescue."

Micheline was puzzled. "A knight? I do not understand."

"Sir Spencer de Shera, my lady," Valdine said, pulling a scruffy scarf over Micheline's head. "He is pledged to Lord Lionel le Vay of Quernmore."

"Where Mara is?" Micheline stood still as the sisters' fussed with the scarf. "Did Mara send him?"

The twins' smiles faded. "Nay, my lady, Lord le Vay sent him." Valdine passed a long glance at Wanda, who finished the sentence. "He came to announce the marriage of Lady Mara to Lord Lionel le Vay."

Micheline's eyes widened. "What?"

The twins hustled her to the landing just outside the door. Wanda closed the panel as Valdine began their reply. "We saw him ride in and..."

"... listened outside the door as he spoke with Edmund. 'Twould seem..."

"... that Edmund sent a missive to le Vay proposing a marriage with your sister. Of course,..."

"... Kirk does not know this. We would suspect that..."

"... Edmund is grateful for the convenience of the Irish uprising to put Kirk far, far away while..."

"... the marriage is carried out."

Micheline was in shock. "Mara is to marry this... this le Vay? My God, she must be devastated!"

The tower was cold, musty, as Wanda took the lead, taking the ladies down the stairs.

"One thing is certain, my lady." It was the first time Micheline had ever heard Wanda speak before her sister. "The urgency to remove you is greater now than ever."

An entire sentence by herself! Had Micheline not been so consumed with distress over Mara's marriage, she would have given praise to Wanda's individuality.

"Why?" she asked quietly, jumping aside as a rat scurried past her feet. "Why more so now, Wanda?"

Wanda remained silent as they neared the second floor landing. Down the hall, a flight of stairs used only by the servants would take them to the kitchens. Once through the kitchens where Gilly and George were standing look-out, it would be to the kitchen yard were Robert waited to make sure the iron gate was open. And Fiona, positioned just outside the outer wall where Spencer should be waiting, carried a bundle of food for the trip.

"Because we saw Johanne near the tower entrance yesterday," she replied belatedly. "She was aware..."

"... that we have been in the tower and no doubt she is curious. It is quite possible..."

"... that her curiosity will cause her to search in places that are better left undiscovered."

Micheline gasped softly. "Why did not you tell me this before?"

"Because we discouraged her with tales..."

"... of my cat lost in the tower. She hates cats."

The second floor corridor was dimly lit, a heavily smoking torch the only light. Wanda grabbed Micheline's hand as the three of them slipped down the hall, silent footfalls to the narrow flight of steps.

The stairwell was dark but Wanda plunged forward. Micheline steadied herself by gripping the stone wall, fearful that she would fall at their fast pace. Smells from the kitchen grew stronger and Micheline was nearly able to breathe a sigh of relief; she was closer to freedom than she had been for days.

Aye, she almost felt a sense of peace. But not yet. The sharp heat of the kitchen slapped her in the face as she emerged into the large, smelly room. And the first thing she saw was a little girl's pale face.

Micheline smiled, suspecting it was one of her rescuers. There was a boy standing next to the young girl, a bit older, his dirty face ashen and strange-looking.

"Are you to help me?" she asked gently. "What are your names?"

"Edmund," came a voice from behind. "And I believe you know my sister, Johanne."

The three women whirled about, gasps of fright echoing off the kitchen walls. Edmund smiled lazily as Johanne stood next to the fat cook and her equally fat assistant, both women bound and gagged. Micheline and the twins watched in horror as Johanne took a roasting spit from the wall and jabbed it into the cook's arm, drawing a stream of blood.

"So good of you to join us for supper, Baroness Bowland," she said, running her finger along the rivets of blood and licking it. "We are to have a great feast tonight. Roasting those who have betrayed the House of de Cleveley."

Micheline's heart sank, trembling so badly that she could hardly speak. "If you are referring to those who would aid an innocent woman, then I believe you are mistaken. They have done nothing wrong."

Behind her, Gilly suddenly bolted, racing from the kitchen and out into the yard. Edmund made no move to stop the girl, instead, retrieving an object behind him. Micheline noticed he had leaned a massive broadsword against the stone wall and, with a sinister smirk, glanced pointedly at his wife.

"You are supposed to be dead, baroness."

He was almost scolding her. Micheline swallowed hard, trying to shield both Valdine and Wanda from what was sure to come. "But I am not. And I do not plan on dying for a long, long time."

Edmund ran his finger across the edge of the sword, a disturbingly deliberate gesture. "Plans are meant to be changed, baroness. I can see now that I must finish Corwin's duty. And when I am finished with you, it will be my pleasure to make Lady Martin and her sister pay for the crimes of my disobedient knight."

Micheline ran cold, taking a step back. In fact, all three ladies were stepping back. "Why would you do this, Edmund? We have done nothing wrong."

Edmund seemed not to hear her words as he continued to inspect the sword. "In truth, I never suspected that Corwin disobeyed me. Not until this very day. When I saw Valdine and Wanda in the yard speaking with Sir Spencer, I thought the knight was somehow coercing them to move against me and I was wise enough to follow them as they fled to the tower. But I never expected to discover the great secret between the knight and the ladies to be my supposedly-dead wife." He looked at the pale faces of Valdine and Wanda. "Isn't that what you were discussing with him, ladies? The woman my loyal knight was supposed to do away with?"

Micheline would not let them further endanger themselves with an admission. "To spare a life is never wrong, Edmund."

Johanne moved away from the captive servants, still clutching the spit. "But to disobey one's liege most certainly is. A conspiracy of lies that is punishable by death." She fixed Micheline in the eye. "This is your fault, Lady Micheline. If you had remained obedient to your husband, we would not have been forced to do away with you. You have your own foolish behavior to blame for the deaths of these people who have helped you."

Micheline turned to Johanne, hating the woman more than she could express. "My behavior may have been foolish, as you put it, but at least it was innocent and pure of heart. Something you yourself can hardly claim."

Johanne flared, the flicker of madness in her eyes. "But I *am* an innocent, my lady, referring to the relationship of which you no doubt speak. To learn the art of passion from a man of the same flesh has kept me pure for my husband. My flesh has not been polluted by the touch of an outsider. If you had understood this, we would not have had to do away with you."

Micheline was baffled. Terrified and baffled. "That's nonsense. Incest is the very worst of sins and certainly you cannot claim purity. And where on earth do you suppose you would find a husband who would agree with your reasoning?"

"The one man who is worthy of me!" Johanne exploded. "I have waited years for Kirk to realize I am the only woman in the world for him, not those foolish wenches who whisper sweet words or taint him with their crude touch!"

Micheline continued to back away, pushing Valdine and Wanda along. "That's madness, Johanne. Kirk can never love you. He loves Mara!"

The taut expression on Johanne's face slackened, melted, drained away. She stared at Micheline, her frail chest heaving unsteadily. Slowly, with the flame of insanity in her eyes growing brighter by the moment, she turned to her brother.

"Is this true?"

"Johanne, I...."

"*Is this true?*"

Edmund's attention was diverted from Micheline. "I sent her away, love. She's no longer a threat to you or to Kirk."

Johanne clutched the spit tightly, the flesh on her face tightening until she was hardly recognizable. As the three ladies continued to shrink from the volatile confrontation, Johanne took on the madness of the Devil himself.

"You bastard," she hissed. "You have known all along. Why did not you tell me?"

Edmund struggled to maintain control. "Because it doesn't matter. She is gone now and you do not have to worry over her."

"But...!" Spittle dropped from Johanne's lips. "Why did not you let me wish her away? *I should have wished her away!*"

"It doesn't matter..."

"It matters!" Johanne shouted. Against the wall, the cook and Robert's mother were weeping with fright, growing louder as their mad mistress bellowed. "Of all the women I have wished away, Mara matters most. If Kirk loves her, then she cannot live!"

Beads of sweat peppered Edmund's brow. The woman he controlled so easily had turned the tables on him and he saw clearly that he was no longer in control. Johanne was lord and master, dominating him, bending him to her will. All of these years Edmund thought it was he who had reigned supreme over the realm of The Darkland, but he could see, simply, that Johanne was the ruler of their world. And it was he who had always submitted to her every whim.

He realized that now. He did not know why he hadn't seen it before. The more Johanne raged, the more frightened he became.

"She's gone, Johanne," he said quietly. "She's le Vay's wife now and you cannot harm her. Nothing can."

Johanne continued to stare at him, her pale eyes twitching ominously. Suddenly, she lifted an eyebrow. "I see now, Edmund," she murmured, a bitter smile coming to her lips. "Oh, yes. I see quite clearly now. You did not *want* to kill her. You love her, too!"

Edmund shook his head. "Nay, Johanne, I do not."

Johanne nodded wildly, her lips hanging open and oh-so-sure of her demented conclusion. "You would not permit me to kill her because you loved her beauty and spirit. You sent her away so that I would not discover the truth!"

"Nay, Johanne!"

"She has taken both you and Kirk away from me!"

"Johanne, listen to yourself!" Edmund pleaded. "You're mad, love, simply mad!"

Johanne growled deep in her throat, bringing the spit up and wielding it like a spear. Edmund screamed but was unable to evade the weapon as she plunged it deep into his belly, twisting the rod brutally and loving every moment of his suffering. Micheline, jolted with horror, shoved Valdine and Wanda toward the open kitchen door.

"Run!"

The women obeyed. Leaving the screaming and grunting behind them, they raced from the kitchen in the same direction Gilly had taken. Emerging into the yard, they were immediately confronted by Sir Spencer. Having been summoned by the terrified young girl, the man was fully prepared to do battle. Micheline pushed the twins in his direction.

"My lord, save us!" she cried. "Johanne has gone mad!"

Spencer recognized the twins, assuming that the frantic woman behind them was none other than Lady Micheline. He charged forward, placing himself between the terrified ladies and the open kitchen door.

"Where is she?"

Micheline and the twins were huddled by the tunnel entrance, trembling with fright. Robert, Gilly and Fiona joined them, creating a fearful flock.

"Inside," Micheline gasped. "She stabbed Edmund and I fear she comes for us!"

Sword raised defensively, Spencer turned to the darkened doorway. It was difficult to see anything but he could hear faint whimpers emitting from inside. Moving slightly to gain a better look, he kept his weapon leveled in front on him.

A long metal spit suddenly came hurling out of the darkness, striking Spencer' sword. He grunted with surprise as the weapon went flying, taking a step back as Johanne emerged from the kitchens. She collected the spit from the ground before the knight could reach it and Spencer raised his armored forearm in time to fend off two heavy blows.

Taking another step back, he slipped on a pile of animal dung and nearly lost his balance. Howling like a fiend, Johanne took the opportunity to thrust the spit at his groin. Spencer could no longer deny the fact that his life was in serious jeopardy. The woman was determined to kill him and he was equally determined to defend himself. But he needed his weapon.

It was several feet away. Robert, seeing that Spencer was in trouble, broke from the frightened cluster of women and children, hurling himself toward the steel blade. Losing his footing, he ended up on his buttocks, spinning wildly through the mud. But the slick motion deposited him next to broadsword and he grabbed the thing, using all of his strength to toss it in Spencer' direction.

"Sir Knight!" he shouted. "Your weapon!"

Spencer' hand was up, catching the clumsy toss. Instantly, he lifted his sword in the path of the screaming lady, knowing that very shortly it would be life or death for one of them. Johanne jabbed the spear again, this time at his neck, and Spencer had no choice but to respond. Without regrets, he deftly parried her thrust and drove his broadsword deep into her fragile chest. Gasping and twisting, Johanne fell to the ground in a dying heap of blood and foam.

Spencer stood over the woman as she cursed him soundly and breathed her last. Raising his visor with a shaking hand, he turned to the huddle of women and children behind him.

"God's Blood," he exhaled slowly. "*What in the hell has happened here?*"

Micheline stared at Johanne's contorted form, her eyes wide with shock. After a moment, she released Valdine and made her way, however hesitantly, toward Sir Spencer.

"She... she went mad, my lord," she breathed, still too fearful to draw any closer to Johanne's corpse as if it would rise up and attack her. "She killed her brother in a rage when she learned that Kirk loved my sister."

Spencer' pale eyes stared at Micheline a moment before passing a long glance at the lady he had killed in self-defense. He simply shook his head.

"I did not want to kill her but she gave me no choice," he said hoarsely. "I fear she would have killed us all."

Micheline nodded firmly, pulling the scarf away from her head. Soft brown hair tumbled down her back as she stared at the dead woman, hardly daring to believe that it was over. The madness, the fear, the torture; with the swift stroke of a broadsword, the conclusion had not been pleasant, but it had been swift. And she wasn't sorry in the least.

"I realize that," she said quietly. "You were simply protecting us, Sir Spencer, and I am ever grateful."

Spencer couldn't decide if he was disturbed over what had happen more than he was satisfied. He had killed a woman, which went against everything he believed in. But given The Darkland's reputation, he suspected he had done a great service to many. And paid vengeance for others.

He turned to Micheline, noticing in a softer, more average way that she resembled her sister. In fact, he thought her to be rather pretty.

"And you, my lady?" His baritone was soft. "Are you well?"

Micheline nodded. "Well enough. Better still now that Johanne and Edmund have been sent where they belong - to the bowels of hell to pay for their horrible sins."

Spencer did not know what else to say. Around them, the occupants of the kitchen yard emerged from their hiding places, daring to come forward to see what had become of their mad mistress. She was dead, as was her brother, disemboweled on the floor of the great kitchen. Though it was wicked to think of celebrating such an event, Micheline realized she was considering that very thing.

Spencer thought he caught a glimpse of a very relieved smile.

CHAPTER TWENTY

The funeral for Kirk's parents had been short, to the point. A lass from the kitchens of Wicklow sang a sorrowful Irish folk ballad, driving Steven to tears as the grave was filled. Ryan Connaught was buried holding his wife, the two of them wrapped in the linens from their wedding bed.

Somberly, the small collection of mourners made their way back to the Castle, the walls slowly rebuilt by a workforce of soldiers and peasants. Kirk had personally screened every one of the Irish peasants before allowing them to repair his beloved Wicklow. Convinced there were no spies or rebels among them, he was satisfied with the progress.

Niles and Albert had already been sent home on one of the de Cleveley boats. With all of the chaos finally quieted and a sense of order taking hold, Kirk had time to reflect on Niles' death and realized he missed his friend a great deal. But he still had Corwin, a fine fighter and companion, and he comforted himself in the fact that he had not lost the both of them. One, most certainly, was enough.

Corwin, too, seemed particularly pensive over Niles' death. But he had been unusually quiet since setting sail for Ireland, going about his duties with silent efficiency, though Kirk had not lingered on the man's subdued mood. Mayhap it was the gloom of leaving his wife, or the distaste of battle altogether. For whatever the reason, he was unconcerned when Corwin wandered up to him after supper on the night of his parent's burial.

The moon was full, the landscape ghostly silent. Kirk glanced at Corwin as the man came to rest beside him on the battlements, exchanging a few pleasantries before slipping into silence. As his eyes swept the countryside and keep, Kirk happened to pass a glance at Corwin and noticed the man was sweating profusely.

"Corwin?" he asked. "Are you well, man?"

Corwin seemed to be shaking. "Why... why do you ask, Kirk?"

"Because you're soaked with perspiration. Are you feeling ill?"

Corwin coughed nervously, the trembling in his body growing more evident. Kirk's brow furrowed with concern.

"If you are ill, then mayhap you should rest. Steven can give up his bed for one night. In fact, you have not seemed well since we arrived in Ireland. Is something the matter?"

Corwin closed his eyes as Kirk spoke, bowing his head as if to block out the question. Before Kirk was finished speaking, he made a strange choking sound and fell back against the stone parapet.

"Oh, God... Kirk!"

Kirk was gravely concerned. He grasped Corwin by the arms to steady him. "Corwin, what's the matter?"

Corwin's brown eyes gushed over with tears. His gaze, wide and frantic, met Kirk. "I cannot... I cannot go on like this any longer! It is killing me!"

"What is?" Kirk demanded softly. In truth, he was a little frightened. "What is killing you, Corwin?"

Corwin suddenly grabbed him, holding his arms so tightly that Kirk lost feeling where the fingers bit into his flesh. "This... silence." He gasped as if it had taken all of his strength to spit it out. "I have been silent for too long and the torment is killing me!"

Kirk tried to remain calm, to make some sense out of what Corwin was trying to say. "I do not understand, Corwin. What silence?"

Corwin drew in a ragged breath, sagging as Kirk held him steady. The auburn head hung slack, lolling from side to side as if losing all control.

"This silence I have carried with me for years," he whispered. "Silence that has eaten away at me, a dark silence that you can hardly comprehend. But I cannot be silent any longer! You must know what is happening!"

Kirk's composure was slowly slipping. "Then tell me, Corwin. What is happening?"

Corwin's head drooped again and he stared at the ground. Finally, he swallowed hard in an attempt to regain his composure. He would need all of his strength to get through this. "Dear God, Kirk, you must forgive me."

"For what?"

"For not being truthful with you. For not telling you what I knew, for not helping you prevent the deaths of nine innocent women."

Kirk stared at him, the flicker of disquiet in his soul bursting into a roaring blaze. "Then be truthful with me now. What do you know?"

Corwin lifted pain-filled eyes. "I know that Edmund ordered me to help him murder those women. He threatened to kill Valdine if I did not help him. He gave me little choice but to keep his dirty secrets."

Kirk drew in a long, steadying breath. "I see," he murmured. The truth as he had always suspected. "Then it was you helping him all along. But the rumors pointed to Niles."

"Edmund started those rumors to take suspicion off me. He knew you suspected that one of us was aiding him and he wanted you to believe it was Niles."

"Because he had leverage against you," Kirk finished softly. "And you did what you felt you had to do in order to keep your wife safe."

Corwin nodded miserably. "I hated myself for being so weak, Kirk. But I had no choice. Edmund gave me no choice!"

Kirk released the man, allowing him to bump softly against the parapet. "I understand what you are saying, lad. But I do not understand why you have chosen this particular moment to confess."

Corwin seemed to pale further, if such a thing was possible. "It... it involves Micheline...."

Kirk grabbed him again, so hard that Corwin yelped with pain. Stone-gray eyes blazed at him. "What of Micheline? You haven't...?"

"Nay." Corwin shook his head quickly. "But Edmund wanted to. He ordered me to kill her, but I couldn't. Instead, I locked her in the tower where she remains to this day. I was hoping you would return from Quernmore in time to take charge of the situation, but instead we were routed to Ireland sooner than expected."

Kirk emitted a harsh sigh, his volatile emotions surging. "Damn you, Corwin! Has she been harmed?"

"Nay."

"What does Edmund know of her death?"

"Only that she is dead. That I disposed of the body, as we have disposed of all the rest."

Kirk released him, roughly, and the knight stumbled back against the stone abutment. But what terrified him the most was the fact that he wasn't finished yet.

"There's more, Kirk."

Kirk was chewing his lip with agitation. "Christ, what more could there possibly be?"

Corwin swallowed. "Edmund promised to kill Valdine if I told you."

Kirk stopped chewing his lip. He did not like the look in Corwin's eye. "Tell me *what*?"

Corwin's trembling increased. In fact, he was nearly cowering. "But Valdine...."

Kirk took a step toward him. "I shall kill her myself if you do not tell me what more there is."

Corwin shrank, averting his gaze. When the mortal blow came, he did not want to see it. "It has to do with his plans for Mara."

As he feared, Kirk went mad. He grabbed the knight, throwing him to the pathway of the battlement. His hands around the man's neck, he half-shoved him over the edge of the narrow walkway, a two-story drop to the ground below. Corwin gasped with terror, but his fear was nothing compared to the look of murder in Kirk's eyes.

"Tell me!" Kirk roared.

"Edmund sent a missive to le Vay proposing a marriage with Mara!" he rattled off. "You carried the missive with you when you went to solicit his support!"

Kirk's mouth went slack, his eyes wide with shock. But the hands remained around Corwin's neck, nearly strangling him.

"A missive?" His eyes closed as realization swept him and he turned away, releasing the knight. "My dear God... the second missive I knew nothing about. A marriage proposal, did you say?"

"Aye."

Kirk could hardly speak. "And I carried it right to him. *Right to him!*"

Corwin scooted away from the ledge, rubbing his sore neck. "Edmund wanted to be rid of Mara because he felt she was a threat to the stability of his Anchorsholme. You had turned against him because of her and Edmund simply wanted to be rid of her."

"Then why did not he kill her like the rest?"

Corwin seemed to be calming now that he had confessed everything. "It was really Johanne who wanted them dead, Kirk. Edmund simply carried out her wishes. And Johanne wanted them dead because they had shown interest in you. And you, as we all know, belong to her."

"That does not answer my question. Why did not he kill her?"

Corwin looked away. "Because Johanne was so focused on Micheline's arrival that she failed to notice the relationship developing between you and Mara. Edmund did not want her to know, and he did not want to risk your wrath by harming the girl, so he chose to send her away. I think the truth of the matter was that he couldn't bear to harm her because she was so lovely."

"So he sent her to le Vay?"

Corwin nodded slowly. "You played right into his plans when you asked that she accompany you to Quernmore. Edmund was going to ask you to take her to Quernmore to show off to the old man, but you beat him to it. Once she was married to le Vay, there would be nothing you could do. You would be forced to forget about her, Anchorsholme would return to normal, and the entire episode would be a distant memory."

Kirk fell back against the parapet, his face glazed with shock. "This is such madness I have difficulty believing it." He turned to the somber knight. "Why, Corwin? Why did you wait until now to tell me all of this?"

Corwin sat dejectedly at the edge of the walkway. "Fear," he said hoarsely. "Fear for Valdine. But I simply cannot sit by while Mara marries another man, or Micheline remains a prisoner. It has to end; all of it. You *must* know."

"Do you still fear for Valdine?"

Corwin shrugged. "I will trust that you will not permit anything to happen to her. Considering you will be returning to England to stop the wedding between Mara and le Vay, I would hope you would take the time to protect my wife from the wrath of our liege."

Kirk pushed himself off the wall. Already, he was moving for the ladder that descended to the bailey. Rising on unsteady legs, Corwin followed.

"Where are you going?"

Kirk did not glance up as he lowered himself on the ladder. "To England."

"Tonight?"

"This very moment."

Corwin watched Kirk as he dropped to the dirt of the bailey, marching toward the darkened keep of Wicklow like a man with a demon on his heels.

"Godspeed, Kirk." He felt sick inside. Sick and full of sadness. "I sincerely hope you are in time."

And time was running out.

CHAPTER TWENTY ONE

Nine days.

It had been nine long and horrific days since Lionel had told Mara of her marital fate. Nine days of tears, of frustration and despair, and nine long days of plotting how to escape the man. She had to break free or die trying.

Lionel knew of her desperation. For the past several days, he had locked her in her room to prevent her from doing anything foolish but Lily had always released her. Still, Lily wasn't entirely oblivious as to why her father had locked Mara in; she kept Mara with her at all times for much the same reason her father kept her locked in her chamber. Neither one of them wanted to see any harm befall Mara her because the woman was so distraught that they were afraid she very well might do something to hurt herself. She was in agony.

The only person Lionel could speak with about the situation was Lily because Spencer had kept a distance from him, but even Lily was somewhat unsympathetic. She made it very clear that she didn't agree with what her father was doing. Her lack of support disturbed him but he wouldn't let it dissuade him. It all came to a head one afternoon when Lionel came to visit Mara and, as usual, found Lily sitting with her.

The day had been unusually cold, a heavy breeze blowing in from the sea ten miles to the west. In Mara's chamber, the same chamber she had shared with Kirk, a fire blazed and the ladies were warmly wrapped. Lionel entered politely, he gazed on Mara as she sat near the fire with Lily. He knew Mara had heard him enter but she would not look at him. She hadn't looked at him in nine days.

"Greetings, ladies," he said pleasantly. "I have come to tell you that supper will be early tonight. A group of traveling musicians have taken shelter with us and have promised to perform tonight. I thought you both might enjoy the entertainment."

Mara didn't move. Her gaze was on the fire. Lily's gaze lingered on Mara a moment before turning to her father.

"I do not believe we will be joining you for supper, Father," she said. "Mara and I will take our meal in her room."

Lionel struggled not to lose his patience. It seemed to him that both women were being unreasonable and that both of them were taking a stand against him. It hurt him that Lily would side with a new friend over her own father. Moreover, after nine days of tension, he was ready to crack. He was tired of it.

"Nonsense," he said. "You have supped every night in your rooms for over a week. You will both come down to sup in the hall tonight, do you hear? We will have a grand celebration this night with music and wine and food."

"Nay, Father," Lily said firmly. "Mara will not go to the hall and I will not leave her. We will eat here."

So much for keeping his temper. Lionel grunted with frustration, turning away from the pair as he struggled to think of something to say that wouldn't set them off. He ended up stomping across the floor towards the chamber door but stopped short of exiting. He turned to them.

"I am at an end with this foolishness," he said flatly. "I realize that Lady Mara is upset by all of this and I realize you are attempting to comfort her. I am grateful for your compassion, Lily. But the time has come for Lady Mara to accept her destiny. All of the weeping and moping is not going to change things. We shall be married very soon and that will be the end of it."

Mara, having been fairly numb and distant for the past several days, suddenly came to life.

"It is *not* the end of it," she snapped. "It is only the beginning, my lord, for if you force me into this sham of a marriage, you will have wed a bitter woman who hates the very sight of you. You have condemned yourself to a life of misery by forcing yourself on a woman who wants nothing to do with you."

Lionel's jaw ticked as he jabbed a finger at her. "If misery is what you want, then that is your choice," he said. "I do not care what you think of me so long as you provide me with a son."

Mara shot to her feet. "There is already a child in my belly that is not of your loins," she fired back. "It is Kirk's son and he will kill you in order to claim what is rightfully his. Is that clear enough for you?"

Both Lionel and Lily stared at her, shocked. The room was taut with silence, a painful sensation as Mara's words hung heavy in the air. Lionel's stunned expression transformed into something peculiar.

"So he has bedded you," he muttered.

It was a statement more than a question. Mara, seething with fury, clenched and unclenched her fists.

"Of course he has," she snarled. "I love him and he will be my husband."

Lionel stared at her a moment longer before emitting a heavy sigh. Furious moments before, he lost all of his fire rather quickly. Confrontation wasn't in his nature.

"It is of no matter," he said quietly. "I will claim the child as my own. Hopefully it is a son to carry on the le Vay name."

"Is that all you care about?" Mara threw up her hands. "A son? Look at me, Lionel; I am a woman of flesh and blood and feeling. I am not a brood mare whose only purpose in life is to provide you with an all-precious son to carry on the le Vay name."

"You serve no other purpose," Lionel bellowed. "You are a bereft woman from an insignificant family and you should consider yourself extremely fortunate."

"Father, you are beastly!" Lily shushed him, turning to Mara with pain in her expression. "Please, Mara, do not listen to him. *Please,* darling."

Mara was beyond rational thought. She turned away from Lily and Lionel, wandering aimlessly to the other end of the room, as far away as she could get from either of them. She struggled to calm herself; oddly, she was reflecting back to the times when she and Kirk had argued. The angrier she became, the cooler he grew. She had never truly known anyone outside of her family or home until he came around, and his very presence caused her to grow up and mature with astonishing speed.

Kirk had helped her understand how to behave with people and how to react. No one had ever done that before. She was coming to see that all of the fighting in the world would not gain her wants with Lionel. The man was determined to marry her no matter what she said which, indeed, left her with little choice. Perhaps she couldn't fight him, but maybe she could delay him just enough for Kirk to return and save her.

Kirk told her that he had no idea how long he would be in Ireland. A week, a month, a year... or perhaps never. Perhaps he would be killed over there and never return. The thought made her stomach churn and brought tears to her eyes. Face to the wall, she just stood there and cried.

Lily came up behind her and put her arms around her, hugging her. Lionel, watching the two women comfort each other, was feeling particularly frustrated. He had always been a benevolent lord, concerned for his family and his subjects, but at the moment, he felt like a beast.

"Lily," he barked. "Come with me now."

Lily was hugging Mara fiercely. "Nay," she said angrily. "I will not."

Lionel would not be refuted. "Come with me now or you shall not like my reaction."

Lily had always shared a wonderful relationship with her father, but the past nine days had seen that deteriorate tremendously. Lily was amiable and sweet, but at the moment, she could only feel anguish. She let go of Mara and went to her father.

"Why are you being so awful?" she hissed. "This is not like you, Father, not at all. What is the matter with you?"

Lionel frowned. In truth, he wasn't feeling very well; he'd awoken that morning with numbness in his legs and a great sharp pain in his belly. He knew the time was drawing to an end for him and that in part fed his bad mood. He wanted to get the marriage over with, and consummate it, but with Mara claiming she was already pregnant with Kirk's child, the situation was markedly changed.

If he married her, any child she bore regardless of the father would be claimed as a le Vay. Perhaps that was all he really needed to do; simply marry her. It was the first step and after that, he would figure out the rest. But gazing at his daughter's angry face, he realized that his first and very necessary step would be to have Lily on his side. If his daughter supported him, then perhaps Mara would calm down and see reason. He could only hope.

"I am sorry," he said, forcing himself to calm. "I... I am not feeling very well. I am sorry if my manner has been harsh."

It was much more like the father she knew. Lily went from angry to concern in a flash. "What is the matter?" she asked.

Ah, sympathy. Lionel was wise enough to play it. "My belly pains me greatly this morning," he said, watching Lily's concern deepen. "And... and I feel very weak and exhausted. I am not trying to be difficult, but it would help me tremendously if Lady Mara would think rationally and understand what I am offering her. All of this turmoil is upsetting me greatly. It is taxing my health. Lily, please help me, my love. Please help Mara to understand.

Lily was greatly torn. "But... Father, she loves Kirk. She does not want to marry you."

He patted his belly, a sour look on his face. "My health, daughter," he repeated softly. "I understand that she loves Kirk. But that will pass. Her duty is to marry me and provide me with a son. You must make her understand this. Don't *you* understand it?"

Lily looked at her father with some uncertainty. He knew she understood the mechanics of marriage. She had spent many years in a rather courtly household and Lionel was well aware that she understood the purpose of an advantageous marriage. Still, he could see the reluctance in her eyes.

"I understand," she said. "But what you are doing is not right. You are hurting two people who never did anything to you, Father. Don't you see that? Kirk has always been a strong supporter and Mara... well, her only crime is loving Kirk. You are punishing her for being young and in love."

Lionel could see he wasn't going to have Lily's full support. It didn't matter that they were flesh and blood relatives, closer than most fathers and daughters were. Lily was taking a stand for what she believed in and it happened to be a stand against him. Lionel didn't like it. If he couldn't coerce her into supporting him, then he could force her. Time was growing short and he had to marry Mara no matter what.

"I am not punishing her," he said, his voice low. "I am not entirely sure why young ladies these days believe that marriage is based on love, but that is a fool's notion. I have summoned a priest who will be here by dinner. You will have Mara properly dressed for the occasion because whether or not she is ready, I am marrying her tonight at dusk. There will be no more delays."

Lily was horrified. "Dusk?" she repeated. "Father, surely you...."

He cut her off, unwilling to discuss it further. "I have waited long enough," he snapped. "Whether we wait nine days, nine weeks or nine months, the result will be the same. Make sure she is ready by dusk."

With that, he swept from the room without a glance to Mara. She was still standing near the wall, weeping softly. When the door slammed in his wake, she jumped, turning to see who was still left in the room. Only Lily remained, looking drawn and anxious. She approached Mara, haltingly, a sickened expression on her face.

"Oh... Mara," she breathed. "He is being most unreasonable. He says he has sent for a priest and you will be married at dusk tonight."

Mara, surprisingly, didn't fall into hysterics. She simply stared at Lily. The hysteria has been replaced by a steely coldness now that a timeline had been put to her fate. It was shock more than anything, perhaps numbness and a sense of harsh realization. Nine days of fighting hadn't solved or changed anything. Her future was still set. She turned away from Lily.

"I will not go willingly," she said.

Lily sighed heavily. "He will call the guards if he has to," she said. "They will carry you down to the hall. They will hold you through the ceremony and force you to wed my father. Is this truly how you wish to behave?"

Mara looked over her shoulder, her bright blue eyes piercing. "How would *you* behave?"

Lily looked pained. She shrugged helplessly. "I do not know," she whispered. "But I would realize there is no use in fighting. Would I wish for everyone to see me screaming and kicking and being held down by soldiers? I would not. I would not embarrass myself so."

"Then help me escape."

"Escape to *where*?"

"Back to Haslingden until Kirk can come for me."

Lily shook her head, exasperated. "My father would find you there just as easily," she said. "Mara, don't you see? You cannot refuse this, darling. I know you love Kirk. I know he will return for you. But he is not here now, and he cannot save you from this marriage. You have no choice."

Mara stared at Lily, a creeping sense of defeat filling her. *But no.* She would not accept it. She couldn't.

"Lily," she said as she averted her gaze. "You have been a true and sweet friend. I... I have never known such friendship and I want to thank you very much."

Lily put a hand on her arm. "As I have never had a friend like you, either," she said. "You are humorous and curious and lovely. I am so sorry this has happened, darling, truly."

Mara patted her hand but then she moved away from it, heading towards one of the small lancet windows that let light into the chamber.

"Will you do something for me if I ask it?" she asked.

Lily nodded. "If I can, you know I will."

"I want you to leave me alone. Please."

Lily wasn't so sure about the request. Mara hadn't been alone since the day of her father's announcement, and for good reason. Everyone was aware of that fact, especially Mara. Therefore, her question had Lily on edge.

"I... I would like to, of course," she stammered. "But...."

"Please," Mara said firmly, turning to look at her. "I swear I will not try to harm myself in any way."

Lily looked at her dubiously. "Do you promise? A promise above all promises?"

"I swore, didn't I?"

"But why do you want to be alone?"

"I just do," she said softly. "I just want to... think. I have so much to think about. Please indulge me, Lily. Just for a little while."

Reluctantly, Lily nodded. "Very well," she said. "I will leave you to your thoughts. Shall I send up some food?"

Mara shook her head. "No food."

With a final lingering gaze, Lily hesitantly quit the room. As soon as the door shut softly behind her, Mara ran to the door and threw the big iron bolt. The door and frame, built like a fortress with great iron supports, was built to withstand a siege.

By dinner, a dozen men were still trying to force it open.

CHAPTER TWENTY TWO

Spencer could see the torches on the battlements of Quernmore in the distance and he sighed with relief; they were almost home. He couldn't wait to see Lionel's expression when he told him what had become of Edmund and Johanne. If Lionel didn't believe him, he'd brought three reliable witnesses with him.

In the darkness of early evening, Micheline rode beside him astride a small gray palfrey, having exchanged her peasant clothing for more suitable attire. Behind them rode Valdine and Wanda, wrapped up in heavy cloaks astride their own palfreys, and terrified of traveling on the open road. Having rarely ventured out of Anchorsholme, they had an unnatural fear of the outside world. Micheline kept glancing back at them to make sure they were well. Since they had tried, and succeeded, in saving her from her prison, she felt an obligation to take care of them.

"They are fine, Lady de Cleveley," Spencer said when she turned around for the hundredth time since leaving Anchorsholme. "You worry like a mother hen."

Micheline looked at him, smiling weakly. "They do not look very well."

Spencer glanced over his shoulder at the pair, riding so close that they were nearly on top of each other. All they could see was their pale faces peering out from behind their heavy hoods.

"How can you tell?" he asked with feigned seriousness.

Micheline giggled. "You'll not make light of them," she scolded softly. "They are brave beyond measure."

Spencer was looking at her, a glimmer in his eye. "I do not make light of them, I assure you," he said. "They were indeed brave to do what they did for you. But I would say, baroness, that you are braver and stronger because you, in fact, survived the Darkland. I have the utmost respect for you."

Micheline blushed demurely. "Were it not for you, my lord, I am not sure what would have happened to us."

Spencer watched her lowered head. She had her sister's nose and soft shape of the face, but her behavior was far more agreeable and sweet.

"I am sure you would have bested Johanne somehow," he said, thinking on what had happened two days before. It had been a freakish and shocking happening, but he pushed it aside for the moment. There were more pleasant things to speak to Lady Micheline about. "Now that you have inherited Anchorsholme from your husband, have you thought about what you intend to do with it?"

Micheline's head came up and she cocked it thoughtfully. "I... I am not sure," she said. "Live there, I suppose. To tell you the truth, I am still rather stunned about what happened. It is difficult to comprehend that both Edmund and Johanne are dead."

The glimmer faded from Spencer's eye. He grew serious. "Not soon enough," he said. "Surely you knew of the rumors of the Darkland, my lady. Everyone in these parts knew of them."

Micheline tried not to look too contrite. "I will confess that I had not heard," she admitted. "My father pledged me to marry Edmund in payment for a debt owed to Edmund's father, Monroe. If my father knew of the rumors, he never told me. I only learned of them after I came to Anchorsholme."

Spencer lifted his eyebrows in understanding. "Now that you know of them, surely you know what a blessing Edmund and Johanne's passing is."

"I am coming to."

He smiled confidently. "Anchorsholme will be an inviting and pleasant place once again under your hand," he said. "I am sure of it."

Micheline was fortified by his kind words, blushing beneath the moonlight. He seemed like such a kind man; she was coming to like him a great deal. "I hope so, my lord. I will do my best."

Spencer didn't say anymore to her after that as the approached the massive walls of Quernmore. It was growing cold and very dark by the time they came upon the great gatehouse with its massive smoking torches, smelling of animal fat. Spencer announced the party to the sentries, who ordered the gates opened. Chains clanked and groaned as the big woodened panels slowly swung open.

They were greeted inside the gatehouse by a few soldiers and a senior sergeant. Spencer wearily climbed off his charger, handing the reins to one of the soldiers and moving to assist Micheline. She was light and slender, sliding easily into his big arms.

"Where is Lord Lionel?" Spencer asked.

"In the keep, my lord," the sergeant replied. "He is attending his bride."

Spencer had just lowered Micheline to the ground but he froze, his hands still on her waist as he looked at the soldier. "They are *already* married?"

The sergeant shook his head. "Nay, my lord," he replied, unaware that the woman in Spencer's grip was the sister of the reluctant bride. "It would seem that his intended has barricaded herself in a room and they are trying to get her out. A priest is waiting for them in the hall once they manage to purge her from the chamber."

Micheline gasped and Spencer glanced at her with concern. Without another word to the gaggle of soldiers, he took Micheline by the hand and began walking, very swiftly, towards the keep. Wanda and Valdine slithered off their palfreys and followed, clutching each other and terrified of all the strange men and the strange surroundings.

Quernmore's keep was a big, square and squat building, four stories including the lower ground floor storage level. It was massive. Micheline skipped after Spencer, hardly able to take the time to view her surroundings as he pulled her through the keep entry and up a rather large flight of spiral stairs that was built into the thickness of the wall. Once they reached the top level, he pulled her down a narrow, arched corridor, ducking his head to avoid the iron wall sconces and their smoking torches.

Almost immediately, they could hear voices and what sounded like a chopping axe echoing in the tight quarters of the passageway. Men were speaking, sometimes barking, and Spencer could hear Lionel's agitated tone. Turning a corner, they could see the situation of a torn-up door and several soldiers trying to break it down.

"My lord," Spencer said as he swiftly approached. "What goes on here?"

Lionel looked surprised to see Spencer. But just as swiftly, his attention was drawn to Micheline in Spencer's grip and the identical women hovering fearfully behind her. His gaze lingered on the women for a moment before he refocused on Spencer.

"Nothing a few dozen soldiers and three months of hard labor will not see resolved," he said, rather exhaustedly. "I did not hear the sentries. When did you arrive?"

"Just now," Spencer told him, still eyeing the door. "What has happened?"

Lionel slumped against the wall as he, too, eyed the door. "The Lady Mara has barricaded herself and we are attempting to free her," he replied. His attention was drawn to Micheline. "Who is your lovely escort, Spencer?"

Spencer looked at Micheline. "My lord, allow me to introduce you to the Lady Micheline de Cleveley," he said, returning his attention to Lionel with a lift of the eyebrows. "Lady Micheline is the Lady Mara's sister."

Lionel's eyes widened. He focused on Micheline. "Lady Mara's sis...?" He couldn't even finish. He pushed himself off the wall and grasped Micheline by the arm. "You are Mara's *sister*?"

Micheline was rather intimidated by the man with the busy dark eyebrows. "Aye, my lord."

Lionel's hope was renewed. "Perhaps she will open the door for you!"

Micheline knew that wouldn't happen; but, then again, perhaps Mara might. The sisters had been separated for a few weeks, more separation than they had ever experienced in their lives. Perhaps Mara would be glad enough to see her sister to forget her stand-off and open the door.

"Perhaps," Micheline nodded, eyeing the soldiers trying to twist the door off its hinges. "But you must send your men away. She will never open the door if she feels threatened."

Lionel began waving his hands at the soldiers. "Cease!" he hissed. "Drop what you are doing and leave at once. *Go!*"

The soldiers, weary and sweaty from hours of exertion, gladly did as they were told. As they backed off from the panel, Lionel turned to Spencer. "You will stand flush against the wall next to the door," he told him. "If Lady Micheline can coerce her out into the corridor, you can grab her from behind."

Spencer's brow furrowed. "Grab her? Why?"

Lionel's features hardened. "Because this girl has put me through nine long days of madness and foolishness," he snapped. "I will stand for it no longer. The priest awaits us downstairs and unfortunately, Lady Mara has chosen to be married by force. I shall be happy to oblige her."

Micheline wasn't at all thrilled with his reply. It was a struggle not to outright refute the man.

"My lord," she said steadily. "I was informed that my husband offered my sister to you in marriage."

Lionel nodded. "He did, and I accepted."

It wasn't in Micheline's nature to resist or go against a directive of any kind. She was too meek. But knowing how Mara felt about Kirk, nothing about this situation made sense to her. She tried very hard to be respectful.

"My lord," she began again, carefully. "I am not sure if you are aware, but my sister has hoped to wed Kirk Connaught. My husband was not aware of this when he sent you the marriage offer. Had he known, he would not have offered Mara to you."

"Aware or not, I have accepted," Lionel repeated. "This is not a subject open to debate. Mara will become my wife before the night is over."

Micheline didn't like the soullessness from the man, and that dislike fed her bravery. "Do you understand that she is in love with another man and he is in love with her?" she asked. "I am sure if you understood this, you would not make such a callous statement."

Lionel eyes narrowed. "It does not matter," he said. "Furthermore, this is a contract between Edmund and me. With all manner of respect, my lady, this is none of your affair and you will kindly stay out of it."

"It *is* my affair," Micheline shot back softly. "My husband is dead; therefore, I have inherited his affairs, this one included. I am rescinding the marriage contract, my lord. You will find yourself another bride or I will not lift a finger to aid you in removing Mara from that room."

Lionel was geared up for a retort when her words sank in; *my husband is dead*. "Edmund is dead, did you say?" he repeated incredulously. "When did this occur?"

"A few days ago," Micheline replied, her manner strong and confident. "His sister killed him and when she tried to murder me, Sir Spencer saved my life."

Lionel looked at Spencer, astonished. "Is this true?"

Spencer was grim. "It is," he said softly. "Johanne was running mad. She murdered her brother and was attempting to murder the baroness when I intervened. When she tried to kill me, I killed her instead. I am not proud of the fact, my lord, but it is the truth. The woman was insane and I had no choice."

Lionel was completely shocked. He stared at Spencer, wide-eyed. "The madwoman attacked you?" he breathed. Then he shook his head. "I have heard tale of what she was capable of, but to attack a fully armed knight? I cannot believe my ears. The woman truly was mad."

Spencer nodded grimly. "She was not particularly strong but she was ruthless," he said. "As much as I did not relish killing a woman, there was no alternative."

Lionel was quickly overcoming his shock, thinking of a world without the horrors of the Darkland hanging over their heads.

"What did you do with Edmund and Johanne?" he asked, looking between Spencer and Micheline. "I am assuming there was no mass said for them?"

Spencer looked at Micheline, who answered without hesitation. "None that I would attend, my lord," she replied. "I paid the local parish priest to bury them in a location he deemed appropriate but I do not wish to know the details. I wash my hands of them both."

"Wise," Lionel concurred. He began to look at Micheline with new, and perhaps respectful, eyes. "Lady Micheline, you seem like a woman with a good head on her shoulders. How is it that you married into that hellish family?"

Micheline repeated the details. "In payment for a gambling debt my father had with Monroe de Cleveley."

Lionel stroked his bearded chin, eyeing her. "I see," he said. "How old are you, my lady?"

"I have seen twenty-two years, my lord."

"And you feel yourself capable of running an established house such as Anchorsholme?"

"I cannot be any worse than my husband was, my lord."

Lionel snorted. He approved of his newest neighbor even though the truth was that he had little choice. It also occurred to him that he needed to establish a good relationship with her from the start and trying to break the woman's sister out of her barricaded room wasn't perhaps the best way to go about such a thing.

"Indeed," he said. "You already seem wise and reasonable. Speaking of wise and reasonable, do you have any suggestions on how to release your sister from her bower?"

Micheline sighed. "I know of no such way, my lord," she said with regret. "She will stay in there until she rots. She is very stubborn."

"Can you not plead with her to open the door?"

Micheline had no real choice in the matter. They simply couldn't leave Mara in the room forever. Again, she signed.

"I can try."

Lionel and Spencer stood back as Micheline went to the door, half-hacked up and wrought with twisted metal. After a moment's hesitation, she knocked on it softly.

"Mara?" she called. "Mara, 'tis me, love. Please let me in."

They could all hear the shriek behind the closed door. Suddenly, the door was rattling as the bolt was thrown on the opposite side. But the door was so warped that it wasn't hanging correctly any longer so the best Mara could do was open it three or four inches. When she saw Micheline in the corridor, she shrieked again.

"Misha!" she cried. "You have come!"

Micheline smiled at her pale-faced sister. "Open the door, love."

Mara jerked at the door until her hair flopped in her face. "I cannot," she said, looking at the warped panel. "Those fools have ruined this door. I do not believe I can open it."

Having heard the conversation from his post several feet away, Spencer moved towards the door.

"Let me try," he said.

As Micheline stood back, Spencer threw his shoulder into the panel and shoved, but it wasn't enough, so Lionel came forward and also threw his shoulder into it. When Mara saw Lionel, she screamed and ran from their field of vision.

"Stay away!" she cried.

"Mara?" Micheline called to her. "Please do not be frightened. Nothing is going to happen to you, I promise."

228

Mara, having spent more than a day in the chamber with hardly any sleep or food, was at her wit's end.

"You... you liar!" she screamed at her sister. "You wanted me to open the door so he would come in!"

Micheline quickly came to understand what her sister meant and she hastened to reassure her. "Nay, love, I promise that is not true," she said. "I simply wanted to see you."

Spencer and Lionel managed to get the door partially open and Mara shrieked again when she saw that it was wide enough for a man to slip through. In a panic, she threw herself into the slender lancet window.

"If you come any closer, I shall jump!"

Spencer was already in the room, coming to a halt when he saw Mara in the window. Lionel was a little slower to enter, struggling his big belly through the narrow opening, but he too came to a halt when he saw Mara in the window that was three stories above the hard-packed bailey. He threw out his hands.

"Nay, Mara," he pleaded. "All will be will, I swear it. You must get out of the window."

Mara inched out of the narrow ledge, gripping the frame of the window for leverage. "I will not get out of the window," she cried. "I will not marry you, do you hear me? If you come any closer, I shall throw myself to the bailey below."

Micheline was in the room now, her eyes wide with fear. She well remembered a situation like this a few weeks ago when Mara had threatened to jump and would have fallen to her death had Kirk not saved her silly neck. She knew Mara wasn't serious but she was also reckless. She could easily slip and....

"*Please*, Mara," she begged softly. "I have not seen you in over a week and there is much to tell. So much has happened. Edmund and Johanne are dead."

Mara had much the same reaction that Lionel had; her eyes widened and her jaw went slack. "Dead?" she repeated. "What happened?"

"Now is not the time to discuss this," Lionel interrupted. He was seriously concerned. "Lady Mara, please climb out of the window."

Mara's attention was back on Lionel, her expression reverting to the panicked frown. "Only if you promise I do not have to marry you."

Lionel wasn't surprised she was striking up a bargain. He knew she was an intelligent creature; she was trying to turn the situation to her advantage. But he knew he could never let her gain the upper hand.

"Would it be so terrible, lass?" he asked quietly. "Would it be so terrible that you would rather kill yourself that become a wealthy baroness?"

Mara's bright eyes flickered. "It would not be terrible under different circumstances," she said, calming somewhat. "But I would rather be the wife of a poor knight whom I love than the wife of a wealthy baron I do not love."

Lionel lifted a bushy eyebrow. "I understand," he said, "but what you have failed to consider is that Kirk might not ever return from Ireland. He went over to fight a battle, my lady. It was not a garden party. Men will aim to kill him and it is quite possible one will succeed. He could be dead right now for all we know and then what will you do? Be a burden on your sister's good graces for the rest of your life?"

Mara turned red. "He *will* return," she hissed. "He will return and he will kill you for what you have done."

"Perhaps," Lionel said softly. "That remains to be seen. Now, come down off the window sill before you fall."

"I will not!"

"Mara, come out of the window, lass."

The words spoken were not Lionel's. Nor were they Micheline's or Spencer's. The voice had come from the chamber doorway and, startled, everyone in the room swung around to see Kirk standing inside of the twisted panel. He'd managed to slip in and no one heard or saw anything. Exhausted, clad in dirty and bloodied armor, he was armed to the teeth as if ready to go to battle at any second.

They could not help but noticed that he did not look pleased.

CHAPTER TWENTY THREE

At the sight of Kirk, Micheline gasped with astonishment. Lionel might have also made a noise. But Kirk had eyes only for Mara.

"Come out of the window, love," he told her again, softly.

For a moment, nobody moved. They were stunned. But then Mara shrieked, propelling herself out of the window and towards Kirk. But the moment she ran past Lionel, within arm's length, the old man reached out and grabbed for her. Mara turned into a wildcat, punching and scratching the man until he released his hold. The next arms that grabbed her were Kirk's.

Mara threw herself against him, sobbing hysterically. Kirk held her tightly, trying not to jab her with sharp and deadly things strapped to his body. He stroked her dark head and kissed her salty cheeks, so very grateful to have her in his arms. He wasn't sure she would ever end up there again.

The truth was that his trip home had been a nightmare of worry and helplessness. Having no idea what had transpired at Quernmore during the time Corwin had withheld this explosive information, it was easy to imagine the worst. Fortunately, the winds had been with him and the trip across the Irish Sea had taken less than the usual day and a night. It had been relatively swift.

The moment the ship docked, Kirk tore off to Quernmore, twelve miles from the port, and made it there in the dark of night. He hadn't stopped moving, or worrying, in days. Now that he had Mara in his arms, the relief was indescribable. But there were still many unanswered questions and he struggled to keep a level head.

"All is well, love," he murmured into her dark hair. "I have returned. All is well."

"Kirk," Spencer's eyes were wide as he took a step in Kirk's direction. "What are you doing here? Has the entire army returned?"

Kirk kissed Mara one last time before turning his stone-gray gaze in Spencer's direction. "It has not," he said, his voice low and deadly. "I have returned prematurely because I was told that Edmund offered Mara to le Vay in marriage. Was this information incorrect?"

Spencer shook his head reluctantly but it was Lionel who spoke. "It was correct," he said steadily. "Edmund de Cleveley, as Lady Mara's legal guardian, offered her to me in marriage and I have accepted."

Kirk's attention shifted to le Vay. "Have you already married her?"

231

Le Vay shook his head. "Not yet."

Kirk relaxed somewhat. Now the most critical issue was answered so he allowed himself a bit of respite from his worry. However, he found that his anger was gaining speed and he struggled to keep it at bay.

"My lord, you are aware that she belongs to me," he said, perplexed. "Why would you accept Edmund's offer?"

Le Vay hesitated. "Because...," he said, paused, and started again. "Because it is my last chance to have an heir, Kirk. With Michael gone, I am in need of a son. I *want* a son. You cannot blame me or deny my wants. It is my right."

Kirk's brow flickered angrily. "*Your* wants?" he repeated. "What about mine? Mara's? Or are you the only person of import and our wants do not matter?"

"I am a wealthy man," Lionel said, summoning courage. Kirk was becoming intimidating. "I was legally offered the lady's hand and I legally accepted. I have done nothing wrong. To want a son to pass my titles and wealth to is not a crime."

"It is not a crime but it is certainly a sin to knowingly marry a woman who loves another," Kirk fired back softly. "You know she belongs to me, my lord. I am shocked and disappointed that you seriously considered this marriage proposal."

Le Vay held Kirk's gaze a moment longer before lowering his head. He couldn't look at the man anymore. He found he was frustrated more than anything.

"So you have returned from Ireland to stop me," he muttered. "Who told you?"

"It does not matter. I have returned to claim what is rightfully mine." Le Vay's gaze flicked up to him. "Rightfully, she is *mine*."

Kirk could see that the man was deadly serious and more than being perplexed by his behavior, he was quickly approaching desperation. He knew that he had no real legal ground to stand on; the contract le Vay had accepted trumped a love story. His thoughts moved to the real problem in all of this; Edmund. His gaze moved to Micheline.

"Where is your husband, my lady?" he asked, grinding his teeth. "I have a need to speak with him."

Micheline was pale and frightened but she met Kirk's gaze evenly. "He is dead," she murmured. "Both Edmund and Johanne are dead."

Kirk didn't react except with a flicker of confusion over his brow. Then his features seemed to slacken. "Dead?" he repeated. "How?"

Micheline sighed heavily, feeling exhausted and sick to the bone. The past few days had been too much to bear.

"Johanne went mad," she said softly. "She did not know that you and Mara were in love. Edmund purposely kept the information from her, I can only assume, out of fear for you. When she found out that he had not told her the truth, she went mad and killed him. When she tried to kill me, Sir Spencer intervened and killed her in self-defense."

Kirk listened intently. He was seriously shocked at the news but, oddly, he found he wasn't particularly surprised. Nothing about events at the Darkland surprised him any longer; he'd grown numb to that place and its poison. He looked at Spencer.

"What were you doing at Anchorsholme?" he asked.

Spencer met his gaze evenly. "I was there to deliver Lord le Vay's acceptance of the marriage offer for Mara."

Kirk fell quiet, digesting the information. His mind was working swiftly, mulling over the facts, the results, and the future. He realized that he felt a great deal of relief at the news of Edmund and Johanne's deaths, more than he ever imagined possible. He had no great love for Edmund and certainly no great love for Johanne. No, he wasn't disappointed in the least. He was glad. But one thought became abundantly clear as he stood there and stewed; he looked straight at Micheline.

"You are Lady de Cleveley and I am sworn to you," he said quietly. "You command an army of one-thousand men and a great Irish empire. Long live Lady de Cleveley."

Micheline, slumped against a chair, stared at him. But she could see the warmth in his dark eyes and she smiled wearily.

"Thank you," she murmured.

Kirk's warmth faded. "That also means that you are responsible for the contracts your husband brokered," he said. "Should you wish to dispute the contract between Lord le Vay and Mara, it is within your right to do so but know he will expect compensation of some kind."

Before Micheline could reply, le Vay interrupted. "I will not give her up," he said flatly. "I am within my legal right to maintain the integrity of the marriage contract."

Micheline showed surprising courage; she wasn't courageous by nature but the past few weeks had shown remarkable growth. She was Lady de Cleveley and the empire of Anchorsholme was now hers. She could either fold or she could meet the challenge; she chose to meet it.

"My lord," she said steadily. "It would seem that we have two choices in this matter; obviously, you know what my sister and Sir Kirk are in love and plan to be wed. Should you choose to go through with the wedding to my sister, Kirk will not fade away. As much as it is your legal right to enforce the marriage contract, it is Sir Kirk's moral right to fight for the woman you are taking from him. He will challenge you and you will lose.

In fact, you will die. Therefore, it would make more sense to dissolve this contract and find a bride elsewhere."

Le Vay looked at Lady de Cleveley with some contempt as well as resignation. Then, his attention turned to Mara. She was still in Kirk's protective embrace and he knew there was no way he would be able to wrest her from the man. But he also knew he didn't have to; he had a champion.

"I choose to fight for what is legally mine," he said quietly. "I feel strongly that I must. Spencer, it would seem you have a task ahead of you."

Spencer knew that. In fact, he'd known all along that it would come to this. He was to face off against Kirk again and not at all looking forward to it. *What an ironic twist of fate*, he thought. Once, he had faced Kirk because he himself wanted Mara. Now it was because le Vay wanted her. He would fight Kirk because he was obligated to, not because he wanted to. If he was in Kirk's shoes, he would want his woman back, too.

"I am not going to do anything with Lady Mara in his grip," Spencer said. "He will have to release the lady before I make a move."

Kirk didn't want to go through the effort of another dark and bloody fight. He knew Spencer was cunning and sly; he also knew he was deadly. He couldn't take the chance that the man would win. Before he could reply, a female voice interrupted.

"Father!" Lily gasped, squeezing around the twisted door to enter the room. "What have you... *Kirk!*"

Lily nearly stumbled in her surprise as her gaze fell on Kirk. The door was destroyed, Kirk had Mara in his arms, and there were women in the room she didn't recognize. Her mouth fell open.

"What on earth is going on here?" she demanded, pointing to the door. "Father, did you do this? What has happened?"

Lionel could see her agitation and lifted an impatient hand to silence her. "Kirk has only just arrived," he said. "Where have you been?"

Lily didn't look pleased. She glanced at Kirk and Spencer as she answered. "I did not want to watch you extract Mara from this chamber as one would extract a rotten tooth from a gaping mouth," she said, unhappy. "You would not listen to me so I left. I have been in the chapel most of the day, praying for a calm solution to all of this. I see that my prayers have brought Kirk returned from Ireland although I am not entirely sure that was the calm resolution I was praying for. I think it may be the more violent option."

Mara let go of Kirk and went to Lily. The woman put her arms around Mara and the two of them hugged tightly.

234

"Lily, your father refuses to release me to Kirk," Mara said. "Kirk will fight for me and your father has ordered Spencer to champion him. Please tell your father not to do this. Please tell him to let me go."

Lily was inflamed. She looked accusingly at her father. "Kirk and Spencer are going to fight for your right to keep Mara?" she was outraged. "Father, I have never known you to be foolish or evil, but what you are doing is wicked. Do you hear me? You are being wicked!"

Lionel would not be reprimanded by his daughter. "Get out of here," he told her. "Go to your chamber. This does not concern you."

Lily wouldn't budge. She held up an angry finger, wagging it at him. "I am ashamed of you," she scolded. "See what your greed and selfishness has done? Kirk will never trust you again and you have even made Spencer miserable. How can you do this to people who respected you?"

Lionel was furious. He was also shrewd. He made his way over to his daughter, who still stood there with Mara. He scowled at his only child.

"It is not your place to rebuke me," he told her. "Things in life do not always work out as we have planned. Life is not a glorious white field of flowers, pure and for the taking. We do not exist from one happy moment to the next. In this world, we must fight for survival and for what we want and if that meets with your disapproval, so be it. I do not answer to you."

With that, he snaked an arm out and grabbed Mara, pulling her against him and throwing his forearm across her neck in a threatening gesture. As Mara screamed, Kirk went for his sword but Spencer was also armed. The broadswords came out and the battle for Mara, in a flash, had begun.

"Defeat him any way you have to, Spencer!" Le Vay yelled as he dragged Mara towards the twisted remnants of the chamber door. "Kill him if you must!"

Micheline, Wanda, and Valdine skittered away from the battling knights in a panic, pressing themselves into the far reaches of the room, as Lily ran for her father. She grabbed Mara's arm and began to pull in the opposite direction.

"Father, no!" she cried as she yanked on her friend to prevent her father from pulling her through the door. "Where are you going?"

Lionel had Mara half way through the door, although Lily was tugging fiercely on her. "There is a priest in the great hall," he bellowed. "I am doing what is my right, do you hear? I will marry Mara and we will be done with this foolish nonsense once and for all!"

Lily dug her heels in. "You will not marry her!" she cried. "Let her *go*!"

Mara, in a bad position, was being torqued quite seriously, but she managed to bite Lionel on the arm. He yelped and let her go, but was able to wind a hand into her dark, luscious hair. He pulled hard as she screamed.

"With me!" he roared. "Lily, let her go!"

The sounds of broadsword against broadsword filled the room, especially when Kirk and Spencer crashed into the massive wardrobe and sent it smashing over onto the floor. Wood exploded all over the room as Kirk managed to grab Spencer by the neck and throw him down onto the demolished pile. Micheline and the twins screamed, trying to move away from the fight, as the battle for Mara not only went on in front of them but also continued at the door.

Unfortunately, Lionel was stronger than his daughter and he had Mara in a painful position, so he was able to wrest her through the door and away from Lily. Lily, horrified and distraught, moved to follow.

"Kirk!" she cried. "He is taking her to the great hall to marry her! You must help her!"

Kirk heard the words and, with a frustrated roar, kicked Spencer as the man tried to get up. It was enough of a blow to cause Spencer to roll several feet away as Kirk made a break for the door. But Spencer somehow ended up on his knees and picked up a piece of the broken wardrobe, hurling it at Kirk. The wood caught him in the legs and knocked him down to one knee, giving Spencer enough time to run at him with his broadsword wielded. Kirk avoided two heavy blows as he struggled to his feet and the battle went on.

Lily had already run from the chamber, following her father and Mara. Mara's angry screams were echoing off the walls as Lionel dragged her down the stairs. Kirk, however, had his hands full with Spencer; as much as he was frantic to rush to Mara's aid, he was in a mortal battle. He needed to subdue Spencer before he could go after Mara.

But time was ticking.

***

Lionel got Mara as far as the entry to the great hall. There was some decorative iron railing in the wall and as Lionel pulled her through the entry, Mara reached out and grabbed it. It prevented Lionel from pulling her any further as she held on for dear life, screaming with pain as he yanked on her hair. When Lionel realized the hair wasn't doing him any good, he wrapped his arms around her slender waist and tried to yank her free that way. Mara tried to kick him in the groin.

Lily, too, was working against him. She came up behind her father, jumped on his back, and wrapped her arms around his neck. She squeezed and squeezed, and Lionel was close to blacking out. He finally had to let go of Mara in order to dislodge his daughter. With Lionel occupied, Mara let go of the iron and ran for her life.

She raced back up the stairs to where Kirk and Spencer were still doing battle, only now they were out in the corridor destroying everything in their path. Mara didn't want to cry out to Kirk and distract him, as she had done the last time Kirk and Spencer battled, because she well remembered what happened that time. Therefore, she ducked into the nearest chamber, hoping to find a weapon. If Lionel laid another hand on her, she was going to make the man pay.

She ended up in a spare chamber, small but nicely furnished. A quick and panicked perusal of the room showed that there were no weapons available. There was, however, a fire poker and shovel. Mara raced to the hearth and collected the iron poker. Taking a deep breath for courage, she ran back to the chamber door because she could hear the battle drawing closer. It was loud and frightening.

Mara was fully prepared to brain Spencer so Kirk could get the upper hand. But what happened next was not as she had planned; it occurred faster than she could comprehend. Soon, it was all spiraling out of control into deadly oblivion.

When she threw open the panel, Kirk and Spencer were right there. In fact, they were practically on top of her. Kirk, seeing Mara in the doorway, was distracted long enough for Spencer to take a huge swipe at his head. Kirk ducked in the nick of time but in doing so, hit his head on the wall and nearly knocked himself out because he was without his helm. He had left it back on his charger when he had arrived at Quernmore.

Mara, seeing Kirk go down, threw herself at Spencer, poker and all, and sent the man sideways into the opposite wall just as Lionel came racing around the corner. The old man was without Lily hanging all over him, running headlong into a battle without a weapon or any armor.

Kirk, dazed as he was, only saw a body. Assuming it was Spencer, he threw up his broadsword and Lionel ran right into it. In the blink of an eye, Lionel was impaled through the gut on the tip of Kirk's massive broadsword.

Lionel groaned as the steel blade carved through him. Mara, hearing the sound, stopped beating up on Spencer and they both turned to see Lionel standing in the corridor with Kirk at his feet and a broadsword through his belly. He was just standing there as if he could not comprehend that he had just been mortally wounded. But swiftly, reality set in as he began to bleed out all over the floor. Blood gushed down his legs and onto the wood. His shocked gaze found Mara, who stood equally shocked gazing back at him.

Lionel smiled weakly at her. "All I wanted," he breathed, "was a son...."

With that, he fell forward, quite dead, against Kirk. Kirk grabbed hold of the man and lowered him carefully to the ground. All they could do was stare at the deceased lord of Quernmore Castle. As swiftly and violently as the battle had begun, it was over. The sudden stillness was overwhelming.

For the longest time, no one said a word. They just stared at Lionel. Kirk moved first; he removed his broadsword from Lionel's soft belly, almost gently. There was a good deal of regret there. His gaze lingered on the man for a moment before turning to Spencer.

"This does not please me," he said, his voice hoarse. "I did not intend to kill him like this."

Spencer looked down at his liege. "I realize that," he said. Exhausted, ill, shocked at the turn of events, he clumsily sheathed his broadsword and slumped back against the wall. "He did it to himself, Kirk. I have always known the man to be stubborn and willful, but never foolish. But... perhaps it is better this way."

"What do you mean?" Kirk asked.

Spencer's focus moved to Lionel, crumpled on the floor. "He was not being entirely selfish," he said softly. "I know it looks that way, but he confided in me recently that he was dying. He saw this marriage to Mara as his last chance to have a son to replace Michael and preserve his legacy, but it seemed as if whatever desperation he felt turned to madness over the past few days. He simply wasn't himself. It was the despair of a dying man, if that is of any comfort. So perhaps it is better that he meet his end quickly rather than looking forward to months of agony as his life slipped away."

Kirk's expression was serious. "Is this true?" he asked. "He was dying?"

"Aye."

"Of what?"

"A mass in his belly. Already, his legs were growing numb and he was in great pain. Ask the castle physic if you do not believe me."

Kirk looked at Lionel's crumpled form through new eyes. He sighed heavily. "Although I am not without sympathy, it still does not excuse what he surely must have put Mara through. If I had not returned when I did, she would be Lady le Vay."

"That is true."

"That selfish behavior is not the man I knew."

"Nor I. Attribute it to his illness if you must."

Kirk's gaze moved to Mara. Still standing against the wall next to Spencer, her lower lip was trembling as she looked at the man she loved with all of her heart. She dropped the fire poker and went to Kirk, collapsing into his embrace tearfully. As they held one another, in exhaustion and in joy, far down the hall, Micheline poked her head out of the chamber with the twisted door. The sudden silence in the corridor had prompted her to find out why.

"Kirk?" she called fearfully, seeing the collection of people at the end of the darkened corridor. "What has happened? Where is my sister?"

Mara let go of Kirk and ran down the hallway to her sister, sobbing as she threw herself into the woman's embrace. The women hugged fiercely.

"Misha," Mara wept. "I did not think I was going to ever see you again."

Micheline smiled as she held her baby sister. "Of course you would see me again," she said calmly, soothingly. "What has happened? Where is Lord le Vay?"

"Dead," Kirk replied for Mara. "He is here, Misha, at my feet."

Micheline could see a body in the dim hall. "Did... did you kill him because he married Mara?"

"He did not marry Mara. He did not have the chance."

Micheline's gaze lingered on Kirk before returning to her sister. Things were still confusing, but Kirk and Spencer were no longer fighting and she found that she was most grateful for that. In truth, she had been quite worried for Spencer.

"It would seem that there was a good deal of madness going on here at Quernmore," she said to Mara. "Would you care to tell me all that has happened?"

Mara nodded, wiping at her eyes, but Kirk spoke from down the hall.

"She can tell you everything tonight at the wedding feast," he said wearily, making his way down the hall and reaching out to collect Mara. "Right now, I understand there is a priest in the great hall. I intend he should marry Mara and I this very moment."

Mara clutched his hand tightly, even tighter when he led her past Lionel as if afraid the man would rear up and grab her. Kirk took Mara and Micheline down to the great hall as Spencer, Wanda, and Valdine tended to Lord Lionel.

They found Lily tied to a chair near the mouth of the great hall, courtesy of her angry father. Kirk untied her and tried to explain what had happened as gently as possible. It wasn't gentle enough; Lily burst into hysterical sobs and raced upstairs to find her father being cared for by Spencer and the twins. Although she did not agree with what her father had done, she still loved him and wept bitterly over his accidental death. He was all the family she had left.

******

Lily stayed with her father's body throughout the marriage ceremony between Mara and Kirk. Mara, although joyful that she now had a new husband that she loved with all of her heart, was nonetheless distraught over her friend's sadness and instead of a wedding night with her very exhausted husband, she sat with Lily all night, comforting her friend just as Lily had spent so much time comforting her. It was the right thing to do.

That night, the hellion finally grew up as her husband slept hard and dreamlessly in their marriage bed, snoring loud enough to rattle the doors. He missed his wife, of course, but he understood as well as encouraged her compassion towards the woman she had once hated jealously.

Now, there was no more jealousy or pain. The love that Kirk and Mara had for one another had come full circle and a bright future was on the horizon. No more horror, no more Darkland.

Kirk, as well as Mara, finally came to know peace.

EPILOGUE

The day was balmy and bright, and a strong breeze blew in off the Irish Sea, snapping the standards of Bowland that flew over Wicklow Castle. The smell of salt was in the air along with a hint of warmth, as the summer season had proven oddly warm during the middle of the day. This morning promised the same weather pattern as the inhabitants of Wicklow went about their business before it grew sticky.

Kirk entered the cool confines of the enormous keep. He had been in the bailey seeing to their baggage, for a cog was moored less than a mile away that would take them to the green fields of England. It had been a trip long planned to visit Micheline and he was anxious to get on with the travel while the weather held good. With baggage and possessions loaded, now it was time to load up his family. With four young children, that would be the tricky part.

He hadn't taken five steps into the keep when he came to a halt and looked around at his feet as if he was missing something. Retracing his steps, his intense gaze roamed the bailey as he shielded the sun from his eyes.

"Ryan?" he called.

A moment later, a small boy with dark hair leapt onto the stone steps. He was a sturdy lad, five years of age, and in his arms he carried puppy. The dog's long body trailed down, the hindquarters swinging as Ryan mounted the steps. Kirk frowned.

"Where on earth did you get that?" he asked.

Ryan Connaught turned his handsome young face to his father. "There was a dog that had puppies by the smithy shack," he told his father excitedly. "I took one!"

Kirk cocked an eyebrow. "I can see that," he said as the boy drew close and extended the puppy for his father's inspection. "A fine beast. But you must return him to his mother."

Ryan's expression fell, looking much like his mother when her wishes were denied. "Papa, I want to take him with us," he said sincerely.

Kirk shook his head. He started to reply but was cut short by first one scream and then another. Kirk turned towards the direction of the screams in time to see one of his daughters shooting out of the keep entry and bash into his legs. When he reached down to steady her, another daughter ran up on her heels and he grabbed them both to keep them from tumbling down the stairs.

"Regan!" Came the cry from inside the keep. "Bridget! Stop immediately!"

Fortunately, Kirk had the two-year-old and three-year-old girls by the arms as Mara emerged from the keep, holding several pieces of garments in her hands. Kirk looked at her curiously until he realized his daughters were only half-dressed.

"You are only now dressing them?" he asked his wife with strained patience. "We are supposed to be departing shortly. What is taking so long?"

Mara cast him an exasperated look. "The baby is screaming and these two will not stand still," she said as she grasped Regan by the arm. "They are both trying to climb onto the windowsill for some reason. I would pull one out and the other one would climb up."

Kirk smirked. "They get that particular trait from their mother."

Mara didn't see his humor. "We are going to have to do something about putting shutters over their windows," she said. "I am terrified that they are going to fall out of the windows."

He looked down at the dark-haired babies at his feet. "I will see what I can do," he said. "But they really should be dressed by now. We must depart."

"Then it would be very helpful if you could lend a hand."

Kirk gave his wife a smile as he grasped the toddlers by the hands and led them gently back into the keep.

"You tend the baby, love," he told her. "I will take the poppets in hand."

Mara reached down and scooped Bridget up. "Bridgie still needs her hose and shoes, and Regan needs nearly everything else," she said as she watched Kirk pick up Regan. "I think she has a splinter in her toe; see?"

Kirk looked at the foot his wife was holding up into his face, kissing the dirty little foot as Regan squirmed and whined.

"I will get it out," he said softly. "I'll not let my baby suffer."

Mara called out to her son, who rushed past his mother up the stairs, still holding the puppy. Mara called to him again but he ignored her, instead taking the puppy into his chamber and trying to hide him behind his bed.

As Kirk took care of Regan's splinter, Mara went into the bed chamber occupied by her sons and wanted to know why Ryan had the puppy stuffed under his bed, but the little lad, being rather persuasive, was able to convince his mother that the puppy was a necessary fixture in his room. Mara didn't have the patience to argue with him mostly because her ten month old son, Brendan, was screaming his lungs out in his pen on the opposite side of the chamber. She picked the baby up, comforting him.

With the baby in her arms, Mara went into the girls' chamber to hurry her husband along but found herself watching him interact with his daughters instead. Over the past five years, Kirk, the big Irish knight with the big voice, had turned into an incredibly soft and attentive father.

In a world where most men didn't participate in child rearing, Kirk had gone out of his way to be a part of his children's world. Ryan was his shadow, Regan and Bridget were his loves, and baby Brendan, with dark hair and his father's gray eyes, was usually a fixture in his arms. While Mara had little patience sometimes, Kirk's patience was infinite, and it made her love him all the more.

She watched him as he plucked the splinter out, kissing and hugging the little girl as he proceeded to pull her little hose on and tie on her little leather shoes. Regan was the oldest at three and a half years, and she was very much her father's daughter, but Bridget, at nearly two and a half, was the image of her mother in both looks and manner. As Kirk tried to tie up the last of Regan's shoe, Bridget wormed her way onto his lap and plopped down. Kirk simply worked around her.

"The boys are dressed and ready," Mara said, entering the room with Brendan on her hip. "Do you need any help?"

Finished with the shoe, he managed to pull a light linen tunic over Regan's head and set her on her feet.

"I do not," he said, taking a similar linen tunic off the bed beside him and pulling that one over Bridget's dark head. "I believe we are finished."

He stood up and Mara handed him the baby as she collected soft-knit caps from the bed and pulled them over her daughter's heads. With the children finally dressed and ready, she surveyed the room to make sure she didn't forget anything.

"Did you pack the parcels for Micheline?" she asked Kirk. "The ones with the baby clothes in them?"

Kirk nodded patiently, going out into the corridor to make sure Ryan was removing the puppy from his chamber. "They were loaded," he replied. "Drew put the packages on himself."

"Are your brothers going with us?"

"They are not. I need someone here to manage Wicklow while we are away."

Mara nodded in understanding, still thinking on their baggage. "I do not want to forget those packages," she said as she took her daughters by the hand. "I spent a good deal of time making all of those items for the new baby. If we forget them, I shall be heartsick."

Kirk was instructing his eldest son to remove the dog to the yard below, making sure the boy was heading down the stairs with the puppy before turning to his wife.

"The new baby has plenty of clothes, I am sure," he said. "In fact, the last missive I had from Spencer said that the baby had more clothes than he did before he was even born."

Mara was undeterred. "It is their first son," she said. "Remember how you felt when Ryan was born? You wanted him to have the very best of everything."

Kirk took the stairs with the baby in his arms, making sure to help his wife and daughters down behind him.

"He *did* have the best of everything," he said flatly. "In fact, Ryan had more clothes than I did before he was even a month old. Why does a baby need so many clothes?"

Mara cocked a dark eyebrow. "This is not just *any* baby," she said. "He is Michael Lionel Edward de Shera, heir to Anchorsholme Castle and the Bowland Barony. You know that Micheline's pregnancy was difficult. There is much to celebrate with my nephew's arrival."

Kirk eased up somewhat; he knew that Spencer and Micheline had suffered some disappointment prior to little Michael's birth. A daughter, Amelia, was born not quite a year after they were married but Micheline had suffered two miscarriages before Michael was finally born. Aye, there was much to celebrate, even if his wife had gone overboard with all of the little garments she had made the child.

His wife. Kirk watched Mara as she came off the stairs, shepherding the children towards the entry of Wicklow's mighty keep with her firm, confident manner. Even though he was lord of Wicklow Castle now, maintaining the Irish lands for Micheline and her husband, the best part of it was Mara. He could lose everything but as long as he still had her and their children, he was a rich man indeed. He adored her more than words could express.

Life over the past few years had been rich and eventful. The wickedness that had once been the Darkland was now transformed into something strong and respectable, and the dark whispers that used to follow them around no longer existed. Micheline and Spencer had seen to that, and a new generation was being born, a generation that would carry on the new tradition of Anchorsholme Castle and her benevolent lords.

When Kirk had first spied that dark-haired lass hanging from the battlements of Haslingden those years ago, never could he have imagined what that hellion of a woman would come to mean to him. The trials, tribulations, and fears that they had gone through in order to achieve their paradise had been difficult but worth the struggle. Kirk couldn't even remember those chaotic days any longer. They seemed like a nightmare, long past.

The baby cooed and he looked down into that handsome little face, seeing his strong Irish heritage mixed with Mara's warm English blood. He saw his father in that little face, his mother, and ancestors long passed. He saw the future. He saw his life. He saw every dream he had ever possessed in a living, breathing form.

Mara called to him and he took his gaze off the baby, once again focused on his lovely wife. With a smile and a return wave, he headed off in her direction. He was looking forward to this visit to reconnect with his sister in law and her husband, and of the good people that now populated Anchorsholme. Wanda, Valdine, Corwin, and even the former servant children Robert, Fiona, Gilly and George… they would all be there. Perhaps even Lily and her husband would visit from Quernmore. Kirk was looking forward to seeing them all again.

Life was good and the Darkland, for all concerned, was no longer dark. It had become home.

Made in the USA
San Bernardino, CA
04 November 2016